MEMORY OF TEA & MAGIC

KATHERINE A. DARLING

Editor: Sandra Darling

Cover design by: Etheric Designs

Internal Art by: Etheric Designs

ASIN: B0C3RMW4W5

ISBN: 978-1-961972-00-1 (Hardback)

ISBN: 978-1-961972-01-8 (Paperback)

To the LGBTQIA+ family. You gave me a place to belong and something to hold onto.

AUTHOR'S NOTE

Please note there is swearing, mentions of gore, mentions of sexual harassment, eye loss, and amnesia in this novel. If any of this bothers you as a reader, you may not wish to continue. Thank you so much for reading, and I hope you enjoy it!

ALSO BY KATHERINE A. DARLING

<u>A First Being Novel</u>

The Drunken Elf
The Royal Elf
Tales of Veridac
The Slumbering Lord
The Encroaching Storm
The Disquieting Reunion

<u>A Bear Creek Novel</u>

A Festive Fiasco

PART ONE

I

The sun shone high above him, blinding him as his eyes fluttered open. Dazed, he glanced around. He was on his back in the middle of a glade, surrounded by pine trees that stretched into the blue sky. Blinking, he sat up and groaned, hand lowering to his stomach. His brow furrowed as his side twinged from the touch; something wet covered his clothes. Pulling his hand away, he stared at the red substance coating his fingers.

Blood, he thought slowly. It was hard to form that single word. Unfocused, he stared at the blood, rubbing his fingertips together. With a shake of his head, he peered at the wound—a single slice along his ribs. It wasn't grievous.

Where am I?

He looked around with no recognition. Nothing, absolutely nothing, told him where was. Green grass spread beneath him and covered the glade. A few flowers and weeds grew randomly, poking out of the ground. Birds chirped, each one like a knife to his ears, and the scent of the damp soil along with something floral made his nose crinkle, overwhelming his senses. His fingers trailed over the soft, slightly wet strands beneath him as he continued blinking, staring at the unfamiliar landscape.

Who am I?

His hands clenched into fists around the grass, uprooting it. He couldn't remember a single thing. Panic clawed under his skin and made his stomach roll as bile burned his throat. With a deep breath, he closed his eyes and searched his mind in an attempt to find something, anything, that would tell him who he was. His brow furrowed. Nothing. There was nothing. His mind was a blank canvas. A black void.

Shuddering, he rubbed his forehead. His breath escaped in quick gasps as his heart pounded, thundering in the empty silence of his mind. How was it possible that he didn't even know his own name? He took several deep breaths in an attempt to calm the ice coursing in his veins.

By the time he opened his eyes, his pulse had slowed. *One thing at a time*, he thought. He would focus on what was right in front of him. He got to his feet, and the world spun. He clutched his abdomen, blood oozing between his fingers. Ignoring it, he looked at the sun, squinting. It hung high overhead—afternoon sun. Turning, he started north. How he knew which direction was which, he had no idea, but he did.

He locked his gaze on a tree in the distance and walked toward it. When he reached it, he picked another tree to the north, moving ever forward in the hope he wouldn't get lost. Blood continued to seep out of the cut, thirst burned his throat, and his head throbbed with every breath, but he refused to stop. He had to find water, people, or help of some kind.

As he trudged under the boughs of the trees, the sun continued its journey across the sky and began its descent. The birds ceased their songs and settled in their nests for the night. A cold wind came from the north, blowing across the two looming peaks capped in snow and chilling him to the bone. With his arms wrapped about his waist, he slogged on.

Eventually, he began to shiver, and the world shifted in his view. His body begged to sit down as he fought to stay conscious, but something deep inside of him refused to surrender. He had to do something. Something important. He couldn't remember what, but he *knew* he had to do it.

Darkness pressed around him as he stumbled toward a tree. Each step burned, becoming harder than the last. Everything within him screamed to lay down. Swallowing, he reached out and grabbed the tree; the rough bark scraped against his palm. He hugged the thin pine for support as he panted in short, hard bursts. Everything hurt. His head throbbed, his side ached, and his mouth was painfully dry.

A crack broke the silence of the forest. His head jerked up as a man rounded a tree. The other man paid him no attention or didn't see him in the encroaching night. The new arrival was tall and lean. His cloak swished around his leather boots and dragged through the pine needles covering the ground. His pitch-black hair fell to his shoulders, flaring in the cold breeze.

A scar slashed through the newcomer's eyebrow, eye, and down to his cheekbone. *I know him*, he thought. He had no idea why he recognized the black-haired man, but he did.

His boots crunched on the pine needles as he stumbled forward, stretching a hand out. The other man whipped around—staff held high in his left hand. It was long, dark in color, and appeared like it was formed from two branches twisting around each other. A deep blue crystal sat on top of the staff, glowing with power.

"What the hell are you doing here?" the black-haired man snarled, prodding the air with the staff.

He didn't hesitate, stumbling toward the mage. *He's a mage.* "I know you."

The man jerked back as he raised the staff between them like a shield. "Of course, you know me."

"I know you," he repeated as his knees gave out, and he collapsed to the ground, face smacking into the forest floor. Footsteps crunched on the dry ground as the sharp scent of pine stung his nose. Something hard poked into his chest and forced him onto his back. Stars glimmered in the night sky before the mage's face blocked them.

A deep scowl covered the other man's face. He focused on the scar slicing down the side of his face. The mage's right eye was milky and scarred while the left was a deep gray—like the stormy ocean.

Suddenly, an image bloomed in his mind of a storm raging over the ocean, waves violently crashing against the shore, and lightning arcing through the sky. He could perfectly imagine it, but he couldn't ever recall seeing it for himself.

His gaze stayed on the scar. "I know you."

"Yes," the mage snapped. "What's wrong with you?"

He grabbed the mage's cloak, which made him snarl. "I trust you," he whispered, realizing it was true. He trusted this man. The other man jerked back, eyes starting to widen. "Who am I?" he asked. The mage's mouth fell open. A heavy weight started to press around his thoughts as he whispered again, "Who am I?"

GREYSON

Greyson gaped at the unconscious man. *Cyrus*, he thought, lip curling. He did not hate anyone as much as he hated Cyrus. He eyed the warrior, who did not carry his usual sword. Greyson scoffed. He'd never seen Cyrus without his blade. So much so, he'd assumed the metal was fused to his flesh.

Cyrus' golden-blonde hair hung around his face, and his square jaw had relaxed from its usual clenched position. Even though Greyson could not see them, he knew Cyrus' eyes were blue—the exact same shade as the sky. Greyson was quite a bit taller than him, but Cyrus was broader and had well-formed muscles, no doubt from swordwork.

He poked him with the end of his staff again. Cyrus did not stir. Blood leaked from his side, but the wound didn't seem severe enough to cause this unconscious state. His last question flashed in Greyson's mind. Cyrus didn't know who he was. The great warrior of the Zaesian Empire, and he couldn't remember. The last eight years of being a pain in Greyson's ass, and he didn't remember any of it.

A sneer crossed his face. Greyson could leave Cyrus here to die, and no one would be the wiser. He stalked off without a backward glance. He was not far from his home, which he'd barely left in the last two, almost three, years since the rebellion ended.

Prodding the uneven ground with his staff, Greyson wound through the forest, though his thoughts returned to Cyrus. That last time he'd seen him was about this time of year when Cyrus had escorted him back to the Griseo Mountains where Greyson had been exiled.

Greyson pushed the thoughts out of his mind. With his head held high, he marched out of the woods. He'd been hunting for herbs and root vegetables while checking his traps and snares. Now that darkness had descended, he had no desire to continue to search, as the low light made it difficult for him to see anything.

As he came to a clearing, he caught sight of his village, Drakcombe, in the distance, surrounded by rich farmland. Lights glimmered from the windows of the few homes nestled in a valley between the Ferrum and Validus Peaks.

He kept walking, ignoring the wooden houses until he came to a path that trailed off into the trees. The path, barely more than a goat trail, led up the mountain and stopped at a cabin—his home—surrounded by towering pine trees.

He opened the door, rested his staff against the wall, and removed his cloak, hanging it on a peg that jutted from the wall. Greyson's home was a one-room cabin with a bed pressed against a wall, a stone fireplace with a wide mantle, a table and chairs, and a simple kitchen to the left. It was not large nor did it hold any luxuries, but it suited his purposes.

After he started a fire, he set a kettle on a hook hanging above the flames. With a sigh, he sank to the oval rag rug in front of the fireplace, warmth seeping into his chilled limbs. Once the kettle released a shrill whistle, Greyson tugged it off with a thick cloth. He put some leaves into the plain white teapot before pouring the boiling water into it.

His shoulders relaxed as he closed his eyes, leaning back on his elbows. Finally, Cyrus would never bother him again. *Nothing like a spot of tea to celebrate*, he mused.

With a deafening crash, the ground trembled, shaking the cabin. His eyes shot open. Light flashed an instant before another peal of thunder roared. The pitter-patter of rain started to beat against the roof. Greyson glanced out the window next to the door as another strike of lightning lit the sky, illuminating the forest.

The image of Cyrus lying on the ground swelled in his mind. His jaw tightened. Greyson had intended to leave him to die of exposure or blood loss. Why should it matter if it started to rain?

Knowing the tea had steeped, he poured a cup and took a sip. The usual pleasure that permeated him at a nice cup of tea did not come. Instead, the bitter flavor clung to his tongue as the hot liquid hit his empty stomach uncomfortably. Greyson clenched the warm porcelain and refused to budge.

It doesn't matter.

Another clash of lightning lit his home, and the ground quaked from the force of the thunder. The pounding of rain grew louder and louder with each passing moment until it was deafening.

Snarling, he slammed the cup down, hot tea sloshing over the rim and scalding his fingers. He collected the cup and teapot, then deposited them onto the kitchen table so he wouldn't trip over them later. Greyson donned his cloak, and, staff in hand, he threw the door open. It almost ripped out of his grasp from the force of the howling wind.

Head down, shoulders hunched, he marched into the pouring rain, prodding the ground with his staff. The darkness plus the rain made it difficult for him to see much, but his feet knew the way. Lightning arced in the sky, making a shiver go down his spine.

I'm going to die trying to save my enemy, he thought, swearing, not that it could be heard over the thunder.

In no time at all, the rain soaked his clothes and made him shiver. By the time he reached Cyrus, he was thoroughly miserable and silently cursing him with each breath.

"I hope you're dead," he muttered, stalking toward the inert man. He nudged Cyrus with the butt of his staff. Unfortunately, he released a whimper. "Well, shit," Greyson said. "You're alive."

He shoved a hand through his dripping hair. His lips pursed as his brow furrowed. A choice lay before him—save Cyrus or leave him to die. Greyson stared at him as it continued to pour and a fierce wind ripped through the trees.

"Shit," he growled.

Grunting, he shifted Cyrus into his arms. "Goddess above and serpent below, you're heavy."

Greyson groaned, knees cracking, and stood with Cyrus thrown over his shoulder like a sack of grain. Using his staff as a cane, he trudged home. The rain did not slow in the slightest, but, thankfully, the thunder grew fainter as the storm moved over Validus Peak.

His back throbbed and his legs trembled while his knees threatened to buckle. Greyson swore again. A spell that could assist him had to exist, but he used magic to fight, not to carry unconscious men. In his exhaustion, his brain refused to produce anything useful. His boots sank and slopped in the mud with every step. And with each step, he cursed himself and his lack of resolve as well as Cyrus.

What the hell is he even doing here?

Finally, the village came into sight, and Greyson wished to abandon his unwanted burden on the ground and leave him behind, but he didn't act on the impulse. Growling, he continued through the downpour. The only good thing about carrying Cyrus was the sweat he worked up had banished any trace of cold.

When he reached the trail to his home, Greyson fought back yet another string of swear words. The rain had made the path slick with mud as rivulets of water cascaded down the hill. Slowly, painfully, he trudged up the steep track until he reached his cabin.

Greyson dropped his charge on the floor with little care. When Cyrus groaned, he smirked. "I'm so sorry," he muttered, sniggering. Greyson left him where he fell and stripped off his wet clothes, then hung them on a rack not far from the fire.

He dried off before pulling on another pair of trousers and a long sleeve shirt. While he rubbed the cloth over his wet hair, Greyson shifted to Cyrus, who lay in a heap. He rolled Cyrus onto his back. Despite the coldness of his soaked clothes, a fire raged under his skin.

"Great," he said. "Now, I have to play nursemaid."

Briskly, Greyson removed Cyrus' clothes, then chafed his skin with a towel. The slice on his side was red and puffy, but it had stopped bleeding. He dried Cyrus' dripping hair before dragging him to bed. By the time he maneuvered Cyrus onto the bed, his back throbbed and his arms ached.

"I swear if you die after all of this trouble, I will find a way to curse your soul in the afterlife," he growled, kneading his tight back.

Stiffly, Greyson removed a simple poultice from a kitchen cabinet that should help with the infection. He smeared the green concoction over the wound, wrapped a bandage around the injury, then tucked the blanket around Cyrus.

Greyson put the kettle on the flames to make tea for himself and some willow bark tea for Cyrus that he would probably have to force down his throat. The willow bark should help with any pain and bring the fever down, though.

He leaned his arms on the back of a chair, and his head slumped. Once the kettle screamed, he poured most of the water into the teapot, leaving some to simmer for a few minutes with willow bark, then he poured it into a cup for Cyrus. He took a drink of the warm tea and his tight muscles relaxed as heat spread from his stomach to his chilled limbs.

After he finished and the willow bark tea had sufficiently seeped and been strained, Greyson sat on the edge of the bed and lifted Cyrus so he rested against his shoulder. Greyson raised the mug to Cyrus' lips. The tea dribbled out the side of his mouth and onto Greyson's shoulder.

Sighing, he wanted to pinch the bridge of his nose, but he had no free hands. "I'm trying here, Cyrus. A little effort would be nice."

Of course, he did not respond.

Containing a snarl, Greyson attempted to get the tea down his throat. Slowly, Cyrus drank the entire cup. When it was empty, he settled Cyrus on the bed.

He stretched his arms over his head, his back cracking in a symphony of pops. Greyson groaned before twisting one way, then the next. He glanced at Cyrus and shook his head. "I should've let you die. I can already tell you're going to be as much of a pain in the ass as usual."

It was too late now.

Shrugging, Greyson poured another cup of tea.

2

CYRUS

As light brushed his face, he woke up. He glanced around with a frown. *Where am I?* The home was empty with very little furniture or clutter. There didn't appear to be anything personal that spoke to the owner's taste. From the red rug to the chairs and table, nothing matched. Everything looked neat and orderly with nothing out of place. He clutched the soft, blue blanket draped over him. The last thing, well the only thing, he remembered was the woods.

The mage.

He knew him. His eyes wandered around the room again, searching for the black-haired man, but he was alone.

He swallowed as a prickling sensation started at the base of his skull and settled deep within his gut. A black void devoured his mind. Empty. He had nothing. A buzzing sound, almost like a hive of bees, filled his ears. The mage's face floated across his thoughts, and his pulse slowed.

Not nothing. I have him.

When he'd relaxed, a sudden remembrance flashed in his mind. He'd been injured. Lifting the blanket, he examined the wound on his side. It had scabbed and only bore a tinge of redness. It didn't even hurt. He couldn't say the same thing about his head. It relentlessly pounded. Even as he rubbed his temples, the pain didn't lessen.

The door creaked, and the tall mage strode in. He didn't wear a cloak this time, but he did carry the staff. The sides of his hair were twisted back while the remainder hung to his shoulders. The light blue shirt he wore was faded, and the brown trousers were sturdy, though patched at the knees.

He hadn't gotten a chance to study the mage's appearance. But as the other man came closer, he examined him closely, trying to spark something in his mind. The mage's deep-set eyes stared back at him, his hollow cheeks appearing gaunt in the morning light. He crossed his arms, drawing Cyrus' attention to his lean, solid form.

"So," the mage drawled, "you're finally awake."

A wide smile crossed his face as Cyrus stared at the mage. The mage jerked back, brow furrowing.

"I know you," Cyrus said.

"Yes," he said in an exasperated tone. "You know me. We know each other. I saved your worthless life."

The mage's tone didn't dampen the warmth blooming in his chest. This person *knew* him. "Thank you."

With a scoff, he replied, "I'm already regretting my decision."

"I'm sorry, I don't remember your name."

"Typical."

"No," he said, sitting up with a slight grunt. "I don't remember my name either. I don't remember anything."

"But you know me?"

"Yes," he answered. "I have this..." He shook his head. "I don't know, feeling that I know you."

He sighed, only through his nose, nostrils flaring. "Just so I understand. You don't remember your name. You don't know who you are or where you're from. You don't know my name, but *somehow* you know that you know me. Is that correct?"

"Yes."

"Right," the mage said.

"What's my name?"

A deep frown formed on his face. "Cyrus. Your name is Cyrus."

"Cyrus," he repeated in the hope that it would stir something. His eyes closed as he absorbed the name, focusing. "Cyrus," he said again. Nothing happened. "It doesn't mean anything to me."

"So sad," the mage said, not sounding the least bit upset.

"What's your name?" Cyrus asked, tilting his head to the side in an attempt to catch his gaze.

The black-haired man didn't even glance in his direction; instead, he remained focused on the fireplace. "Greyson."

Cyrus nodded in approval. It fit him. His pale skin bore a grayish tinge to it, and his left eye was gray. "Greyson," he said slowly. Greyson tensed. "Greyson," he repeated, brow furrowing. A spark flashed in the chasm of his mind. The name meant something—something important. Whatever he'd been doing before he lost his memory had to do with Greyson.

"What?" Greyson snapped.

"Your name means something to me."

Greyson's lip curled. "I have no idea why it would."

"Well, we know each other, right?"

"Yes."

"How?" Cyrus asked.

"What?"

"How do we know each other? What's our relationship?" he asked again.

GREYSON

Greyson tried not to gape at Cyrus who stared innocently at him, not at all like the Cyrus he'd met across the negotiation table or on the battlefield. Not like his worst enemy. Honestly, Cyrus resembled a lost puppy, and it made Greyson want to punch him in the gut.

What should he tell him? That they hated each other? That he was the golden boy of the Zaesian Empire, the same empire Greyson had rebelled against years earlier? Only three or so years ago, his people had tried to claw their way to freedom from the Zaesian Empire, but they lost. The empire was too vast and powerful to escape from. They wanted the mountains for the venetus gemstones that resided deep within them and the mages born here.

No one knew why, but more people were born with magic in the secluded mountains than anywhere else in the entire empire. Both the gems and mages were the reason the Zaesian Empire conquered the Griseo Mountains several hundred years ago.

Greyson had no idea why Cyrus had traveled to this part of the empire, as he had no business being in the Griseo Mountains. The best option was to tell Cyrus the truth and send him on his way. Something in him rebelled against that plan. Instead, another formed—a far riskier and stupider idea.

I could mess with him for a few weeks while I figure out why he's here. Cyrus might regain his memories at some point, depending on how he lost them in the first place, and this opportunity was too good to pass up.

"We're...friends," Greyson said.

"Yeah?"

"Yes," he replied in a tense tone. "We met in the army and became friends."

Cyrus' brow furrowed. "I must've been coming here, to you. That's why your name means something."

"What do you remember?"

"Waking up in a glade, bleeding. I was doing something important," Cyrus said, rubbing his forehead.

"What were you doing?" he asked, interest piqued.

"I don't know." Cyrus kept rubbing his forehead, wincing.

"Does your head hurt?"

"Yeah."

Greyson grabbed Cyrus' chin, lifting his head so he could look into his blue eyes. They were clear. Letting go, Greyson inspected Cyrus' head. There were no bumps or sensitive parts, so he probably hadn't hit his head. If he had, his memory wouldn't have been the first thing to be affected. His speech was sound, his movements steady, so probably not a head injury, but Greyson wasn't a true healer.

"Do you know any mages?"

"Besides you?" he asked with a smile. Greyson frowned. Cyrus grinned wider. "Not that I remember. Why?"

"I think someone scrubbed your mind with magic. Crude but efficient," he answered. An action he wouldn't have chosen to do, even to Cyrus. Why erase someone's mind when it was easier and more permanent to kill them?

"Why would someone do that?"

"No idea," Greyson said with a shrug. "When you're feeling better, we'll go back to the glade and see if I can find anything of use. Though, I doubt it because it rained heavily the night I found you."

Cyrus smiled again, the skin around his eyes crinkling. "Thank you for that."

He grunted. He didn't know if rescuing Cyrus was the best idea he'd ever had. It probably would have saved him a lot of pain and suffering in the future if he'd let Cyrus die. Greyson snorted. It was too late now.

"Are you hungry?" Greyson asked.

"Food sounds amazing."

A frown pulled at his lips. Greyson wasn't used to Cyrus sounding so chipper. It felt unnatural and nauseating. Brushing it off, he made a simple meal of eggs and a slice of bread with a little butter on it.

Cyrus ate with gusto, inhaling the food.

"Easy," Greyson cautioned. "You've been asleep for a couple of days. Your stomach will need time to adjust."

Almost the instant he said it, Cyrus' face clenched as his tan skin paled. Growling, Greyson shoved a bucket at Cyrus, who promptly threw up. The pervasive smell of bile made Greyson's nose wrinkle and churned his own stomach. Cyrus retched again, and Greyson swallowed, eyes darting to the side. When he finally stopped, Greyson whisked the plate and bucket away as Cyrus leaned against the flat headboard, sweat dotting his brow.

"That's why I told you to be careful."

Cyrus did not respond.

Greyson popped the kettle on the flames to make tea. Once it was done, he handed Cyrus the cup and ordered, "Sip it."

Without a single protest, Cyrus did what he was told. Greyson's brow furrowed as worry pricked down his spine; Cyrus always fought. Greyson placed a hand on his forehead. His smooth skin was the same temperature as Greyson's. No fever, which was good. The last thing either of them needed was for him to become sick again.

Leaving Cyrus to his tea, he searched the cabinets, but they held little in the way of food or supplies, as he didn't need much to get by. Unfortunately, Greyson had nothing to make a broth with. He would either have to purchase something from another villager or go hunting.

As he stood there, pinching the bridge of his nose, he knew his purse was emptier than his kitchen. He could always trade for it, but then he would have to make something of value, which would probably take more time. He snagged his bow and quiver of arrows.

"Stay in bed," Greyson ordered. "I will return."

CYRUS

Cyrus stared at the closed door for several long breaths before taking a drink of tea, wincing. It was much too bitter. His stomach gurgled unhappily as the hot liquid started to rise up his throat. Swallowing convulsively, he clutched the mug.

Once his stomach settled, he glanced at the door again. So he and Greyson were friends. *It makes sense*, he supposed. That must be the reason why he was in the area—he'd come to see Greyson. It had to be why Greyson's name resonated with him when his own meant nothing.

However, Greyson didn't seem happy to see him or happy they were friends. That could be his normal personality, but Cyrus had no way of knowing. Greyson had saved his life, though, and Cyrus remembered the relief that surged inside of him when he saw Greyson. They must be close.

After he finished the bitter tea, he sank back on the bed, tired. Even though he'd just woken up, Cyrus was exhausted. He lifted the blanket to his chin. The scent of leaves, bark, and dirt tickled his nose—the smell of the woods. With a smile, Cyrus fell asleep.

The door slammed open, and he shot awake, reaching to his hip as his pulse thundered in his ears. His fingers clasped nothing. Something should rest on that hip. Even as he concentrated, the sensation slid out of reach, and Cyrus was left, yet again, with nothing.

Greyson strode in carrying a large bird—maybe a turkey. He didn't say anything as he cut the cleaned bird into manageable-sized pieces. Then he got the fire going in the kitchen stove, even though the room was uncomfortably warm, before shoving the meat and bones into a large pot. Cyrus watched the precise movements as Greyson peeled and dumped vegetables into the pot before pouring several different spices into the concoction.

"I'm making soup. You should be able to keep the broth down," Greyson said as he sat at the table.

"Thank you."

Greyson nodded.

"You went hunting?" he asked, desperate for conversation to fill the emptiness of his mind.

"Yes."

Apparently, Greyson didn't talk much. Sitting against the headboard, Cyrus tried again. "Tell me about yourself."

"Why?"

"Because I don't remember anything. If you don't want to talk about yourself, tell me about...well, me."

Brow furrowing and jaw tightening, Greyson ground out, "You're an expert swordsman."

"That's something," Cyrus said. He hoped Greyson would say more, but he didn't. Cyrus' eyes gravitated to the scar on the right side of Greyson's face. He wanted to ask about it but didn't know if it would be a welcome question.

"Do you know anything else?" Cyrus asked.

"Like what?"

"My age, my family, anything else about me, please."

Greyson pinched the bridge of his nose. He had a good nose for it, as it was long and thin, starting high on his face. "I don't know your exact age. I believe you're in your twenties. You never speak of your family. You're ruthless. Loyal. Dogged. Clever. Excellent schemer."

Nodding, Cyrus watched him closely, longing for any information. He needed something, anything to hold on to, or else he feared the panic would drag him away. When Greyson stopped talking, he asked, "How old are you?"

"Twenty-seven."

"Do you have any family?"

"No," Greyson said with a shake of his head. "They're all gone."

"I'm sorry."

"It was not your doing." He stood and stirred the soup. The savory scent filled the home and awoke Cyrus' stomach.

"It will be fun to get to know you again. Well, fun for me. Repetitive for you."

Greyson snorted, which made Cyrus smile for some reason. Already that sound had started to become familiar. Something familiar. That thought alone was comforting. He watched Greyson as he continued to make the soup, never turning toward Cyrus.

Eventually, Greyson ladled some into a bowl and brought it over to the bed. "Eat it slowly."

The delicate scent made saliva fill his mouth and his stomach gurgle. Swallowing, he blew on the spoonful before placing it in his mouth. The flavor of the turkey mixed with the taste of herbs and vegetables danced along his tongue. It was delicious. His stomach grumbled in demand for more. He wanted to devour the bowl but held back, not wanting to vomit again. Slowly, he ate spoonful after spoonful.

Returning to the kitchen, Greyson sat at the table to eat. Not once did Greyson look at him. On the other hand, Cyrus couldn't help but stare at him. A niggling sensation started in the back of his mind and told him that Greyson was important. That he had to tell Greyson something. But even as he tried to follow the feeling, it slipped away. Cyrus let it go. It would come to him eventually.

He finished the soup, and his stomach rumbled for more. "Can I have another bowl?"

"No. You need to wait a bit. Give it an hour, and then you can have some more."

"Okay." Cyrus swallowed, staring at him. Needing to fill the silence, he asked, "When can we search for the glade?"

"Not today. You need to heal."

Smiling, he smoothed the dark blue blanket. "Okay."

3

GREYSON

It took another three days before he was satisfied with Cyrus' healing for them to leave the house. The day was sunny and moderately warm for the fall. As Greyson strode down the trail, Cyrus moved to his right, which made his heart beat slightly faster because he disappeared from sight. Clearing his throat, Greyson nudged Cyrus with his staff toward his left side.

"Stay on this side," Greyson ordered.

"Why?"

"Because."

Cyrus' eyebrows scrunched together, but he complied.

Greyson led Cyrus through the village, head swiveling back and forth. The villagers gawked at Cyrus, who obviously did not belong with his bright blonde hair and warm sandy skin. All of Greyson's people resembled him: pale, gray-tinged skin and dark hair. No one said anything, nor did he explain.

Cyrus smiled at everyone, chipper. Greyson didn't know what to do with a happy Cyrus. It wasn't what he was used to. A ghost of a memory surfaced. Cyrus with his arms crossed, face a hard mask as he stood beside Emperor Caspian, his sky-blue eyes never straying from Greyson. He peeked at the Cyrus next to him; the two versions of him were so different. It was hard to reconcile the disparity.

They headed south past the village to where he'd found Cyrus among the trees. Greyson doubted he would've wandered far in his injured condition. Cyrus looked around with a relaxed expression, his stride long and loose. The birds chirped, and the pine needles squished under their boots while the fragrant scent of pine, mixing with the smell of wet dirt, tickled his nose.

Surprisingly, it was pleasant enough to walk next to Cyrus, especially when he remained quiet. Cyrus seldom stopped talking. Greyson shook his head; he would've never guessed. Unbidden, he peered at Cyrus.

"Do you recognize anything?"

With a slight frown, Cyrus said, "No."

Cyrus should have known this region, as he'd fought several battles in this area. "We're close to where I found you," Greyson said.

"Okay," Cyrus replied with a warm smile.

Clearing his throat, Greyson faced forward. They wound among the soaring pines until they reached the place where he'd found Cyrus. "Do you know where you came from?"

Lips pursed, Cyrus said, "I remember heading north."

"So we go south."

Scouring the ground with his good eye, Greyson searched for any sign of someone moving across the forest floor, but the storm had destroyed any trace. It took about half an hour before they entered a glade. The moment he stepped into the open field, his heart clenched.

The first battle of the short rebellion had happened on this ground. This is where he and Cyrus met in battle for the first time. Greyson had known the golden boy of the empire before that day, but this had been the defining event of their relationship.

Taking a deep, shuddering breath, he buried the rage that sprang up in his stomach like a persistent weed. He viciously wished he'd let Cyrus die, but the rain had made him weak. Greyson remembered what it was like to be injured, cold, and wet, all the while longing for someone to help him.

His gaze shifted to his staff. If someone had performed magic here, he could potentially sense or track it, but the rain had probably washed any remnants away. Nothing scrubbed nature clean of the taint of magic better than rain. What to do? On the one hand, it most likely wouldn't result in anything. On the other, what if it did?

In the end, it was better to check than not.

He drew on his magic; it bubbled under his skin, ready as always. The wooden staff grew warm beneath his fingertips, vibrating with power. It had been a while since he'd last used magic, but it came to him as if no time had passed.

Greyson moved the staff in a slow, clockwise circle as he channeled his magic down his arm, through the staff, and into the surrounding area. His eyes fluttered closed as he waited for the spell to blanket the glade, searching for any residue of magic. Nothing flared. Trying again, he drew out the circle, going slower with exaggerated movements to allow time for the spell to charge and give it more power. Still, nothing happened. He loosened his hold, and the magic slid like water between his fingers. The staff cooled as the magic dissipated.

With nothing else to do, he searched the clearing for any sign of disturbance. When there was none, he was unsurprised.

Coming to a sudden halt as something glinted among the damp weeds, Greyson nudged it with the end of his staff, freeing it from the tangle of grass and flowers. "Over here."

Cyrus, who was on the other side of the clearing, jogged toward him. "What?"

Prodding a sword on the ground with his boot, he said, "This is yours."

Squatting, Cyrus picked up the blade. The second he grasped the hilt, his brow furrowed. His breathing slowed as he gripped the sword. Greyson's hand tightened around his staff, waiting. If anything would stir Cyrus' memory, it would be his blade.

"Do you remember anything?" Greyson asked.

"No," Cyrus said. "I had a familiar sensation, but it left as soon as it came."

There was no indication that Cyrus was lying with his open expression, staring at the trees while he loosely held the sword. Then again, Greyson wasn't well enough acquainted with Cyrus to know for certain.

When Cyrus said nothing more, appearing lost, Greyson continued, "There's nothing here for us."

"Okay."

"Come on." He strode out of the clearing, longing to be free of it. Once they stepped the treeline, his shoulders relaxed and some of the tension left.

"What now?" Cyrus asked.

"Now, I will contact a friend to find out if he knows why you wandered all the way from the capital to out here in the middle of nowhere."

"A friend of mine?" Cyrus' eyebrows raised, expression expectant.

"No." Greyson had already decided to stay as close as possible to the truth. It would be easier to keep the lie straight. "He's my friend, not yours, but he might know something."

"Okay."

"You trust me, don't you?" he asked, stopping to face Cyrus.

"Of course. I told you that when you found me. I don't know why, but deep down I have this feeling that I'm supposed to trust you."

"Good," Greyson said as he started home. *Bad mistake, Cyrus. Probably the worst of your life.*

CYRUS

Imposing trees pressed around them, not quite blocking out the sun. Birds sang, pine needles squashed under their boots, and the day seemed beyond peaceful. Cyrus kept watching Greyson from the corner of his eye, unable to pull his gaze away for more than a few seconds at a time. He completely trusted Greyson. They were friends after all. His friend, though, seemed much quieter than him.

"Who is this friend you're writing to?"

Sighing, Greyson looked heavenward. "He's a mage from here who now works as a royal mage for the emperor."

"Will he help?"

"Yes."

"Will he know anything about me?" Cyrus asked, anxious for the conversation to continue.

"I won't know until I write to him," Greyson ground out.

"Will you write to him when we get home?"

"Yes."

Lips pressed together, Cyrus tried to remain silent. Pressure built in his chest, slid up his throat, and compelled him to keep talking, but he swallowed it. He didn't know if it was in his nature to speak so much, but the silence grated on him. Maybe it was because he couldn't remember anything. He could recall things like the ocean, a sunrise, maps, and anything that didn't pertain to him as a person. Like when he held the sword, he'd known how to grip it, the muscles in his arm already responding. But Cyrus couldn't remember sword lessons or the like.

It was infuriating to know nothing.

He peeked, yet again, at Greyson, who didn't even glance in his direction. There was something about Greyson's serious features that appealed to him. Greyson's gaze finally darted toward him, expression pinching.

"What?" Cyrus asked.

"Is it possible for you to remain quiet?"

"I don't know, is it? At this point, you know me better than I do."

Greyson stopped. He swallowed, throat bobbing, and nodded with a scowl. "I suppose that's true."

He didn't know why, but he liked that scowl. It was familiar. "Do I always talk?"

"I suppose so." Greyson started to walk again.

Cyrus paced along beside him. "How did we become friends?"

"Disagreeable happenstance."

He moved in front of Greyson and walked backward. "It couldn't be. You said we're friends."

"Watch out," Greyson said, grabbing him, staff digging into his shoulder. "You almost crashed into a tree."

Long fingers gripped Cyrus' shoulders as Greyson practically growled at him. Cyrus' stomach clenched and his eyes drifted up. Greyson towered over him, squeezing his shoulders, their bodies close together. Something about this position felt right.

Greyson shook him, frowning so deeply two lines appeared between his eyebrows. "*Now* you choose to stop speaking. You need to watch where you are going before you damage yourself further."

Smiling, he shifted even closer. "You're worried about me."

"No," Greyson said in a clipped tone. "I don't want to play nursemaid again."

"Hmm."

"It's true." Greyson released his shoulders.

"How did we become friends?"

"I met you in the capital about eight years ago," Greyson said as he started moving again. "I was with the spokesperson from the Griseo Mountains. We mine for a rare gem here, venetus. The emperor was demanding an exorbitant amount of it. My people had wanted to be paid more and to have smaller quotas."

"And we met at the meeting?"

"Yes. You were there. That's how we met."

Cyrus nodded, brow furrowing. "How did it end?"

"What end? We're still here...friends."

"Not that, the meeting. How did it end?"

Eyes narrowed, Greyson said, "Not well. Years later, it ended in a rebellion, which my people lost."

"You said we were in the army together. We lost together, then."

"I suppose."

"Misery loves company."

Greyson snorted. Cyrus grinned.

Cyrus did his utmost to remain quiet, but it was difficult. They strode through the forest until they reached the mountain village consisting of a smattering of homes and buildings. A stone well sat in the center of the town with a worn red roof that was covered in moss and a bucket hanging from a rope. The wooden homes were small, and flower boxes hung beneath their windows, each one bursting with plants. Everything seemed well-cared for and full of life from people going about their chores to the chickens clucking in the middle of the dirt road.

As they approached, people gawked at him again. The villagers stopped whatever they were doing and gaped at him. No one moved toward him or returned his smile.

Touching Greyson's elbow, he asked, "Did I ever visit because people keep staring at me?"

"I only saw you in the capital. People here are not used to strangers."

"Maybe I need to make friends with them."

Greyson sneered. "I don't think so."

He ignored the comment and rushed toward an old woman who attempted to draw a bucket of water from the well. Cyrus hoisted it, the rope rough in his hands.

"There you go."

The old woman with gray hair, innumerable wrinkles, and kind brown eyes said, "Thank you."

"You're welcome. I'm Cyrus."

Before she responded, Greyson came to his side. "Widow Abney, I hope he's not bothering you."

"Of course not," she croaked and patted Cyrus' cheek with a gnarled hand. "He's a good boy."

"Yes," Greyson said, planting his staff into the ground.

She patted his cheek one more time. "Come see me sometime, Cyrus."

"I will."

"Good boy," Widow Abney said in her gravelly voice, then ambled to a house that had colorful flowers bursting from the window boxes.

"If you're done making friends, I should get back to write that letter. It takes a considerable amount of time for mail to reach the capital," Greyson said in a hard voice.

Cyrus followed after him, jogging to catch up with his much longer strides. "Maybe we can come back later, so I can meet more people?"

His eyes turned heavenward once again. "If we must."

"It'd be nice," Cyrus said, swiveling in front of him so he could see Greyson's face.

Growling, Greyson hauled Cyrus back to his left side. "Watch where you're walking."

"Sorry." He liked that growl. Just like the scowl, Greyson's growl was familiar and calmed him. Continuing, Cyrus said, "I would like to meet more people."

"I haven't decided if it is a good thing or not for you to meet people. A mage might have scrubbed your mind clean, and we might not want to run into them."

"You'll protect me," Cyrus declared immediately as he peeked at him. Greyson's eyebrows drew together, forming a slash across his forehead. "You will, won't you?"

Greyson stopped and pinched the bridge of his nose. "Yes, Cyrus. I will protect you."

A huge smile stretched over his lips. "It shouldn't matter, then."

"Nonetheless, let me think about it first. And you are no slouch with a blade; you should be able to protect yourself," Greyson said, starting toward home.

He glanced at the sword on his hip, the weight and feel familiar. Cyrus followed Greyson, grinning at his back. He should worry about the mage who'd attacked him, if it was a mage, but he couldn't. Right now, Cyrus was completely content. Jogging, he caught up to him and stayed by Greyson's side.

4

GREYSON

Greyson carefully wrote a letter. Each time he wet the quill's nib, he placed his opposite hand next to the inkwell before dipping it into the black ink. He did not know if his friend could help, but this was the sole chance he had to find out why Cyrus traveled north from the capital. Frederick worked in the palace as a royal mage for Emperor Caspian. Hopefully, he would know something about Cyrus and this unexpected trip.

The quill scraped across the paper, then he dipped it into the ink and glanced up. Cyrus watched him with a slight smile on his full lips. Greyson shifted in his seat, chair rocking slightly beneath him, and went back to the matter at hand.

He continued to write and tried to ignore Cyrus' presence, which was more difficult than it should have been. Cyrus, for once, remained silent, but Greyson felt his eyes boring into him. Shifting, he refused to check.

Sealing the letter with a bit of wax, he finally looked up. Cyrus still stared at him. Greyson frowned and cleared his throat. "I will send this with the messenger who takes the letters to Woodhurst."

"Woodhurst?" Cyrus asked, head tilting to the side.

With a deep scowl, he stowed the letter in his satchel. "It's where the representative for the emperor, Lord Darius, lives."

"Why does the emperor have a representative?"

It took everything Greyson possessed not to snarl. He pinched the bridge of his nose. "It was the outcome of the rebellion. The best possible option to be honest."

"I don't understand."

"I told you about it. You remember?"

"Yes, but you didn't explain much besides that we fought the emperor's forces for mining rights."

"Yes," Greyson said. "The emperor didn't want to pay us market value for the gemstones we mined because he owned the land. He set a quota we had to meet quarterly. Everything we mined over that we could sell to others, yet every quarter he raised the quota to how much we mined the quarter before. The emperor wanted to control all of the venetus without paying us much.

"We were dying." Greyson could not believe he had to explain this to Cyrus, who'd sat in every meeting and played an integral part against the rebellion. "To meet the quota, my people were dying of exhaustion. We had no money. The emperor threatened to charge us every time we did not meet it.

"So to try and enact change, the different villages of the Griseo Mountains sent a spokesperson, Charlotte Williams, to meet with the emperor. I traveled with her. We went every summer for three years to propose changes. Some we were successful with, others not so much. After three years of negotiations, the emperor decided to stop paying us entirely, and my people spent the next year planning a rebellion before we acted.

"Long story short, after we lost the rebellion, the emperor dropped the quotas to a reasonable amount and agreed to pay us for the venetus, not market value, but more than previously. Also, we have the chance to appeal for raises each year. We sell the extra for a higher price. To ensure his gems reached him, the emperor elected a lord to watch over the main mining village, Woodhurst.

"I'm sending the letter to Woodhurst, so it can be sent on to the capital. Do you understand now?" Greyson finished tersely.

"I understand," Cyrus said, expression downcast.

An odd stabbing sensation started in his gut. He cleared his throat. Cyrus and his emotions should in no way affect Greyson, yet he felt guilty for upsetting him. Though, he absolutely refused to apologize to the warrior that had ended the rebellion his people had needed to win.

Cyrus met his gaze and smiled, albeit sadly, then bit his lip. Greyson could not help but stare. He'd never seen Cyrus anything but confident. The nervous movement completely transfixed him. When Cyrus finally let go of his lip, Greyson averted his gaze.

"How long will it take for it to reach the capital?"

"It depends on the weather, but a month, maybe more."

Nodding, Cyrus bit his lip yet again. Greyson locked on to the motion. He didn't know what about the movement captivated him so much, but he could not look away. Cyrus let his lip go and asked, "What do we do now?"

"That is the question."

Expression lightening, Cyrus said, "You could tell me more about myself."

He swallowed. Greyson knew next to nothing about Cyrus. What exactly would he say? "Maybe," he said, not meeting Cyrus' earnest gaze, "you can discover what you like and think for yourself?"

"But we're friends, you can just tell me."

"I could," Greyson lied, "but it might help you remember to figure it out by yourself."

"Are you sure?" Cyrus asked with a furrowed brow.

"Yes," he replied firmly.

"Okay. You're my friend, and you know me best after all."

The stabbing sensation returned, more powerfully this time. It twisted his stomach. Greyson shoved the feeling aside and answered, "Yes, I do."

CYRUS

Cyrus moved toward Greyson, who scowled when he got close, which made him grin. That scowl. He knew that scowl. Leaning his hip against the table, arms crossed, he asked, "So what do we do until your letter comes back from the capital?"

"I'm not sure."

Greyson wouldn't look at him. Moving even closer, Cyrus tilted his head as he swiveled in front of him, trying to catch his gaze. When Greyson's eyes finally met his, he asked, "What do you usually do?"

"Check my traps, search for herbs, make poultices and potions, and that's about it. I don't farm, though I do help with the planting and harvest, and since the quotas have been dropped, I don't have to work in the mines. Also, this isn't a mining village."

"Then," he said, "we can do that."

"I suppose."

"What should we do first?"

"We can check my traps." Greyson collected his staff, then his bow and arrows before he stalked out of the house, leaving Cyrus to chase him. He expected Greyson to take the path to the village, but he didn't. Instead, Greyson headed in the opposite direction, further north.

He followed Greyson while trying to remain silent. It was difficult. Cyrus wanted to ask more questions, but Greyson became snappy when he spoke. A frown pulled at his lips. How were they friends? Yes, Cyrus didn't know much about himself or Greyson, but they seemed so different. Though, even as he watched him, a feeling of trust swelled in his chest.

Rushing forward, Cyrus reached Greyson's side. "Where are your traps set?"

"I rotate where I place them, so I don't thin out the game too much."

"Do you ever hunt with your bow?"

"Yes, but I do better at short range than anything at a distance."

His brow furrowed as he moved in front of Greyson. "Why?"

Greyson's expression clearly showed he thought Cyrus was an idiot. "My eye."

Unable to stop himself, Cyrus ran his fingers along the scar. Greyson froze, his breath growing jagged before yanking back. Cyrus bit his lip, then whispered, "Sorry."

Shifting away, Greyson scrubbed a hand through his black hair. "It's fine. Let's check the traps."

With a nod, Cyrus followed silently after him, fingertips tingling.

Greyson deftly led them through the forest, making nary a noise. He checked his traps and snares before picking them up. He'd only caught a couple of hares, which he shoved into a sack. The entire time Greyson scoured the ground, head swiveling, and occasionally, he picked some plants and stuck them in his bag. As the sun started to set, Greyson headed back.

When they arrived at the cabin, Cyrus asked, "Is there anything I can do?"

"No, it's fine," Greyson said as he began to clean the hares.

Cyrus didn't know what to do besides watch. Greyson was clearly used to being alone. He didn't need or want any assistance. Once finished, Greyson went inside with nary a word or look in his direction, and Cyrus followed, biting his lip.

When he turned around, Greyson focused on his mouth. Greyson stood there, frozen, for a few moments before clearing his throat and moving to the stove. He started cooking dinner—a simple meal of rabbit and some root vegetables. Cyrus wouldn't have minded helping, but Greyson seemed perfectly fine. Sitting on a chair, he leaned an elbow on the table and rested his head in his palm as he followed Greyson's every movement.

As soon as Greyson finished preparing the meal, he placed the food on the table, gaze averted. Cyrus said, "Thank you."

Greyson glanced up, frowning as usual, and nodded before shifting back to his meal. Staring at his own plate, Cyrus stabbed some of the food with his fork, then put it in his mouth. Flavor exploded on his tongue.

"This is excellent," he said, trying to start a conversation.

Nodding, Greyson ate a vegetable.

The silence unnerved him. It was empty inside of him with very few memories to contemplate. "What's your favorite color?"

"What?" Greyson asked, looking up.

"Your favorite color."

With a sigh, Greyson said, "Orange."

"What's mine?"

His mouth opened for a second, then his eyes slid toward the fireplace. "You will have to find out for yourself."

"That's right," he said. Greyson wanted him to discover everything for himself. "You must miss your friend. I'm sorry."

Brow furrowed, Greyson asked, "What?"

"Your friend, me. You must miss the me that I was."

Pinching the bridge of his nose, Greyson muttered, "Serpent below." He took a couple of deep breaths, then said, "You are still you. Don't worry about it."

"I'll try and remember. I promise."

"Fine," Greyson said, then went back to his meal.

5

GREYSON

Greyson sat before the crackling fire, drinking a cup of strong tea. Cyrus was across from him, staring blankly. There wasn't much in the way of entertainment. He had a few books, but they were magical theorem books that his mother had brought with her when she returned from her studies and enlistment in the capital. A couple he'd stolen from the royal library when he visited. None of the books would interest Cyrus nor did Greyson want to reveal he owned them in case Cyrus recovered his memories and recalled them.

"You should go to sleep."

Cyrus' gaze shifted to the lone bed. "Where are you going to sleep?"

"On the floor."

Eyes widening, he said, "I can't let you do that."

A sigh broke out of his lips. He'd sighed more in the last few days than he had his entire life. "It's fine, Cyrus. Go to sleep." Cyrus opened his mouth, but Greyson snapped, "Just sleep."

Expression falling, Cyrus undressed before he settled on the bed. "Thank you, Greyson."

His eyes flicked to Cyrus, who stared at him as he rested on his side. "It's fine."

Greyson kept his gaze on the flames until he was absolutely certain that Cyrus had fallen asleep. Once he heard snoring, Greyson took three blankets from the chest pressed against the wall, then used the thickest as a mat, one as a pillow, and the final to cover himself. After he'd stripped off his clothes, Greyson stretched out.

Almost immediately, his back began to protest. He rolled to his right side and saw Cyrus sleeping on his back, mouth open, and blonde hair falling over his forehead.

What am I doing? Greyson thought. This was not a good plan or even a well-thought-out one, which was unusual for him. He'd acted before thinking, saving Cyrus with little regard for the future.

Maybe I could poison him?

A plan started to form in the back of his mind. He could slowly poison Cyrus while searching for the reason he'd traveled this far, and maybe he could figure out who'd wiped Cyrus' memory. If Greyson did find who'd erased his memory, they might know something about this journey Cyrus had taken.

The only problem was the emperor. If he found out, he would blame the entire Griseo Mountains and punish them, though no one besides his village had seen Cyrus yet. They wouldn't say anything. Greyson shook his head. It would've been better if he'd let Cyrus die.

Counting silently in his head, Greyson forced himself to fall asleep.

CYRUS

Cyrus awoke with a smile because Greyson was on his side, facing him. Cyrus tucked an arm under his head. In the void of nothingness around him where he couldn't recognize anything, Greyson and his familiarity were like a mooring rope that kept him from floating adrift. Their friendship was a balm to his soul and the bone-deep terror he felt with not remembering anything.

Even as he watched Greyson, Cyrus couldn't help but wonder. Greyson didn't act like they were friends.

Greyson jerked back. "What the hell? Why are you staring at me?" He rolled to his other side, then stood and stretched. Greyson wore nothing besides undershorts, which gave Cyrus an excellent view. Greyson didn't have well-defined muscles, but he was in no way out of shape. He donned some clothes before striding outside.

Cyrus threw the covers off. Standing, he put on his own clothes. The door opened, and Greyson returned. Cyrus went outside to take care of his needs, then headed back into the cabin.

The smell of food already filled the air, as Greyson started cooking breakfast. Cyrus sat at the table and watched him, stomach growling. Greyson deposited a plate in front of him with eggs and a slice of bread.

"Thank you."

Grunting, Greyson put the kettle on the flames for tea.

"Are we going into the village to send the letter?" he asked between bites.

"Yes," Greyson replied as he sat across from him. "We also need more bread. I usually buy it from Widow Abney."

"I'm surprised you can't bake bread."

"I can," Greyson said, "but I like to support her. Also..." He trailed off as his gaze wandered over Cyrus.

A blush started to rise to his cheeks from the close inspection. "What?"

"We'll have to do something about your clothes. Eventually, they'll have to be washed. If you weren't so short and broad, I would let you wear mine, but you won't fit into my clothes." Greyson pinched the bridge of his nose. "I'll have to ask Window Abney or Annabeth to make you some."

"Who's Annabeth?" A tightening sensation started in Cyrus' chest and stole his appetite.

"A woman in the village, and the closest thing we have to a seamstress." Greyson took a sip of his tea before eating his eggs.

Cyrus nibbled on his bread. "It would be nice to meet other people."

"Hmm."

Cyrus whistled jauntily as they entered the village. In the distance, he could see a few people in the fields doing who knew what. A couple of boys led a herd of bleating goats into the trees while a little girl of five or six chased after some chickens.

Several women huddled near the well, talking, and their eyes kept darting in his direction. Cyrus gave the gaggle of women a friendly wave, which they didn't return. Instead, their whispers intensified.

"Is there something wrong with me?" Cyrus asked, patting his body.

Greyson swiveled toward him, brow furrowed. "Why? Do you feel ill? Do you need to go back?"

"No." His eyes shifted to the women. "They keep looking at me."

With a frown, Greyson glanced at the group of women, who instantly became a flurry of activity. "There's nothing wrong with you. People here are not used to travelers or visitors. Ignore them."

"If you're sure," Cyrus said.

Greyson grunted, then stopped in front of a single-story house that had abundant orange flowers growing in the wooden planters under the windows. He knocked on the door with a brass knocker, and it creaked open, revealing Widow Abney.

Her wrinkled face stretched into a smile as she pushed the door all the way open. "What can I do for you two boys?"

"I was hoping you had some bread that I could purchase?" Greyson asked.

She waved them in. "Of course. I can whip some up and give it to you tomorrow. Why don't you two come in?"

The house boasted a decent-sized kitchen, a light wood table with matching chairs, a fireplace, and a bed. It was cozy and decorated in bright shades of yellow and blue. A strong smell of baked sugary treats filled the small space, lending a homey air, and it made him moan in appreciation.

Widow Abney ambled to the stone fireplace and put a kettle on the flames. "I assume you want tea, Greyson."

"You know me too well," he said as he sat at the table.

Cyrus sank onto the chair beside Greyson. "Do you come here a lot?"

"Yes. I lived with Widow Abney for a bit in my teenage years. Also, since her sons died, I've been taking care of her."

He nudged Greyson with his shoulder. "You're a nice guy."

Grunting, Greyson rolled his eyes, which made Cyrus chuckle. Greyson gave him the barest hint of a smile in return. Cyrus swallowed and his pulse raced as they stared at each other. Time slowed. Something powerful strung between them. Greyson's smile dimmed, but his eyes stayed soft. Cyrus leaned closer.

The tea kettle let out a shrill whistle, making them jump.

Widow Abney loaded a tray with a yellow teapot decorated with small white flowers, cups, and cookies. Cyrus jumped up and snatched it from her, so she didn't have to manage the tray as well as her cane. He set it on the table, teapot and cups rattling.

She sat across from them, resting her cane against the table, then poured them each a cup of tea. Cyrus took a drink and fought back a frown. It didn't taste as bitter as the tea Greyson made, but it clung unpleasantly to his tongue.

"This is good," he lied, setting the cup down and pushing it away.

"Widow Abney makes the best tea," Greyson said.

The old woman released a croaky laugh as she prodded the plate of cookies toward them. Cyrus gratefully accepted one. It was soft and melted on his tongue. Shaking his head, he thought, *This is amazing*.

"It's magic," she said, almost like she'd read his mind.

"What?" he asked, mouth falling open.

"Magic," Greyson repeated. "Not many people in the Griseo Mountains are traditionally trained, but almost everyone possesses some form of magic. Some people can tell with perfect accuracy what the weather will be or where someone lost something. Anything Widow Abney cooks tastes amazing. It's her gift."

Cyrus gaped at her. "That's the best gift possible."

Chuckling, she offered him another cookie while Greyson rolled his eyes and took a sip of tea. "Well, it has come in handy," Widow Abney said.

"I don't suppose you could make Cyrus some clothes? I will pay of course," Greyson asked, dipping a cookie in his tea.

"My hands are not what they used to be," she replied.

"I understand. I will have to ask Annabeth."

A frown immediately pulled on Cyrus' lips. He didn't know why, but he despised the idea of Greyson spending time with someone else. Widow Abney glanced between them for a couple of breaths before returning her gaze to Greyson.

"No need," she said. "My son's clothes should fit Cyrus."

Greyson took her hand. "Are you sure?"

"Yes, I'm sure."

"Okay," Greyson said, pulling back, then looked at Cyrus. "Can you find your way back to my cabin?"

Blinking, Cyrus asked, "Where are you going?"

"Check my traps, hunt for herbs, and such."

"Oh," he said, peeking at Widow Abney, who watched them with a curious expression. "I'll be able to get back."

"You promise to not search for me and go straight to the cabin?" Greyson asked as he rose.

"I'm not a child."

Scoffing, Greyson said, "That's debatable."

"I will go straight home."

"Good." Greyson nodded at Widow Abney and strode out of the house, closing the door behind him.

"Thank you for the clothes," he said.

She patted his hand. "You're a good boy."

They both sat in amiable silence for a few minutes as she finished her tea, and he ate the rest of the cookies.

Once she finished, Widow Abney slowly walked to a trunk under a window. Opening it, she rooted through the clothing, then waved her cane at him. "What are you doing? Get over here."

Cyrus came to her side and peered into the trunk. It was filled with clothes that appeared like they belonged to several different people, as they were different sizes and styles. "Whose are these?"

"My sons' and husband's. They're all gone."

"I'm so sorry."

"Thank you." She picked up a stack. "I think my eldest's clothes should fit you."

He accepted the clothes, trying them on. The shirts were a tad long, but overall, everything fit well. He changed into a green long-sleeved shirt made of soft wool and sturdy brown trousers. Widow Abney tugged on the hem of his shirt with a sad smile on her face, eyes wet. He didn't know what to say in the face of her grief.

Searching for anything to break the quiet, Cyrus asked, "How did you and Greyson come to know each other?"

"It's a small village. I've known him since he was born. I helped his mother bring him into this world. But since our families passed, we've gotten closer. We're both alone."

"I'm glad he has you."

"Now," she said, tugging on his shirt again, "he has you."

"Yes." He nodded. Greyson had him now.

"Well," Widow Abney said, "you better get home."

"Okay. I'll see you soon."

Bright orange blossoms caught his gaze as he opened the door. They were round balls with countless petals. Their vibrant orange contrasted against the light green stems. Looking over his shoulder, he asked, "Can I pick a couple of your flowers?"

"Of course. Why?"

"Orange is Greyson's favorite color."

Widow Abney smiled at him, sinking onto a chair. "I'm glad you came."

"Me too. The old me might not have agreed, but I can't know for sure because I can't remember."

"I'm still glad you're here." One hand clutched the top of her cane while the other gestured to the overflowing planters. "Help yourself."

"Thanks." Cyrus picked several, then waved goodbye to Widow Abney and headed home.

GREYSON

Greyson stepped into the one-room cabin, exhausted. Arms going above his head, stretching, he looked around. Stopping, his gaze froze on the orange flowers, King Zinnias, in his favorite cup. He glanced at Cyrus, who was sprawled on the bed like a giant cat, asleep.

What in the world am I doing?

His worst enemy had brought him flowers and slept in his bed. This could not be worth any chance of information or even killing Cyrus.

He touched one of the soft, smooth petals, flattening it. While he would have to relocate the flowers to a different cup, it was a nice gesture. He peeked over his shoulder at the sleeping man. Cyrus was on his back, arms thrown out and mouth open with thunderous snores escaping him. His feet moved to the bed, and Greyson peered at Cyrus. The golden boy of the capital. Warrior. Enemy. The greatest pain in the ass. How could Cyrus lay there completely at ease?

"You need to remember who you are and soon."

A loud snore erupted out of Cyrus' mouth.

Never in his life would Greyson have thought he would want to see Cyrus—the real Cyrus. This unshielded, vulnerable man before him unnerved Greyson. Keeping his back to Cyrus, he stoked the flames and carefully placed a kettle on for tea. Once the water boiled, he poured it into the teapot.

Setting the teapot down, Greyson pinched the bridge of his nose. *Why do the flowers bother me so much?* He could throw them outside if he wanted. They were just flowers—flowers that Cyrus had picked for him. Greyson refused to contemplate it. He strode to the cabinet and removed another cup, standing a bit back from the table as he poured tea into it, spout resting on the rim of the cup. He sank onto a chair as his gaze moved to the flowers. He would switch them to another cup. Tomorrow.

6

CYRUS

Cyrus rolled over, and there was a figure stretched on the ground. In the darkness, he couldn't see Greyson's features in detail, but he heard the gentle sound of his breath going in and out. Cyrus tucked an arm under his head and stared at him.

Groaning, Greyson shifted. His face scrunched, looking uncomfortable, then his expression smoothed as he fell back asleep. Worry plucked at Cyrus' heartstrings. The floor couldn't be comfortable. Greyson made another noise, but this one sounded upset—scared even.

He scooted to the edge of the bed to pat Greyson's arm in an attempt to soothe him. "It's alright, Greyson," Cyrus whispered, watching his face closely.

Greyson's eyebrows squished together as he whimpered. Cyrus grabbed Greyson's hand and continued to make calming sounds. Eventually, Greyson settled back into a deep slumber and fell quiet.

He would have to talk to him about trading nights on the bed, so Greyson didn't spend every night on the floor. *Of course*, he thought, *we could always share*. He smothered a smile. That prospect didn't bother him in the slightest. Somehow, he didn't think Greyson would be amiable to that idea.

Laying on his stomach, Cyrus squeezed Greyson's fingers as he fell asleep to the sound of even breathing and the warmth of skin.

GREYSON

Sunlight filtered in from the windows, waking Greyson. With a blurry gaze, he squinted at the bright light in confusion as his back throbbed. He'd overslept. Normally, he arose before the sun, but for whatever reason, he'd slept longer than usual. He started to stand when something stopped him.

Cyrus held his hand.

He gaped, unable to move in the slightest. Calluses covered Cyrus' hand, probably from the constant sword work, and scraped against Greyson's skin. His palm was wide, fingers thick and stubby, almost swallowing Greyson's much thinner one. Greyson's hand felt warm, and, surprisingly, comfortable in the warrior's grasp.

Cyrus slept on his stomach, face relaxed as he quietly snored. Greyson had never been this close to him before.

Well, at least not when he wasn't angry or fighting Cyrus. It was odd to be so close, to see his sleeping face.

He twisted out of Cyrus' grasp and got to his feet, stifling a cry. His back ached. He lifted his arms above his head before twisting side to side. His bare feet dragged across the wood floor to his clothes, which he donned before striding outside to take care of his needs.

When he re-entered, he threw some kindling and logs onto the coals. They quickly caught, sending a pleasant heat throughout the cabin. With winter coming, the air had grown cold, especially in the morning. Once the flames steadily burned, Greyson started the water for his morning tea.

Cyrus still slept, sprawled across the bed. Greyson shook his head and began making breakfast. Cyrus would be hungry when he woke up, as he'd slept through dinner. Greyson tried to move as quietly as possible to not wake him.

As he prepared the tea, he couldn't help but stare at the cup full of bright orange flowers. He'd planned to transfer them to another container, but Greyson found he couldn't. It was like they belonged where Cyrus had placed them.

Shaking his head, he refused to think about it because it didn't matter. He would either kill Cyrus, or the man would remember who he was and this charade would end. At the thought of ending Cyrus' life, Greyson's gaze flicked toward the kitchen before darting back to the bed. Cyrus had not moved.

He removed the false back on the top shelf of the cabinet. A handful of innocent-looking berries sat in the cubby. The rubrum berries' bright red color contrasted against the dark green of the leaves. Sweet to the taste, it would be easy to add them to Cyrus' food. Slowly, he would fall sick—vomiting, fever, chills—then he would die after a week or two. Of course, if Greyson fed him all of the berries, Cyrus would die in an hour or so, screaming as he clutched his stomach.

Carefully, he held the berries by the twig they clung to. Greyson twisted them one way, then the next, the light glinting off their shiny skin. His jaw clenched. Should he poison Cyrus? It would be easy. Barely an effort. Add a berry here and there, and Cyrus would be gone.

Unease twisted his gut. It felt almost underhanded. It shouldn't.

During the rebellion, Greyson had poisoned the enemy soldier's food stores and water. It had become a trademark of sorts for him in the short but deadly war.

I should've let him die, Greyson thought. He thoroughly cursed his soft heart and the rain.

"Good morning," a groggy voice said.

Greyson shoved the berries into the cabinet, then put the false back in its proper position before turning to Cyrus. "You're finally awake."

Cyrus' arms went above his head as he yawned loudly. He stood, then went outside in nothing more than his undershorts. Cyrus would freeze in the chilly mountain air. Greyson took a sip of warm tea, then finished making a simple breakfast of hotcakes and eggs. When he set the food on the table, the door creaked open and Cyrus rushed in, rubbing his arms.

"It's freezing out there," Cyrus complained.

He scoffed. "No one told you to go outside basically naked."

Not bothering to get dressed, Cyrus sank down across from him. Greyson rolled his eyes, not commenting, as he prodded a cup of tea toward Cyrus, who grinned in response. Cyrus plunked most of the hotcakes on his plate, then spread a heaping amount of butter on them before taking a huge bite.

"Delicious," Cyrus groaned, mouth full of food.

"Shut your mouth."

Cyrus grinned, cheeks full like a chipmunk. Greyson frowned and placed a spoonful of eggs on Cyrus' plate. He nodded his thanks, chewing the mouthful of hotcakes. Greyson frowned again and took a reasonable-sized bite of food while he stared at the flowers resting in the middle of the table.

"Did you get those for me?" he asked, not looking at Cyrus.

"Yep. You said you like the color orange."

Nodding, he glanced toward Cyrus and then away. "Thank you."

"I'm glad you like them."

Greyson cleared his throat, guilt surfacing about his earlier murderous thoughts. It shouldn't bother him; Cyrus deserved it. Nevertheless, the annoying sensation persisted. "It was a nice surprise. Did you get them from Widow Abney?"

"Yes. She didn't mind me picking them. She also had plenty of clothes that fit me."

Greyson poked at his food, not even glancing at Cyrus. A hushed, muttering came from across the table, and unable to help himself, he studied Cyrus. His face was pinched as he mumbled under his breath.

"Did she say something to upset you?" Greyson asked. He had not explicitly told Widow Abney or anyone else to not say anything to Cyrus. He was counting on people's general dislike to keep Cyrus from finding out the truth. Not a great plan, but none of this situation had been well thought out.

"No," Cyrus said, then shook his head. "Well, yes. Her family died."

"Yes, they did. Her husband died years ago, then her sons died in the rebellion."

"Your family's gone too?"

"Yes."

"I'm sorry."

Greyson had waited years to hear an apology from Cyrus, but this is not how he'd imagined it. He wanted it when Cyrus kneeled on the ground, defeated. He pushed the image out of his mind. "My family was not your fault."

"I can still feel bad about it."

"They died over ten years ago. It's fine," he said, returning to his breakfast. The eggs had gone cold and rubbery. Greyson forced himself to eat them and the hotcakes before downing the remainder of his tea.

"So," Cyrus asked between bites, "what are we doing today?"

"I suppose that means you want to come with me?"

"Of course."

Of course, Greyson thought with a shake of his head. He pushed his empty plate to the center of the table, then poured himself another cup of tea. Leaning back in his chair, he contemplated what to do. It would take a month at least for the letter to reach the capital and another month to return with Frederick's response.

Greyson could check his traps, harvest roots and herbs, then pick up the bread from Widow Abney, not leaving the area. Or he could take Cyrus around and see if he could find the person who wiped his memories. Even if by some miracle he found the mage, it would hardly matter. It was impossible to restore Cyrus' memory. But they might have vital information about why Cyrus was here. Maybe he'd said something and that was why his memories had been taken?

Of course, if Cyrus had merely hit his head, then Greyson would be out of luck.

He could spend the next two months twiddling his thumbs or he could rustle up some information. Though if he showed Cyrus around, Greyson couldn't kill him. Poison or not. Too many people would have seen him at that point, and if Cyrus died, word might reach the emperor's ears about his presence in the Griseo Mountains.

Despite that, he went so far as to pick the rubrum berries yesterday, but could he actually use them?

A callous hand rested on top of his, making Greyson jerk. "Are you alright?" Cyrus asked.

Warmth seeped into his skin from the simple contact. Cyrus' brow furrowed, forming two lines between his perfectly arched eyebrows, and his mouth curled down. As Greyson stared at his enemy's face, he didn't know if he could go through with his earlier plan.

Could he end his life? Destroy that easy smile?

"Greyson?" Cyrus asked, squeezing his hand.

"I'm fine," he lied, withdrawing from his warm grasp.

CYRUS

Cyrus watched Greyson, whose expression didn't change as he extracted his hand from Cyrus' grip. He immediately missed the contact, but let it go. "So what did you want to do today?"

"Gather supplies."

"Supplies for what?"

"Your memory loss has two possibilities: head trauma or someone magically scrubbed your brain."

"Okay," he said slowly.

"I can't do anything about a head injury. Magic, though, we might be able to find the person who did it," Greyson explained.

"Could they reverse it?" Cyrus didn't know if he wanted his memory back or not. He should want it to return, to remember his life, his friendship with Greyson, but his stomach churned. What if he remembered something bad? While, presently, he felt like a flag in a windstorm, it was manageable with Greyson by his side. But what if he remembered something he didn't like?

"No. At least, I don't think so. But we might be able to find out why they did it. It could tell us something, maybe."

That didn't sound very definitive, but Cyrus let it go. "How do we find them?"

"I figure we travel to different villages in the Griseo Mountains, and I'll talk to the mages I know, hence the supplies."

"You think a mage did this to me?"

Greyson took a drink of tea. "Everyone here has magic, but there are basically no trained mages; my mother was an exception and she taught me. So it could be someone with a little magic and no training. It doesn't take much to scrub someone's mind. It's rather crude."

"Do you think I can regain my memories?"

"I honestly don't know."

"Well," Cyrus said, shrugging, "let's get supplies, then talk to your mage friends."

7

GREYSON

As Greyson readied for their trip, back aching from sleeping on the floor, Cyrus was sprawled on the bed, asleep. He didn't bother to be quiet, stomping from one end of the cabin to the other while growling under his breath. Despite the noise, Cyrus did not stir.

Frowning, he kicked the bed. "Wake up."

Cyrus lifted his head. "Greyson?"

"Yes. Wake up."

Jerking back, Cyrus didn't say anything but gave him a sad smile and put on his clothes before exiting the cabin. Greyson ignored his hurt-puppy act as he made a simple breakfast of eggs and toast, as well as tea.

They ate in silence for several minutes until Cyrus commented, "I think hotcakes are my favorite."

Unable to stop it, a chuckle broke out of his lips. "You've tasted hardly anything, and you're ready to commit to hotcakes as your favorite?"

"Yes," Cyrus said. "They're my favorite."

He swallowed as he stared at him. Cyrus focused directly on him, his expression intent and serious. He almost resembled his old self. "Well, today you have eggs," Greyson ground out, heart beating rapidly as fear pumped through his veins.

Greyson did not know if he wanted to see the real Cyrus face-to-face again, even though he'd wanted that a few days ago. The small glimpse of the warrior hiding beneath this facade scared him more than he wanted to admit.

The expression disappeared, and Cyrus grinned innocently. "What's your favorite?"

"Cinnamon buns."

"You should make some when we get back."

"They take a long time," Greyson said.

"Oh. You should still make them."

"Fine," Greyson said in a clipped voice.

They finished their meal in silence. Once the dishes were clean, Greyson collected his cloak, staff, and bag, throwing it over his shoulder before he shifted toward Cyrus, who stood in the middle of the cabin, arms swinging at his sides. Greyson sighed and grabbed another cloak—the one that Widow Abney had given to Cyrus. He threw it over Cyrus' shoulders and fastened it.

"Thank you," Cyrus said, staring at him with a wide smile.

He pulled back, swallowing. "Where's your sword?" Cyrus didn't bother to answer as he secured the blade and strapped it on. Greyson handed him a pack. "Let's go."

CYRUS

The morning air was crisp, and his breath came out in foggy gasps. His hands were cold and stiff. He kept curling and uncurling them, but it didn't seem to help. He walked right next to Greyson's left side. Greyson, unlike Cyrus, seemed completely comfortable in the chill, but then again, he lived here in the mountains; whereas, Cyrus lived...he actually didn't know where he lived.

"Is it always so cold?"

Snorting, Greyson stepped lightly over the frosted ground. "It's only going to get colder."

"Oh." He did not like the sound of that. "Have I ever lived anywhere cold?"

Greyson's eyes darted in his direction before facing forward again. "I don't know, but as far as I'm aware, no. You always lived in the capital, which is right next to the southern coastline."

"So it's warm?"

"Yes."

They continued up a steep hill. Pine needles scattered the ground and crunched under their boots, releasing a sharp scent. Even this late in the season, birds sang from the trees. Cyrus smiled, head leaning back as a light breeze ruffled his hair. It was peaceful walking next to his friend. It also felt familiar. The feel of the ground, the creaking of the trees, the forward movement. If Cyrus had to guess, he would assume that he'd spent a considerable amount of time trekking across the land.

When the sun hung high above them, Greyson stopped. "We should eat lunch."

Cyrus sat right next to Greyson, leaning against a craggy rock that jabbed into his back. He had to reposition several times as he munched on hard cheese, dried meat, and an apple. The thin pines shifted in the wind, and in the distance, a creek gurgled.

Cyrus asked, "How long until we reach the village?"

"Tomorrow evening."

"That's not long."

With a shake of his head, Greyson said, "It's the closest village to mine, and my good friend Elizabeth lives there."

When Cyrus heard the woman's name, he frowned. Taking a bite of his crisp apple, juice flicking his chin, he stared at Greyson, whose expression didn't change in the slightest. "How well do you know her?"

"Well enough."

"What does that mean?"

"Why?" Greyson asked.

"Why not?" Cyrus didn't know why, but the thought of Greyson being close to someone else bothered him.

Greyson studied him before shrugging. "I trained Elizabeth. We fought in the rebellion together. We're friends."

"Does she know me?" he asked, lips pursing. If the woman had fought in the war, maybe they had met, as he'd served with Greyson.

"In passing, I think."

He nodded, not saying anything else.

After they both finished, Greyson brushed himself off. His head tilted to the side, black hair falling around his sharp cheekbones. "Are you coming?"

Smiling, Cyrus got up. "Of course."

"Then let's go."

Cyrus watched Greyson for a moment, then chased after him.

GREYSON

When the sun set, they stopped near a babbling brook. Trees surrounded them, and there was a fallen tree that was starting to rot to the left of their camp. Greyson filled his waterskin, hands dipping into the frigid water; his fingers turned red almost immediately. He dried them off, then checked on Cyrus, who huddled on the ground, shivering. Cyrus already had his cloak drawn tightly around him.

Greyson rifled through the pack next to Cyrus, then removed a green woolen tunic. Without bothering to speak, he unclasped Cyrus' cloak and tugged it over his head. Cyrus obliged by putting his arms into the sleeves, shaking, then Greyson draped the cloak over his shoulders.

"I'm so cold," Cyrus said, teeth chattering.

How would Cyrus ever survive the harsh winter in the Griseo Mountains? "I'm going to make a fire. You'll be fine."

Gathering wood and stones, he scraped aside the pine needles with the edge of his boot before placing the stones in a ring and starting a fire. Cyrus scooted as close as possible. Greyson watched him to make sure he was staying safe as he began making dinner.

Shockingly, Cyrus remained quiet. Greyson didn't think Cyrus knew how to be silent. Apparently, he was wrong. Greyson added several vegetables, bits of dried meat, and seasonings to a pot. Before long, a savory scent wafted from the bubbling soup, making his stomach grumble. He was not alone. Cyrus continued to huddle near the flames, but his wide eyes were fixed on the pot, as his throat bobbed with frequent swallows.

Greyson had to fight back a chuckle at Cyrus' hungry expression. "It'll be done soon."

Cyrus nodded but didn't reply.

He stirred the soup for several more minutes before it was done. Greyson gave Cyrus a cup of tea, half a loaf of bread, and a bowl of soup. He accepted the bowl, dunking the bread into the broth before shoving it into his mouth.

Satisfied that Cyrus was eating, Greyson turned to his own food. The soup was flavorful and rich, and the bread was delicious, as Widow Abney had baked it. They continued to eat in silence. Once Cyrus finished, he asked for more, which Greyson gave him. Cyrus polished off the remainder of the soup, though he only drank one cup of tea.

Once they were done, Greyson collected the dirty dishes, washed them, and put everything in the bag. Then he spread one of the bedrolls next to the fire and dropped the extra blankets he'd brought on it. He'd known Cyrus would become cold in the open night air.

"Lay down before you freeze to death."

Cyrus flopped onto the bedroll, and Greyson repositioned the blankets over him with a shake of his head. *Always the nursemaid*, he thought. He gathered more wood, throwing a few pieces on the flames, then stacked the rest so they could add to the fire as needed.

He peered at Cyrus, who continued to shiver, even under the thick blankets. Greyson's jaw worked side to side. Coming to a snap decision, he dropped his own bedroll next to Cyrus, lifted the blankets, and settled against him.

"Greyson?"

"Yes?" he asked with his back pressed against Cyrus. Cyrus rolled over, scooting close to him. Greyson's hand curled around his staff.

"Nothing's going to eat us, right?"

A startled laugh broke out of his lips. "No. The fire will keep the predators away, and I have my staff right here."

"So I'm safe?"

Greyson swallowed. "Yes. You're safe."

CYRUS

Settled next to Greyson, Cyrus was chilled but not as frozen as earlier. The fire warmed his back while Greyson warmed the rest of him. Greyson's breath came out slow and even, deep asleep. Slowly, carefully, Cyrus snaked an arm over his waist and drew Greyson against his chest. Greyson groaned but did not wake. Cyrus' breath became shallow and harsh as his heart bashed against his ribs, threatening to escape.

The feel of Greyson's body against his felt right. Greyson fit perfectly in his embrace. Cyrus buried his cold nose against Greyson's neck and breathed in the scent of pine and soil. His body relaxed. This felt right. Cyrus had no other way to describe it.

Maybe we were once like this? he thought, not that Greyson acted like it. Closing his eyes, Cyrus snuggled close.

8

GREYSON

Greyson blinked at the gray light filtering through the crowded branches. Warmth surrounded him, and he felt surprisingly comfortable on the hard ground. Stretching, he suddenly stopped when an arm tightened around his waist, pulling him against another body.

His pulse skittered as he patted the frost-covered ground for his staff. The instant his fingers touched the twisted wood, he held it in a white-knuckled grip. Greyson tried to move, but Cyrus held him fast, warm breath rushing over the back of his neck.

Swallowing, Greyson touched Cyrus' arm, the muscles stiffened under his fingertips. Slowly, he trailed down his arm until he reached Cyrus' hand, his palm rough and wide.

Cyrus nuzzled him. "Good morning."

"Good morning," he said between his clenched teeth.

They lay there silently as Cyrus held him and Greyson's thoughts whirled. He wanted to lash out, scold him, but the words wouldn't come. With every moment that passed, his body grew warmer and his breath turned rougher.

Unable to think of anything else, Greyson said, "We need to get a move on."

"Alright." Cyrus loosened his hold and stretched with a loud yawn.

The second Cyrus let him go, Greyson bolted up, staff in hand. His heart pounded and his neck felt oddly hot as his thoughts lingered on the feel of Cyrus' arms around him. He'd never been so close to Cyrus, not once in their entire acquaintance. He strode toward the trees to answer nature's call with a little bit of privacy and to collect himself.

When he returned, Cyrus sat in front of the fire that he must have restarted. Greyson could not look at him as he began breakfast. Once they finished eating, Greyson led them east toward Creekside. They should arrive near nightfall, thankfully. He didn't want a repeat of last night.

After a couple of hours of quiet, Greyson glanced at Cyrus who had a thoughtful expression on his face as his eyes wandered over the woods. He didn't know why Cyrus' silence unnerved him, but it did. Shaking it off, he continued.

In the middle of the day, they stopped for a short respite. Greyson gave Cyrus a couple of pieces of dried meat, an apple, and a hunk of hard cheese. Cyrus accepted them with a smile, which made his heart thump. Sitting, Greyson scanned the trees. The area did not appear any different than the woods that surrounded his home. Of course, the Griseo Mountains all basically appeared the same until you reached the peaks or the icy coastline in the north.

Cyrus kept glancing in his direction, but neither of them spoke. The only sounds were the chirping birds and an occasional rustling from game animals like rabbits or turkeys, even though Greyson did not see any. Once they finished their meal, they started walking again.

The temperatures dropped drastically as the sun started to set, and Cyrus hunched his shoulders, curling in on himself. Greyson stopped when he heard Cyrus' teeth chattering.

"You should put on your woolen tunic," Greyson said, frowning.

With a nod, Cyrus shakily dropped his bag, though his hands trembled too much to open it. Greyson ripped open the brown sack, then took out the thick tunic Cyrus had taken off earlier this morning. Not bothering to ask, he undid the clasp of Cyrus' cloak, then slipped it over his head. Once Cyrus put it on, Greyson draped the cloak back over his shoulders and clasped it.

Satisfied, Greyson started off again. While the additional clothing seemed to help, Cyrus continued to tremble. They traveled in the dark for a couple of hours until they came to a village that consisted of almost a dozen houses. Creekside, much like Greyson's village, was a farming village that helped provide food for the whole of the Griseo Mountains. They also raised sheep and goats and fished in the stream.

By the time he could see the village, Cyrus' teeth chattered so loudly that Greyson feared they would shatter.

He glanced at Cyrus for the hundredth time. "We're close," he said, not able to see him well in the low light. Cyrus only nodded. Greyson headed straight to a home on the edge of the village and knocked on the door. It cracked open and revealed a tall woman with black curly hair and a round face that radiated kindness from the fine wrinkles around her deep brown eyes to the perpetual smile on her thin lips.

"Greyson," she said, waving him inside.

"Hello, Elizabeth." Greyson followed her inside and dragged the shivering Cyrus behind him. Her eyes widened and her mouth dropped open when she caught sight of Cyrus. Greyson shook his head, and she snapped her mouth close. He made Cyrus sit next to the fire, then he looked at Elizabeth, who gaped at him.

"Do you have tea or something warm to drink?"

"You know where it is," Elizabeth said, covering her mouth as she stared at Cyrus, face pale.

Greyson removed a kettle and a green tin from a cabinet in the kitchen. He stuck the kettle on the flames before securing a teapot and a couple of cups. The whole while, Cyrus watched him but said nary a word. Greyson tried to ignore his gaze, but it made his shoulder blades itch. Elizabeth kept watching them, eyes bulging.

"Greyson," she said in a calm voice.

"Give me a moment." Greyson's gaze flicked back to Cyrus. His face had regained some color, and his teeth had finally stopped chattering. "Are you okay?" Greyson asked, and Cyrus nodded. As he started to stand, Cyrus latched onto his arm. Greyson's brow furrowed. "What?"

Cyrus didn't say anything as he continued to hold on. Frowning, Greyson pressed his free hand to Cyrus' forehead, worried he'd started to get sick again. He didn't feel warm, but Greyson studied him before patting Cyrus' arm and saying, "I'll be right back."

Standing, Greyson strode closer to Elizabeth who immediately asked in a squeaky voice, "Are you insane?"

Peeking at Cyrus, who watched them with a furrowed brow, he said, "Later. I'll explain everything later. I promise."

She crossed her arms. "Fine, but you'd better have a good explanation for this."

Greyson smiled tightly at Elizabeth who stared at him with an arched eyebrow. There really wasn't. He wished he had one, but he doubted his feeble excuses would satisfy her. "I do."

He poured the boiling water into a white teapot painted with pink roses, Elizabeth's favorite flower. After the tea steeped, he gave a cup to Cyrus, who accepted it with cold fingers.

"Elizabeth, would you like some?"

"No," she said, standing on the opposite side of the house, pressed against the wall with wide eyes.

They sat in silence, and Elizabeth did not move from her position while a thick tension filled the air. Greyson couldn't find the words to dissipate it. She had good reasons to despise Cyrus, very similar to Greyson and most people of the Griseo Mountains.

His gaze flicked over the small home with a modest kitchen, matching table and chairs, a fireplace with a couple of rocking chairs in front of it, and a single door near the back, searching for evidence of another person. But besides the blanket thrown over the back of a chair and a stack of books, he couldn't find anything out of place. It wasn't surprising that she was alone, but Greyson did not want to put Cyrus in danger from a random person appearing.

After a bit, Greyson puttered around her kitchen, making a dinner of eggs and toast. Cyrus wandered over to the table, gaze darting to Elizabeth. She finally peeled off the wall and sat at the table as far from Cyrus as possible, staring at him.

Greyson scooped some food onto a plate for Cyrus and poured him another cup of tea before serving Elizabeth. "How are you?"

She grunted.

"Any beaus I should speak to?" he asked, even though he knew the answer.

Her eyebrows raised. "Seriously?"

He smiled in response, and she just ignored him as she continued eating. Elizabeth's husband had died last year, and she hadn't moved on yet.

"Cyrus, are you warm?" he asked, trying to fill the silence for some unknown reason. It picked at him, making him squirm.

"Yeah." Cyrus poked at his eggs without eating them.

The remainder of the meal passed in tense silence until Elizabeth rose, chair scraping on the floor. "I think I'll go to bed."

Immediately, Cyrus seized his arm, expression urgent. Greyson frowned. He had absolutely no idea what was going on with Cyrus. Shaking his head, Greyson said to Elizabeth, "Goodnight."

With her hands fisted in the skirt of her lavender gown, she headed into a bedroom off the main room, closing the door behind her.

When Cyrus did not let go of his arm, Greyson considered him with a furrowed brow. "Are you alright?"

"Yes."

"Finish your tea." Greyson took a long drink; it was a different blend than his but delicious regardless. Cyrus took a sip, face scrunching. "Do you not like it?"

"No. Apparently, I'm not a tea person."

Who doesn't like tea? He could not even fathom someone disliking it. Greyson supposed it made sense in some cosmic way because Cyrus was his enemy. Though, at this moment, sitting in the warm house and staring into his open expression, it was hard for Greyson to think of Cyrus as his foe. Putting it out of his head, Greyson snagged the cup and set it aside.

"You could've said something. You don't have to drink it."

"How well do you know this woman?" Cyrus asked, gaze averted.

"I already told you, twice I believe. We're friends."

"But you've been here before?"

"Yes," Greyson answered slowly. "We're friends."

"You've been here so many times that you know where she keeps her tea." Cyrus would not look at him, instead, staring at the shifting flames.

"Let me tell you a secret."

Cyrus shifted toward him, mouth opening.

Stifling a chuckle, he continued, "I pretty much know where everyone keeps their tea."

With a wide grin, Cyrus asked, "You like tea?"

"I do." He took another drink, and they both fell silent.

Once he finished, Greyson placed the dishes in the kitchen. He would wash them in the morning. Then he dropped a bedroll right next to the fireplace for Cyrus, dumping the blankets on top of it, before putting his own some distance away. He didn't want a repeat of last night.

Even as he thought about it, his heart started to thump and he felt oddly warm as the skin between his shoulder blades tightened. Clearing his throat, Greyson lay down.

"What are you doing?"

"What do you mean?" Greyson asked.

"You're sleeping all the way over there."

"Yes, because it's too warm next to the fire," he lied, rolling onto his right side, back to Cyrus.

The only sound in the open room was the occasional snaps and pops of the fire. Greyson shifted on the hard floor, wincing. He rolled his cloak up, then shoved it under his head.

A dragging noise started, followed by a soft thump as someone settled behind him.

"Is this okay?" Cyrus asked. "I feel more comfortable next to you."

Greyson wanted to say no; instead, he replied, "It's fine."

Blankets covered him as Cyrus slid an arm over his waist, pulling him close. "Goodnight."

"Goodnight." Warmth encased him while the sound of Cyrus' even breathing began to lure him to sleep.

CYRUS

Cyrus held Greyson in his arms. Greyson's breath eventually evened into slumber. He didn't know what was going on with them, but he liked Greyson resting in his embrace. His thoughts shot back to the woman whose house they stayed in—Elizabeth. She seemed attractive enough, he supposed, in her mid-to-late twenties like Greyson.

For some reason, when she smiled at Greyson, something curled in his stomach and made him uncomfortable, edgy. He didn't like it. Greyson seemed calm enough when he talked about her, but it made Cyrus uneasy.

A scared moan came from Greyson that drew him to the present. Cyrus tightened his hold, pulling him as close as possible. "You're okay," he whispered. "I'm here."

Greyson's breathing quickened as he started to twitch. Cyrus rubbed his arm and nuzzled his neck. "Shh, it's okay, I promise," he said, trying to soothe the nightmare. Greyson didn't calm, so Cyrus grabbed his hand and held it over his stomach, squeezing him tight.

Eventually, the dream passed, and Greyson quieted.

Cyrus closed his eyes with a relieved smile as Greyson relaxed. He pressed his face against Greyson's neck while he rubbed his arm, hoping to soothe any lingering stress. Waves of sleep started to draw him in, and Cyrus reveled in the warmth and comfort. His last conscious thought was of Greyson and how Cyrus never wanted it to end.

9

GREYSON

"Are you out of your mind?" Elizabeth asked the next day.

Greyson stood outside, not far from Elizabeth's house, and watched Cyrus kick a ball around with a group of teenagers in the middle of the village. The sun was decently warm for the late fall day without a single cloud in the sky.

All morning, she'd held her peace about bringing the golden boy of the capital into her house, but now that they were alone, she did not hold back.

"You brought the emperor's nephew, his only nephew, *here*. What's going on?"

This was a bad idea—a very bad idea. He didn't have a good explanation for her, but he had to come up with one. Unable to, he scanned the village, searching for differences since the last time he'd been here. Most of the homes were single-story while a few were two stories with shops on the ground floor. All of the buildings were wood with thick windows, shutters, and full planters. There were a couple of buildings toward the center of the village that were three-story and under construction.

Creekside, like a few other villages, had started growing now that more money was starting to enter the Griseo Mountains.

Elizabeth coughed.

"Cyrus doesn't remember who he is," Greyson said, even though it was not much of a reason.

"So take him to Woodhurst and leave him with the emperor's representative. Lord Darius will take care of it."

"I need to know why he's here, and if it spells trouble for us all."

She twirled a frizzy curl around her finger. "Did you ask anyone from the capital?"

"Yes," he replied, eyes following Cyrus as he chased after the children, laughing uproariously. "But it'll be at least a couple of months before I receive a response."

"You might not find anything out, and even if you did, what would it matter? We couldn't survive another war."

Elizabeth was right. The information was probably not worth the risk. Nonetheless, Greyson couldn't send him to the representative yet, for reasons he did not understand. He had a hard time explaining the complete unwillingness to send Cyrus away that resided in his very muscles, making them tense at the very thought. It was irrational, but it wouldn't be banished.

In an attempt to defend his rash decision, he said, "We can prepare better if we know what the emperor plans."

Elizabeth scoffed. "Yeah, right. What plan could withstand the force that he would rain down upon us?"

Greyson had no argument to dispute that, so he remained quiet, watching as Cyrus raced back and forth with the teenagers who were too young to know who he was and to fear him for it. At the same time, they were also too old to fear him for simply being an outsider.

"He'd better not die," Elizabeth said abruptly.

"Why?"

"If you'd kept him secluded in your home, it wouldn't matter. But," she said, gesturing to all the people around them, "too many people have seen him now. If he dies, someone might mention his presence to the wrong person, and Emperor Caspian would blame us. I swear I will rat you out for the preservation of the rest of us."

"I know," Greyson said, "I was already having second thoughts about killing him."

"Just pass him off to Lord Darius, Greyson. He's not your problem, and you could endanger us all."

She was right again, but as Greyson watched Cyrus smiling broadly, he didn't want to take him to Woodhurst. It would spell the end of all his chances to find out why Cyrus had traveled from the capital to here—the middle of nowhere. If something happened to Cyrus, it could be disastrous for all of his people. The emperor was not a kind man, and he lurked in the background, waiting for a chance to tighten his grasp on them once more.

"Do you know who could have wiped his memories?" he asked.

"Are you sure someone scrambled his mind?"

"Pretty sure, yeah. He didn't even know his own name. He had no head injuries that I could find, and it happened here."

"Honestly, I don't know. I didn't do it if that's what you're asking. Where did it happen?"

"I can't know for sure," he told her, "but Cyrus told me he woke up in the glade."

Elizabeth nodded. He did not have to specify what glade. Everyone in the Griseo Mountains called that area "the glade," the location where the first battle in the short war had taken place. He'd lost his eye there, and many people had lost their lives. It was a graveyard for both sides.

"Do you think he could've come upon someone doing something they shouldn't be doing?" she asked carefully.

"Necromancy," he stated blatantly. It was a rare gift, exceedingly rare, and one they did not talk about. In general, some people looked unfavorably at mages, and they didn't know about necromancers. They were an anomaly, a well-kept secret. There could be uncomfortable questions if it was found out that some mages dug up bodies and used them in their arts.

"There are many bodies buried there, and they are soaked in blood and anger. Potentially, the bones could be quite powerful."

Elizabeth grimaced. "It's distasteful and makes my skin crawl, but I suppose, yes." Shaking her head, she continued, "Imagine someone digging up a body, then the emperor's nephew stumbles upon them. Of course, they wiped his mind. He's lucky they didn't kill him."

"Well, we don't know for certain, but that's a possibility."

"You know where necromancers usually come from."

Greyson pinched the bridge of his nose. "Davies."

"Yep."

The Davies family had given birth to most of the known necromancers. They lived on the icy coast on the other side of the Griseo Mountain range. The head of the family, Charles Davies, and Greyson had an *interesting* relationship. They had almost come to blows over a misunderstanding.

"I'm sure he's forgiven me," Greyson reasoned. "It's been five years."

"He thought you were trying to seduce his daughter. I don't think five years is enough."

"It was a misunderstanding. She asked for me to demonstrate a spell, to which I agreed, and then I tried to show her. When Charles passed by, I happened to be standing quite close behind her. She and I both explained nothing happened, but he refused to listen. I mean, Julia was only seventeen at the time, a child, and we were planning a rebellion. I would have never even thought about it. I wouldn't even contemplate it now. It's ridiculous."

"It didn't seem to matter to Charles," Elizabeth remarked. "But you shouldn't completely discount Julia. She is beautiful, talented, and extremely kind."

Greyson shrugged. He had very little interest in romance. It had never been a factor in his life. When he would've started courting, his parents and sister died and his entire world became taking his mother's place, teaching others to wield magic and making potions as well as poultices. He dabbled a little in romance, but he'd never really cared. Now, he had no interest in upsetting his life for the slight chance of falling in love.

Unwillingly, his gaze shifted to Cyrus. Already Greyson's life had been upended; he didn't need anyone else screwing it up. All of sudden, Cyrus stopped playing and met his gaze. Cyrus grinned and started to head in their direction.

"Don't say anything to him. I haven't told Cyrus anything," he said quickly.

She raised her eyebrows but didn't respond.

Cyrus jiggled his left arm. "Did you want to play?"

"No."

Expression falling, Cyrus asked, "What are you two talking about?"

"I was simply asking Elizabeth if she had any idea who erased your memories."

"Any idea?" Cyrus asked her.

"No, unfortunately not. I suggest you ask Charles Davies," she offered, smirking.

"Who?" Cyrus asked.

"Oh, no one," she said in a sing-song voice, twirling a curl around her finger. "Greyson just had a little encounter with his daughter, Julia."

"What?" Cyrus' eyebrows scrunched together.

"Nothing happened. She's basically a child."

"Twenty-two is not a child. She's only five years younger than you," Elizabeth said.

"Whatever," Greyson said with a wave. It hardly mattered. They were friends and nothing else. "Besides, I think she got married."

"I have no idea. But are you going to travel all the way there?"

It would be a long journey, and winter had started to settle on the mountains. They could travel to several different villages on the way and see if anyone knew anything. Also, the coast was lovely—the low roar of the sea, the icy water, and the rocky beaches, and he hadn't been there in a couple of years.

"I don't know," Greyson said. "I would need to stock up on supplies, and it would take quite some time to travel there." Winter was fast approaching, which meant storms, snow, and freezing temperatures.

"I'm going with you, right?" Cyrus asked, gripping his arm. Elizabeth gaped at Cyrus' hand on his arm, eyes wide.

"Of course. I would never leave you behind." Greyson could hardly leave Cyrus to wreak havoc in his absence. Cyrus grinned, squeezing his arm.

Elizabeth smirked. "I should go. I have things to do." She raised her eyebrows at Greyson before strolling in the direction of her home.

"Are we going to leave today?" Cyrus asked, biting his lip.

Greyson froze, gaze latching on Cyrus' perfect white teeth sinking into his plump lip. An odd heat flooded his body as he went stock-still, every thought leaving his mind while he stared at Cyrus.

Cyrus shook his arm and asked again, "Are we leaving today, Greyson?"

Blinking, he cleared his throat. "No. It's too late now. We'll head home in the morning."

"What should we do?"

"Why don't you meet more people while I'll buy supplies?"

With pursed lips, Cyrus looked at the ground and said as he walked away, "Okay."

Part of Greyson wanted to follow him, in case someone said something that would end this charade. Though, he couldn't help but wonder if the truth coming out would be best. Of course, Greyson could accomplish that by taking Cyrus to Lord Darius in Woodhurst.

Instead, Greyson wandered around the village, gathering the necessary items for the short trip home. People stopped him multiple times to request potions or ask him to demonstrate certain spells.

The rest of the day passed in a haze of questions and faces. It wasn't until late afternoon, not long before sunset, that Greyson saw Cyrus again, chatting with the same pack of teenagers. Greyson stopped near them, watching Cyrus as he motioned dramatically with his arms. Unable to stop it, a smile tugged on his lips.

Elizabeth came to his left side and asked, "Is there anything going on between you and Cyrus?"

"Like what?" he asked with a scoff.

"I don't know. He seems protective."

"I'm the only person he knows. Of course, he's protective," Greyson said. Cyrus and the teenagers spoke in low voices, gesturing to a three-story building that was under construction. Cyrus smirked, then grasped a plank and started climbing. Sighing, Greyson toward the structure.

"Really, Cyrus?" he asked.

Cyrus smiled but kept climbing until he reached the top. "I win," he told the teenagers, who cheered. Apparently, Cyrus was a child at heart. Cyrus lifted his leg over a beam, so he could climb down, and slipped.

Greyson acted without thought, flicking his staff in a sharp, jerking motion. Magic caught Cyrus by the ankle. The magic rebelled against his control as Greyson had only cast half a spell. It writhed, struggling against his iron hold. With a groan, Greyson tried to lower Cyrus to the ground. Cyrus hung in the air, his mouth open and arms stretched. Greyson's muscles tensed, and his teeth clenched together as he held Cyrus, struggling to fight back the rest of the spell.

The spell he used was to grab and then fling someone, but he did not want to fling Cyrus. If he'd thought about it, he would have used something different.

It was too late now.

Elizabeth raced forward. Her green ring grew bright as her magic hooked onto Cyrus, holding him. Another man moved under Cyrus with a large rock in his grasp. He glanced between Greyson and Elizabeth, then asked, "Ready?"

"Ready," she said.

Greyson nodded, unable to speak. The third mage said, "On my count." After they both nodded, he began to count. "One. Two. Three!"

On three, the third mage threw the stone toward Cyrus as Elizabeth yanked on him. Greyson relaxed the magic just enough, so it let go of Cyrus and enclosed around the rock. The second Cyrus was free, he flung the rock toward the forest. It smacked into a tree, which splintered, sending chunks of bark and wood into the air, and broke in half with a deafening crack.

He sank to his knees, breathing hard. His muscles ached and everything hurt. The only reason a mage would hold back a spell was to charge it, pouring more magic into it, but it cost the mage more energy.

Greyson swallowed, falling onto his backside and staff landing on the ground. His body vibrated with excess energy as black spots flashed before his eyes. He wanted to scold himself. Greyson had let himself get out of practice. In the past, this wouldn't have been enough to knock him out. He didn't fight the darkness edging his vision or the buzzing noise in his ears.

"Greyson!"

The pounding of feet sounded and someone grabbed him. Greyson opened his eyes and saw Cyrus who wore a familiar expression. One Greyson recognized all too well. Cyrus' eyebrows had squished together while his mouth curled down in a harsh frown.

Greyson touched Cyrus' face. "There you are."

"Greyson?"

Darkness consumed him.

CYRUS

Greyson lay in front of the fireplace, unconscious. Cyrus kneeled beside him, stomach churning. When Greyson fell, two men carried him into Elizabeth's house while Cyrus picked up Greyson's staff. The twisted wood was still in his grasp. Power thrummed through his fingers, like an itch he couldn't scratch, uncomfortable, though, at the same time, it felt oddly familiar, almost like Greyson.

"What's wrong with him?"

"He only did half the spell, catching you, and did not fling you. Once a spell is cast, you have to complete it, which is why I grabbed you and Franklin threw the rock as a substitute."

He brushed Greyson's soft black hair. "He'll be okay, though, right?"

"Yes," she answered, following the movement of his hand. "He just needs to sleep it off."

"Thank the goddess," Cyrus whispered, head coming down to rest against Greyson.

"You'll want to be careful with his staff."

"Why?" he asked, straightening.

"His staff. If it breaks, Greyson won't be able to use magic. Once a mage bonds to an artifact, they can't join with another one or use magic without it."

He squeezed the black staff in his grasp, power vibrating up his arm. This was the source of Greyson's power, or at least, how he used magic. He maneuvered the staff, so it was right next to Greyson. Cyrus would keep it safe for him. All the while, Elizabeth watched him with a curious expression.

"How did he come by it?"

She shook her head. "You really don't remember?"

"What do you mean?"

"You were there when Greyson got it. The staff is ancient and was in the emperor's vault. On the first meeting he had with the emperor, the staff flew out of the treasury, through the palace, and landed on the floor next to him."

Cyrus asked, "That's unique, right?"

"Yes," she said. "Old artifacts pick who they want to bond with. They're rare and powerful."

Smiling, he stroked Greyson's hair. Cyrus knew Greyson was special, but now, he knew he wasn't alone in that regard.

"Well," she said, "I will leave him in your capable hands."

After Elizabeth exited the house, he snagged one of the blankets he'd used last night and draped it over Greyson.

Settling next to Greyson, Cyrus placed an arm around his waist.

He couldn't know this for certain, but Cyrus didn't think he'd ever been more frightened than when he saw Greyson fall to the ground. Not even slipping off the half-built building could compare. Even recalling it made his mouth dry and his pulse throb.

Stroking Greyson's cheek, Cyrus said, "You better not do this again."

Head snuggled on Greyson's shoulder, Cyrus waited for him to wake up.

IO

GREYSON

His eyes opened, and needles immediately stabbed his head, making him close them. Even through his eyelids, the room was too bright. His muscles ached as if he'd run for miles. He hated overpowering spells. If it didn't knock him out, it always gave him a throbbing, unrelenting headache.

It had not been that long since he'd found Cyrus, and already it was taking a toll on Greyson. He constantly sighed. His solitude had been destroyed. And now, he'd overpowered a spell to save Cyrus' worthless life. What had Greyson's life come to?

Cyrus coming into his life was clearly a mistake, and now, he didn't even have the consolation of killing him at the end of it.

Greyson winced at the bright light filtering in from the windows. He could not tell the time of day, but from the amount of light, he assumed late afternoon. His gaze roved over the room but stopped when it landed on Cyrus, who was next to him, asleep.

Cyrus' mouth hung open and soft snores escaped. His blonde hair had fallen over his forehead. Unable to stop himself, Greyson brushed the silky-smooth locks back. For the first time in his life, he truly studied Cyrus' features from his golden-blonde hair, warm brown skin that was the same shade as sand, square jaw, and full lips. Cyrus reminded Greyson of the summer—warm and bright.

All of sudden, Cyrus snapped his mouth closed as his face scrunched. Muscular arms going above his head, he arched his back and yawned. The second his gaze landed on Greyson, a smile pulled on his lips. Cyrus cupped his cheeks. Heat seeped into Greyson's skin from the contact and made him swallow.

"You scared me," Cyrus said, shaking Greyson's face between his calloused palms.

"*I scared* you? You climbed on a building and fell off, nearly killing yourself."

"I would've been alright."

Greyson ignored the comment and stood, slowly. His knees trembled and his breath became shallow. Cyrus instantly came to his side and grabbed him around the waist, supporting him. Greyson wanted to shove Cyrus back but didn't. He was not used to people helping or caring for him. He'd been alone for a long time.

"Where's my staff?" he asked suddenly, frantically searching as his pulse thundered in his ears.

"Over there." Cyrus gestured to the corner near the fireplace. His staff, along with Cyrus' sword, leaned against the wall. "I kept it safe for you."

"Thank you." For a moment, Greyson imagined the worst. His staff broken in two. Powerless.

Cyrus squeezed him, drawing Greyson back to the present. "Where do you need to go?"

"Outhouse."

When they returned, Greyson sank into a chair by the table. Everything ached, but the second he sat, relief seeped into him.

Cyrus crouched, hand on Greyson's knee, as his eyebrows scrunched together. "Do you need anything?"

"Tea would be nice."

With a smile, Cyrus strode across the room and put a kettle on the flames. Greyson leaned back in the chair, shoulders slumping. He would feel better in the morning, but it would take a couple of days before he completely healed.

I'm out of practice, Greyson thought as he pinched the bridge of his nose.

When the rebellion waged, and before it, he used to be able to cast spell after spell, even when he was exhausted, hungry, and injured. Now, he hardly ever used it, except when he taught.

A rattling followed by a quiet thunk sounded just before Cyrus nudged the teapot closer to him. Greyson waited for the tea to steep before pouring himself a cup. He glanced at Cyrus, who sat across from him, chin in his palm, watching him.

"You know you might like tea with a bit of cream and sugar. I don't usually use either because they're expensive, but when we get back, you can try it," Greyson said, taking a sip of the warm tea. His body relaxed as the heat seeped into his aching muscles. Tea fixed everything.

"It's okay. I don't mind not drinking it."

"You should at least try it."

"Okay," Cyrus said with a shrug.

Greyson had no idea why he was so insistent on Cyrus trying tea a different way, but it felt like a shame if he couldn't get him to like it. Besides, he didn't want to drink tea with Cyrus staring at him. If they both enjoyed it, then they could both drink it, and Greyson would not feel awkward. He might sacrifice his original plan of killing Cyrus, but he would not give up tea.

"How long will it take for you to recover?" Cyrus asked.

"I'll be fine to travel home tomorrow morning."

Cyrus stretched across the table, his touch light. "Are you sure?"

"Yes," Greyson ground out as he slid out of his grasp. His fingers oddly tingled.

"I just want to make sure," Cyrus whispered, staring at the table.

He fought back a sigh. He hadn't meant to hurt his feelings. Scowling, Greyson patted Cyrus' hand roughly. "Sorry."

Cyrus' wide fingers closed around his hand. "It's okay."

Clearing his throat, Greyson withdrew from his touch, then drank his tea.

CYRUS

Cyrus sat at the table, head in his hands, watching Greyson as he made breakfast. Elizabeth was near him, leaning against the counter, but Cyrus studiously ignored her. He followed Greyson's every movement as he thought back to sleeping next to him. It felt secure and safe next to Greyson.

Greyson said, drawing Cyrus out of his reverie, "I'm making hotcakes for breakfast."

"My favorite," Cyrus said with a smile.

"Yes," Greyson said with a scowl, which only made Cyrus smile broader.

After a bit, Elizabeth pushed away from the counter to hang a kettle above the flames. It seemed like everyone in the Griseo Mountains loved tea. He personally didn't see the appeal of hot, bitter leaf juice, but if it made Greyson happy, it made him happy.

She came to Greyson's side and stared directly at Cyrus before winding her arm around Greyson, who did not react. Cyrus, on the other hand, started to stand before he controlled the motion, sinking back into the chair. Elizabeth smirked, then retrieved the kettle before sitting across from him.

After a silent breakfast, in which he spent the entire time glaring at Elizabeth, Cyrus packed their bags while Greyson cleaned the dishes. He shoved their bedrolls and blankets into the sacks, then leaned back on his heels as he searched the room to make sure they didn't leave anything behind. All that remained were his sword and Greyson's staff, which leaned against the wall next to each other.

"Are you ready?" Greyson asked from behind him.

He glanced over his shoulder at Greyson who wiped his hands on a towel. "Yes."

Cyrus strapped on his sword, flung a bag over his shoulder, then picked up the staff. It vibrated beneath his fingers, alive. When he turned around, he saw Greyson's eyebrows were a slash across his forehead as he focused on the staff. His breathing was harsh bursts and his hands had curled into tight fists. Cyrus slowly stepped toward him, holding it out. With trembling fingers, Greyson accepted it, clutching the staff to his chest. Cyrus didn't know what was wrong or what to say, so he remained quiet.

"Thank you," Greyson said, eventually.

"Of course." Cyrus picked up the other pack and held it out. Greyson took it and slung it over his shoulder before striding out of the house. Cyrus followed, more than ready to go home.

GREYSON

Greyson walked into the chilly morning air, breath coming out in a cloud. His heart beat against his ribs as he squeezed the staff in a white-knuckled grip, wood digging into his palm. When he saw Cyrus holding it, a terrible vision of the warrior snapping it in half and leaving him helpless raced across his mind's eye. The panic lingered, even though nothing had happened. Cyrus had no reason to break the staff, as he didn't remember the animosity between them. Greyson clenched it again, magic zinging beneath his palm, and took a deep breath.

Chickens clucked as they wandered through the village, scratching the dirt. In the distance, people tended the fields, readying them for winter, while fishers carried nets toward the stream. Greyson greeted several different people, some he knew better than others, as he searched for Elizabeth. He wanted to say goodbye before leaving.

A touch on his arm stopped him. Greyson looked to his left, and Cyrus said, "I want to say goodbye to the kids."

"Fine."

Cyrus jogged toward the group of teenagers next to the half-built building, who waved excitedly at him. As the group talked animatedly, Elizabeth hooked an arm through his, startling Greyson. "You're leaving us?"

"Yes," Greyson said, trying to calm his racing pulse. When people walked up on his right side, he couldn't see them. Even all these years later, it startled him when people suddenly appeared as if out of thin air.

"You should be careful around Cyrus."

"What do you mean?" Greyson shifted in her direction so he could see her face.

"I think he likes you."

Scoffing, he replied, "He thinks we're friends; of course, he likes me."

"Not like that."

"You're being ridiculous."

"No," she said, shaking her head. "I'm not. You're attractive enough and you're all he knows."

Greyson did not bother to respond as he looked at Cyrus, who'd stopped talking to the kids and watched them. He would not deny that Cyrus was attractive, not that he'd ever thought that before. Greyson paused, mouth opening a fraction, as he realized he'd never thought of another man as attractive before now. But it did not matter, there was nothing between Cyrus and him. There never had been.

"You want to test my theory?" Elizabeth asked, eyebrows raised.

Before he could respond, she clamped onto the back of his neck and yanked his face to hers. Eyes widening, Greyson froze. His stomach twisted. He'd never kissed her nor had he ever wanted to. Jerking out of her grasp, Greyson wiped his mouth off, swallowing convulsively. He opened his mouth to shout at her when Elizabeth nodded in Cyrus' direction. Unwillingly, his gaze shifted to Cyrus who wore a thunderous expression as he stalked toward them.

"I told you," she said in a sing-song voice. Elizabeth raised a single eyebrow, then sauntered toward her house, whistling.

Cyrus nudged his left arm. "What was that about?"

"Nothing. Let's go." Greyson strode toward the trees, thoughts whirling. He'd seemed upset, but Greyson did not want to believe what Elizabeth said or Cyrus' obvious anger. It had to be for another reason.

"Hey," Cyrus called.

"What?" he asked in a clipped tone.

"Are you alright?"

Greyson scratched his cheek, replaying the incident. There had to be some way that he could have avoided it. He shook his head. This wasn't his fault, and why should he feel guilty? Elizabeth shouldn't have done that.

"I'm fine," Greyson said after a bit, ignoring the hard lump in his stomach. "Elizabeth was joking around. There's nothing going on between us."

"Really?"

"Yes," he ground out. "Elizabeth is still in love with her husband who died last year."

"Oh." When Greyson didn't say anything else, Cyrus entwined his arm with Greyson's and started toward the treeline. "Let's go home."

II

CYRUS

When they entered the one-room cabin, Cyrus sighed, shoulders slumping. Night had fallen a couple of hours ago and with it the temperature. Water dripped off his hair, sliding down his cheeks. Wet clothes clung to his frame and chilled him to the bone. The trip back to Drakcombe had been as cold as the journey to Creekside. The only time he'd felt warm was when he and Greyson curled next to the fire under the blankets.

This time had been worse for one glaring reason—it had started to rain about an hour ago.

Greyson immediately started a fire as Cyrus huddled near him. When the fire burst into life, heat rushed over him, almost hurting in its warmth. Greyson scowled, two lines deeply etched between his eyebrows. Cyrus ached to trace the divots, to feel the smoothness of his skin, to ease the tension.

"Your lips are blue," Greyson said, frowning even more deeply.

Cyrus would have answered, but his teeth wouldn't stop chattering.

Greyson took off Cyrus' soaking-wet cloak, then ordered, "Take off your boots and clothes."

Shaking, Cyrus moved to comply. The moment his wet clothes were off, Greyson whisked them away, hanging them up to dry, then draped a thick blanket from the bed over his shoulders. Cyrus nodded his thanks, but he didn't know if Greyson noticed because he rushed around the cabin, taking his own cloak off and emptying the bags.

Towel in hand, Greyson briskly rubbed it over Cyrus' hair. Shivers continued to wrack his body, but Cyrus grinned and leaned into the touch, pleased, even if it made Greyson grumble the entire time about nursemaids.

"I swear," Greyson growled, "if you get sick, I'm not taking care of you."

Cyrus smiled because he knew it was a lie.

Continuing to mutter under his breath, Greyson stripped off his own clothes and boots, then stuck the kettle on the flames before sitting across from Cyrus in nothing but his undershorts. Cyrus stared at Greyson, who dried his shoulder-length black hair.

He'd seen Greyson without clothes on before, but he'd never really gotten a chance to closely examine him. He took in Greyson's lean muscles, tracing the lines. The smattering of dark hair on his chest trailed down his stomach. The strength of his arm and hands. Two long scars stretched over his right side and a burn marred his left shoulder.

Stomach warm and fluttery, Cyrus stared at the scars. He wanted to touch them, feel them beneath his fingertips, and ask where they came from. That thought made him look at Greyson's face and the long scar that went through his right eyebrow to the top of his cheekbone, blinding him. Cyrus itched to touch it. To kiss the length of it. His breath became sharp as a tingling sensation began near the base of his skull and his heartbeat accelerated.

Greyson stood, startling Cyrus. Either Greyson hadn't noticed his blatant staring or he simply didn't care. With a thick cloth, Greyson lifted the beat-up kettle off the flames, then poured it into a teapot before sitting again.

"Are you warming up sufficiently or do you need another blanket?" Greyson asked, carefully adding the loose tea leaves to the teapot.

Clearing his throat, Cyrus said, "I'm fine. I can finally feel my toes."

Immediately, Greyson's gaze shot to Cyrus' feet. "You should've told me that earlier." Greyson grabbed his feet, inspecting them. Cyrus couldn't stop the blush that raced to his face.

"Do they hurt?"

"No," he choked out as Greyson continued to examine one foot, then the next before letting them go and readjusting the blanket over them.

"Next time, tell me immediately. You could lose a toe if your feet get wet, then freeze." Greyson strode to the sink and washed his hands before sitting next to the fireplace again.

Cyrus didn't know what to say, so he silently watched Greyson as he drank a cup of tea, smiling softly as he obviously enjoyed the beverage.

"Have you always liked tea?" Cyrus asked.

"Yes. I grew up drinking it. Didn't you?"

"How would I know?"

Mouth falling open for a second, Greyson snapped it closed. "Of course."

"I don't suppose you know?"

"No," Greyson replied, eyes shifting to the side. "We never really discussed it."

"And you didn't know that I don't like tea."

Greyson scoffed. "It never came up."

Cyrus' lips pursed as Greyson placed the teapot and cup in the kitchen and braced himself against the counter, back toward him.

"Are we really friends?"

"What a question." Greyson didn't even glance in his direction.

"Greyson, are we friends?" Cyrus needed to know the answer to that question.

"Yes."

"Okay." Cyrus focused on Greyson's tight back and his hands that gripped the edge of the counter. "I trust you."

"I know." Greyson turned around, eyes shifting around the cabin, looking anywhere besides Cyrus. He wanted to question Greyson, to demand a more definite answer, but he didn't, afraid of the response he would receive.

Deciding to let the matter go, Cyrus said, "Tell me a story."

"What?" Greyson asked, mouth agape.

Cyrus huddled next to the crackling fire and repeated, "Tell me a story."

Greyson sat in front of him. "What kind of story?"

"Anything."

"Alright." Greyson focused on the fire, brow wrinkling in thought. Cyrus drew his knees to his chest and waited. Finally, Greyson began to speak. "I will tell you how the Griseo Mountains came to be."

Cyrus rested his head on his knees as he listened to the rumble of Greyson's voice.

"It is said that three dragons came from a distant land and made this area their home. The eldest and strongest was Validus. He made a bargain with the humans that lived here. He would help them and teach them the ways of magic if they allowed him and his younger siblings to stay. The humans agreed.

"Validus taught them and protected them from anyone who would do them harm. His younger sister Sarcio healed the humans and taught them all she knew of herblore. Both easily found their place in the new land, making a home. Ferrum, the youngest of the three, did not. He struggled, for humans wanted no part of his magic, necromancy. They saw darkness in it when there was none.

"Years passed, and Ferrum secluded himself from the humans while Validus and Sarcio intermingled with them. As Ferrum made his home on the icy coast, he was the first to see the newcomers. More dragons. Hundreds. They had left their homeland in search of another. Validus welcomed them, but he made it clear that these were his lands and the humans were under his protection. They stayed and made no trouble, integrating with the humans. Eventually, the humans and dragons intermarried, giving birth to the mages.

"As the years continued, one by one, the dragon all fell into a deep slumber. Their bodies became the Griseo Mountains. The most prominent peaks: Ferrum in the west, Sarcio in the east, and Validus in the center. The stories say the dragons could wake again and shake the world."

"You're descended from dragons."

Greyson laughed. "It's a story, Cyrus, nothing more."

Cyrus scooted closer. "I believe it."

"Of course, you do," Greyson said with a quirk of his lips.

The silence stretched between them, only broken by the pops of the fire. It was like a current stretched between them. Cyrus wanted to bridge the gap and snuggle against Greyson, but he didn't know if he should. His eyes flicked to Greyson's lips. *I wonder if they're soft.* Ever so slowly, he slid closer, but Greyson stood.

Clearing his throat, he said, "We should go to bed, though the extra blankets are wet."

"So?" Cyrus commented. "It's not like we can't share."

With a curt nod, Greyson headed toward the bed, but before he could position himself next to the wall, Cyrus beat him to it.

"What are you doing?"

"What?" Cyrus asked, keeping his eyes wide and innocent.

"Whatever." Greyson sat and readjusted the blanket over them. As he lay down, Greyson rolled onto his right side, facing Cyrus. "You did this on purpose."

Cyrus smirked and settled next to Greyson, warmth surrounding him.

GREYSON

Greyson could not fall asleep. Cyrus was pressed against his chest, arms wrapped about his waist, and his head tucked under Greyson's chin. They'd never slept face-to-face, and he found it a tad suffocating while at the same time, his skin was flushed and his muscles relaxed. He'd never been one to snuggle, even in the past, nor had he ever thought to be in such a situation with Cyrus. Despite that, it was not as bad as he would have guessed. Comfortable, even, if he let himself admit it.

It had been a while since he'd spent this much time with someone, as he was a loner by nature and choice. But right now, he and Cyrus always remained in each other's company, never separating except for a few hours at most.

Cyrus shifted slightly with a sleepy snort, and Greyson sighed. He should shove Cyrus away but some part of him didn't want to. Unbidden, Elizabeth's words came back to him.

Could Cyrus like him? He scoffed. No. That was impossible. Besides, Greyson had lied to him, planned to kill him, and they were enemies. If Cyrus suddenly regained his memory while they were like this, he would slay Greyson without hesitation.

Nonetheless, as his arm closed around Cyrus' muscular body, his heart pounded faster. He didn't hate this. Greyson had never been attracted to another man before, not that he thought about it one way or the other. Sex and romance had never been important in his life. He'd never given himself the opportunity to explore. Now was not such a time. Especially with who lay in his arms.

CYRUS

Cyrus carried a pail of water from the well, through the sheets of rain, and toward Widow Abney's home. The old woman leaned heavily on her cane as she stood in the door frame, waiting for him.

"You should have a pump installed like Greyson." He took off his damp cloak and hung it near the fireplace so it would dry before Greyson came to get him.

Widow Abney sat at the table. "I've always carried the water in this way my entire life, and I will continue to do so until I die."

He shook his head, hands stretched toward the flames.

"So," she started, "why aren't you with Greyson today?"

"The rain. He was afraid I would get sick."

She knocked her cane against the floor. "He seems to care for you a great deal."

"He doesn't like to 'play nursemaid' as he says. Also, we're friends."

"So he says."

His lips pursed. Cyrus opened his mouth, then closed it. He would believe Greyson, for now. Besides, did he actually want to know the truth? Changing the subject, he asked, "Is there anything else I can do for you?"

"You're a good boy."

"Thank you."

"It's nothing but the truth."

"Do you need anything?"

"What? Are you anxious to return to your mage?" An odd grin played over the woman's wrinkled face.

"No," he replied. "Greyson said he would come and get me. He explicitly told me, several times, to wait here."

Widow Abney offered him a cookie. "That man is way too overprotective."

Cyrus shrugged, snagging one. He took a bite, and it broke apart in his mouth. Around the sugary treat, he said, "I like it."

"The cookie or his attitude?"

"Both."

"You two are well-suited for each other." She put a kettle on an iron arm, then swung it over the fire.

A sudden flash shone through the window followed by a peal of thunder. Cyrus glanced out, but there wasn't much to see. Rain poured, and it was dark outside. The longer he peered out the window, the more tension built in his chest, suffocating him. Greyson was out in the storm.

"We're friends; of course, we suit each other."

"Hmm."

Thunder rolled as lightning lit the sky and the ground quivered. Cyrus swallowed. Standing, he headed to the window. There was nothing. Just gray darkness. Fingers tapping a rapid tattoo on the sill, he kept watch, waiting.

"You could go look for him."

"I promised him I'd stay here. I'm sure he's fine."

Widow Abney made another non-committal grunt as she walked across the room, her feet and cane thumping with each step. Cyrus didn't pay her any attention as she made tea and kept searching for a glimpse of Greyson.

"Come have some tea," she said a few minutes later, porcelain rattling.

He shook his head. He didn't even like tea. Nothing could tempt him from the window.

A dark figure appeared, steadily heading toward the house. When they got a little bit closer, a flash of lightning arced in the sky right before thunder roared, revealing the figure's face—Greyson.

Cyrus yanked the door open and rushed into the storm. Rain poured down his face as his boots slid in the mud, practically crashing into Greyson. He seized Greyson's arm, the fabric squelching under his fingers, and hauled him inside.

The instant they were out of the rain, he gathered Greyson into his embrace. Tension seeped out of his muscles, and he sagged against Greyson's chest. It was like all the weight had left his body, making him light as a feather.

Greyson did not return the hug and moved out of Cyrus' hold, then closed the door. Water dripped off Greyson, his black hair soaking wet and sticking to his face.

"Are you okay?" Cyrus asked, scouring him for any sign of injury.

"I'm fine," Greyson answered with a scowl.

His expression didn't bother Cyrus in the slightest. He pressed a hand to Greyson's forehead. It felt chilly and damp. Greyson frowned and shifted away from his touch.

"We'll be taking our leave if you don't need anything," Greyson said, looking at Widow Abney.

Her eyes flicked between them. "No. You two best get home with the storm. It'll probably worsen as night falls."

Greyson nodded, then said, "Oh." He removed a dead rabbit out of the bag slung over his shoulder. "I caught this and thought you might like it."

"Thank you. You know rabbit stew is my favorite."

"I do indeed," Greyson said.

Getting to her feet, Widow Abney said, "You two best go."

"I'll see you later," Cyrus said with a wave.

The rain came down in icy sheets and froze him. Cyrus took Greyson's arm as they headed toward the cabin. His boots slid on the muddy path, making it hard for Cyrus to traverse the steep hill. Greyson had to practically drag him while Cyrus struggled to keep up, shivering.

When they finally crested the hill, the cabin came into view, and all Cyrus wanted to do was sit in front of the fire and warm up. Greyson ushered him into the dark cabin, muttering something Cyrus couldn't understand.

"Hang up your clothes," Greyson said.

Cyrus stripped as Greyson started the fire, which dimly lit the house. He tugged off his boots, then padded barefoot across the room. Greyson chucked a towel at him. Cyrus caught it and rubbed his hair.

Greyson took off his wet clothes before pulling on a thick sweater and dry trousers. He dropped another set of clothes next to Cyrus before sinking to the floor. Cyrus held out the towel, and Greyson accepted it, drying his long hair.

"If it's raining tomorrow, you should stay home," Cyrus said, studying his pale face. He didn't want Greyson to get sick; being out in this weather could not be good for him.

"We'll see."

Cyrus frowned.

With a long sigh, Greyson said, "I'm sure I can think of something to do here. Besides, you almost froze simply walking back."

He smiled as an arrow of warmth shot him squarely in the heart.

12

GREYSON

Rain came down in thick sheets while the wind whipped around the cabin, howling, but the fire kept the one-room home warm and cozy. Quietly, Greyson slipped outside to get an armload of wood. Coming back into the cabin, his eyes shot to the bed. Cyrus was sprawled on his stomach, asleep. Greyson set the wood in the metal firewood rack and hung his cloak before stoking the fire to make sure the house stayed warm for Cyrus.

Cyrus was always cold.

He was still deciding whether to make the journey to the northern coast. They would have to travel over Validus Peak, and with winter approaching, the temperature would start to drop drastically. His brow furrowed as his lips pursed. They could wait for the letter to arrive from the capital, but he didn't like the idea of sitting here, doing nothing.

I could always take him to the representative, Greyson reasoned. A vise squeezed his lungs, stealing his breath. *That* was not an option.

While keeping Cyrus was not the wisest plan, it was the only chance at finding something out. Well, that and Frederick. His thoughts went round and round, arguing the different sides—take Cyrus to the representative or keep him. In the end, it might be best to take Cyrus to Lord Darius because what would Greyson do if Cyrus planned to hurt them? Would he kill Cyrus?

The very thought made him go cold.

Greyson shoved it aside. It didn't matter. He would simply plan for the immediate future. If he was going to travel across the mountains, he would need to have warmer clothes made for Cyrus. He'd been saving the pelts of the animals he'd trapped for quite some time now.

A plan began to form. He would take the pelts to Annabeth and have a fur-lined cloak and vest made for Cyrus. He might even have enough for a blanket. That should be enough to keep Cyrus warm.

He pulled some herbs, fresh and dry, from the cupboard, then removed his mortar and pestle. Greyson would need money to pay Annabeth, though she would probably trade the work for some of his poultices.

Time passed quickly, and the world disappeared as he steadily worked. The soothing motions of creating healing poultices and the grinding of the stone in his ears made all the tension flee his body. Greyson could almost hear his mother's gentle voice as she instructed him in the delicate art.

She'd taught him well, and he'd surpassed her skills, crafting near-perfect potions and poultices, even though he did not share her healing magic.

Sitting up straight, eyes closed, Greyson stretched his tight shoulders. Looking up, he started. Cyrus sat not far from him, watching him.

"You're awake from your nap?" Greyson asked, his voice tight.

"I woke up a while ago."

"Why didn't you say anything?"

Cyrus smiled softly. "You seemed so serious."

Scoffing, Greyson stood, back tight. "You should've told me so I could make dinner."

"It's fine."

The fire was dying, so Greyson chucked a couple of pieces of wood onto it. They did not immediately catch. Crouching, he blew on the red-hot coals. After a moment, they sparked to life. Greyson hung a kettle over the flames, then turned around, and Cyrus watched him with an intense gaze. His serious expression made Greyson's stomach flutter. Clearing his throat, he stalked to the kitchen, head down.

As he passed by, Cyrus snagged Greyson around the waist and held him against his broad chest. "I'm okay. You don't have to make anything."

Greyson wiggled out of his hold, as he tried to banish the thrill that went down his spine. Ignoring Cyrus' comment, he made a quick meal. Once it was finished, Greyson poured a bit of tea, then added a dollop of milk, careful not to overfill the cup, and stirred in a couple of spoonfuls of sugar. He pushed the cup toward Cyrus, who shook his head but accepted the tea.

Taking a sip of his tea, Greyson asked, "What do you think about traveling to the coast?"

"I don't really care."

His brow furrowed. "You don't care? Don't you want to find the person who did this to you?"

"You already said they can't restore my memory, so it doesn't matter."

That seemed odd to Greyson, but maybe he was more of a revenge person than Cyrus? He suggested, "We can wait for my friend to respond and see why you're here in the first place."

Whatever Cyrus saw in his expression made him grin widely. "You don't like waiting around, do you?"

"Not really."

"Then we can go."

"It'll be cold," Greyson said. "And long."

"If you're with me, I'll be fine."

He nodded, swallowing. Trying to find anything to say, Greyson said, "You should try your tea."

Cyrus lifted the cup to his lips and took a sip. His face immediately scrunched, and he set it down. "I don't like it."

"Heathen."

Unexpectedly, Cyrus laughed. "You'll have to enjoy it by yourself, I guess."

"I guess, I will."

The next day, the sun shone brightly, and the air held a crisp edge that Greyson quite liked. He and Cyrus strolled to the village with a bag full of pelts slung over his shoulder. Cyrus snaked an arm through his left arm and stepped in time with him. Greyson rolled his eyes, but let Cyrus keep ahold of him. He kept doing that, allowing Cyrus to come closer, and he refused to contemplate why.

"Why are we going to Annabeth's?"

"One, so you can meet her, and two, so she can make fur-lined clothes for you so you don't freeze on our trip."

"You'll stay with me, right?"

"No," Greyson replied. "I need to start gathering supplies. You'll be fine. Annabeth is very nice, and when she's done, you can see Widow Abney."

Cyrus frowned, visibly deflating. Greyson swallowed as his chest unexpectedly tightened. He bumped Cyrus with his shoulder. Cyrus smiled and returned the bump. Averting his gaze, Greyson continued toward the village with Cyrus by his side.

When they reached the outskirts, Greyson shook off Cyrus' arm and strode to Annabeth's house—a one-story home with fragrant herbs growing in planters under the windows. Greyson rapped on the door. A few moments passed before it opened and revealed a slim woman with black hair and hard features.

"Greyson," she said, opening the door the rest of the way. Her light brown eyes darted to Cyrus, and her lips flattened into a tight line. Greyson wondered in the back of his mind if he'd made a grievous mistake. Annabeth had lost her older sister and brother in the rebellion—the last bit of her family.

"Annabeth," he said. "I need a favor."

She glowered at Cyrus, not reacting. Greyson had no idea if Cyrus had directly killed Annabeth's siblings, but he'd been the face of the war much as Greyson had been the face of the rebellion.

"I don't know if I'm inclined to grant that favor."

He pinched the bridge of his nose, then glanced at Cyrus. "Can you give us a moment?"

Cyrus frowned deeply, lines forming between his eyebrows. He looked between them, unmoving for so long Greyson thought Cyrus wouldn't leave. Stiffy, he moved back, leaning against the stone well with his arms crossed.

"Annabeth," Greyson started.

She interrupted him, "How could you bring him here? To my house?"

"He doesn't remember."

"And that's supposed to make this better? I've seen him traipsing after you, and all I can think about is my family. Gone. Dead."

Greyson scrubbed a hand through his hair. "The war is over."

"Really?" She scoffed. "*You're* going to say that to me?"

"Please. Someone wiped his memory, and I need to find them. I need to know why Cyrus is here and what that means for us."

"And this concerns me how?"

"I need you to make him fur-lined clothes so he can survive the journey to the northern shore."

"The poor baby gets cold." A mean sneer pulled at her lips. "Let him freeze." She slammed the door in his face.

"That went well," he muttered and strode toward Cyrus, who watched him with narrowed eyes.

"What happened?"

"She doesn't want to help us."

"Why?"

"For unimportant reasons," Greyson answered.

"Did you used to court her?"

What does that have to do with anything? "Years ago for a short while."

"Maybe she's still upset."

"Trust me," Greyson said, "that has nothing to do with it."

"Okay," Cyrus replied, voice deepening. "What are we going to do?"

"What I always do: ask Widow Abney."

CYRUS

Widow Abney stood in front of Cyrus, taking his measurements with sure movements. Greyson had left as soon as the old woman agreed to sew the garments, not saying even a word as he disappeared outside. Cyrus peered out the window, hoping to catch a glimpse of Greyson, even though it was pointless.

Wrapping the measuring tape around his chest, she asked, "What's troubling you?"

"Nothing."

She pinched his side. "Don't lie to me, young man."

"I wanted Greyson to stay," Cyrus said, "but he insisted on leaving me behind, again."

With a shake of her head, she remarked, "You're a bit needy."

"Excuse me?"

"You're only apart for a short time and you're already pining for him."

"I guess. I like being with him."

"I noticed," Widow Abney said.

Strong emotions swelled in his chest. He desperately wanted to see Greyson. They'd only been apart for a short while, and Cyrus wanted to be with him, walking next to him, talking, or even doing nothing.

Widow Abney studied him. After several long moments of silence, she placed a wrinkled hand on his arm. "You're in love with Greyson."

"What?"

"You're in love with Greyson."

He swallowed. *Love. In love with Greyson*, he thought. The word scorched him to his very soul. "I'm in love with Greyson."

"Yes," she said, continuing to take measurements. "I noticed."

"How did that happen?"

"The usual way. You saw him, talked to him, and fell in love. It happens," Widow Abney said with a shrug.

"I can't believe it."

"I can," the old woman said. "I saw you mooning over him the first day he brought you into the village."

"Still."

"It's not revolutionary. You just fell in love with someone. It happens to the best of us."

"But it happened so fast," Cyrus remarked, shaking his head.

"Maybe you liked him before you lost your memory."

Cyrus froze. That was possible. But Greyson didn't act like they had any romantic relationship previously. Of course, he might have never told Greyson.

The mere thought of Greyson was enough to send his pulse racing. Images of his scowl, the way his hair fell around his sharp cheekbones, his long fingers, his body, and the way Greyson took care of him, even when he said he wouldn't, played through his mind. Cyrus had a hard time believing it, but Greyson had apparently claimed his heart.

"How in the world am I going to tell him?"

"That's your problem," she said with a croaky chuckle.

13

CYRUS

Cyrus bolted through the woods, feet crushing the pine needles scattered on the ground. Blood seeped from a wound on his side. His breath escaped in quick gasps, lungs burning. He gripped his unsheathed blade. North. He had to keep heading north.

Greyson, he thought. *I have to get to Greyson.* Danger was coming for him, and Cyrus had to warn him.

Feet pounding on the ground, he broke into a clearing—a clearing he recognized. As he glanced around, his heart thrashed against his ribs. He was still some distance from the village. There was a sharp, stabbing sensation with each breath, but Cyrus refused to let it deter him. Greyson needed him. He continued north, racing across the old battlefield.

A gasp came from behind him. Whirling around, he caught a flash of black hair and a slight form before a cloud of magic encased him. Agony tore him apart, shredding his mind, as darkness circled. His last conscious thought was of Greyson and the danger circling him.

Cyrus shot up; sweat soaked his clothes and the sheets beneath him. His eyes darted around the cabin. Greyson had left earlier this morning, alone, as the weather was cold and he didn't want Cyrus to get sick. Panic flared in his chest. Greyson was in trouble.

Leaping out of bed, Cyrus ran out of the cabin without a second thought. He paused when his bare feet slammed into the cold dirt. He took a second to put on his boots, then raced into the woods.

He tore over the ground, searching the pine trees for any sign of Greyson's passing. He had to find Greyson. Cyrus didn't know what danger threatened him, but he wouldn't allow anyone to hurt him. His boots slid on the wet ground, but Cyrus kept running, ignoring the freezing cold that nipped at his skin. He would not stop until he found Greyson.

Cyrus didn't know how much time passed or even where he was, but the ice that coursed in his veins would not abate. His head whipped in each direction, but he saw nothing except trees. Not knowing where to go, he started north when several things happened almost at once. A deer scampered away, and at the same instant, an arrow whizzed past him, sinking into a tree trunk with a loud thud.

"Are you insane?" a voice yelled. "I almost shot you!"

Rustling sounded as Greyson appeared from behind a bush. The second Cyrus saw him, something in his stomach relaxed. Greyson kept yelling, but he didn't care. Cyrus walked straight up to Greyson, who continued to shout, red-faced, but he ignored it. He clamped onto the back of Greyson's neck, dragged his face down, and kissed him.

GREYSON

As Cyrus' lips touched his, something snapped in his head. The simple touch seemed to create a disconnect between his brain and body. Greyson stood there, stock-still, as Cyrus held the back of his neck, kissing him fervently.

Greyson broke away, gripping Cyrus' shoulders. Cyrus didn't stop him, but he searched Greyson's face like he was looking for something. Greyson stared at Cyrus, his breath coming out quickly while his heart thudded loudly in his ears. Cyrus returned his look, face void of expression as his grasp remained tight on the back of Greyson's neck. Not knowing why, Greyson brushed his lips against Cyrus' mouth.

Cyrus kissed him back, frantically. One of Cyrus' calloused hands stroked Greyson's cheek while the other slipped into his hair, gripping him tightly. Greyson clasped Cyrus' back, holding him as close as possible. He had no idea what he was doing, but it did not feel weird. Truthfully, it felt good.

He calmed the frenzied movements until Greyson slowly caressed his full lips. Cyrus' hand loosened on his hair as he returned the kiss, gently and fully. Greyson's tongue flicked out, tasting Cyrus, who opened his mouth. When their tongues mingled, Greyson moaned, and Cyrus pressed against him. Cyrus' fingers slipped from Greyson's face and gripped the front of his shirt.

The kiss slowed, becoming almost achingly perfect. Greyson cupped Cyrus' cheeks before moving back a fraction, breath harsh. Cyrus smiled. Greyson lowered once more and brushed a lingering kiss on his lips, then shifted back. His fingertips skimmed over Cyrus' face as Greyson studied him.

What am I doing? he thought.

Greyson could not take his eyes off Cyrus. Never in their entire acquaintance had he thought of Cyrus in a romantic sense. Now, the very sight of his sky-blue eyes made Greyson's heart pound while his arms ached to hold him.

Unable to stop himself, Greyson pressed one last kiss on Cyrus' full lips, then he stroked Cyrus' cheek. "What happened?"

Quickly, the story about the dream poured out. Brow furrowed, Greyson listened. It seemed it was about Cyrus' memories being stolen. Absent-mindedly, his arms went around Cyrus, crossing over the small of his back. Someone *had* wiped his mind. Greyson had figured it was the work of magic, but now, he knew for certain.

"Could you recognize the person if you saw them again?"

"No," Cyrus said. "All I saw was a flash of black hair."

Scoffing, he said, "That won't help." Pretty much everyone in the Griseo Mountains had black or dark brown hair.

Cyrus jostled him. "You're in danger."

Greyson was always in danger. The emperor had placed a bounty on his head when the rebellion started and he became the face of it. As far as he knew, the bounty was still in effect, an incentive for him to remain in exile, though his staying here hadn't hindered some people or their desire for money.

He'd been attacked by several entrepreneurial bounty hunters who wanted to force him out of the Griseo Mountains and claim the reward. On two separate occasions, he'd been attacked but had managed to escape before they could abscond with him.

"I'll be fine," he replied, not worried in the slightest.

Expression darkening, Cyrus' eyebrows scrunched together to form a slash across his forehead. "I will not allow anyone to hurt you."

Swallowing, Greyson tried to fight against the sudden emotions that cascaded through him. No one had ever tried to protect him. He always stood at the front lines, shielding others. Also, that expression reminded him of the old Cyrus, which oddly enough didn't bother him.

"Thank you."

With a wide grin, Cyrus said, "Of course. Let's go home."

Greyson stretched out on the floor next to the fire with an arm around Cyrus. Cyrus' fingers traced Greyson's shirt while they rested, side-by-side, not speaking. The sun had set some time ago, and the fire crackled, warming the cabin. Greyson rubbed Cyrus' arm, the thick fabric soft under his skin, as his thoughts raced in hundred different ways.

The main thing Greyson fixated on was the fact he'd kissed Cyrus, multiple times. His enemy. Golden boy of the capital. Nephew of the emperor. And Greyson had kissed him. Not just that, he'd enjoyed it. Even now, he thought about doing it again.

Cyrus snuggled closer, nuzzling Greyson's chest. Greyson placed a kiss on his blonde hair, inhaling his scent—the pine fragrance of their soap. His arms tightened around Cyrus' solid frame.

What am I doing? he thought for the thousandth time. *This* could not happen. They could not happen. Yet here in the peaceful darkness of his home, Greyson wanted to believe it was possible.

Cyrus rubbed his chest. "Were we ever like this?"

His hand stilled on Cyrus' arm. "No."

Nodding, Cyrus leaned up on his elbow, hovering over Greyson. "I like this." As Cyrus' fingertips touched the edge of his scar, Greyson shifted to the side. "What's wrong?"

"I don't like people touching my scar," he stated, voice tight. Cyrus was the one who'd given him that scar, years ago, during the first battle of the short rebellion.

Slowly, gaze intent on Greyson's face, Cyrus skimmed his fingers along the scar. Greyson swallowed, pulse-quickening, and closed his eyes. Cyrus kept running his fingertips over the scar, up and down, until Greyson completely relaxed.

"Do you want me to stop?" Cyrus asked.

"No."

A breathy laugh came from above him, but he didn't open his eyes. He could feel Cyrus shift against him before warm lips met the tip of the scar, right above Greyson's cheekbone. With every touch, Greyson tensed, his skin too tight and over-sensitive.

Cyrus kissed up his scar. When Cyrus reached the top, just above his eyebrow, he murmured, lips brushing his skin, "I won't hurt you." Then he continued to place whisper-soft kisses along his scar.

When Cyrus stopped, Greyson asked, "What's wrong?"

Cyrus hovered above him, expression serious. "I don't want to remember."

His brow furrowed. "What?"

"I don't want to remember."

"Why?"

"Because I don't want to go back to a time when you and I weren't like this," Cyrus said, motioning between them.

Greyson didn't know what to say, so he cradled Cyrus in his arms.

As the night deepened, he could not stop thinking about what Cyrus said. Greyson stared at the dark ceiling as Cyrus sprawled on his chest, asleep. The bed was soft, the cabin warm, but he couldn't fall asleep even when he lay on his side.

Cyrus' words plagued him. Would Cyrus, the real Cyrus, choose this? Choose him? Greyson highly doubted it.

He tightened his arms around Cyrus. Greyson didn't want to give this, him, up. Pressing a kiss to the top of Cyrus' head, he had to do what was right for Cyrus, even if the very thought tore his heart out.

I4

CYRUS

Cyrus headed down the mountain path with a lump of ice in his chest. The cold wind didn't even bother him, as he stared unseeingly in front of him. He was numb, utterly numb. Something had happened in the space of a few hours, and he didn't understand what.

This morning, he woke up alone. Cyrus had searched, not leaving the area around the cabin, but Greyson was nowhere to be found. As it approached the afternoon, Greyson had finally appeared, he was distant. He wouldn't even look at

Cyrus, and when he attempted to hug Greyson, he slithered out of his embrace. He tried to press Greyson for an explanation, but he wouldn't answer.

Eventually, Greyson said they couldn't be together and that Cyrus had to remember.

Shaking his head, Cyrus paused as his face lifted to the clouded sky. He didn't understand. Everything had been perfect, and he'd been hoping to recreate that magic today, though, apparently, Greyson didn't feel the same.

His feet continued on the path toward the village, sliding every couple of steps in the mud. The pine trees creaked in the breeze, and the clouds covered the sun, blocking out the light. His boot slammed into a deep puddle, and water splashed over the edge of his boot, soaking his foot. Cyrus froze, tears prickling. He didn't understand. He would never understand it.

Cyrus plodded down the muddy lane until he reached Widow Abney's home. She opened the door and frowned. "Why do you appear so down?" Widow Abney asked in her croaky voice.

The words couldn't escape his tightened throat. Widow Abney drew him inside, and they sat at the table. She poured him a cup of tea and nudged a plate of scones forward. Cyrus ignored the food, tracing the whirl patterns in the wood of the table.

"Cyrus?"

"I told Greyson how I feel," he said, voice dead. "At first, he seemed happy about it, then he suddenly changed his mind."

Her lips pursed. "Did he say why?"

"No. He just said I have to remember and that we can't be together."

She nodded, taking a scone and tearing it apart. "Do you want to be with him?"

"Yes," Cyrus said, arms crossing on the tabletop. "I don't know much right now, but I *know* I love Greyson."

Widow Abney offered him a scone. "What are you going to do?"

"I don't know, but I can't give him up. Last night was perfect." Cyrus slumped, head plunking onto the table.

"Hmm," was all the old woman said.

GREYSON

Greyson strode through the village, shoulders slumped. The sun had begun its descent, and the air grew cold, nipping at his exposed skin. As he started toward his cabin, a voice called out, "Greyson."

Widow Abney came toward him, cane in hand. "I would like a word."

"Of course. What's going on?" he asked.

She linked an arm through his, directing him toward her home. "Cyrus told me what's going on between the two of you."

A sigh escaped his lips before Greyson could stop it. He steeled his heart. Cyrus, the real Cyrus, would not choose to be with him. He and Greyson had too much baggage between them to even have a chance at a future. Greyson had done the right thing by putting some distance between them—distance he desperately needed or he would relent and do something they'd both regret in the end. Cyrus' sad, puppy-dog expression flashed in his thoughts. Greyson pinched the bridge of his nose. He was trying to do the honorable thing. He and Cyrus could not be together.

"Did he now?"

"Yes," she said, tugging him along to her house with a surprisingly strong grip.

"I know you have an opinion on the matter, so you might as well speak your peace," he ground out. Widow Abney had an opinion on everything; besides, this situation could not get any worse nor would he change his mind.

Widow Abney patted his arm, not speaking. Even now, he could see the bright flowers in front of her home, bobbing in the slight breeze. He glared at the orange puffballs, uncomfortable, as a vision of a smiling Cyrus bloomed in his mind. Greyson snorted, banishing the wayward thoughts. The flowers would be dead in a matter of days when the icy weather of winter came upon them, and they would no longer bother him.

When they reached her door, she waved him inside. Greyson did not want to go in nor did he want to hear what the woman had to say. With no other option, he followed her. Widow Abney sat, motioning to the chair opposite of her. Stiffly, he sank down.

"You rejected him," she said bluntly, taking a scone off the plate in the middle of the table.

"Yes. Cyrus would not care for me if he had his memories."

"That is a possibility," she said with a nod.

Greyson scoffed. "It's a fact. You know who he is. You know we're not friends."

"Yes. He's the emperor's nephew, who you hate."

"He's the one who brought troops to our mountains and killed your sons," Greyson spat out.

A guttural laugh burst out of her throat. His mouth fell open. Widow Abney took a bite of a scone, a smile pulling at her lips. "Cyrus is no more responsible for Emperor Caspian winning the war than you are for us losing it. He was the face of the army as you were the face of our rebellion. Cyrus didn't even lead the troops as you did not lead ours."

"You don't blame him for your sons' deaths?"

"No."

"You blame the emperor, then?"

"No."

"I don't understand."

She patted him. "There is no one to blame for Caleb and John's deaths, just as there are no words to describe the pain of losing them. They died protecting our people. There was no winner or loser in that war. Both sides had their reasons, and everyone lost someone or something."

He shook his head. "The emperor had no reason beyond greed."

"That is a very simplistic way of looking at it. Did he want all the venetus because of greed? Maybe. Venetus gems are used to create magical artifacts, tools, and so many things that help our lives. But they're also used to make weapons. Before the emperor demanded the entirety of what we mined, we would sell to other nations, who could make weapons that they then could use against us. Should the emperor have paid us more? Yes. But I think many factors went into the war on both sides."

The chair scraped on the floor as Widow Abney rose and came around the table. She placed a hand under his chin and forced him to meet her gaze. "Cyrus protected his people much as you did yours. You both did your duty to the best of your abilities. I no more blame him than I would you. Besides, he endeared himself to me forever on two counts.

"After we unconditionally surrendered, the emperor wanted to take the venetus for no money, but Cyrus fought for us. The only reason we are being paid now and have reasonable quotas is because of him. More importantly," she said, firmly gripping his chin, "he saved your life, Greyson."

Greyson wanted to look away, but she would not let him.

"The emperor wanted to execute you for being the face of the rebellion, and Cyrus convinced him not to. He saved you, Greyson, and I will forever be grateful."

"So you think I should accept him because he saved my life?" he asked, his voice hard.

"No," Widow Abney said, stroking his cheek. "You don't have to accept him or return his affection. That's up to you. But give him the respect of believing what he says to be true.

Just because he doesn't remember everything doesn't make his feelings any less valid. Right now, Cyrus cares about you. Whether that feeling will fade with time or the return of his memories, I don't know. But at this moment, he cares for you, and you should believe him."

"But he's so different. How can I believe what he says when he acts nothing like the man I remember?"

"If the burdens of the past and responsibilities were suddenly gone, you would be different too. I think what we're seeing is the real Cyrus that hid beneath all of the responsibilities he shouldered and the memories he had to bear."

Of course, Greyson would be different if the weight of the past, the responsibilities of the present, and the fears of the future didn't rest upon his shoulders. Could Widow Abney be right? There were times when he caught glimpses of the Cyrus he remembered.

"You think he actually likes me?"

"Yes. I do."

Greyson did not want to believe that Cyrus' feelings were real because it would make it harder to reject him.

She started to speak again, drawing his attention to her heavily wrinkled face. "Whether you return or reject his feelings is up to you. But I want you to think about something. Maybe just maybe, all that anger and hatred you feel for Cyrus is nothing more than the fact that you stood on separate sides of the negotiation table. And maybe, you both deserve to set the past aside for the chance of a better future, together."

CYRUS

Cyrus turned from the fire as Greyson walked into the house. He'd been gone most of the day, though when he was here, it hadn't mattered. He treated Cyrus like a ghost, ignoring him or pretending he couldn't see him. It twisted his chest and stole his breath.

He tried to smile, but it was forced. Greyson's blank mask didn't alter as he strode directly toward him, and a sudden spark of hope burned Cyrus. Maybe he'd changed his mind?

Crouching, Greyson said, "This is what's going to happen. First, we wait for Widow Abney to finish your fur-lined clothes. Second, we'll travel to the coast. Third, we try to find the mage who stole your memories. Last, and most important, we stay only friends, nothing else."

"Why?" Cyrus asked, squeezing Greyson's arm.

He wrenched out of Cyrus' grasp. "You wouldn't want this, Cyrus."

"You don't know that!"

"Yes," Greyson snapped, standing as he fisted a hand in his hair. "Yes, I do."

Cyrus shook his head. "I don't believe you."

Greyson continued like he hadn't spoken, "This is what we're going to do, or I can take you to Lord Darius in Wood-hurst who can arrange for you to go to the capital for treatment. Those are your choices, Cyrus."

"Fine," Cyrus replied as he turned back to the flames. "Let's go to the coast."

15

CYRUS

Pine trees pierced the sky, crowding around the muddy, dirt path as they headed up a steep hill on Validus Mountain while Ferrum, smaller but more jagged, hovered in the west, capped in snow. The blue sky stretched before them without a single cloud to mar its perfection. Besides a few large boulders, some bushes, fallen trees, and underbrush there wasn't much to see. There weren't even game animals or squirrels, though he heard a few birds singing.

They'd begun their journey north to the coast that morning. It would take a few weeks depending on the weather, as winter started to encroach on the land. They would travel along a road that led through three different villages that were situated against the mountainside before reaching the coast.

The thought of the ocean made Cyrus beam. He could remember what the ocean looked like, smelled like, and even sounded like, but he possessed no personal memories of it. Even now, he could picture the warm sand, the sun glinting off the blue-gray water, and the low roar of the waves all the while the briny scent tickled his nose.

Something about that scene called to him. He stared at Greyson's lean back as he walked in front of him. He and Greyson would be at the beach together. His stomach knotted in an odd excitement.

Thanks to the fur-lined vest, cloak, gloves, and knit hat, Cyrus remained warm in the late fall air. It was chillier than he would've preferred, but the air didn't bite at his skin. Of course, it was only morning.

He tried to remain cheerful as the day passed, but it was hard, as Greyson gave him the cold shoulder. If Cyrus could have walked next to him or chatted quietly, it would've been more pleasant, but Greyson rebuffed him anytime he got close or tried to start a conversation. So the day passed in an oppressive silence until the afternoon when they took a short break.

Greyson gave him some dried meat, a hunk of cheese, and an apple. Cyrus accepted them with a smile, which wasn't returned. They sat right next to the road with some rocks at their backs and pines in front of them. He ate the meal quietly and drank from his waterskin, all the while watching Greyson, who sat, cross-legged, some distance away with his gaze on the treeline.

"Are you expecting danger?" he asked, thinking about his dream. It felt like an age ago.

"No."

Cyrus scooted closer, back scraping on the rocks. "How long until we reach the village?"

"Three days."

As he shifted even closer, the pine needles crackled beneath him. Greyson finally looked in his direction. Cyrus bit his bottom lip as his gaze trailed over Greyson's face. Greyson focused on his mouth as his posture stiffened. Cyrus' pulse skittered. Only days ago, he'd found out how soft Greyson's lips were. A palatable tension hung between them. He let go of his lip as his mouth opened to speak.

That small movement broke the moment, and Greyson jerked back, hands fisting on his thighs. Clearing his throat, Greyson brushed himself off. "We should go."

With a nod, Cyrus followed him.

GREYSON

As the sun set, Greyson made camp not far from the path in a copse of trees that shielded them on the off-chance another traveler journeyed the same road. Seeing that Cyrus had already started shivering, Greyson quickly gathered wood for a fire, having no trouble finding any. Once the flames burned bright, he riffled through the bags, removing the fur blanket and an extra blanket for Cyrus. He immediately draped them over Cyrus' broad shoulders, fighting the urge to gather him into his embrace.

"Stay here," he ordered. "I'm going to get water."

Cyrus nodded, teeth chattering.

How by the serpent below was Cyrus going to survive the winter?

Greyson stalked through the trees toward a stream that was about five minutes from their camp. The clear water rushed over the rocky streambed, curving through the trees and disappearing from view. A massive tree had fallen and crossed the creek, serving as a bridge if he wanted it. His gaze instinctively swept the area for any herbs or moss that may be of use. When he didn't spot anything, he crept down the steep embankment to fill the waterskins, kettle, and a pot.

The walk back, while short, became precarious. When he entered the camp, Cyrus smiled and almost made Greyson drop what he carried. Cyrus plucked the pot from the crook of Greyson's arm, his hand skimming over Greyson, which set off a riot of tingles.

Nodding his thanks, cheeks uncomfortably warm, Greyson put the kettle on the flames, then took the pot from Cyrus. Quickly, Greyson started dinner by adding chunks of dried meat, vegetables, and herbs.

Unable to stop himself, Greyson peeked at Cyrus from the corner of his left eye. He'd missed Cyrus, which was ridiculous because he was right there. Cyrus was always right there beside him. Nonetheless, he couldn't help the longing that rose within him, so powerful it stole his breath. He missed the easy touches, comfortable conversation, and sleeping with Cyrus in his arms.

It was necessary, or at least, he told himself it was.

He stirred the bubbling soup as a savory scent suffused the air and made his stomach growl. His gaze flicked to Cyrus, whose shoulders were hunched. Suddenly, blue eyes met his. Greyson jerked back, swallowing.

"Are you warming up?"

"Yes," Cyrus replied, rubbing his arms. "You don't happen to have a warming spell, do you?"

"No," he said. "I'm sure there are warming spells, but I don't know any."

Brow furrowing, Cyrus asked, "I thought you were a trained mage?"

"I am and I'm not."

Cyrus' mouth hung open as his eyebrows squished to-gether, which made Greyson chuckle. "My mother was a court-trained mage. She was taken from the Griseo Moun-tains when she was ten because of her healing ability. It's a very rare gift. It took her twenty years to pay off her contract and come home. She married my father and had me. She taught me. I never went to school, though, because she didn't want to send me. There is a lot I don't know. I'm most skilled in battle magic. Basic spells that most trained mages would know, I don't."

"What do you mean 'contract?'"

"Court mages don't have to pay for schooling. Instead, they have a contract price that has to be repaid before they can end their service to the emperor. The price depends on the person's skill."

"So your mom was taken?" Cyrus asked, moving toward him.

"Yes."

Cyrus leaned closer to him, almost touching. "Couldn't you go to school now if you wanted?"

"It's in the capital."

"So?"

Greyson tried to organize his thoughts for a response. There was so much Cyrus no longer understood. "I can't go to the capital. I can't leave the Griseo Mountains."

"Why?"

"After the rebellion ended, the emperor was going to exe-cute me for the part I played. I was the face of it, after all."

A hand latched around his. "What?"

Fingers tingling, he extracted his hand from Cyrus' grasp. "In the end, I wasn't executed, obviously, but I was exiled. I can't leave the Griseo Mountains. If I do, there's a bounty on my head. Incentive, I guess, to stay put."

"You won't go back, right?" Cyrus asked, eyebrows forming a slash across his forehead.

"No. Why would I ever want to leave here? I love the Griseo Mountains."

Smiling, Cyrus said, "I'm glad. I like it here too."

He did not respond, and Cyrus' grin dimmed.

When the soup was finished, Greyson and Cyrus ate in silence, seated near each other. The fire gave enough light for him to see, and enough heat to keep Cyrus comfortable. An owl hooted in the distance followed by a long With wide. Wide eyes on the trees, Cyrus scooted even closer, almost pressing against Greyson's side and making him spill his tea.

"What's wrong?" Greyson asked, wiping his stinging fingers on his thighs. He shifted to the side to give himself much-needed space.

"We won't get attacked by anything, right?"

His brow furrowed until another howl pierced the air, too distant to bother them. "The wolves will leave us alone. The fire should keep them at bay. Besides, we're both armed."

Cyrus stayed close to his side, eating his bowl of soup, focus never straying from the darkness.

Greyson set the two bedrolls on opposite sides of the fire before stacking up a pile of wood. When Greyson sank to the ground, Cyrus hovered next to him, arms swinging.

"We're not sleeping next to each other?" Cyrus asked, feet shuffling.

"No. The fur should keep you warm enough."

"Okay."

Unable to stop himself, Greyson watched as Cyrus arranged the blankets. Greyson forced himself to lie on his right side, facing the fire with his staff resting on the ground in front of him. Settling, he held his staff and tried to fall asleep.

"Goodnight," Cyrus said from across the camp.

"Goodnight."

CYRUS

A series of yips broke the silence and made Cyrus squeeze the blanket. The cold air pierced him through the many layers and numbed his face. He drew the blanket tighter around him, curling into a ball. It didn't help.

The low fire gave off enough light that Cyrus could discern Greyson's sleeping face. He wanted to close the distance between them and wrap his arms around Greyson, to feel the warmth seep into him.

He shifted again, trying to get comfortable, an impossible feat on the hard ground. No matter where he moved, a rock or a stick jabbed into his side, making him reposition yet again. A howl sounded in the distance followed by more high-pitched yips.

His breath quickened as sweat gathered on his palms. "Greyson?"

Greyson didn't react.

Tightening his hold on the blanket, Cyrus tried to let it go. The trees creaked above him, swaying in the wind. He stared at them, swallowing. Rustling came from behind him, and Cyrus flipped over, reaching for his sword while his pulse thundered in his ears. His eyes flicked back and forth, searching as if something would suddenly materialize from the shadows.

His gaze shifted back to Greyson, who was sound asleep. Safety was right there. Cyrus swallowed, hands curled into fists.

"Greyson."

With a growl, Greyson snapped, "What?"

"Can I sleep next to you?"

"No," Greyson said, shifting to his back.

Cyrus bit his lip and kept lying on his side. Eventually, Greyson rolled back onto his right side. "Are you okay?"

"The wolves are making me nervous."

"You are safe. I promise." Greyson threw a couple more pieces of wood onto the fire, sending sparks into the night sky.

"I trust you."

"I know."

16

CYRUS

Appearing like magic, a village emerged as they crested a hill. About a dozen homes that were built from wood stood in a glen, ringed around a simple, stone well; the others were carved right into the side of Validus Peak. The rocky ground was sparse with greenery, only boasting a few scraggly, brown weeds. Chickens clucked in coops near the homes, and goats munched on the few offerings.

"Stay close," Greyson said.

He wanted to take Greyson's left arm but didn't. "Why?"

"People here in Cliffside are not used to strangers."

"How would they know I'm a stranger?"

Greyson didn't respond, rolling his eyes, as he started forward. Cyrus followed him, gaze wandering over the people. They all wore unadorned, sturdy clothes. Everyone had the same aspect as Greyson—dark hair and pale, gray-tinged skin. There were not too many people in the village proper, as it was the middle of the day.

As soon as they got closer, the townspeople stopped whatever they were doing and gaped at him. Greyson stepped in front of Cyrus, blocking him from view. Cyrus gripped his sword. He didn't care who these people were, he wouldn't let anyone hurt Greyson.

A man with light brown hair, green eyes, and a square jaw approached. "Greyson," he said in a pleasant voice. He dragged Greyson into a hug, slapping his back a couple of times.

Cyrus struggled to breathe while a dark emotion coiled in his stomach like a snake about to strike. He wanted to rip the newcomer's arms from Greyson.

The new man's gaze landed on Cyrus, and his expression cooled. "What is *he* doing here?" he asked with an arm draped across Greyson's shoulders. He was maybe an inch taller than Greyson and several inches taller than Cyrus.

Before Cyrus could respond, Greyson shielded him from Liam. "He doesn't remember, Liam."

"What?" Liam asked.

"I lost my memory. A mage erased it," Cyrus replied as he moved to stand by Greyson's left side.

"So? Why are you here?" Liam crossed his arms.

"It's a long story," Greyson said. "We're on our way to the coast. I was hoping you'd let us stay with you."

Liam glared at Cyrus for several moments. "Fine. Keep him close so someone doesn't kill him."

Cyrus glanced at Greyson. "What's going on?"

His gaze darted to the side. "Nothing." Greyson reached across his body with his right hand and squeezed Cyrus' fingers. "Stay close to me."

"You will tell me later, right?"

Greyson merely said, "Let's go."

GREYSON

A heavy tension hung in the air. Liam sat on one side of the table, glaring at Cyrus, while Cyrus crossed his arms and glowered. Greyson had no idea why Cyrus instantly disliked Liam, but he had.

Glancing between them, Greyson said, "I should make a pot of tea."

"Good idea. I always wanted to have tea with Cyrus," Liam said, sarcasm dripping from every word.

This was a very bad idea, Greyson thought. The people of Drakcombe trusted him as did the people of Creekside, so they didn't say anything or do much more than glare at Cyrus. Here? Greyson did not have the same assurances. Though he was well-respected and beloved throughout the Griseo Mountains since he took over for his mother as a teacher, Cyrus' presence tested his people's faith in him.

The truth would come out eventually, and he didn't know what to do.

"Tea would be good," Cyrus said.

"I can make it." Greyson started to stand, but Liam waved him off, getting to his feet.

Cyrus placed a hand on his thigh, whispering, "What's going on?"

"Liam doesn't like you. I didn't think it would be a problem," he answered. It was the truth but not the complete truth.

"Did you two used to court or something?"

"No," Greyson said, brow furrowing. "I taught him magic, like many *many* others. Besides, I've only courted a couple of people."

"Ah." A quick smile appeared and vanished so quickly on Cyrus' lips that Greyson couldn't be sure he'd actually seen it. Cyrus asked, "Why doesn't he like me, then?"

"It's complicated."

With a deep frown, Cyrus stared at him. Greyson swallowed. Cyrus was going to figure it out.

After several minutes, Liam returned, carrying a tray with a teapot and three teacups, then poured each of them a cup. Greyson opened his mouth to say Cyrus didn't like tea when Cyrus grabbed his leg, silencing him.

As they drank their tea, Liam and Cyrus glared at each other. Greyson wanted to say something, but he didn't want to say the wrong thing or start a fight. Once they finished, Liam asked, "Can I speak with you alone?"

Cyrus clamped down on his knee, expression darkening. Greyson peeled his fingers off. "Yes. Let's go outside." Greyson leaned toward Cyrus. "I will be right back."

"I'll be right here if you need me."

"Liam is my friend. Everything is fine."

"If you say so," Cyrus replied.

Greyson hovered near the table, staring at Cyrus—the serious mask plastered on his face was familiar. Cyrus appeared like his old self. This same expression had been on his face every time Greyson and the spokesperson, Charlotte Williams, met with the emperor. Cyrus would stand behind his uncle, arms crossed, with this same blank mask. Shaking his head, Greyson cleared the dual image before going outside.

Liam had not gone far, pacing right in front of his home, his boots crunching on the loose stones. He was quite different from most people of the Griseo Mountains with his light brown hair, bright green eyes, and tan skin. His mother came from the capital and gave Liam his coloring.

"Are you insane?" Liam asked.

Unable to stop himself, Greyson laughed.

"What?"

"Elizabeth asked me the same thing when I brought Cyrus to Creekside."

"Well, the question bears repeating. Why do you have Prince Cyrus with you?"

The story slipped from his lips—a pared-down version. Greyson had no intention of telling his friend about the kisses he and Cyrus had shared. Liam listened, not commenting.

When Greyson stopped talking, Liam said, "You should've let him die, Greyson."

"It's too late now."

"Yes," Liam bit back. "You paraded him around, so now if he dies, the emperor will blame us."

Greyson said, "I need to find out why he's here, and to do that, Cyrus needs to regain his memory."

"And you think Davies is going to help you?"

There was only one village along the icy coast, and Charles Davies was the headman. "I don't know, but Elizabeth theorized that a necromancer may have erased Cyrus' memories."

"Why?"

"Because he woke up in the glade."

Liam nodded, understanding. "And of course, the Davies have produced more necromancers than anyone else."

"Yes."

"This is a bad plan," Liam said. "Just give him to the representative, and he'll take Prince Cyrus to the capital and out of our hair."

His breath rushed out as if someone had punched him in the gut. He did not want to separate from Cyrus, not yet. Greyson had started to get used to his presence. Clearing his throat, Greyson said, "I need to know."

"I don't think this is a good idea."

"You won't tell him anything?"

"What do you mean?" Liam asked.

Rubbing the back of his neck, Greyson said, "I lied and told him that we were friends."

Liam started laughing, shaking his head. "It's not going to take much to shatter that lie."

"I know. And when Cyrus remembers, hopefully, he won't kill me."

CYRUS

Cyrus glared at the closed door. He wanted to charge into the cold air and keep Liam away from Greyson. Thoughts of punching Liam in his perfect face made Cyrus grin. He shook his head to banish the violent images. Greyson said it was fine, and Cyrus had to believe him.

Dread curled in his stomach. Liam obviously hated him, and Cyrus didn't want him to sway Greyson. It also didn't help that Liam was attractive. While Liam and Greyson hadn't courted in the past, things changed. Cyrus snorted. Currently, he was attempting to change his and Greyson's relationship.

He examined the space, searching for a flaw. Begrudgingly, Cyrus had to admit the home was cozy with its stone fireplace, wood mantle adorned with trinkets, round rag rug, and couch with a knitted blanket. A single bookshelf graced the wall to the right of the door, bursting with books. A basic kitchen with light cabinets and stone counters was to the left of the door, and a square table, plus matching chairs, was not far from the kitchen. There was a single door near the fireplace that was closed. Everything was clean and organized, though it resembled pretty much every other home he'd seen here. Thankfully, it was one of the wooden homes on the ground, not on the cliffside. He shuddered at the very thought.

The door opened, and Greyson strode in, alone. Cyrus stood. "Are you okay?"

"Yes," Greyson replied slowly. "Why wouldn't I be?"

"I don't know."

Greyson chuckled.

Stepping closer, he asked, "What's going on?"

"I already told you," Greyson said, looking at the door.

"*What* is going on?" Cyrus repeated in a hard tone. Greyson didn't say anything, swallowing, which made his long throat bob. Cyrus was almost positive that Greyson was lying to him about something. What exactly, he didn't know.

"Liam said we could stay here for the night."

"Fine."

Greyson and Liam went in and out of the house all day while Cyrus stayed inside, curled up on the couch under a blanket. He tried to follow the first time, but Greyson told him to stay where it was warm. So much for showing him off to people in the hopes of finding the mage who scrubbed his memory.

Once the sun set, they came inside, a smile playing on Greyson's lips as Liam said something. Liam bumped his shoulder, and Greyson grinned. The happy expression tugged on Cyrus' heartstrings.

When they noticed him, Greyson nodded while Liam's expression morphed into something hard and frigid. A sudden tension bloomed, filling the home. The snaps from the fire were the only thing to break the oppressive quiet.

"I can make dinner," Greyson offered, the wood floor creaking as he shifted his weight.

"I'll help you," Cyrus said.

Greyson raised an eyebrow but didn't comment. Liam merely scoffed and went into the lone bedroom, closing the door behind him. Greyson said, "Don't mind Liam."

Together, they made a simple soup, which suited him fine. No matter what Greyson cooked, it tasted delicious. Once finished, Cyrus carried it to the table, and Greyson set a thick cloth down to protect the wood from the heat of the pot. Placing it on the table, Cyrus glanced at Greyson, who stared at the closed door.

"I should get Liam." Greyson knocked on the bedroom door. After a moment, he went inside, closing the door behind him.

Arms crossing, Cyrus tried to breathe evenly. He very much doubted he'd ever been more jealous in his entire life, though he couldn't confirm that. Several minutes passed before the door opened again, and Greyson appeared.

"Liam wasn't hungry," Greyson said.

"He really hates me doesn't he?"

"Yes."

They ate in silence. Occasionally, Cyrus would glance at the closed door, but Liam never came out. Once they finished, he said, "I can clean the dishes."

"I can do it. It's fine," Greyson said, standing. After the dishes were cleaned, Greyson set his bedroll across the room from Cyrus. An annoyed grunt came out of his lips.

"What?" Greyson asked.

"Why are you lying so far away?"

"You know why."

"I know, but it's not necessary."

Greyson sat on his bedroll, scowling. Cyrus wanted to run his fingers over it, tracing every aspect of Greyson's lips. Greyson lay down, back facing Cyrus, and broke the moment. He settled on his own bedroll, flames warming him as his view was filled with Greyson's back.

"Goodnight."

"Goodnight, Cyrus."

GREYSON

Guilt clogged his throat, choking him. He kept hurting Cyrus; he'd lied and kept lying. Greyson stared at Cyrus, who slept on his stomach, arms sprawled, mouth hanging open, and hair in his face. Unable to stop himself, he brushed the golden strands back.

"Cyrus," he said, voice coming out softer than he intended.

Cyrus' face scrunched, but he didn't wake. Greyson caressed his cheek. He did not understand how his emotions changed so quickly where Cyrus was concerned.

Something shuffled, and he turned his head and froze. Liam leaned against the bedroom door frame, arms crossed. Greyson swallowed, hand falling.

"This is an interesting development."

"Liam." Greyson glared at him. He and Cyrus could not be together, but he refused to let Liam judge him.

"What are you doing?" his former student asked, eyebrows pulling together.

Greyson ran a hand through his hair. "I don't know."

"This will not end well."

"I know," he whispered, stroking Cyrus' soft hair.

"Well, I warned you."

Scoffing, he said, "You can tell me 'I told you so' later."

"Not if you're dead," Liam joked, striding out of the house.

His fingers skimmed over Cyrus' cheek and tingles shot up his arm. Cyrus shifted toward his touch, a sleepy smile on his face.

"Greyson," Cyrus muttered.

Could Widow Abney be right? Could the *new* Cyrus simply be him without the burden of responsibility or memories of the past? Unable to stop himself, Greyson cupped Cyrus' cheek, thumb sliding over his cheekbone. Cyrus grinned.

Greyson shifted back. Whether Widow Abney was right or not didn't change anything. He and Cyrus had too much history that could not be overcome. Also, if Cyrus had his memories, he wouldn't choose this.

Cyrus moved to his knees. In their current positions, they were almost the same height. "What?"

"Nothing."

"That's a lie."

Greyson nodded. "It is."

Cyrus held Greyson's face between his calloused palms. "Tell me."

His gaze darted to Cyrus' lips before shooting back to his eyes. Brow furrowed, Cyrus leaned ever so slightly forward. Shaking his head, Greyson withdrew from his grasp. "We should get ready to leave."

"Alright."

17

CYRUS

They left the village with no trouble. Cyrus remained close to Greyson's side, and he didn't say anything, which wasn't unusual. He was always quiet, but this silence felt more pensive than normal. They continued north, up the side of the mountain. The path steadily grew steeper and made Cyrus' thighs burn with exertion while his breath grew jagged. The only good thing about the steep road was the sweat he worked up. Finally, he was warm.

Greyson strode ahead of him, seemingly unbothered by the fast pace or the hike. Shaking his head, Cyrus tried to keep up.

When Greyson finally stopped for lunch, Cyrus fell to the ground—exhausted. Footsteps crunched on the ground and a shadow came over him.

"You're getting soft."

"What?" Cyrus asked, breath uneven.

"You used to be much fitter. You've gotten soft from sitting around my cabin," Greyson said with a slight smile.

He arched up. "I guess I need more activity."

Greyson cleared his throat and stepped back. Cyrus sank to the cold ground, panting. The footsteps receded, then returned before a slight thump sounded as Greyson sat right beside him.

"You should eat," Greyson said before taking a bite of a crisp apple.

Cyrus sat up, and Greyson gave him some food. He took a bite of dried meat, then took a sip of his waterskin. "How long until we reach the next village?"

"About a week."

"Is the path this steep the whole way?"

"Pretty much."

A groan escaped his lips, and Greyson chuckled. Cyrus chewed on his lip as a tension stretched between them. Greyson's gaze shifted to him, and the smile on his face dimmed into something softer as he stilled. That expression drew Cyrus in like a moth to the flame as the urge to touch Greyson, to feel his skin, flooded him. Cyrus shifted closer, boots scraping on the rocks beneath him.

Greyson jerked toward the treeline.

Cyrus went back to his meal as a sharp stabbing sensation started in the region of his heart. He squashed it. At least Greyson sat close to him.

When they finished, they started off at a brisk pace and continued until sunset. The pattern held the same for the next three days. On the afternoon of the fourth day, a cold drizzle started, changing the path into a mud pit and chilling Cyrus to the bone.

They pressed onward until they reached the side of the mountain and a cave system. Greyson shoved him under an overhang before, staff held out, and investigated the cave for inhabitants.

The mouth of the cave was wide and gaping, much taller than Greyson. Cyrus peered around the long tunnel as Greyson's staff lit up the darkness. The walls were shiny with water and there was a deep pool in the back as well as a few large stones. Thankfully, though, it was empty.

"Get undressed before you freeze, and I'll build a fire." Greyson went back out in the rain while Cyrus shakily took off his soaked clothes before wrapping himself in a damp blanket. Greyson returned several minutes later and quickly built a fire near the entrance, then hauled Cyrus toward it. The second Cyrus sank next to the flames, heat washed over him. Stretching his hands to the roaring flames, Cyrus glanced at Greyson.

Greyson stripped off his clothes, and Cyrus couldn't help but watch. The line of his muscles. The way he moved. His long, capable fingers. Even the black hair scattered over his chest. All of it was perfect. Cyrus sighed. Greyson paused, and Cyrus looked up at his face, only to blush. He'd been caught staring. Greyson rolled his eyes and spread his clothes out to dry before pulling on another pair of trousers and a shirt.

Crouching in front of him, Greyson tucked the blanket tighter around his shoulders. "I shouldn't have even tried this journey. You're going to freeze before we even reach the coast."

Smiling, he touched Greyson's arm. "I'm fine, Greyson."

Scoffing, Greyson pushed his hand back under the blanket and covered him again. "Stay under the blanket."

After a quick dinner, they settled down for the night. The drizzle had transformed into a downpour as lightning flashed across the sky followed by a roar of thunder. Greyson placed their bedrolls next to the fire, then tossed another piece of wood onto the flames before lying down. Cyrus glared at the space between them. Apparently, the rain was not enough to draw Greyson close.

Facing Greyson, he asked, "What are we going to do if it doesn't stop raining?"

"Just go to sleep."

Cyrus nodded, staring at Greyson as the fire warmed his back.

When the morning came, the rain hadn't slowed. Greyson stuck his hand out from the cave, then glanced back at Cyrus. He watched him with a slight smile, and Greyson scowled. "We'll have to wait until the rain stops to travel again."

"So we'll stay here?"

"Yes."

A wide smile tugged on his lips. Cyrus didn't mind the rain. Greyson settled against the cave wall as he played with his staff. Cyrus watched the movements, but nothing magical seemed to happen. Greyson grinned before he twirled the staff. The rocks nearest to him rolled over. Cyrus' eyebrows rose. With a breathy chuckle, Greyson performed the same flipping, twirl motion with his left hand. The rocks rolled again.

"How does it work?"

"Repetition of movements with your dominant hand and learning how to channel magic appropriately."

"Do something else," Cyrus demanded as he drew his legs to his chest.

Greyson arched a single eyebrow, but amusement danced in his eyes. He swept the staff in a long arc, and a gust of wind rushed into the cave, making the fire sputter. Cyrus smiled, though a shiver went down his spine from the sudden chill. Greyson's brow furrowed, but Cyrus asked, "What else can you do?"

He shrugged. "A lot and not so much."

"Which is it?"

"Both."

"Do you like magic?" Cyrus asked, genuinely curious. Greyson didn't use it often and never seemed to talk about it.

"That's like asking me if I like water or breathing. It's a part of me. But yes, I like it well enough. Though," he said with a shake of his head, "I prefer making potions and poultices. I like healing people."

"What else do you like?"

"Many things."

Cyrus extended his lower lip as he silently pleaded for Greyson to keep speaking.

"I like cooking," he said, eyes averted. "I like making something delicious from nothing. I started cooking when my family died. It was something I could control, something I could master. I love herblore and wandering the mountains. No matter how much I explore them, I always find something new."

"I want to do that with you," Cyrus said.

"What?"

"Explore."

Greyson laughed. "You'd freeze."

"Not if we go in the summer."

His eyes darted toward the rain coming down in sheets. "That's true."

Cyrus wanted to close the distance between them, feel the smoothness of Greyson's skin, and the warmth of his body. He wanted Greyson to want him back. With everything that Cyrus learned and every day that passed, his love grew stronger, though it grew progressively sharper like a knife that twisted in his heart. He needed it to be returned, but Greyson pulled back whenever they got close.

After a bit, Greyson spoke again. "Do you want to hear another story?"

"Of course." Cyrus rested his chin on his knees.

"I can tell you a story about Ferrum. Ferrum Peak is the only mountain within the Griseo Mountain range without any venetus."

"Why?" Cyrus loved the sound of his voice and the way his face moved as he spoke.

"Just listen," Greyson snapped, but he gave Cyrus a smile. "Ferrum lived on the icy coast where the wind always blows and the ice crashes upon the rocky shores, which is where we're going by the way. Humans in general did not like Ferrum unlike his older siblings or the other dragons that came. He used the bones of the dead to wield magic and spoke to those across the veil. They saw darkness in it, the serpent's influence, so to speak. But there was none. He helped those souls that couldn't cross yet. He made use of the dead bones left behind. He used his magic to protect, much as his siblings did."

"That's sad," Cyrus interjected but fell silent with a sheepish grin when Greyson glared at him.

"One day, a ship crashed upon the shore. Ferrum saved the people aboard from the icy depths. These humans did not see darkness, but rather, someone who saved them when he had nothing to gain. They stayed by the shore so he would not be alone, and he taught them his magic.

"Years passed, and the village thrived. But Validus and Sarcio, as well as most of the other dragons, had taken their long sleep, forming the mountains. Ferrum wanted to as well, but he couldn't no matter how hard he tried. It would not come for him. So he went to Validus Peak to speak with his brother. Validus' soul came forth and told Ferrum that he hadn't completed his life's task. Something waited for him.

"Ferrum did not believe him. What would wait for him? He wasn't the eldest or the strongest in magic like Validus. He didn't heal or guide like Sarcio. He only spoke to the dead, and no one wanted to hear what they had to say.

"So he appealed to the human who became leader of the Griseo Mountains after Validus. She helped him."

"With what?" Cyrus asked.

"Sleep. She and many others worked together to help him sleep. The story doesn't say if it was accomplished by a spell or potion or some combination of the two."

"He became Ferrum Peak."

"Yes," Greyson said with a nod. "But unlike the others, it wasn't natural. The leader at the time said Ferrum would one day wake to finish his uncompleted task."

Cyrus asked, "Why isn't there any venetus in Ferrum Peak?"

"My mother had a theory. She said the dragons died in their sleep, and when their bodies broke down, they became venetus. Ferrum didn't die. He's spelled asleep. So there is no venetus because of it," Greyson said, sipping some tea.

"But you don't believe it?"

"No. It's a story. There are no dragons."

His arms tightened around his legs. "I believe it."

"Why?" Greyson asked with a laugh.

"Because you're like Validus. Strong and you protect every-one with that strength."

The next morning the rain stopped, and they continued their journey. Greyson set off, at a slower pace because of the mud, and kept casting glances over his shoulder at Cyrus. He tried to keep up as best as he could. The next two days passed in the same pattern as their earlier travels. On the afternoon of the third day since the cave, they came to a tiny village that consisted of six homes huddled close together.

All of the buildings were wood and plain. There was no color anywhere, even in the empty flower boxes and barren gardens next to the homes. A few scrawny chickens clucked as a few people in threadbare brown clothes went about their chores.

"Stay close," Greyson ordered.

"Is it like the last village?"

"Yes and no. I don't have a close friend here, and this village is extremely secluded. The people here don't like outsiders, nor do they trust me as much." Greyson started forward, and Cyrus followed right behind him. It took a little bit for people to notice him, but the second they did, it was like a current went through townspeople. They all stopped and swiveled toward him.

An older man with weathered features and thinning hair approached. "He's not welcome."

"Cyrus is with me," Greyson said, holding his staff out. The gem on the tip began to glow.

"He is not welcome here," the man repeated in a deeper voice.

Cyrus grasped the hilt of his sword. He didn't want to hurt anyone, but he wouldn't allow any harm to come to Greyson. Greyson stood in front of him, so Cyrus couldn't see his face, but his shoulders were tight while he clenched the staff in a white-knuckled grip.

"Let's leave," Cyrus said.

"We're just passing through," Greyson said, staff glimmering with power. "Come on," he whispered over his shoulder.

As Cyrus passed by a woman, she glared at him, then spat. He recoiled as warm saliva hit his cheek, dripping down.

"Murderer," she growled.

18

GREYSON

Anger seethed under his skin, rolling along his veins like fire, as Greyson jumped in front of Cyrus. The woman immediately drew back, blanching. "Anyone who tries to hurt Cyrus will have to deal with me."

People started to drift away, disappearing. While they may not like him as much here, no one doubted his skill. The Griseo Mountains were his, and no one who'd challenged him here had ever won. Greyson used the edge of his own cloak to wipe the spit off Cyrus' cheek. Cyrus simply stared, eyes wide. Greyson took Cyrus' hand and stalked out of the village, staff held high.

Cyrus did not utter a single word as they walked, and Greyson could not see Cyrus because he was on his right side. Greyson kept his hand tight around Cyrus' as rage pounded inside of him. He'd known people would recognize Cyrus and that it could potentially be a problem, but seeing someone angry at Cyrus stirred his protective fury.

As the sun began to set, Greyson made camp a little distance from the road in an open expanse. Trees stood behind them and the mountain before them. If someone wandered down the road, they would undoubtedly see him and Cyrus, but Greyson would protect him if such a situation arose.

He took the bag from Cyrus' shoulder, and Cyrus would not even look at him, expression drawn. Cupping his frigid cheeks, Greyson said fiercely, "What she said doesn't matter. Do you hear me?"

"What was she talking about? Why does everyone seem uncomfortable around me?"

With a hand behind Cyrus' neck, Greyson yanked him closer. "Don't think about it, alright?"

Cyrus shook his head and moved out of his arms. Greyson watched him as he got a fire started. The temperature started to drop drastically once the sun set, and he did not want Cyrus to get cold. He made dinner, but Cyrus wouldn't eat. He curled up on the bedroll, arms wrapped around his stomach with his eyes squeezed shut while his breath came out in short bursts. No matter what Greyson did, Cyrus refused to speak.

Greyson dropped his bedroll right beside Cyrus. Laying on his left side, he gathered Cyrus close. "Don't think about what she said, alright?" Tightening his hold, he pressed his face against Cyrus' neck, breathing in his sweet scent. "It'll all be alright. I promise."

"I need to know what she was talking about."

He swallowed. Greyson did not want to confess the lies. Not now. He buried his face against Cyrus' shoulder. "I know."

Cyrus wiggled out of his embrace. Greyson let him go, reluctantly. Cyrus did not go far; he simply rolled over and cupped his cheeks. "Something is going on."

Greyson frowned. Calloused thumbs stroked his cheeks, creating tingles in their wake. Without thinking about it, he moved closer to Cyrus, whose hands slid from his face and around his back.

"I wish you'd trust me," Cyrus said.

He did not respond.

They lay in silence, holding each other. The only noises in the darkness were the crackling of the fire and the occasional hoot of an owl. Cyrus snuggled against his chest and whispered, "You should roll over, or else you won't be able to sleep."

Greyson agreed, but he was enjoying this moment with Cyrus. The warmth. The easy touches. The perfectness of it. With a grunt, he rolled onto his back and brought Cyrus with him. Cyrus gave a startled squeak, and Greyson kept shifting until he was on his other side.

Cyrus clutched the front of his shirt, laughing breathlessly. "What are you doing?"

"Rolling over."

"I don't understand you," Cyrus said, shaking his head.

Greyson finger-combed Cyrus' hair. "I don't understand me either."

"That's okay," Cyrus remarked, nuzzling his chest. "I still like you."

"I know." His arms tightened around Cyrus, warmth permeating his skin, and he fell asleep.

CYRUS

Cyrus groaned as a shaft of light directly shone on his face. He tried to resituate, but solid arms wouldn't allow him to. A familiar, intoxicating presence encircled him. With a smile, he snuggled closer, and Greyson rubbed his back. Cyrus kept his eyes closed, hoping the attention would continue, but Greyson said, "I know you're awake."

"I'm not. You're dreaming."

"Hmm, dreaming?" Greyson lifted his face. Cyrus opened his mouth, shifting closer. Before their lips touched, Greyson pinched his side.

"Ow."

"So, not a dream," Greyson remarked with a smirk.

"Spoilsport."

Chuckling, Greyson shifted to his back. "Come on. It's already late."

Cyrus reached for him, but Greyson was already standing. With a yawn, Cyrus followed suit, stretching, then paced around the clearing next to the muddy trail to wake up. The fire had died, leaving nothing but coals in the ring of stones. The air held a chill, and a dense fog hung around them, obscuring his vision, not that he would see much. Everything appeared the same since they'd started traveling.

His gaze landed on Greyson, who knelt next to the dead fire, his black hair falling in front of his face. Cyrus wanted to push it back, to feel the soft strands slide between his fingers.

His expression dimmed as the events of yesterday washed over him. Something was awry. *He's lying to me, I think.*

Suddenly, Greyson met his gaze. He gave Cyrus a slow smile, which made his heart falter. Cyrus returned it, a blush heating his cheeks.

Clearing his throat, he asked, "How long until we reach the next village?"

"I think we're going to go straight to the coast."

Brow furrowing, he asked, "Why? Aren't we supposed to be showing me around in the hope to find the mage who magicked my memories?"

"We didn't do that at the other villages, so I'm sure it'll be fine to skip the next one." Greyson wouldn't look at him.

He sank to the ground in front of him. "Do you have a friend there?"

"Yes. James. But we don't have to speak to him."

Cyrus took Greyson's hand, placed it on his thigh, and ran his fingers over Greyson's palm, tracing the lines. Greyson's fingers twitched under his gentle ministrations. "Is this about what happened yesterday?"

Greyson closed his hand around Cyrus' fingers. "Let's head to the coast, alright?"

After a moment, he nodded. "Okay. How long will it take?"

"About a week to two depending on the weather."

The days disappeared quickly, though, with every day that passed, Greyson withdrew, further and further, until he would no longer hold hands or sleep next to Cyrus. But Greyson continued to answer questions. Over the journey, Cyrus learned more about Greyson like his love for the peace of the mountains and his fear of horses and heights.

"You don't like the capital?"

Greyson sipped a cup of tea. "It's not just the capital. I don't like any city."

"Have you ever lived in a city?"

"Not long term. I stayed in the capital for a few months at a time when we were negotiating with the emperor."

"You didn't like it?"

"No," Greyson said.

"We met there, though, right?" Cyrus watched Greyson closely; his expression tightened as his eyes darted to the side. Every time he asked Greyson a personal question about their previous relationship, he would look away.

"Yes. We met there."

"Why don't you like the city?" he asked, changing the subject.

His shoulders relaxed. "Lots of reasons."

"Which are?"

"First, the smell. Second, the people. Third, the tall buildings. And so many other reasons."

"I guess we'll have to stay in the country."

Greyson asked, "Do you like the country?"

"I mean, I don't remember the city. Well, I know what it looks like, but I don't have any personal memories of it. But yeah," Cyrus said, glancing around at the towering pine trees, then the gleaming stars. "I like it here."

"That's good."

"Yes, it is. That way we can stay here together."

"Together," Greyson repeated quietly as he prodded the fire. The light played on his hollow cheeks, making them appear gaunt as his gaze never wavered from the flames.

The next few days flew by while the weather grew steadily colder. Until the last night before they reached the coast, snow drifted from the sky. Cyrus stared in wonder, mouth open, at the sight. Lifting his face, he spun around. He didn't know if he'd ever seen snow before, but looking at it now, Cyrus quickly decided he loved it.

Hands settled on his waist, stopping his movements. He peeked over his shoulder at Greyson. "It's snowing."

"Be careful, you almost hit a tree."

"Do you like snow?"

"Yes." Greyson held out a hand, catching the flakes. "I've always loved the first snow."

"I don't know if I've ever seen snow before."

"You have," Greyson said.

"I have?"

"Yes."

"When?" Cyrus asked. Greyson seldom spoke about his past. Cyrus bit his lip. Maybe, just maybe, Greyson wasn't lying about them being friends.

Greyson stared at the sky, snow falling on his face and clinging to his black hair. "When the rebellion ended, you brought me back to the Griseo Mountains. It snowed the night before you left and went back to the capital."

"Did we stand side by side like this?"

"Yes, though not exactly like this." Greyson's expression was drawn.

Cyrus stepped closer, gawking at the flurries hanging off his hair. He wanted to bring the black strands to his lips and brush them away. Cyrus desperately wanted to close the distance between them. His fingers ached to touch him. Instead of doing any of that, he held Greyson's hand, their fingers interlacing, and stared at the clouded sky.

After a bit, Greyson shook him off and started to pick up pieces of wood. Sadness pierced his chest. Cyrus didn't understand why Greyson kept moving away from him. Taking a deep breath, he began to collect wood and stacked it.

Greyson started a fire, and Cyrus huddled as close as possible, rubbing his hands together. Greyson removed the fur blanket from one of the bags, then draped it over his shoulders.

"Thank you."

With a nod, Greyson began dinner, soup again. Cyrus, with his chin on his knees, watched Greyson's precise movements and his long, trim fingers.

"You're staring," Greyson said, dumping potatoes into the pot.

"I can't help it."

Greyson rolled his eyes. "You can. Simply look elsewhere."

"Sorry." Clearing his throat, he asked, "How far from the ocean are we?"

"A few hours. We'll get there tomorrow afternoon if the snow doesn't slow us down."

"I can't wait to see the ocean," he said. For some reason, the thought of being at the seaside with Greyson made his stomach churn in excitement.

"I promise it's not like the ocean you're used to," Greyson said, laughing.

His head tilted to the side. "What's it like?"

"Rocky shore. Cold water covered in ice. Like I told you in the story about Ferrum."

"I'm still excited."

Once dinner was done, Greyson gave him a bowl of soup. Cyrus put a spoonful in his mouth, groaning as the savory taste danced along his tongue. "I swear to the goddess," he said between bites, "everything you cook tastes the best."

A pleased smile pulled on Greyson's lips as a blush warmed his gray cheeks. It was adorable, and Cyrus wanted to touch the redness to see if it was warmer than the rest of his skin. He bit his bottom lip at the thought. Greyson focused on his mouth, motionless. A sudden tension bloomed. Cyrus let go of his lip, and Greyson looked into his eyes. Cyrus wanted to kiss him, but the instant he moved, the tension shattered, and Greyson's gaze darted to his own lap.

When they finished eating and cleaning the dishes, he set up his bedroll near the fire. It was cold even next to the flames, and snow continued to float from the sky, dusting the ground. He shivered and stared at Greyson, eyes wide and lower lip extended.

"It's cold," Cyrus commented. Greyson scowled, and Cyrus smiled.

"Fine," Greyson ground out. He dropped his bedroll next to Cyrus and sank to the ground behind him. Cyrus draped his blankets over the both of them, and Greyson hooked an arm over his waist, drawing him close.

Nestled against his chest, Cyrus exhaled. "Now I'm not cold."

Greyson scoffed. "You're shameless."

Cyrus didn't mind being shameless if it led to snuggling. Greyson pushed an arm under his neck, then pressed his face into Cyrus' shoulder. It didn't take long for Greyson to fall asleep, his breath becoming shallow and even.

He brushed Greyson's arm. "Goodnight, my love."

19

GREYSON

Greyson led Cyrus across the snow-crusted ground, their boots crunching loudly, toward the ocean. He heard the soft roar of the waves and smelled the briny scent, but he couldn't see it yet. Nonetheless, a grin was plastered on Cyrus' face as he strode beside Greyson, a hop in his step. It was hard to keep the smile off his own face at Cyrus' eager expression, but he managed it, though he couldn't stop looking at him.

A little bit after noon, they broke through the treeline and onto the rocky shore. A cold wind whipped over the ocean, making his hair flare and his nose run.

Cyrus rushed forward, looking over his shoulder with a glowing expression. Greyson's pulse quickened as his stomach clenched. He followed at a more sedate pace as Cyrus raced toward the water, yelling in obvious joy.

The ocean was a stormy gray while ice covered its surface, which the tide pushed onto the rocks. Cyrus stopped right on the edge of the ocean, arms extended. Greyson grabbed Cyrus and yanked him back before the freezing water crashed into him.

"Careful. Make sure you don't get wet. I don't want you to lose a toe," Greyson snapped.

Cyrus snaked his arms around Greyson's waist. "I'll be careful."

He frowned while his pulse thundered in his ears. Cyrus yanked Greyson flush against him, hands locking in the small of his back. Greyson swallowed. Everything inside of him wanted to kiss Cyrus. He started to lean forward, and Cyrus opened his mouth. Shaking his head, he jerked out of Cyrus' embrace.

"I don't get you."

"I know." Greyson faced the ocean. "Come on."

Together, they walked along the coastline toward the village. As the day deepened and the wind never ceased, it grew colder and colder. From behind him, he heard Cyrus' teeth chattering. Worry coiled in his stomach. Greyson peered over his shoulder and saw Cyrus' lips were tinged blue while his skin had become shockingly pale. Cyrus' shoulders were hunched clear up to his ears as he shook.

Stopping, Greyson tugged Cyrus' cloak tighter around him. "Are you okay?"

"I-I'm f-f-fine," Cyrus said through his chattering teeth.

Greyson frowned, touching his cheek; Cyrus' skin felt cold beneath his palm. "We're getting close."

Cyrus nodded again, not bothering to speak.

The wind swelled, growing stronger, and made Cyrus' trembling worsen. Greyson hoped Charles Davies would let them stay the night, as he didn't know anyone else very well and Cyrus wouldn't survive a night in the open.

They continued along the beach for a couple of hours until, finally, a village came into sight. A couple dozen buildings rested on stilts above the crashing waves. The homes were long with prominent main ridges and large chimneys, and the entire village was connected by decks and bridges. When a breeze rushed over them, it brought the brine of the sea mixed with the smoke from the many chimneys.

When they reached the platforms, he walked up the creaky, wooden steps. Cyrus did not follow him and eyed the deck.

"It's safe. I promise."

When Cyrus continued to hesitate, Greyson stretched out his hand. Cyrus slipped his fingers into Greyon's waiting grasp, holding it tightly, and joined him. Greyson smirked. "I've never seen you afraid of anything before."

Cyrus didn't reply, probably because his teeth chattered too much to get a word out. Greyson towed Cyrus along the platform, winding through the houses. He didn't see anyone, which didn't surprise him because people made their living fishing. Most of the villagers would be on the ocean until evening.

Finally, he came to a two-story house on the edge of the platform. Greyson hid Cyrus behind him, shielding him, then knocked on the door carved with twisting sea serpents. The door cracked open and revealed a woman in her early twenties with long black hair, light green eyes, and pale grayish skin.

"Greyson," she said, eyebrows raising in surprise.

"Julia. Is your father home?"

"No," she said. "He's out on the water. Why?"

"Can we come in?"

"*We?*" she asked, brow furrowing.

He shifted, allowing her to see Cyrus.

Her mouth fell open as her eyes widened. "Goddess above."

Cyrus waved.

"Greyson, why is he here? Are we in trouble?" she asked, hand on her throat.

"No. I mean, I don't know." Greyson scrubbed a hand through his hair. "It's a long story. Can we come in?"

She pursed her lips, gripping the door, then she pushed it open and waved them inside.

Greyson directed Cyrus to the fireplace and forced him to sit on the thick, woven rug. Removing the bags from Cyrus' and his shoulders, he yanked the fur blanket out and draped it over Cyrus' shoulders.

"Are your feet wet?" Greyson asked, concern shooting through him as he held Cyrus' frozen fingers. It seemed the gloves were not enough to ward off the icy temperatures.

Cyrus shook his head, teeth chattering loudly.

"Here," Julia said, giving Cyrus a cup. "I just made some tea."

"Thank you," Cyrus said, accepting the cup and holding it between his hands.

"You're welcome," she said with a warm smile.

"Thank you," Greyson told her with a nod.

"Of course." Julia left the living room, giving them space.

Greyson tucked the blanket tighter around Cyrus, then draped another blanket across his legs. "I'm going to go talk to Julia, alright?"

"I'll be here."

He went into the kitchen. It had been five years since he'd been there. It hadn't changed much. The long table with matching chairs. The generous kitchen with stone countertops and dark cabinets. A large window with shutters that looked out over the ocean. A door that led to a private deck.

Paintings of sunflowers and irises hung on the wall along with copper pots and pans. Julia's mother, Gertrude, had painted the pictures before her death almost ten years ago.

Julia looked up from the bread she kneaded. "So Prince Cyrus?"

An unbidden laugh broke out of his lips as he sank onto a chair. "I've had this conversation multiple times in the last few weeks."

"I believe it. You have Cyrus, your sworn enemy, with you, and clearly, something is going on between the two of you."

The story of finding Cyrus and the subsequent lies and kisses slipped out of his lips before he could stop it. Though as the words poured from his mouth, it felt like a weight lifted off his shoulders. It was freeing to be honest.

She nodded as she shaped the loaves. "I'm guessing you're having second thoughts about the lies."

"Yes, but that's not why we're here. I'm here about a necromancer who might have wiped his memories."

"I don't know of anyone, but in the past, people tended to keep that talent to themselves so I wouldn't expect to know of one now," Julia said. "Besides, as you and your mother taught me, they can't restore his memory. Some of the time it comes back on its own."

"I am aware," he said. Finding the mage who erased Cyrus' memories wouldn't change anything, but Greyson had to do something instead of waiting for Frederick's letter. Besides, they might have a clue as to why Cyrus traveled this far north.

"You know it doesn't have to be a necromancer, right? Anyone here could have done it," Julia said, drawing him out of his thoughts.

"Yes, but he woke up in the glade. Why else would someone be there?"

Julia shrugged as she covered the floured loaves with a gingham towel. Greyson frowned as he stared out the window at the white-capped waves, thoughts circling. Who had stolen

Cyrus' memories? It probably didn't matter, but what else could he do?

"So," Julia started, "back to the interesting part, you like Cyrus."

"What? Now that you're married, you want to match everyone up?"

"Something like that. Though, as I recall," she started, eyes twinkling, "you mentioned several kisses."

Heat rushed to his cheeks, but Greyson refused to respond.

"Besides," she continued, "Victoria and I worked out. We even adopted two kids."

Glancing over his shoulder at the closed door, he said, "You and Victoria didn't hate each other, nor did you plan to kill her, or lie to her."

"All true, but we didn't like each other at first, and my father hated her," she said.

"Your father hates everyone who courted you or who he thought wanted to court you."

"Very true. Now, he likes her. Of course, we did give him grandchildren."

"Always helpful."

Julia wiped her hands on her apron. "I missed you. Five years is much too long."

"I missed you too. You were always my favorite student."

"You're not supposed to say that," she joked, coming to sit across from him.

Greyson smiled for a moment, then his expression dimmed. "Do you think your father will let Cyrus and I stay?"

"Probably. He's been in a good mood."

His shoulders sagged. "That's good. Cyrus doesn't handle the cold well."

Julia said, "You should give the two of you a chance."

He rolled his eyes and got to his feet. Julia hooked an arm around his waist, then they walked back into the front room.

CYRUS

Cyrus studied the room as he waited for Greyson. It was sizable with two large windows near the door. There was an elegant staircase with a banister carved in the shape of a sea serpent. A massive stone fireplace with a wide mantle took up most of one wall. Several chairs sat near the fireplace along with a couch. Red pillows embroidered with gold thread were haphazardly scattered over the furniture while a maroon wool blanket draped over the back of the couch. A few paintings of mountains, a lake, and forests hung on the walls.

The door opened, and Greyson and the woman entered. Her arm was slung about his waist while he had an arm draped over her shoulders. Cyrus swallowed, jealousy, hot and caustic, coiling in his stomach. He supposed she was attractive enough and maybe twenty or so years old. The two of them looked well together with the same lithe grace and height, but Cyrus did not like it.

"Cyrus," Greyson said, "this is Julia."

"Hello," he said stiffly.

The woman raised an eyebrow, but before she said anything a high-pitched voice squealed, "Mama."

A child of two or three bounded into the room and threw her thin arms around Julia's legs. "Ruth. Did you come back with Papa?"

"Yep," the child replied, bouncing and sending her two black braids over her shoulders.

Greyson moved to his side as a man walked in. He had hard features, green eyes, short black hair, and a broad, muscular form. When he spotted Cyrus, a deep frown marred his face. Greyson moved in front of Cyrus and blocked his view.

"Charles," Greyson said, hands fisting at his sides.

"Why is he here, Greyson?" Charles sounded almost tired to Cyrus' ears.

"I can explain," Greyson said, slowly. "We would like to spend the night if you'll let us."

"Why are you here?" Charles repeated, looking directly at Cyrus.

Cyrus came to Greyson's side. "My memories were erased by a mage. A necromancer, Greyson thinks."

Charles' brow furrowed as he stepped closer. Greyson yanked Cyrus behind him, hiding him. Charles leaned to the side, staring at him, and asked, "You don't remember anything?"

"No," Cyrus replied.

"I don't know any necromancers, but I can ask around."

"You'll let us stay?" Greyson asked, surprise obvious in his tone.

"Of course," Charles said as he picked up his granddaughter.

Cyrus moved to Greyson's side with a smile. The little girl caught sight of him and shyly tucked her head into her grandfather's shoulder.

"She gets nervous around new people," Julia commented.

"I can sympathize," Greyson said.

The door opened and another woman with a long brown braid and a round face came inside, trailed by a boy of seven or so. She froze in the doorway, drawing the boy against her side. Cyrus took a deep breath in preparation for whatever she would say.

"What's going on? Is that who I think it is?"

Julia nodded.

"Does everyone know me?" he asked Greyson.

"Yes."

"Victoria, dear, why don't you and I take the kids to the kitchen for a bite?" Julia said, plucking the little girl from Charles before herding her family out of the room.

Charles said, "It's a bit shocking to have you here. I'm going to check on them."

When the door closed, leaving them alone, Cyrus swiveled toward Greyson, who avoided his gaze. "So everyone does know me."

"I said yes."

"I don't suppose you'll tell me the truth?"

"The truth is you're very famous," Greyson replied, walking after them.

When the door closed, Cyrus scoffed. "Right."

20

CYRUS

After dinner, Cyrus followed Greyson out to the private deck behind the headman's house. The air was crisp, and a low roar from the crashing waves resounded in his ears. Greyson stood next to a large brazier; flames twisted and twined within the iron, gleaming in the darkness. His expression appeared drawn as the shadows made his hollow cheeks appear gaunt. Greyson hadn't said a word during dinner, which was awkward enough, but he wouldn't even look at Cyrus.

Straightening his spine, he strode toward Greyson. When Cyrus reached his side, Greyson shifted a few steps to the side. Frustration welled within him, making his hands curl into fists. He truly didn't understand. Sometimes it seemed like Greyson wanted to be with him, and others, it felt like he couldn't get far enough away.

"Greyson," he started, determined to get at least one answer.

"You should go inside, it's cold."

"Greyson."

"Maybe we both should go inside," Greyson said, moving toward the door.

He stalked after Greyson. Before he could go inside, Cyrus pushed him against the side of the house. Greyson tried to slide left, but he raised an arm barring his escape. He lifted his other hand, planted it firmly on the wall, and trapped Greyson.

"Stop running."

GREYSON

Greyson's pulse boomed in his ears as he stared at Cyrus, whose jaw was clenched while his eyebrows pulled together to form a slash across his forehead. He recognized the expression, as Cyrus often wore it when he was mad.

"I'm not," he lied.

Cyrus banged the wall with a fist. "You are. You never answer any important questions, and anytime we get close, you flee. I cannot take it anymore."

"What do you mean?" Greyson asked, numbness spreading down his limbs. Was Cyrus going to leave? He didn't want that. Cyrus had invaded every aspect of his solitude, and Greyson did not know how he could go back to before.

"I need to know. Do you like me? Do you not like me? Do you want to be together? Do you want me to leave you alone? You're switching from hot to cold so quickly I can't keep up. I know there are things you're not telling me. I just need you to be honest about one thing. I know nothing here. I just need one true thing to hold onto. Just one."

Greyson stared at Cyrus—a man he used to hate. Glassy eyed, Cyrus stared at him while his muscular arms tensed. Greyson couldn't imagine not remembering anything. How confused Cyrus must be, and he had not helped. Of course, in the beginning, Greyson hadn't thought it would matter. Now, the lies had piled up, burying him. It was not only the lies, though. Their history of animosity was like a wall between them. How could he ever cross it?

"Greyson," Cyrus whispered. His lyrical voice slid over Greyson's ears and made him shiver. "Please, tell me the truth."

One brick at a time, Greyson thought. He realized he wanted to climb that wall, or rather, tear it apart because he wanted Cyrus. No matter what had happened between them, he wanted Cyrus.

"The truth is," Greyson said, cupping his cheeks, "I love you."

Cyrus' mouth opened and closed like he searched for the words to say. Greyson did not bother to let him respond and captured his lips. Cyrus shoved him into the wall and gripped the front of his shirt, lips moving frantically. Greyson clutched Cyrus' face, matching his urgent pace. It felt like time had stopped as the sound of the ocean and the fire disappeared. All Greyson could pay attention to was the softness of Cyrus' lips and the thundering of his heart.

Sliding his fingers into Cyrus' golden-blonde hair, Greyson moaned. Cyrus' tongue flicked out and grazed his. Deepening the kiss, Greyson hooked an arm about Cyrus' waist and yanked him as close as possible; their hips pressed together, igniting even more sensations.

He could have never guessed that this is where life would take him, but Greyson was perfectly fine with this outcome.

Cyrus wrapped both of his arms around Greyson's neck and leaned against him. The passion softened as he kissed Cyrus, slowly, fully, and gently. Greyson trailed away from Cyrus' lips as he brushed kisses along Cyrus' jaw and cheekbones, then over his eyes. Greyson wanted to kiss every inch of him. At that thought, heat raced to a certain part of his body and made him jerk back, his head hitting the wall with a thunk.

"Don't go," Cyrus whispered, voice husky.

"I'm not going anywhere. I just need air."

Chuckling breathlessly, Cyrus nuzzled his face against Greyson's neck. "You love me."

"Yes." Greyson clasped his hands behind Cyrus' back. "I love you."

"I don't know why that surprises me so much, but it does."

"Well, I should hope so. It shocked me."

Cyrus said, "I love you too."

Something clenched in his chest as the backs of his eyes burned. Greyson placed a slow kiss on Cyrus' lips. "I could have never guessed I would ever hear those words out of your mouth."

"It's the truth." Cyrus' expression was so serious, it made him appear like his old self.

Brushing the tip of his nose along the edge of Cyrus' nose, Greyson replied, "I believe you."

CYRUS

"Go to sleep," Greyson said as he cradled Cyrus against his chest.

"One more question," he pleaded. Cyrus couldn't stop staring at Greyson in the dim firelight. *He loves me*, Cyrus thought for the thousandth time.

"No," Greyson snapped. While his tone was harsh, his touch remained gentle on his back.

"Please," he begged quietly.

Greyson scowled, which made him grin. Leaning forward, Cyrus pressed a kiss between his scrunched eyebrows. Greyson groaned. "Tomorrow. Go to sleep for now."

"Fine," Cyrus said. After a long pause, he whispered, "I love you."

"I love you too."

The fire crackled and sent out waves of warmth. Occasionally, smoke would waft out of the fireplace and sting his eyes as the wind howled outside. But he just burrowed closer to Greyson. Safe.

Eventually, Greyson's breath evened into slumber. Cyrus brushed his fingertips over Greyson's eyelashes, which fluttered.

"You're lying to me, aren't you?"

Greyson grunted in his sleep, shifting. Cyrus rubbed his back.

Cyrus asked quietly, "We were never friends, were we?"

Greyson, of course, did not answer. Cyrus stroked Greyson's hair, then snuggled against him. "It's okay," he whispered. "I don't want to be your friend anyway."

GREYSON

A low cry pierced the air. Greyson's eyes shot open. The room was dark, barely lit up by the coals in the fireplace. His brow furrowed as he glanced around, having a hard time seeing. His hand stretched out and connected with an empty bedroll. Cyrus must have rolled away from him. Squinting, he peered around the room, trying to discern what the shadowed blobs were. Some distance in front of him was a long shape—Cyrus, he assumed.

Another whimper sounded. Frowning, Greyson scooted closer. Cyrus' face was pinched and sweat dotted his forehead. Cyrus moaned, tears slipping down his cheeks.

"Cyrus, you're alright."

Cyrus cried again. Greyson rolled him over and brushed his cheek. His sky-blue eyes popped open, then his face scrunched in obvious confusion.

"You're okay," Greyson said.

"I was dreaming."

"About what?"

"About you. I was arguing with someone about you. I remember crying," Cyrus said.

He stroked Cyrus' cheek, wiping the tears. "It's okay."

"You were in danger."

"I'm fine." Greyson shifted onto the bedrolls and folded Cyrus into his arms. Settling Cyrus against his chest, Greyson held him close. "It's all fine. Go to sleep."

Arms tightened around his back as Cyrus pressed his face into his chest. Greyson rubbed his back, trying to soothe him. "I won't let anyone hurt you," Cyrus said, squeezing him.

Greyson swallowed as sudden emotion clogged his throat. Cyrus held him even tighter, almost hurting him. Greyson hugged him back, wiggling. "I'm okay, Cyrus."

Cyrus would not loosen his hold no matter how much Greyson patted his back. He winced. "Cyrus, you're hurting me."

Slowly, Cyrus relaxed his grip. "Sorry."

"It's okay," he said, rubbing his face against Cyrus' blonde hair. "Go to sleep. I'm right here."

"I'll keep you safe."

"I know."

Greyson scowled as he tugged the cloak tighter around Cyrus. "Why do you even want to go?"

Cyrus shrugged. "It seems like fun."

Last night, he confessed his feelings. He had a hard time believing it, but the evidence was in his hands. They had not slept much afterward because Cyrus had a nightmare. Cyrus had clung to him, but Greyson had been unable to soothe him into more than a light doze. Now, Cyrus wanted to go traipsing around, not rested, and without him. Greyson gripped the fur-lined cloak, pulling Cyrus closer, unwilling to let him go.

"Are you sure?" Greyson asked.

"It's only fishing."

"On the freezing ocean, and you don't handle the cold," he snapped. Cyrus raised his eyebrows. Greyson frowned. "You won't fall in the water?"

"I'm not a kid."

He pinched the bridge of his nose. Everything in him wanted to keep Cyrus close, which was ridiculous because he could take care of himself. "It's not like I can stop you."

"You're the one who doesn't want me to go with you as you talk to people and gather supplies."

That morning, Greyson had decided not to travel back through the villages. He did not want to repeat what happened with the woman who called Cyrus a murderer. The other way home was shorter and crossed over much rougher terrain, but it was better than risking someone upsetting Cyrus.

Also, he had to chat with people about the possibility of a necromancer. Greyson thought it would be easier to get people to talk if Cyrus was not with him. Not to mention, he didn't want someone to utter something they shouldn't. He was not quite ready for the truth to come out and what it would do to his and Cyrus' relationship.

"Well, be careful."

Cyrus drew him down for a simple kiss, but Greyson dragged him flush against his chest. They had an audience, yet he didn't care in the slightest. He nibbled Cyrus' bottom lip before backing up and caressing his blushing cheek.

"I'll be waiting for you."

"He's not going off to war," Charles called loudly. "He's fishing. He'll be back in a few hours." Charles tossed his grandson, who gawked at them, over his shoulder and stepped onto a boat.

Julia smirked. "I'll keep your boyfriend safe."

"You were always my favorite student for a reason."

"You know," Charles said from the boat, "I like you a lot better now."

Greyson remarked, "All it took was for your daughter to be married to someone else."

"Yep."

Tugging on Cyrus' cloak, Greyson said, "I'll see you later."

"See you in a few hours." Cyrus waved as he hopped onto the boat. Greyson watched him until they disappeared.

Victoria moved to his side, holding Ruth's hand. "They'll be back."

"I know, but I don't have to like it."

Less than a day together and he didn't want to let Cyrus out of his sight. Not a good sign. He needed to get a hold of himself. With a shake of his head, he shifted toward the woman. Ruth pressed against her mother's side, hiding. He tilted his head to the side as he shifted closer to the child.

Crouching, he held out his hand. "Let me see you."

Ruth pressed into her mother's side, chewing on her finger. Greyson gently tugged her closer so he could see her face. Something about her spoke to him, making his magic tingle under his skin. He lifted his staff and twisted his wrist to the left, the blue stone glowing with the movement. The little girl pulled her finger from her mouth and reached toward his staff. A simple testing spell coiled around Ruth, glowing brightly.

"You are very blessed."

"She has magic?" Victoria asked, eyebrows raising.

"Yes. Ruth is very powerful."

Her face fell. "What are we going to do?"

Standing, he said, "Don't worry. I'll train her."

"How will we find an artifact?"

That was an issue. Artifacts were not easy to come by, and no one in the Griseo Mountains crafted them, not anymore. Before the Zaesian Empire conquered them a few hundred years ago, they made them. But after they were conquered, the empire would not allow them to create artifacts, so the knowledge had been lost.

Once bonded, a mage couldn't pick a new artifact. That was the reason his mother held off binding him to one. It wasn't until he reached the capital at nineteen that he received one—the staff. It came flying out of the royal treasury. Ancient artifacts had a mind of their own. His gaze shifted to the little girl with waves of power coming off her.

"I might have something," he said, rubbing his chin. "Next summer, bring her to see me. My mother's ring may choose her. If not, I'll figure something out."

"Do you think it will work?"

"I don't know," he said honestly. "My mother's ring is ancient. It chooses the mage, not the other way around."

"I'll talk to Julia, but I imagine she'll agree. My wife loved you and your mother teaching her," Victoria said, shaking her daughter's hand.

"She is my favorite student and my close friend," Greyson said. Looking at the little girl, he said, "I think I'll enjoy teaching you too, little Ruth."

"That's if Julia and I can convince her father to let us move to your village for a while."

"Have fun with that," Greyson remarked.

Training Ruth would take a few years, and Charles loved his only child immensely. Julia had come and visited every summer when she was younger, but Greyson doubted she would want to do the same and leave Ruth in his and Widow Abney's care for a couple of months each year.

Greyson had been teaching people since his mother died when he was fourteen, even before he was bound to an artifact. That was how desperate people were for a magic teacher. But being a teacher is what made him so beloved in the Griseo Mountains. That and how powerful he was.

"Yeah," Victoria grunted. "Come on, Ruth."

The little girl smiled, giving a wave before she left with her mother.

21

GREYSON

He walked around the village, wood creaking beneath his boots as the waves rolled under the stilts. Greyson greeted various people, a heavy bag slung over his shoulder. He'd already bought plenty of dried meat and hard cheese for the journey home.

Greyson headed down a thin bridge, which rocked with every movement, toward a house on the outskirts of the elevated village. Mildred Mowsley lived there with her family. While he didn't know her well, he knew enough. She was a prolific gossip and hoarder of knowledge. If anyone had heard of a hidden necromancer, it would be her.

The house loomed above him, near the size of Charles' home, with a prominent main ridge and smoke curling out of the stone chimney. He knocked on the wood door carved with pine trees. Feet scurried on the other side, followed by low voices. He tightened his grip on his staff as he waited.

Eventually, the door cracked open and revealed a woman in her early twenties. Greyson's brow furrowed as he tried to recall her name. She'd studied with him, but she'd been exceedingly quiet and scurried to and fro, head down and face obscured by her long hair.

Agatha, his mind supplied. She was Mildred's granddaughter. Decent magic user. Unbound, like most people in the Griseo Mountains.

"Agatha," he said with a nod.

"Mage Greyson, what are you doing here?" she asked, her hand tight on the door.

"I wanted to speak to your grandmother. Is there a problem?" Greyson frowned. Most people within the mountains were excited to see him, or at least more welcoming than she was.

"Of course not." Agatha waved him inside.

The house was long with three doors off the main room. A warm fire burned in the stone fireplace while an older woman sat in a rocking chair, which creaked with every movement. There were a few chairs and a couch covered in red fabric scattered around plus a bookshelf against the wall, giving the room a full and lived-in feel.

Over the wide mantle hung a painting of Ferrum Peak. It showed a crack in the side of the mountain, jagged and rough, that was surrounded by trees. Greyson had been to that cave. It led deep underground, and it was unstable and dangerous to explore.

Greyson moved toward the older woman. Long black hair with gray strands hung around her weathered face. She had heavy jowls and a pinched expression as she carefully stitched an intricate embroidery pattern.

"Mildred," Greyson said.

She grinned, revealing several missing teeth. "Greyson. What are you doing here? I haven't seen you in a few years. Are you and Charles finally over your spat? What happened? Did Julia abandon Victoria to be with you? Was it scandalous? I bet it was!"

"No, Julia did not leave her wife, but Charles and I are over our fight."

"Good. Good. What exactly happened? Spare no details."

"I came with my boyfriend."

"Ah." She nodded. "That probably helped. Though, grandchildren have calmed Charles." Mildred glanced at her granddaughter who poured them each a cup of tea. "I would know. No greater blessing."

"Hmm," he replied as he accepted a cup of tea from Agatha, who smiled shyly at him.

"So who are you courting?" Mildred asked, taking a sip of tea. "Everyone will want to know."

He doubted many people cared about his love life, but this revelation would certainly be shocking. He fought back a smile. "Cyrus."

She coughed, tea spattering her blue dress, and Agatha dropped the teacup. It shattered on the wood floor, shards of porcelain and tea covering the ground. "Excuse me?" Mildred asked, patting her chest. "I must have heard wrong. You don't mean Prince Cyrus, right?"

Giving into the growing urge, Greyson snickered. "Yes, I mean Prince Cyrus. We're together now."

Her mouth opened and closed a few times as she blinked rapidly. "Well, that is a development. One even I didn't see coming."

"Indeed. His memory was scrubbed."

"Your doing?" she asked before taking a long drink of tea. Agatha quickly cleaned up the shards of porcelain and puddle of tea, then whisked the mess out of the room and returned with another cup.

"No. Necromancer. I assume at least."

Mildred's thick eyebrows raised. "Do you know who?" she asked, leaning closer, the chair creaking beneath her. "I haven't heard nary a whisper of a necromancer existing. It's rare. That last known one was Charles' grandmother and my aunt, and she died a long time ago."

Greyson leaned back. "I was hoping you would know."

"What makes you think it was a necromancer?" Agatha asked, her voice quiet and soft.

"Cyrus was in the glade when he lost his memories."

Nodding, Mildred said, "Bones soaked in blood and magic."

"Yes." Those bones would be strong and powerful for any necromancer.

"I haven't heard anything, but I guarantee I'll start asking around. A necromancer. The first in years." Mildred shook her head, jowls shaking. "I'd almost thought that magical line had died out, but now...there's hope."

Necromancy was the rarest type of magic, and it had been dwindling to the point of extinction. Many mages, like Elizabeth, did not see that as a bad thing. But Greyson viewed the death of any magic as a tragic loss. It was all beautiful. Not voicing his opinion, he asked, "Has anyone been missing from here for any length of time?"

"People travel," she said with a shrug. "But, no. No one has left that I've noticed."

"Will you ask around for me about a necromancer?"

"Of course, Greyson. Do you think that person can restore Cyrus' memories?"

"No, but maybe they know why Cyrus came in the first place."

Her brow furrowed as she asked, voice full of censure, "But you're courting him without his memories?"

"Yes." Greyson paused, then merely said, "It's complicated."

"I imagine so," Mildred said before taking a long drink of tea. "Scandalous as well."

Agatha chuckled but didn't say anything.

CYRUS

Cyrus ambled off the boat, shivering. He hadn't fallen in, but the spray from the ocean had soaked him. Being on a boat, though, had felt natural. The ebb and flow. The wind rushing past him. He had to have sailed before.

He scoured the pier, searching for Greyson, who was nowhere within sight. Disappointment shot through him. He liked kissing Greyson and hoped for another upon his return.

He loves me, he thought, beaming.

Julia hooked an arm through his. "Let's get you inside before you freeze and Greyson kills me."

"H-he w-w-on't b-be mad," Cyrus stuttered.

"Yeah," she said with obvious sarcasm. "I'm sure when you lose a toe, he'll just laugh it off as he transforms me into a frog."

He tried to laugh, but his teeth were chattering too much. Swallowing, he asked, "C-can he do-do that?"

"Greyson can do whatever he wants."

Cyrus glanced at her, but Julia merely led him toward her home. When they approached the house, the door opened. Greyson took one look at Cyrus before he scowled deeply.

"What the hell happened?"

"He got wet from the sea spray," Julia replied.

Cyrus tried to smile reassuringly, but it came out more like a grimace and made Greyson's scowl deepen. Greyson yanked him away from Julia, glaring at her, then draped an arm over Cyrus' shoulders and ushered him into the house.

Heat washed over Cyrus. It hurt his chilled skin while, at the same time, it made him moan in relief.

Immediately, Greyson started to yank his clothes off.

"Greyson," Cyrus protested.

"You need to get out of your wet clothes," Greyson snarled.

Charles came inside, pausing in his step. "Would've never guessed the two of you would get together." He guffawed as he directed his daughter and grandson upstairs to give them some privacy.

Shivers wracked his body as Greyson helped him undress, then made him sit in front of the warm flames before placing a blanket over his shoulders.

"You shouldn't have gone," Greyson said, scrubbing Cyrus' wet hair with a towel.

"I liked sailing."

"Of course you do. You grew up on the coast."

"I've been sailing?"

Kneeling in front of him, Greyson dropped the towel as his gaze met Cyrus'. "Yes."

"Have we been sailing together?"

"No."

Cyrus hooked his arms around Greyson's waist. "We should go some time."

"Hmm," Greyson said as he began drying Cyrus' hair again.

A week later, he and Greyson stood outside the headman's house. "Thank you for hosting us," Greyson said.

"Of course. I didn't find any likely candidates for erasing Cyrus' memories, but I will keep asking around," Charles said.

"Thank you," Cyrus said, but his brow furrowed. He hadn't seen Charles speak to anyone about it, though that didn't mean he hadn't. Of course, Greyson made him stay in the house most of the day while he and the others asked around, leaving him with Julia, who was nice enough.

"I like you more than I thought I would," the headman remarked.

"I'm not sure how to respond to that," he said.

Greyson squeezed his arm. "Ignore him. It was nice to see you, Charles."

"Sure."

"Julia," Greyson said. "Always a pleasure."

"It was nice to see you, and, Cyrus, it was nice to meet you," Julia said.

"It was nice to meet you as well," he replied.

"We need to go," Greyson said. "We're wasting daylight."

They waved goodbye, then, hand-in-hand, they strolled along the beach. The waves slapped against the rocky shore. Snow dotted the ground, and his breath came out in long, foggy gasps. As he held Greyson's right hand, Cyrus peeked at him. Since they'd raced out of that small mountain village, Greyson had been holding his hand more often.

Biting his lip, Cyrus peered at him. "I thought you wanted me to stay on your left side."

Stopping, Greyson faced him. "I don't mind now."

"Why?"

Greyson shrugged.

"Because you love me?"

Rolling his eyes, Greyson started walking again.

As they continued, Cyrus studied the gray-blue water. "I think this is my favorite color."

"Really?" Greyson asked, stopping again.

"Yes," he said. Cyrus was almost positive that this was his favorite color. Greyson gave him a slight smile, then tugged on him.

When the sun started to set, Greyson made camp, and Cyrus huddled near the flames, shivering under his blanket.

With a furrowed brow, Greyson caressed Cyrus' face, but he didn't say anything.

"I'm fine." Cyrus yanked Greyson onto his lap and wrapped his arms around Greyson's waist, holding him tight. Inhaling the sweet yet sharp scent of pine, he rubbed his face against Greyson's back. "Now, I'm much better."

Greyson shook his head.

Cyrus tightened his hold. Greyson fit perfectly in his embrace. Solid and intoxicating. He nuzzled his neck. Cyrus knew, at this moment, that he wouldn't ever let Greyson go.

"I need to make dinner," Greyson said, but he didn't move out of Cyrus' arms and, instead, he leaned back.

He enfolded the blanket around Greyson, then tightened his hold. "You should stay right here."

"You're impossible."

It took close to three weeks for Drakcombe to come into view. Never had a sight looked so appealing. Lights gleamed from the windows as smoke curled from the chimneys. The sun had already set, and the air held a crisp tinge as thick clouds covered the sky.

They walked up the thin trail toward home. When they reached it, Greyson placed him before the empty fireplace. Greyson got a fire going as he kept peeking at Cyrus, whose teeth chattered loudly.

"Are you alright?" Greyson asked, brow furrowed.

He nodded, shakily, but didn't respond. Greyson cupped his face and brushed a thumb along Cyrus' cheekbone. "Stay here. I'm gonna get more wood."

The last three weeks of trekking over the rough goat trails had been hard, but at the same time, it had been amazing. Greyson had held his hand, snuggled against him at night, and answered questions. It had been perfect, except for one glaring reason.

Every time they got close, Greyson would pull away, though he wouldn't go far. Greyson would continue kissing him but wouldn't go any further. Cyrus knew he was interested, but Greyson wouldn't do more.

The door opened, and Greyson came in, carrying an armload of wood. He chucked a piece onto the hot flames. "Let me make you some food."

Snatching his hand, Cyrus yanked Greyson beside him. "I'm fine."

"Then I would like to make tea."

"Stay with me," Cyrus whispered in his ear.

Greyson shifted toward him, frowning. "I have not left your side once. Tea would be nice."

"Fine," he grumbled, "make your tea."

Chuckling, Greyson moved to his knees and softly kissed him. Cyrus drew him close. He cupped Greyson's cheeks as he nibbled on his lips. Greyson pressed against him, hands moving around his back. Cyrus shrugged off his cloak before undoing Greyson's, then clutched the front of his shirt, keeping him close. Greyson groaned, tongue pushing into Cyrus' mouth as he fell on top of him.

Cyrus slipped Greyson's shirt off, fingers exploring his chest. Greyson moaned. Needing to feel his skin against Greyson's, he pulled his own shirt off. Greyson shifted back, panting. Cyrus drew him down. Greyson hesitated before he lowered onto Cyrus and took possession of his mouth. Cyrus undulated beneath Greyson, his movements smooth and liquid. Every touch inflamed him.

He grabbed Greyson's pants, but Greyson seized his wrists, lifting them over his head and trapping them against the floor. Greyson continued to kiss him, his lips firm and relentless. Cyrus frowned slightly. He ground against his hips, and Greyson moaned. They were both hard.

Rocking against Greyson again, Cyrus tried to wrest his hands from Greyson's hold. When Greyson didn't release him, he shifted back, chest heaving.

"What's wrong?" Cyrus asked. Greyson moved back, and Cyrus sat up. "Greyson, what's going on?"

Greyson would not look at him.

Cyrus cupped his cheeks, lifting his face. "Talk to me. We *clearly* want each other, but you keep pulling back. What's going on?"

"I can't do this."

Pain flashed through him. "What?"

"I love you, Cyrus. I do. But..."

"But what?"

"I've been lying to you."

I know where this is going, he thought. Cyrus nodded. "I know."

"Excuse me?"

22

GREYSON

Greyson gaped at him. *He what?* How did Cyrus know? No one had said anything to him. When Cyrus did not say anything, he snapped, "What?"

"You're the one that lied to me and *you're* upset?"

"No. I mean—yes." He ran a hand through his hair. "What do you mean you know?"

"I may not remember anything, but I'm not stupid."

"I never said you were stupid."

"Greyson," Cyrus said, "I know you lied. I don't know exactly what you lied about, but I figured some things out. Like I'm pretty sure we were never friends."

His eyes flicked to the side as guilt washed through him.

"Yeah, that's what I figured. I mean you know very little about me, and anytime I ask, you look away. Just like now."

"What else have you figured out?"

"No one seems to like me, besides you, so I'm going to guess I didn't fight for the Griseo Mountains in the war, did I?"

"No," Greyson replied.

Cyrus scooted closer, their knees bumping. "Tell me now. Tell me everything."

Taking a deep breath, he tried to calm the panic that buzzed under his skin. Greyson met his gaze and began, "You and I are not friends. We're enemies. You hate me."

"What?" Cyrus asked, brow furrowing. "That's not possible."

"It's the truth. I also hated you."

Expression dropping, Cyrus jerked back.

Greyson did not let him go. He hauled Cyrus onto his lap. "I don't anymore. I swear."

Nodding, Cyrus stayed within his grasp. "Continue."

"It started eight years ago. That was the first time the Griseo Mountains sent a spokesperson to the capital to appeal to the emperor. I traveled with the group, mainly the spokesperson, Charlotte Williams. My parents were gone, and I'd taken my mother's position as a teacher of the magical arts, even though I hadn't bonded to an artifact. During that first meeting is where I met you. You were by the emperor's side."

"Why?"

"You're Emperor Caspian's nephew. He raised you."

Cyrus gaped at him, stock-still. Greyson simply waited for him to shift off his lap, but Cyrus didn't. Cyrus stared at him for quite some time before pressing his face against Greyson's shoulder and saying, "Continue."

"I hated you from the second I saw you. You stood behind the emperor's shoulder, not speaking a single word." Greyson could easily recall Cyrus' stony expression. Cyrus had stared at him throughout the meeting with his sky-blue eyes. Shaking it off, Greyson continued, "I got my artifact during that meeting. It belonged to the emperor, but my staff decided it wanted me. After that, anytime I was in the capital you would follow me everywhere.

"About four years later, the war started. You became the golden boy of the capital. The face of the emperor's forces. I became the face of the rebellion. We met each other in combat a few times."

Shifting back, Cyrus slowly traced the scar that ran through Greyson's eyebrow and down to his cheekbone, blinding him in one eye. "I didn't do this, did I?" Cyrus asked, eyes glassy.

He wished he could lie. It would be simple, but Cyrus wanted the truth. "You did," Greyson said. "You gave me the scar." When Cyrus started to move off his lap, Greyson locked his hands behind Cyrus' back, keeping him in place. "You could've killed me, Cyrus, but you didn't."

Unbidden, memories of that first battle surfaced. Greyson had been in the middle of the rebels—protected. He was their strongest mage. But Cyrus and his men had pushed through to find and no doubt kill him. When they met, Greyson started to retreat. He did better at a distance than in close combat. At the same moment he stepped back, Cyrus swung at him, the tip of his blade slicing through his eye.

Even now, years later, Greyson recalled screaming as blood dripped down his face. He'd been completely open for another attack, but Cyrus did nothing. The battle sounds had faded as Cyrus stood in front of him, eyes wide and mouth hanging open. The masses of fighting men and women separated them, and Greyson retreated for treatment. Magic had saved his eye but couldn't restore his vision.

Brushing Cyrus' cheek, Greyson repeated, "You didn't take your opportunity."

Cyrus leaned against him. "What happened next?"

"About four months of you and your soldiers chasing us through the mountains and small skirmishes before we surrendered unconditionally to the emperor."

"How long ago was that?"

"About two almost three years ago," Greyson answered.

"We didn't see each other after that?"

"No, we did. After we surrendered, the emperor demanded my head as recompense. I was the face of the rebellion by choice, and I knew if we lost that would be my fate."

Suddenly, Cyrus grabbed his hand, face scrunching. "What happened?"

"The emperor executed me. What do you think?"

Glaring, Cyrus asked, "Did you give yourself up?"

"Yes, I surrendered. I left my staff in the mountains because Emperor Caspian would've broken it in two regardless of its age. I was arrested and taken back to the capital for execution."

"Why did you give yourself up?"

"Because I didn't want the emperor to send soldiers to hunt for me and for him to hurt anyone."

"What happened?"

"I was kept in a cell and awaited public execution for about five months. But you saved me."

"I did?"

"Yes. You showed up in my cell, and I thought you were there to kill me, but you told me you were going to take me home. And you did. We traveled back to the Griseo Mountains together. When we reached the base of the mountains, you told me I'd been exiled and I couldn't leave and there was a bounty on my head if I did, which was fine with me. You also negotiated with the emperor, so we would receive more payment for the venetus we mined and reduced the quotas.

"I hated you for saving me," he admitted.

"Why?"

He laughed humorlessly. "It was a strike against my pride. You so easily fixed my people's problems and saved me with no apparent effort, and I never understood why. It irked me to have to be saved by you."

"We saved each other," Cyrus said, wrapping his legs around Greyson's waist.

It was true, he supposed. Though Cyrus saved Greyson in ways that he could never say. Greyson wasn't alone anymore.

Nuzzling his forehead, Greyson said, "We did." Cyrus' lips brushed his, and Greyson shook his head. "I'm not done."

"What else is there?"

Unease coiled in his gut as his throat closed. Greyson didn't want to tell him this, but Cyrus deserved the truth. "When I found you in the woods, I left you to die in the rain. Then I grew weak and brought you back. But then, I planned to kill you."

"What?"

"I was going to poison you, Cyrus. I mean, I gave up the plan almost immediately, but regardless, I was going to kill you."

"What stopped you?"

The uncomfortable feeling he had when he studied the berries rushed back to him. Greyson pressed his forehead against Cyrus. "I don't know. I just couldn't stomach the thought of going through with it."

"I believe you."

Scoffing, he said, "I left you to die, then thought about hurting you."

"I know, but you didn't, and that's enough for me."

Leaning forward, Cyrus' lips caressed his. Greyson yanked him closer, grasping his back. Part of Greyson felt surprised that Cyrus even wanted to kiss him after everything he revealed, but Greyson was glad he did. Fisting a hand in Cyrus' soft, blonde hair, he groaned. Greyson could not believe that he'd fallen in love with him. It seemed impossible. But now, he couldn't imagine his life without Cyrus.

Cyrus pushed him, shoving, until they fell back. Cyrus flopped on top of him as his hands roamed Greyson's chest and his hips ground against him. "Cyrus," Greyson protested, turning his head away from Cyrus' insistent lips.

"No," Cyrus gasped. "Don't leave now."

"I just told you I lied and plotted to kill you."

"I don't care," Cyrus said, kissing him again. "I forgive you."

He wanted to laugh, but Cyrus' mouth was on his. Losing himself to the sensations running through his body, Greyson forgot what he intended to say. After a moment, he rolled on top of Cyrus, who burrowed against him. Greyson's fingers skimmed along Cyrus' muscles. His every touch made Cyrus moan and grip his sides tightly.

It was not enough. Greyson needed more.

Heat burned him, and sweat dotted his brow. Cyrus let go of his waist and started undoing the ties of Greyson's pants. That jolted him out of the pleasant sensations. Greyson grabbed Cyrus' wrists and held them above his head.

Panting, Greyson said, "No."

"Why?" Cyrus asked, voice uneven. "You want this as much as I do."

"I do," Greyson agreed. He had never wanted anyone as much as he wanted Cyrus. Need consumed him and actively destroyed all rational thought, making him want to stop talking, but he couldn't. "Cyrus, if you had your memories, you wouldn't want this."

"You don't know that."

Greyson let go of his hands while remaining on top of Cyrus. His fingers trailed over Cyrus' perfect face. "You're right. I don't, but I'm pretty sure."

"I want this right now. I may never get my memories back, Greyson. Am I supposed to never be with you? Because that sounds horrible."

"I get that and I agree, but it's difficult for me. *This* is difficult for me."

Cyrus held his face and whispered, "What do you need from me? What words will soothe your anxiety?"

"I don't want to take advantage of you."

Laughing, Cyrus arched his hips into him so Greyson could feel his desire. "You are not taking advantage of me. I want you."

He placed a firm kiss on Cyrus' lips. How Greyson wanted to lose himself in the moment, but he had reservations that could not be talked away. "I can't," he said, breaking away.

"What is the problem?"

"You could be married, Cyrus. A spouse and kids could be waiting for you." Greyson honestly had no idea if Cyrus was married as he'd never cared one way or another before now. Cyrus was in his early twenties. It wouldn't be too crazy for him to have already married.

"Oh." Cyrus' head fell back against the floor. "That's possible. Though I'm gonna tell you right now if I am married, it's not to a woman. I'm gay. Just a thought."

"That doesn't change the fact that you might be married," Greyson snapped, sitting up. "I can't sleep with you until I know that you're actually mine."

"We've already slept together," Cyrus remarked with a smirk.

"Seriously?" When Cyrus did not respond, Greyson said in a clipped tone, "Fine. I can't have sex with you until I know you're not married."

"Okay," Cyrus said. "But just so you know, I'm already yours. Whether I'm married or not, I'm yours, Greyson."

At those words, Greyson groaned and yanked Cyrus closer, kissing him hard. "You have to not say things like that."

"It's the truth," Cyrus said against his lips.

It took everything he had to pull back from Cyrus when all Greyson wanted to do was continue until they both got lost in each other. "I can't believe you want to be with me after everything. I tried to kill you."

Cyrus trailed a finger over his bottom lip. "I love you, Greyson."

"Still," he persisted. If the situation had been reversed, Greyson wouldn't have been as forgiving.

He shrugged. "I know you don't want to hurt me anymore, and you didn't go through with it. You and me, Greyson. We belong together."

They did, but Greyson couldn't believe that Cyrus was so forgiving. Despite that, he let it go. He had to trust Cyrus. "First," he said, "we wait for the letter to arrive from my friend in the capital. He may have some notion as to why you traveled so far. Second, we will figure out if you're married."

"How?"

"By taking you to the representative in Woodhurst. Lord Darius would know, though he'll want to send you back to the capital for treatment."

Cyrus immediately said, "You can't go to the capital."

"No."

"I would have to go without you."

"Yes," Greyson said, swallowing the lump that formed in his throat.

"I won't go, not without you."

"In the end, we might not have a choice. The emperor is going to send soldiers to search for you. I wasn't going to keep you here forever because it could endanger the people of the Griseo Mountains."

Their time would come to an end soon, whether they willed it or not. It was simply the reality before them. Greyson may not want Cyrus and him to separate, but in the end, they probably wouldn't have a choice.

Cyrus' arms wrapped about his neck. Greyson shifted to his knees and returned the hug. Cyrus tightened his hold until it was almost painful. "I will not go without you."

"Cyrus," he said. "You may or may not be mine, but I am most definitely yours, wholly and completely. If you have to go back to the capital for a few months or even years, I will be here, waiting for you."

Cyrus did not respond; he simply held Greyson even tighter.

CYRUS

He snuggled in bed next to Greyson, who slept on his right side, like always, with his arms around him. Greyson's breath came out slow and even, deep asleep. Sleep wouldn't find Cyrus. He nuzzled Greyson, pressing as close as possible.

Nonetheless, sleep would not come. He shifted on the bed, trying to get comfortable. His gaze moved to Greyson's face, tracing it, as tension tightened his muscles. Everything. Cyrus knew everything now. It hadn't been shocking to learn they weren't friends. He'd already suspected. Also, fighting for the Zaesian Empire wasn't surprising. Other people's reactions suddenly made complete and total sense.

Though, he hadn't even suspected his relation to Emperor Caspian. Cyrus was his nephew. Prince of the realm. How was he supposed to accept that? Not that it mattered much right now, but it felt like a weight settled on his shoulders. There were responsibilities with the position, even if he didn't remember them.

Greyson moaned in his sleep, shifting against Cyrus and drawing his attention. Greyson had hated him. Cyrus bit his lip as his chest tightened. When Greyson confessed, he was fine with it. Now, the image of Greyson holding the poison berries replayed in his mind over and over. It wouldn't vanish. He'd left Cyrus to die, then later tried to kill him. How was he supposed to get over that? Yes, Greyson wouldn't do it again, and they had a history of animosity that fueled his actions, but still, he'd plotted to kill him.

Arms tightened, drawing Cyrus tight against a solid chest. A woodsy, pine scent tickled his nose and soothed him. He clutched Greyson's back as he pressed his face into his shirt. Cyrus didn't want to be angry, and he wasn't. He didn't think so, at least. He was...Cyrus didn't honestly know. His emotions were a jumble. Greyson had lied, plotted, and concealed things from him. Nonetheless, Cyrus loved him and wanted to be with him.

Cyrus traced Greyson's face. Nodding, he took a deep breath. He would have to let it go. As hard as it was, he would have move on. They had enough problems, and from what little Greyson said, there were enough things in their past to separate them without dwelling on this. Cyrus could put it behind him because no matter what he didn't want to live without Greyson.

Now for the other pressing problem—sex. Cyrus wanted Greyson, badly. It was like an ache that wouldn't ease. While honorable, Greyson wanting to hold off because of his lack of memories and the possibility of Cyrus being married was irritating. He wanted Greyson right now, and that should be enough. Also, Cyrus truly didn't think he was married. He was Greyson's. It was as simple as that to him.

The chances of his memories returning were slight, even though he had a few vague ones, so they had no way of knowing whether he was married or not without going to the representative. His heart hammered at the thought. He didn't want to travel to the capital, at least, not without Greyson. As much as Greyson said he would wait, Cyrus didn't want to separate from him. They belonged together.

Everything that happened in the past would have to stay there. Cyrus wanted nothing to do with it. All he needed and wanted was Greyson.

23

GREYSON

Greyson skimmed the letter, gaze roving over the ridiculously neat script. Frederick had come through as expected.

Greyson,

I urge caution. About six months ago, I heard whispers from the royal family, mainly Empress Quinn and Crown Princess Jade, urging Cyrus to finish what he started. That if he could not get over it, it was better to push forward. The prince did not say anything, at least to my knowledge, but he has been seen moping around the capital.

Many say he misses the war and regrets not destroying us. I don't know if that is true or not. I hope not, for the Griseo Mountains could not withstand another attack.

Finally, about eight weeks before I received your letter, I overheard Emperor Caspian yelling at Cyrus. I did not hear the whole argument, though it sounded heated, but I do recall hearing the emperor shout, "He'll probably kill you, but if that's what you want to do, I'm not going to stop you."

I suspect Prince Cyrus has traveled to the Griseo Mountains to kill you. Everyone knows of your animosity. Please be careful, my friend. Cyrus is not an opponent to underestimate. If you could manage to not slay him, that would probably be best for our people, for the emperor loves him dearly.

I was going to send the above by itself, but today I overheard something else. The emperor is worried that he has not heard from Prince Cyrus. He was sending regular letters to his cousin and aunt, but they stopped. The emperor is planning on sending someone out to search for him.

Greyson, if you are holding Prince Cyrus captive, let him go or it could prove deadly for our people. If the prince has met his demise, make sure you or none of our people can be implicated. His body can always be disposed of to the wolves or in a sunken mine shaft. Take care of it and make sure to burn this letter.

Frederick.

Greyson shook his head in amusement, leaning against the kitchen counter. Of course, Frederick assumed he'd killed Cyrus. That had been the original plan.

So Cyrus had left the capital to do something important, most likely kill him. Could he long to finish what he'd started with the people of the Griseo Mountains? It was possible, but

Greyson did not think so. Cyrus had argued for their freedom. Why would Cyrus change his mind so easily?

Could Cyrus have left the capital to kill Greyson? That was a possibility. The old Cyrus bore no love for him. All it would take was a couple of falsified reports of Greyson causing trouble, and Cyrus might feel obligated to kill him.

"What are you reading?"

He started. Cyrus had come in so quietly that he hadn't noticed. Cyrus had left a while ago to help Widow Abney with something.

"What are you reading?" Cyrus asked again.

"A letter from my friend in the capital."

Cyrus immediately reached for it, and Greyson held the piece of paper high in the air. Cyrus kept trying to snatch it, pulling on Greyson's shoulder, but to no avail. He was five inches taller than Cyrus.

Finally, Cyrus stopped. "Your boyfriend wrote you back, didn't he?"

A laugh broke out of his lips as he brought the missive down. "No. Frederick, my married friend and student, wrote me back."

"So you're not cheating on me?" Cyrus asked, grinning.

He pursed his lips as he pretended to think about it. "Hmm. I don't think so."

Cyrus wrapped his arms around Greyson's neck, heedless of the letter. "Good."

Greyson pressed a gentle kiss on his lips, but he couldn't stop his arms from instinctively gathering Cyrus against his chest. Quickly, the movement changed from soft to passionate. Once his skin felt flushed and he kept tugging on Cyrus' clothes, frustrated, he shifted away, eliciting an annoyed mutter from Cyrus.

"Your friend didn't happen to mention how very single and unmarried I am, did he?"

"I think that would have been the first thing I said."

"Too bad." Cyrus sat in a chair and read the letter while his expression remained casual. Greyson watched Cyrus, content, as he sipped his cup of tea. When Cyrus reached the end of Frederick's letter, he paused. "Would you have disposed of my body to the wolves or in a mine shaft if you'd killed me?"

"No. Mage fire. I would have burnt you to ash, then dumped your ashes in the river."

"Efficient."

"I thought so."

Returning to the letter, apparently skimming it again, Cyrus asked, "What's this important thing I was going to do?"

"Maybe kill me?"

"No."

Pushing off the counter, he joined him at the table. "Do you remember?"

"No," Cyrus said as his face twisted in thought. "It's right on the edge of my memory. I know it was important, but I can't remember. I have a few random memories. You are much younger and staring at me in a fancy room." Cyrus rubbed his temples. "You're in a dingy room, asleep on a cot. It was dark and I'd been crying, fighting with someone. A man who looks similar to me. Two women, one much older than the other. Then the glade when I was injured and running to you because you were in danger."

He pried Cyrus' hands from his face. "Are you in pain?"

"When I try to remember, my head starts to hurt."

"It's okay. You don't have to remember right now."

"I don't think I came here to kill you, Greyson. I was coming to you for a reason, though. I wish I knew what it was. And I wish I knew what danger lurked around you."

"I'll be fine," he said, stroking his cheek.

"What are we going to do?"

Greyson knew what they had to do, he just didn't want to. "The emperor is worried about you and is going to send someone to search for you. We have to go to Lord Darius. We can't put the Griseo Mountains in danger because I don't want you to leave."

"I don't want to leave either." Cyrus leaned forward, pressing his forehead against Greyson.

"I know," he said, hand on Cyrus' thigh. "We'll prove to Lord Darius that you're alive and send a letter to the emperor, then we'll go from there."

"I'm not going to leave you, Greyson."

"I will always be here for you, Cyrus."

CYRUS

"Aren't those the berries you were going to kill me with?" he asked. The red berries, wrinkled and withered, hung on a branch with dried leaves. Their bright color contrasted against the clean snow that surrounded the cabin, almost looking like drops of blood.

"Yes," Greyson replied, his tone crisp. Cyrus opened his mouth, but Greyson scowled at him, silencing another question, then went back to work. He hauled a stone mortar and pestle from the shed right behind the cabin. It was not the same one Greyson kept in the house. He donned a pair of gloves, then picked the dried berries off the twig and placed them into the mortar. "Stay back. These are much more poisonous when dried."

Cyrus obliged but snorted at the caution. If Greyson was fine crouching right over the berries, Cyrus would be fine standing next to him. Greyson slowly ground the berries, using steady circular motions with the pestle. When they were nothing but a fine, red powder, he poured them into a glass bottle, then shoved a cork in the top.

Shivering in the cold air, Cyrus asked, "Are you almost done?"

"I didn't make you leave the house, you chose to," Greyson said, not even glancing at him. He started a small fire before placing wax in a copper spoon, then held it over the flames. Once it melted, Greyson poured it over the cork and top of the bottle, sealing it.

Kicking snow over the flames, Greyson returned the mortar and pestle to the shed along with the gloves. Cyrus reached for Greyson, but he skittered out of range. "Let me wash my hands thoroughly first. I don't want any chance of contamination."

Greyson repeatedly cleaned his hands, the bottle, and the pump with a bar of soap. By the time he finished, his fingers had turned cherry red. When Greyson approached, Cyrus hooked an arm about his waist and led him toward the house. As soon as they were inside, he led Greyson to the fire, then took his frozen hands. Cyrus held them, chafing them, before he tugged his shirt up and tucked Greyson's hands against his bare skin.

"What are you doing?" Greyson asked.

"Making sure your hands warm up."

A smile stretched over Greyson's lips as he looked down, but not fast enough because Cyrus caught a glimpse of pink staining his cheeks. He swore Greyson blushing was the cutest thing he'd ever seen.

"So," Cyrus asked, "are we poisoning someone?"

"No, unfortunately not. These berries are rare, very rare, and therefore expensive. I know where they grow. Not many people take the risk to dry and grind them, but I do, occasionally. I'm planning on bribing Lord Darius with them. Though he'll probably kill me with the powder, it could help us stay together, at least until the emperor writes back."

"Are you in danger?" he asked, breathless. The thought of Greyson dying caused him physical pain. Cyrus couldn't even contemplate it.

Greyson scooted closer. "No. I promise. I've done this before, many times, and I'm very careful."

"That's not what I meant. Are you in danger from Lord Darius?"

"I'll be fine," Greyson said.

Cyrus wanted to argue, but instead, he asked, "When are we leaving?" He didn't want to go to Woodhurst, but Greyson was right. They couldn't endanger people because they didn't want to separate.

"I'll need a couple of days to gather more supplies. I swear I haven't traveled this much in the winter in a long time."

He didn't possess many memories of Greyson nor did he have much time to reflect on, but Cyrus felt like he'd known Greyson forever. He couldn't imagine living apart from him, not now. "I love you."

Another smile crossed his lips. This time, though, Greyson did not hide his face. "I love you too. It'll all be okay."

"How do you know?"

"I don't," Greyson replied, leaning closer. "But against all odds, we found each other, so it has to work out."

"I suppose it does."

24

GREYSON

Greyson and Cyrus headed west over the rough terrain. It would take five days to reach Woodhurst, where Lord Darius lived. The trip would not be easy, though. There was a road, but it was a much longer, circuitous route that went through a couple of towns. He did not want Cyrus to experience anything similar to the woman calling him a murderer, so they avoided the path and journeyed through the woods.

Cyrus trailed along, shivering. The cold wasn't his friend. Now if they stayed in the house or spent very little time outside, he seemed to enjoy winter.

Of course, Greyson thought with a shake of his head, *Cyrus becomes handsy at every opportunity.*

Memories of when they were alone resurfaced. Cyrus's lips on his. The warmth of his skin. The way his fingers explored Greyson's chest. Greyson scoffed, which made Cyrus raise an eyebrow. He smiled but didn't say anything. Cyrus had respected the boundary of no sex, but he definitely tested it. Greyson had a feeling that as soon as the word 'unmarried' was out of Lord Darius' mouth, Cyrus would drag him to the first private space he found.

Fire raced in his veins and made his skin tingle at the thought. Part of him didn't mind at all. Another part of him worried. He'd never been with another man. Greyson loved Cyrus, but it concerned him a bit. Shrugging it off, he knew, in the end, it would be what it was, and Cyrus loved him so it would work out.

Shaking his head, Greyson wanted to laugh. Romance had never been important to his life. His parents and little sister had died when he was fourteen from a plague sweeping through the empire. After that, everything became about teaching and making potions and poultices to help his people.

There had been no time or inclination for romance. He'd courted a couple of women, nothing serious or long. Cyrus was the first man Greyson had been attracted to. Cyrus was also the first and only person he'd ever fallen in love with.

"What?" Cyrus asked, trembling.

"Nothing," he said. "I just like being with you."

"Me too," Cyrus said, moving closer.

Greyson faced forward, walking over the steep, snow-covered ground. He carefully wound through the pine trees, all the while focusing on Cyrus' hand in his.

CYRUS

Cyrus huddled next to the fire, frozen. Snow covered the ground, and the air was so cold, it burned his skin and made needles prickle his lungs with every breath. He desperately longed for the cabin Greyson called home. Cyrus wanted to stay with Greyson in their small home. He didn't care that he was a prince or about whatever waited for him back in the capital.

While he shivered next to the fire, Greyson cut branches from the trees, not even bothered by the frigid temperatures.

"I'm almost done," Greyson said, black hair hanging in front of his face.

"What are you doing?"

"Making something for you to sleep on. The cold ground doesn't bother me much, but this should offer you some insulation." He continued to work, layering heavily-needled branches on the ground, then covered them with one of the extra blankets they'd brought before holding out his hands. "Come here, love."

The endearment made Cyrus beam. Standing, he went to Greyson, who wrapped his arms around him. With a smile, Greyson kissed him, slowly and gently. Cyrus wanted to groan in frustration. Every touch made him want more. Every time he kissed Greyson, a panicked frenzy would grow in his chest and make him want to kiss him harder, faster, like it would be their last chance.

Much quicker than he would have liked, Greyson lifted his head. Cyrus held back a frustrated sigh. Some of it must have leaked out in his expression because Greyson stroked his cheeks.

"I'm sorry," Greyson said.

He seized the front of Greyson's shirt and shook him slightly. "You have nothing to apologize for. I understand your hesitation. It's very honorable."

Greyson's eyebrows raised. "I believe that is the first time anyone has called me honorable." Cyrus chuckled, and he continued, "You have to admit it's a possibility."

"Yes," he said. "I understand your worries, but I don't share them. I know I'm not married."

"How?" Greyson asked, brow furrowing.

Cyrus shrugged. He couldn't explain the certainty he felt deep within him. "I don't know. I just do."

Leaning down, Greyson pressed his forehead against his. "I hope you're right."

"I know I am."

The next four days passed in a haze. Cyrus had never been so cold in his life, and every day the temperature dropped. Even at night, wrapped in Greyson's embrace, did not banish the chill that had settled into his very bones. He promised himself most heartily to spend the future winters in the house and sparingly outside, not traipsing around the mountains.

The sun hung in the west as Greyson continued to lead him on an unseen path. Constant shivers wracked his body as his teeth chattered. Cyrus swore viciously and repeatedly in his mind. He would have spoken out loud if he could've managed it without biting his tongue off.

Greyson kept glancing over his shoulder at him, but each time, Cyrus would wave off the obvious concern. He didn't want to stop. All he desired was to reach Woodhurst so he could sit in front of a fire and thaw out.

Finally, after another hour or so, they came up a steep slope. In the distance, Cyrus spied a village—a proper settlement of a few dozen buildings, dirt roads, and people. Validus Peak, capped in snow, loomed over Woodhurst and pierced the sky. To the east, he saw Sarcio Peak, his first sighting of it. It was taller than Ferrum but it was quite a bit smaller than Validus.

"Thank the goddess," he muttered, which elicited a chuckle from Greyson. Unable to stop himself, Cyrus grinned. The last few days, actually since Greyson confessed everything, he'd been laughing more.

"Soon we'll be inside, and you can warm up," Greyson said as he directed Cyrus to the wide road.

"I would like that," he muttered. But even as the excitement for a warm fire grew in his stomach, worry began to gnaw at him. What would the representative say? Cyrus was pretty sure he wasn't married, but what if he was? What if Lord Darius separated them or hurt Greyson? His hands clenched as his back straightened. He would allow no one to hurt Greyson while he breathed.

"What's going on?" Greyson asked, shaking his hand. "You're hurting me."

Cyrus immediately loosened his grip. "I'm sorry."

"It's alright. What's bothering you?"

"You don't think you're in danger, do you?"

"From Lord Darius?" Greyson asked, stopping in the middle of the road.

"Yes."

"It's a distinct possibility, but I should be fine," Greyson said, eyes averted.

"You're lying to me," Cyrus responded, completely certain. When Greyson didn't reply, Cyrus demanded, "Tell me the truth. Are you in danger?"

Meeting his gaze, Greyson answered, "Yes, but I can't let the emperor punish or hurt my people. I was willing to die for them before, and I still am."

He yanked Greyson's face down. "I will not let anyone hurt you, ever." Then Cyrus tried to kiss him firmly, but his numb lips made it more clumsy than he intended, though Greyson didn't seem to mind. Greyson belonged to him, and he would not let him go. Not now. Not ever.

Pulling back, Greyson said against his lips, "Thank you."

Unfortunately, Greyson shifted back and continued toward Woodhurst. Cyrus would've much rather have stayed in the middle of the road, kissing, even if it meant he would freeze the entire time. But Greyson, as usual, remained focused on the task at hand. Together, they walked down the dirt path, which was full of ruts and covered in a light dusting of snow.

People stopped and gaped at them or him; Cyrus couldn't tell which it was. Greyson did not let the crowd stop him. He nodded at various people and called out greetings, which were returned, continuing to a two-story home with a steep gable roof in the middle of the village.

It had wide windows, empty flower boxes, and dark brown siding that contrasted against the white paint. There was a red brick wall around the side of the home that disappeared behind it. Peeking out behind the home was a long building with a fenced-in area with targets in the distance. *Barracks and lists*, he assumed.

When Greyson reached the large home, he rapped on the door, a frown already forming on his face. The dark red door with a black iron knocker loomed before them and made Cyrus swallow. Cyrus squeezed his hand, and Greyson gave him a slight smile.

It took a few minutes before a slight maid with golden-blonde hair, tan skin, and light blue eyes opened the door. Immediately, Cyrus knew she couldn't be from the Griseo Mountains. Pretty much everyone he'd seen looked like Greyson—grayish skin and dark hair.

When she saw him, a surprised squeak came out of her mouth. Throwing the door open, she bowed low. "Prince Cyrus."

If he possessed any doubts that Greyson had lied about his heritage, this alone would have assuaged them. Cyrus nodded, distinctly uncomfortable. "Is the representative available?"

"Of course, Lord Darius will see you," she said, bowing again.

"We need to speak with him immediately," Greyson said.

The maid's expression cooled. "Mage Greyson. You are not welcome here."

As Cyrus studied him, he could find no evidence that the maid's words hurt him. Returning his focus to the woman, he said, "Greyson is with me."

Her eyes darted to their joined hands, widening. "Of course, your highness." She, with yet another bow, allowed them to come in.

Warmth immediately washed over him. Cyrus shuddered. He couldn't wait to sit in front of a fire. He glanced around as the maid led them into a front-facing parlor. Paintings hung on every wall. Statues in the corners. Finely carved and well-polished furniture decorated every space, and thick rugs spread over the polished wood floor. In the short time he'd been in this house, Cyrus had seen more evidence of wealth than in the entire time he'd been with Greyson.

Once they entered the parlor, the maid bowed and closed the door. Greyson immediately shoved him into a chair closest to the ornate marble and gold fireplace, then crouched before Cyrus.

Cyrus tried not to laugh. Greyson may complain about being a nursemaid, but he did it well. "I didn't freeze to death." Swallowing, he fought against the worry coiled in his chest. "I'm nervous."

"For yourself or me?"

"Both."

"Don't be. We will both be fine."

He pointed to the staff on the ground next to Greyson. "You have your staff, and you *will* use it to defend yourself," Cyrus ordered.

A sigh escaped his lips as Greyson's eyes shifted to the fireplace.

Cyrus gripped the front of his shirt. "I'm serious, Greyson."

"I know."

"You'll protect yourself, then?"

"I will protect you and decide what to do about myself in the moment, should it arise."

When the door opened, Greyson started to move away, but Cyrus held fast. "That's not good enough."

With a quiet chuckle, Greyson picked up his staff, then sat beside Cyrus. Unwillingly, his gaze shifted to the intruder who sauntered in wearing fine deep blue clothes. Lord Darius was a man in his fifties with blonde hair, green eyes, and soft features. No doubt in his youth, the lord would have been considered attractive, but he had a weasely look about his face and slim body that made Cyrus immediately dislike him.

"Prince Cyrus," Lord Darius said, his voice high and nasal. "How unexpected. I received word from the emperor that you would be heading in this direction months ago. In fact, a couple of days ago, I received an urgent message that you were missing, but here you are with Mage Greyson."

Cyrus froze. He and Greyson hadn't discussed what to say. Greyson calmly said, "His journey took an unexpected detour."

"You don't say," Lord Darius remarked with obvious sarcasm as he gestured to Greyson.

"On his journey north to see me, Cyrus met with someone else and was injured," Greyson stated in a bland tone.

Lord Darius whipped in his direction. "Are you alright, your highness?"

"Yes," Cyrus said. "I was minimally injured. Greyson saved me."

His thin eyebrows shot up. "How unbelievable."

"It's true," he said, grabbing Greyson's hand. Lord Darius blinked at the movement, mouth opening.

"Unfortunately, Cyrus has lost his memory," Greyson said.

Scoffing, Lord Darius said, "*That* I believe." Then the lord turned to him and asked, "You remember nothing?"

"No. Well, very little. I had no idea who I was until Greyson informed me and brought me here."

"So," Lord Darius started. "I'm supposed to believe that you," he broke off pointing at Greyson, "saved Prince Cyrus' life, but *somehow* the prince has lost his memories?"

"Yes, because it is the truth," Greyson answered.

"I don't believe it," Lord Darius said, legs crossing.

"You don't have to," Cyrus said, his voice cold and hard, "because I do."

Lord Darius paused for all of one second at his tone, then continued, "No offense, your highness, but I could tell you that your esteemed aunt was a talking bird and you'd believe me. You're not exactly the image of reliability."

"I have no memories, but I'm not stupid," Cyrus growled, anger boiling in his stomach.

Lord Darius continued like he hadn't even spoken, "So this is what I'm going to do. I'm going to arrest Mage Greyson, and if he resists, I will punish random citizens. Then I will write to the emperor while sending you to the capital with an armed escort, and when he orders me to execute Mage Greyson, I will do so."

GREYSON

Cyrus immediately leaped to his feet, snarling, "You will do no such thing."

Greyson had known where this would lead, and *shockingly*, Lord Darius had acted predictably. He yanked Cyrus back into the delicate chair with flower and vine covers.

"Enough, Cyrus," he said, holding on to him. He studied Lord Darius for a few breaths. His overplucked eyebrow was arched as he stared at where Greyson held Cyrus' arm. Greyson pulled the bottle of poison out of his pocket, twirling it between his fingers. The glass gleamed in the firelight as the red powder slid around the cylindrical bottle.

"Is that what I think it is?"

"Yes," Greyson said, nodding. "Very rare and illegal." He twirled it faster. "I'm one of the few who makes it. You can have it if you allow Cyrus to write a letter and stay here until the emperor decides my fate."

Lord Darius' lips pursed. "What's to stop me from simply taking it?"

"Nothing besides the fact that the prince of the nation, the capital's golden boy, and beloved of the emperor will see you take it. Me? I have nothing to lose. You? You could be stripped of your title and land."

"He'll see me either way," Lord Darius remarked, hands folding on his legs.

"Yes, but Cyrus will say nothing if you agree to the terms." It was not much, but it was all he had. Greyson wanted to scoff. He was holding out hope that the emperor he hated had a heart and would allow them to stay together.

When the lord did not say anything, Greyson continued to twist the bottle full of deadly red powder between his fingers. "Think about it. There's enough to kill a hundred people or one person if you really want to make sure they're dead. You seem like the overkill type. Here? Not much you can do with it. But when you return to the capital with the venetus, think of the people you could kill that are in your way."

Lord Darius followed the bottle's every movement. Of course, he didn't want to be stuck in the middle of nowhere, surrounded by people who hated him. The assignment had to be a punishment. But if he was cleverer than he seemed, Lord Darius could get what he wanted. Most likely, Lord Darius would end up poisoning himself because he would not be careful enough, but it wasn't Greyson's problem.

"Deal, but you don't get to keep your staff."

Greyson fought back the sudden panic that stole his breath and made his stomach roil at the thought of his weapon and the only link to magic in the hands of a man who would simply break it in half. He looked at Cyrus, who watched him with wide eyes. Cyrus was worth it. He started to toss the bottle to Lord Darius when Cyrus clamped onto his arm.

"You can take the staff," Cyrus said coldly, "but you can't break it. If you do, I will tell my uncle. It is a prized royal artifact."

Lord Darius frowned. "Fine."

Cyrus let go of his arm, and Greyson tossed the vial to Lord Darius, then handed his staff over. As Lord Darius' fingers closed around it, his heart clenched. It physically hurt Greyson to see him holding it.

"I don't suppose you know if I'm married or not?" Cyrus asked, which made Greyson roll his eyes.

Lord Darius' focus shifted from the two prizes clutched in his skeletal-like hands. "What?"

"Am I married?"

"No," he said, eyebrows squished together. "At least not as far as I know. News takes a while to travel this far, but I probably would have heard about you marrying."

Cyrus said triumphantly, "I told you so!"

Before Greyson could respond, a loud racket filled the air.

25

GREYSON

Greyson peered out the window. From this angle, he couldn't see much besides people gathering in the village square. A few he recognized, as they were his students.

"What's going on?" Cyrus asked, coming to his side.

"I don't know."

"We best go see," Cyrus said. When Lord Darius did not move from the settee, Cyrus frowned. "You're coming with us."

Lord Darius, rather unwillingly, led the way out of the house and into the street. In the middle of the road were five people, two men and three women. They all wore plain clothes with thick cloaks. Two, Greyson recognized—bounty hunters.

On two separate occasions, he had met them when they tried to abduct him and claim the reward from the emperor. This same scheme had been enacted by many people over the three years he'd been exiled. His bounty was exorbitantly large.

"What do you want?" Lord Darius asked, squinting. "I won't stand for any trouble."

"We want no trouble," the woman he'd recognized said as she ran a tan hand through her short, pale hair. Her solid form was loose and ready as her green eyes remained on Greyson and Cyrus. "We simply want Mage Greyson."

"Oh," he said. Nodding, Lord Darius shoved him forward, causing Greyson to stumble. "You can have him."

He glared at him over his shoulder. Of course, Darius would give him up. Cyrus moved closer to his side, a hand on the hilt of his blade. "You cannot have Greyson. Be gone," Cyrus ordered, sounding more like his old self than ever before.

Scoffing, the woman, maybe the leader of this little troop, said, "You survived our earlier encounter."

"What?" Cyrus asked, eyes flicking toward him.

Greyson did not bother replying to his question as he moved in front of Cyrus, shielding him. "Really?" he asked, shaking his head. "You want to do this *again*? How many times has this been?"

"I brought more people this time."

"I see that," he remarked, sneering. "But you're attacking me in the middle of a village with plenty of witnesses and in front of Prince Cyrus. Not your smartest move."

"You never seem to leave his side," she said. "Besides, he killed two of my people. I had to replace them."

"This might just be me," Greyson commented, "but this doesn't seem worth it."

"Your bounty increased again. Your weight in gold," she replied.

"The emperor is getting desperate, huh?"

No one responded, not that he'd thought they would. The emperor had raised the bounty every few months. But Greyson's weight in gold was ridiculous, even for the emperor, especially when he'd done nothing to merit it. Stance widening, his left hand closed around nothing.

"Where's your staff, mage?" she taunted in a sing-song voice.

Numbness raced up his spine as Greyson peered over his shoulder just in time to see Lord Darius running away. "Come back with my staff, you idiot," he yelled. When the lord did not stop, Greyson said, "Shit."

The bounty hunters charged toward him. Greyson moved back, bumping into Cyrus. "Run, Cyrus," he ordered. Without his staff, Greyson was powerless, and he wasn't a good hand-to-hand fighter.

Cyrus yanked Greyson out of the way before drawing his blade in one smooth motion. "Get your staff."

Greyson didn't argue; he raced toward Lord Darius, who had stopped right in front of his house. Three bounty hunters followed him while the other two engaged Cyrus. He could hear the ring of steel meeting steel, but he didn't turn around. As he was about to reach Lord Darius, someone snagged the back of his cloak and wrestled him to the ground.

A swear ripped out of his mouth as Greyson fell. He tried to get up, but two men pinned him to the ground while the third, a woman, tied his wrists together. "Don't just stand there," Greyson yelled at Lord Darius, who sneered. "I swear when I get out of this, I'm going to kill you."

He struggled against the ties futilely. Greyson was plenty strong, but he could not overcome the three people. A cry rang through the air and stilled his heart. Greyson tried to see Cyrus, but all he could glimpse was him sprawled on the ground, unmoving.

The breath left his lungs at the sight. "Cyrus!" Greyson screamed as he thrashed in the men's grasp. Frantically, he swept the area and landed on Jessica, one of his students. The gangly teenager watched him with wide eyes and an open mouth, her black hair trapped in a messy braid. By her side were two more people, older men in their thirties, and also his students. Normally, he wouldn't get any of his people involved, but Cyrus was in trouble.

"Help me," he begged.

It took no more than that. Jessica raced forward, hand extended with a glowing ring. The bounty hunter that held his legs was lifted into the air, then went flying. His other two students joined the fray, and the two bounty hunters left him and joined their associates to face the new threat.

Greyson got to his feet, bound, and charged Lord Darius, who watched the fight. He tried to enter his home, but Greyson grabbed his cloak and yanked. With his wrists tied, he couldn't pull Lord Darius much, but it was enough. Darius stumbled, then elbowed him, catching Greyson in the nose. Blood dripped down his lips as tears gathered in his eyes, but he refused to stop.

Grabbing Darius near his neck, he leveraged the other man around. Lord Darius kicked him, keeping Greyson's staff out of reach. Grunting as he took the hit, Greyson reached out and his fingertips brushed the wood of his staff. Power immediately shot through him and the staff, sending Lord Darius flying into the side of his home with a loud thud.

He did not give the fallen lord a second thought. Hands wrapping around the warm wood, Greyson concentrated on channeling his magic into the rope, which almost instantly snapped. He ran toward Cyrus, who was motionless on the dirt road.

Jessica bled from a cut on her arm, but the teenager kept fighting. The bounty hunter she'd thrown had returned. The five of them worked in unison to defeat the three mages, but other people in the town joined in. While most were not bound to an artifact, which made them weaker mages, they still had skills.

The ground rumbled as Elric, a large miner with rough features, stomped his foot, making the bounty hunters wobble. An old woman with white hair waved a hand at the snow, which morphed into ice around the bounty hunter's feet.

Breaking through the ice, the leader captured Cyrus before Greyson could reach him. She held a knife to his throat and ordered, "Call them off, Greyson, or Prince Cyrus dies."

"Why should that deter him?" Jessica asked, sniggering.

Everyone knew how much he hated Cyrus in the past. Greyson had been vocal about Cyrus' annoying presence in the capital during the negotiations, then later, when he was the face of the emperor's troops. What they didn't know is how that had changed.

"The emperor will blame you," the bounty hunter said.

"He'll blame me either way." Greyson's thoughts whirled. He could not let her hurt Cyrus, but at the same time, he wouldn't give himself up to the bounty hunters. Greyson tightened his hold on his staff and twisted it in the dirt; the ground trembled and began to shift.

"Stop it, Greyson," she ordered, knife pressing against Cyrus' neck.

Greyson shrugged like he couldn't care less while sweat slid down his neck. "Kill Cyrus, and you die. Leave now, and live to fight another day."

The ground rose about their legs, holding them in place and squeezing them like a snake.

A soundless snarl twisted her features, but she sheathed her knife. "I will succeed one day."

"Many have tried, but none have succeeded because these are *my* mountains." Greyson slammed the butt of the staff into the ground and it shifted violently, making the houses creak in strain. Exhaustion seeped through him, black spots floating through his vision, but he kept pressing forward before it could consume him.

The bounty hunters gave him one last look before they fled. Greyson wasted no time, he sank to the ground as his hands ran over Cyrus, who'd been stabbed in his shoulder and had a long slice along his right thigh, plus another cut on his stomach. His cheek was starting to bruise like he'd been hit.

"Cyrus," Greyson called, patting his uninjured cheek.

Cyrus did not wake.

Picking him up, Greyson draped Cyrus over his shoulder and straightened with a loud grunt, back and knees protesting. "Why are you always so damn heavy?" he asked. People gaped at him. "I need somewhere to take Cyrus to," Greyson said in a strained voice.

The old woman who'd controlled the snow gestured to a two-story house not far from them. "Over here." She headed to the back of the building where a narrow staircase led to a separate room.

Greyson silently swore at the wooden steps but walked up, hand on the banister, and silently counted in his mind as was his habit, ignoring the pain in his back and legs. Cyrus was much too heavy for him to carry. Agonizingly slow, he trudged up the stairs and into a small room. It had a bed, table, fireplace, and kitchen, but there was nothing personal and a thin layer of dust covered everything.

He lowered Cyrus onto the bed, then asked, "Do you have any herbs, bandages, anything?"

Her brown eyes wandered over Cyrus and Greyson as her lips puckered. Her weathered face and white hair spoke of her advanced age as did the spots on her hand that rested at the base of her throat. Greyson didn't know her name, but he'd seen her before. Not speaking, he waited for her to decide.

She scrutinized them for several long moments before she nodded. "I will see what I can round up."

"Thank you."

Immediately, he stripped Cyrus' clothes off so he could inspect the wounds. None of them appeared deep enough for him to have fallen unconscious nor had he lost that much blood. Greyson strode to the kitchen and filled a bowl with fresh water. A little digging provided a cloth.

He cleaned the wounds as he whispered, "Cyrus," over and over again.

The door opened, and he jerked toward it, hoping the old woman had returned. Greyson was disappointed. Lord Darius stood in the doorway, flanked by two hulking soldiers.

"Mage Greyson, you are under arrest."

"For what?" he asked, gripping his staff.

"For trafficking in illegal substances and attacking Prince Cyrus."

"What?"

"Arrest him," Lord Darius said, waving the two soldiers forward.

Greyson snarled as he lifted his staff, the blue stone glowing. "Take one more step, and I'll kill you all."

"You'll be executed for murder," the lord said.

"You'll still be dead, which I'm beginning to think is worth it."

Cyrus moaned behind him. Unable to stop himself, Greyson peered over his shoulder. Cyrus was still unconscious as his wounds continued to bleed. Taking a deep breath, he faced Lord Darius. "Do you have a healer?"

"For the prince? No," the man replied with a sneer.

"You would allow the emperor's nephew to die?"

"What has the royal family done for me? Nothing. They banished me to this hellhole when the bitch empress complained I'd been handsy with her. No. Prince Cyrus will die, and I will blame you," Lord Darius said.

He could kill Darius and his soldiers, but the emperor would punish the people of the Griseo Mountains. They needed Cyrus to live, so the emperor would have mercy, though Greyson would most likely not survive either way. But he *needed* Cyrus to live. He could not imagine a world without that perfect smile, easy laugh, and kind heart. Swallowing, he glanced at Cyrus. Cyrus was worth it. He was worth everything to Greyson.

"I'm the closest thing he's got to a healer, then. Lord Darius, if Cyrus survives, I will give myself over to be arrested. If he dies, I'm going to kill you and all your men, then surrender myself to the emperor. I would suggest you leave, so I can save him and your lives."

"There are no deals to be made, Greyson," Lord Darius said. "If you do not comply or fight, I will order my guards to start killing citizens."

"Fine. No deal. Try me. I'm willing to die. Hell, I'm willing to risk another war. Cyrus is worth it. I will kill you and all the soldiers who stand against me, then throw myself on the mercy of the emperor. If I die, at least I'll have saved Cyrus."

"You think you can beat us all?" Darius asked, chortling.

"He's not alone," a voice said. In the doorway stood the old woman, Elric, and Jessica. "We will all stand with him," she said.

Lord Darius turned around, swallowing. As Darius and his two guards moved, Greyson saw more people lining the stairs. Pride swelled in his chest at the sight. His people supported him, even if they didn't understand.

Clearing his throat, Lord Darius said, "I accept your deal. Cyrus lives and you hand yourself over."

It was the only way to keep everyone safe long-term.

"Staff," he demanded.

"No. Once Cyrus is safe, I will turn it over but not before to keep you honest. You will hurt no one or our deal is void, and I kill you, which I'm beginning to think I'll like," Greyson answered, pointing his staff at him.

Lord Darius snarled and tramped toward the door, shouting, "Get out of my way." The people shifted, and he disappeared down the stairs followed by his two guards.

Greyson sank to the bed, and the old woman settled near him. "Thank you," he told her as sincerely as possible. "Thank you all."

"Of course. We will always stand with you, Greyson, no matter what," the old woman said, pushing her white braid over her hunched shoulder. "I am Widow Jones."

His brow furrowed. Her surname was familiar, though Jones was common enough, then it hit him. "Your Hugh, Jemima, and Elric's grandmother."

"I am."

He'd taught all three of them, though they were all close to a decade older than him.

Together, they cleaned Cyrus' wounds as villagers brought bandages, poultices, and other offerings. Greyson carefully spread a green paste over the wounds to fight off infection, then started to wrap them. As he shifted Cyrus, he glanced at Widow Jones, who examined Cyrus with a bent finger on her lips.

"I don't think," she said, "these wounds are bad enough to knock him out."

"Me either," Greyson remarked, pulling a thick piece of cloth taut over Cyrus' well-muscled stomach. As he moved Cyrus again, Greyson paused. There was a sizable patch of blood on the pillow. As he finished tying the bandage around Cyrus' stomach, Greyson swallowed. Head wounds were unpredictable. Shaking, he ran his fingers through Cyrus' hair, stopping when he came to a wet spot.

The amount of blood did not bother Greyson, what worried him was the softness he felt in the back of Cyrus' skull. It should not be there.

Clearing his throat, Greyson said as calmly as he could manage, "There's a soft spot."

"How big?"

"Pretty big," he replied, emotion clogging his throat. "I think one of the bounty hunters must have hit him with the pommel of their sword."

The cuts he could treat, the injury to Cyrus' head he couldn't. All they could do was wait and see. But from the size and softness, he didn't know if Cyrus would survive it. Greyson methodically cleaned the wound, put a paste on it, then wrapped a cloth around the injury.

Squeezing Cyrus' hand, he said, "You are not allowed to die, especially from something as stupid as protecting me. Do you understand?"

His lungs struggled to take in air as ice filled his veins. Greyson could not lose Cyrus, not now. He wouldn't survive it.

A hand settled on his arm, and Greyson looked at Widow Jones. She stared directly at him with her serious brown eyes as she said, "You're in love with Prince Cyrus."

"Yes," Greyson said, not bothering to deny it.

"I'm going to get my great-granddaughter."

"What?" he asked, brow furrowing.

"She's unbound, but she's already showing signs of healing ability."

His mouth fell open. Healing and necromancy were the two rarest abilities. "Why didn't anyone tell me?"

"We don't want her to be taken. But we were going to bring her to you this summer, to learn."

"I will figure something out about getting her an artifact." He paused, then continued, "If I don't survive this, write to

Widow Abney in Drakcombe and she will write to Frederick in the capital. He'll figure something out."

"Thank you," she said.

He clutched Cyrus' lifeless hand. "No, thank you."

As Widow Jones left, tears began to burn the backs of his eyes. "Cyrus, don't do this to me. Not now."

Cyrus did not respond.

Greyson lowered his head to Cyrus' arm. *Maybe the little girl can save him?* he reasoned. Maybe Cyrus would be fine? A sob caught in his chest. Lifting his head, Greyson placed a shaky kiss on Cyrus' lips, then whispered, "I love you."

26

CYRUS

Everything hurt. His head pounded and his muscles pulsed as bile climbed his throat. Cyrus had no idea what was going on. *Where am I?* he thought. Everything was muddled. He tried to think back to what he last remembered. He'd been attacked, then he was running, and—*Greyson*. He was in trouble.

He started to sit up, but something across his waist stopped him. Cyrus stilled. Greyson lay next to him, asleep. His pulse quickened as his mouth opened. *How is this possible?* Slowly, he lifted a hand, stopping when his shoulder twinged and made him moan.

Greyson jerked, arm tightening, then blinked at the bright light. His eyebrows drew together as he looked around before his gaze settled on him. Cyrus tensed, unsure. Greyson's face scrunched in a strong emotion that Cyrus couldn't identify.

"Cyrus."

Before Cyrus could react, Greyson kissed him. Cyrus froze. He couldn't move a single muscle as Greyson pressed against him, gripping his face. An awareness bloomed within his body. Cyrus returned the kiss, movements frantic. His head throbbed and his body ached, but at the moment, Cyrus couldn't care less. Greyson's lips were soft and gentle against his. Cyrus moaned, and Greyson's tongue delved into his mouth.

I'm dead, he thought. *This is paradise.* While he assumed paradise would involve less pain, Cyrus was all for it because Greyson was beside him.

Greyson pulled back, and Cyrus cried, "Don't go."

"I'm not going," Greyson replied with a smile.

His soft black hair brushed Cyrus' face, and his breath quickened from the contact while his heart thrashed from that expression. Cyrus had never seen Greyson smile in their entire acquaintance, not once. He clutched his woolen tunic, ignoring the throbbing in his head. "I'm dead, aren't I?"

A chuckle broke out of Greyson, making Cyrus' breath turn jagged. "No," Greyson said. "You're simply with me."

"I like the sound of that."

"Good." Stroking his cheek, Greyson's brow furrowed as emotion filled his eyes. "I thought you were going to die."

"I can't believe you found me," Cyrus said with a shake of his head. How in all the goddess' grace did Greyson find him?

Thumb pausing in its arc, Greyson blinked. "What?"

"You found me."

"You were right beside me," Greyson said slowly as his hand slid away.

"No, I wasn't. I was running from the bounty hunters." All of sudden, Cyrus remembered and seized Greyson's hand. "Greyson, you're in danger. Bounty hunters are on their way to get you. I killed a couple of them, but I couldn't get them all."

Greyson sat up, face pale. "Cyrus, what is the last thing you remember?"

"Running through the old battlefield near your village. My side was cut open. I remember a person with black hair. Can't recall their face. Then pain. Lots of pain."

Climbing out of bed, Greyson panted. "Oh, goddess."

Cyrus tried to sit up but couldn't. "What's going on?"

"You don't remember any of it?" Greyson asked, voice breaking.

"What are you talking about?"

"Cyrus," Greyson said, staring at him, "that was almost three months ago."

"No," he said. "It just happened!"

"I am not lying to you. I saved you almost three months ago."

It was the start of fall. He'd traveled from the capital to see Greyson. Cyrus shook his head as the world faded around him and a buzzing like angry bees filled his ears. *It's not possible.*

"Cyrus." Greyson's harsh voice cut through the terror. Greyson had become deathly pale as trembles wracked his body. "I need to go outside. I will come back and explain everything." Greyson practically ran out the door, and it swung closed behind him.

Cyrus sagged back on the bed, trying to calm the storm swirling inside of him. He could barely see his surroundings as his pulse thundered in his ears. It wasn't possible. None of this was possible. Greyson had to be lying to him. They weren't friends, and he had no reason to tell the truth.

When he shifted, his side throbbed. The bounty hunters had cut his side. With careful movements, he slipped the blanket down and examined where he'd been injured. A perfect white scar sat exactly where the bounty hunter had cut him. He had other bandages for wounds he didn't remember. He looked at where Greyson slept not long ago, and he paused.

A staff, Greyson's, was on the bed not far from him. Cyrus had never seen Greyson without his staff since he got it. Like he'd been struck by lightning, he thought, *Greyson kissed me.* Greyson had kissed *him.* His pulse accelerated. *Is it possible?*

Throwing the blanket off, he got to his feet, then tilted dangerously as his knees buckled. Cyrus forced himself straight. His head throbbed with every movement while his muscles cried and exhaustion weighed him down. He refused to stop; he had to know what the kiss meant.

He yanked the door open, and a world covered in white greeted him. Cold air enveloped his naked body as he gaped at the snow. Piles of it covered the wooden buildings, pine trees in the distance, and Validus Peak. It was not possible. How couldn't he remember the last three months?

Greyson hadn't gone far. He stood on the stair landing, leaning against the railing. His black hair hung around his gaunt face as each breath he released turned into a cloud. Cyrus stretched a hand out to him, feet scuffing on the icy wood.

"Cyrus," Greyson snapped. "What the hell are you doing?"

His knees buckled, and he started to sink to the landing. Greyson's arms wrapped about his waist, holding him up. Cyrus gripped the front of his tunic. "Greyson, you kissed me."

"Seriously?" Greyson started to drag him inside. "We can talk about that later. You're injured."

He wanted to protest but couldn't find the strength to do so. Cyrus leaned heavily on Greyson. He'd never been so close to him. The sharp yet sweet scent of pine wafted off his skin and made Cyrus take another deep breath. As they moved into the room, Cyrus half expected Greyson to let go of him, but he didn't.

"Why are you so heavy?" Greyson asked, practically carrying him.

Greyson helped him onto the soft bed, panting. He lifted his legs and tucked the blanket around his shoulders. Cyrus could feel exhaustion taking him, but he held on. He seized Greyson's hand. "You kissed me."

"You need to sleep, Cyrus."

"No," he said, even as his eyes started to close. "I don't understand, Greyson."

"I know," Greyson said. As sleep started to take Cyrus, a gentle touch on his lips warmed him. "Everything will return to normal once you wake."

Cyrus shook his head. He didn't want to go back to how it used to be. "Greyson," he cried sleepily, but Greyson did not reply.

PART TWO

27

CYRUS

The first sense of awareness he had was pain. His head throbbed and his body ached. Cyrus swallowed as he tried to breathe through it, but it didn't lessen. With a narrowed gaze, he inspected his surroundings.

It was a small space. He lay on a bed pressed against the wall. Directly opposite was a tiny kitchen, a window over the sink, and a square, knotty pine table with matching chairs. A stone fireplace, a round woven rug on the floor before it, that burned bright with flames sat on the other wall. There was a lone door with a long window next to it. There was not a single personal item. Nothing.

"Greyson," Cyrus called, even though he was alone.

Frowning, he tried to sit up, and the world immediately spun. His various wounds protested and his head hurt so viciously, he had a hard time seeing. Swearing, Cyrus took a deep breath and waited for the pain to dim. He had to find Greyson and make him explain.

What if it was a dream?

Cyrus had dreamed about Greyson so many times, but they had never felt so real or vivid. He shook his head, regretting the movement as his vision swirled and nausea clawed at his throat.

No. It was real, and he had to speak with him.

He stood and his breath came out in short gasps as his knees trembled. Chilly air wrapped around his naked body, raising gooseflesh. He located a pair of trousers and a shirt he'd never seen before. Painstakingly, he donned the clothes, only to have to sit on a chair halfway through because buzzing filled his ears and black spots danced before his vision.

Once his sight cleared, Cyrus leveraged himself up and trudged to the door, hoping Greyson was right outside. He opened it, and a soldier, not Greyson, was on the stair landing.

"Your highness," the man said, bowing.

"Where is Mage Greyson?"

"He was arrested."

Arrested? What's going on? Swallowing, he ordered, "I want to see him immediately."

"Lord Darius said you lost your memory. We can't follow your orders. I'm sorry, your highness."

"Lost my what?" he asked. Not bothering to let the soldier respond, Cyrus continued, voice deepening, "Lord Darius was mistaken. I demand to see Mage Greyson immediately or there will be hell to pay."

The other man jerked back slightly. Cyrus hadn't quite mastered the "royal voice" as his uncle liked to call it. Despite that, people had a hard time not obeying him.

"Please understand, your highness, you've been sick," the soldier pleaded.

"Either you bring me Mage Greyson or take me to see Lord Darius this instant," Cyrus said coolly.

"I will bring them both here, your highness."

"Excellent."

Bowing, the soldier slunk away to hopefully follow his orders.

The cold air made Cyrus shiver. He wanted to follow the soldier or at least wait outside for the other man to return, but he hadn't found his boots. Barefoot, he stepped into the warm room and sat at the table.

His head throbbed with every beat of his heart. Gingerly, he raised his arms, one shoulder twinging, and massaged his temples to ease the discomfort. It did not help. Minutes passed and no one appeared. Cyrus was about to search for Greyson himself, barefoot or not, when someone rapped on the door.

"Enter," he said.

Lord Darius strolled in followed by two soldiers, who dragged Greyson. He had a black eye, a split lip, his nose had been broken, and he limped badly.

"Cyrus, a pleasure to see you as always. Though to be honest, I'm having a hard time seeing you," Greyson remarked.

He moved as fast as possible toward Greyson, shoving the two soldiers aside. Slowly, Cyrus grabbed his chin. Cyrus expected Greyson to shake him off like he always had in the past, but he didn't.

"Did they do this to you?"

"Yes."

"Lie," Lord Darius spat.

Cyrus whirled around. "So he did it to himself?"

The lord blustered, turning red. Cyrus shook his head. He hated Lord Darius. He'd only been assigned this post because of his inappropriate conduct with the empress. Cyrus had protested against it, but the emperor ruled it a fitting punishment for him.

Looking at Greyson, Cyrus finally noticed the ropes around his wrists. "Knife," he demanded, holding a hand out.

"He's under arrest," Lord Darius protested.

"Knife," Cyrus repeated louder.

A soldier unsheathed a dagger and slapped the hilt into his waiting palm. Cyrus quickly cut through the thick ties, ropes falling to the ground.

"Thanks."

Cyrus swallowed; he'd never heard those words from Greyson before, not even when he'd saved Greyson's life.

After he returned the dagger, Cyrus faced Lord Darius once again. His head pounded, making his vision waiver, but he had to resolve this matter before he could talk to Greyson. "Why is Mage Greyson under arrest?"

"I know you've lost your memories—"

"I've lost nothing."

"Oh, you regained them. Excellent," he said in an insincere voice.

"Why is he under arrest?" he repeated with a slight growl.

"Illegal trafficking and hurting you, your highness."

"Liar. You sniveling coward. You accepted the poison, and the bounty hunters hurt Cyrus, not me," Greyson yelled.

"Poison?" Cyrus asked, perking up. During the war, Greyson had been known for his poison-crafting abilities.

"I confiscated rubrum poison from his person when I arrested Mage Greyson. He was probably going to kill you," Lord Darius said evenly, hands stretching out wide.

Greyson limped forward, anger radiating off of him. "I was alone with Cyrus for almost three months. If I wanted him dead, I could have easily killed him. You accepted that poison as a bribe in front of Cyrus."

Cyrus held out an arm to stop Greyson from getting any closer to Darius or his guards. He expected Greyson to push him out of the way, but he merely stopped. Cyrus glanced between them. He believed Greyson, mostly.

Holding his hand out, Cyrus said, "I want the poison."

"Excuse me?" Lord Darius said.

"I want it. Now. I'm confiscating it in the name of the crown," Cyrus said, wiggling his fingers. He would never let Darius keep something so dangerous.

"I don't have it on me," he said, eyes flicking to the side.

His voice lowered as he ordered, "I want it, Darius. I will follow you to wherever you hid it. It had also better have the wax seal Greyson puts on all his poisons or I'm charging you with murder."

Lord Darius pulled a bottle out of his pocket and handed it over. Cyrus took it, then immediately gave it to Greyson, ignoring Lord Darius' snarl of protest. "Is it sealed?" he asked.

"Yes," Greyson replied, surprising him by giving it back.

"Since it was in your possession and you lied to me, I'm not willing to accept that this belongs to Mage Greyson," Cyrus lied. He had no doubt, whatsoever, that Greyson made the poison.

"He confessed," Lord Darius said.

"I heard he gave it to you as a bribe. Are you confessing?"

The man sputtered.

"I will take that as a no," Cyrus commented. "The matter is dismissed, and you can't hold him."

Lord Darius pointed at Greyson, snarling, "He hurt you."

Cyrus swallowed. That he believed.

"I did not!" Greyson shouted, moving closer. "The bounty hunters hurt him. There are a dozen witnesses."

"Your people. Who would lie for you."

"Not just my people. You soldiers saw it and did nothing," Greyson said.

The lord's mouth fell open as he started to sputter again. Cyrus ignored him and focused on the soldiers. "I want the truth. Did Mage Greyson injure me?"

Both of the soldiers glanced at Lord Darius before one said, "No, your highness. Bounty hunters attacked you, and Greyson, with the help of some villagers, saved your life."

"Lies," Lord Darius snapped, raising his fist to strike the soldier, but he dodged the blow.

"No, it's the truth."

"Lord Darius," Cyrus said, drawing his attention, "that's twice you've lied to me. I do not believe this is the right posting for you. You will be confined to your home until I write to my uncle about a more proper placement."

"Like the tower," Greyson suggested.

Lord Darius' mouth fell open in obvious horror.

"Yes," Cyrus said with a nod. "Some time with the monks on their island, far from everything in silent contemplation, might be what you need."

"I could always kill him," Greyson said. "I think I'd enjoy it."

A chuckle slipped out of his lips. "Not at the moment." Turning to the soldiers, he ordered, "Take Lord Darius home and see that he stays there. I will speak to your captain later."

The soldiers bowed, then one opened the door. "My lord?" he said, waving Darius through it.

As soon as the door closed, Cyrus faced Greyson, then scanned the room. "Where's your staff?"

"Darius took it. I imagine he's snapped in ten half by now."

He raced to the door, ignoring the pain. Greyson couldn't do magic without the staff. If it broke, he would be powerless.

"Wait!" Cyrus ran down the stairs, clutching the railing as he slid on the frozen steps.

The soldiers halted. Cyrus winced as he strode barefoot across the snow. "Where is Greyson's staff?"

Lord Darius refused to meet his gaze. "Gone."

He grabbed the front of his cloak. "You will procure it or I'm throwing you in whatever hole you locked Greyson into." When he did not respond, Cyrus let him go and continued, "Better yet. Drop him in a mine. I will tell my uncle he wandered in like an idiot. No one will question further."

The guards started to haul him away, and Cyrus steeled his heart. Lord Darius had hurt Greyson and taken his magic. He was willing to kill him if need be.

"Wait," Darius said, trying to wrench his arms free from the soldiers' grasp. "I will give you the staff. I'd rather live with the monks than die."

He followed the lord to his home and secured the staff. As he touched it, power raced up his arm. Cyrus could say, with some certainty, that he'd never held Greyson's staff, but it felt so familiar. Ignoring it, he returned to the room he'd been staying in, and hopefully, to where Greyson waited. The cold burned his feet and chilled the rest of him. Shivering, he headed up the stairs and was met by Greyson.

Greyson stood in the doorway, arms crossed. Cyrus tensed, holding out the staff, but Greyson ignored it and instead, drew him inside. "Are you insane?" Greyson demanded. "It's winter and you went out in the snow."

Cyrus gaped, unsure of what to say.

Greyson pushed him in front of the fireplace. "Give me that," Greyson demanded, tugging on the staff.

He let it go, searching for his sword. Before he located it, Greyson stalked to the corner, with a very pronounced limp, and leaned his staff right next to Cyrus' blade. The sight of the two weapons together did something to Cyrus. A tingle raced down his spine as heat filled his stomach. A strong emotion that he couldn't identify swelled in his chest. It was nice. His and Greyson's weapons so casually leaning in the corner, right next to each other, as if they belonged together.

Greyson continued to fuss over Cyrus as he draped a blanket across his shoulders, then stiffly sat, inspecting his feet. A blush shot to Cyrus' cheeks as Greyson pulled the frozen appendages onto his lap, holding them in his warm grasp.

"Don't come crying to me when you lose a toe," Greyson grumbled.

Unable to stop himself, Cyrus stared at Greyson. His eyes darted away from the scar on the right side of his face. He'd done that to Greyson. It made him sick to think about it.

"Are you in pain?"

"What?"

"Are you in pain, Cyrus?"

"Yes," he answered, blinking. "My head's killing me and everything hurts."

"That's to be expected. You need to sleep."

"Are you alright?" he asked, taking in all the bruises.

"Broke my nose. Pretty sure several ribs are cracked. The rest is just bruises. I'll heal."

"Darius did that to you." Cyrus drew his feet from his grasp and tried to scoot closer, but a sharp stabbing in his shoulder and thigh made him stop with a grimace.

"Stop moving. You're going to hurt yourself. And no, Darius didn't do it himself. He had the soldiers do it."

"What?"

"I will live, Cyrus. I've had much worse." Cyrus opened his mouth to protest, but Greyson interrupted him, "You should go to sleep."

Without a word, Greyson got to his feet, grimacing, then hooked his arms around Cyrus and tried to lift him, but swear words ripped Greyson's mouth as he hugged his waist. "Oh goddess, I hate broken ribs."

Cyrus got to his feet by himself, then Greyson pushed him toward the bed and made him sit. "Greyson," he said, grabbing his hand. "We need to talk."

"I suppose we do," Greyson replied, staring at their joined hands before he withdrew from Cyrus' grasp. "But you need to rest. Having your brain scrambled, then unscrambled is trying. Not even to mention your other wounds. Shit," Greyson said, staring at him. "I need to check them."

"Later." Cyrus waved him off, heat rushing to his cheeks. He had to try very hard to think of innocuous things instead of Greyson seeing his unclothed body. "I think," he said, clearing his throat, "you should tell me what happened."

GREYSON

Panic coiled under his skin. His side stabbed with every single breath, his face hurt, and he could barely see, but none of that compared to the agony of realizing Cyrus didn't remember falling in love with him. Now, Greyson had to explain it all to Cyrus, who'd saved his life, yet again. Stiffly, he sank onto the chair.

"I came upon you in the woods near my home. You were injured and you passed out."

"You saved me?" Cyrus asked, looking at him with his perfect sky-blue eyes.

"No, I left you to die."

"What?" Cyrus released a startled laugh.

Staring straight at him, Greyson told the truth. "I left you to die and went home. Then it started to rain, and I felt guilty, so I went back and brought you to my cabin. When you woke up, you didn't remember anything. So I lied and told you we were friends, all the while planning on poisoning you. Hence, the poison you currently have."

Cyrus held the bottle up. "You were going to kill me with this?"

"Well," Greyson admitted, "I was going to use the fresh berries, but I decided not to pretty quickly."

"Continue."

"I wanted to know why you were here and how that would affect my people. Also, I wanted to know who erased your memories. Whoever did it wasn't very good. Some of your memories had started to return and look at you now," he said, gesturing to Cyrus, "you got everything back."

"You didn't do it?" Cyrus asked, studying him with a closed expression.

"No, I favor permanent fixes like death." When Cyrus did not say anything, he continued, "I wrote a letter to my friend in the capital to see if he knew of anything. While waiting for his response, I took you to several villages to see if I could find the mage that wiped your memories. No one knew anything. Though, several people pointed out that I couldn't kill you because the emperor would blame us all."

"Is that what stopped you?" Cyrus asked.

"Partly. Anyway, when my friend wrote back, all he knew was that you'd traveled here to do something important, and the emperor was searching for you. So I took you to Lord Darius," Greyson finished. He'd left out so much, but how could he explain what happened?

"That's not all," Cyrus said, standing with a groan. "Why did you kiss me?"

Greyson swallowed as tears burned the backs of his eyes. He could not find the words. When he saw Cyrus awake and alive, he'd been so happy. He loved Cyrus, even now, but Cyrus didn't remember any of it.

Cyrus nudged his chin until their gazes met. "Were we together?"

"What?"

"Were we together during the time I can't remember? Were you with the me I've forgotten?"

A pounding sounded in his ears. Greyson had no idea how Cyrus would react if he told the truth. *I love him enough*, he thought fiercely. He loved Cyrus enough to fight for him.

They were perfect together, and Greyson would prove it. He captured Cyrus' hand, squeezing his fingers.

"Yes. We were together."

Mouth falling open, Cyrus took a step back, though he stayed within Greyson's grasp.

Greyson said, his voice desperate, "I didn't use you, Cyrus. I promise. You and I just...fell in love."

"What?"

"I'm in love with you," Greyson said honestly, standing and stifling the subsequent moan. "I love you, Cyrus."

Cyrus shook his head.

Pain that had nothing to do with his injuries made his breath turn harsh. "Please," he begged. "Please give me the chance to prove it. To show you how good we are together."

"Do you know why I traveled to the Griseo Mountains?" Cyrus asked quietly.

"I don't." Greyson did not know if he wanted the answer, for it could shatter his soul.

"I came to tell you that I am in love with you," Cyrus said, tugging Greyson against his chest.

"What?" Greyson asked, his voice coming out rougher than he'd meant.

"I have been in love with you since the first time I saw you."

"That's not possible."

"Honestly, I'll admit, it was lust that became love," Cyrus said. "Anyway, my aunt and cousin thought I would get over it after you were exiled, but I didn't. So they told me to come here, confess, and have you reject me. My uncle was certain you'd kill me, though my aunt said you were smarter than that."

He covered Cyrus' mouth, stopping him. It did not seem possible. All those years, Cyrus had loved him. "You love me?"

"Yes," Cyrus said against his fingers.

There was a lot they would have to work through. Also, he feared when Cyrus got to know him, he would fall out of love.

But at the moment, he didn't care. Greyson kissed him. Cyrus wrapped his arms around him, squeezing him as his mouth moved against his. Greyson broke away, fighting the cry that wanted to escape.

"Did you not like it?" Cyrus asked, looking at the ground.

"Don't be stupid," Greyson snapped. "I'm in pain. My lip is split and you squeezed my ribs."

"Oh," Cyrus said. "Sorry."

"It's fine." He held Cyrus close with his hands locked behind his back. "We're both too injured for this."

"Later?"

"Later," Greyson promised.

28

CYRUS

Cyrus stared at Greyson in wonder. *Greyson loves me.* He couldn't believe it. Absurdly, he felt jealous of the him that he couldn't remember. That person had stolen his firsts with Greyson. Yet at the same time, he was ridiculously grateful. Never had Cyrus been able to break through the wall Greyson enclosed himself in, but now, he had, somehow.

He had never spoken of his attraction, subsequent crush, and ultimately falling in love with Greyson. His uncle would have never approved because of who Greyson was. During the war, Cyrus had to work very hard to bury his emotions and follow his orders. To this day, he could clearly remember that first battle.

Greyson had been wiping out his soldiers with powerful spells, so they coordinated an attack to simply kill him. Cyrus had hardened his heart to prepare himself for what actions he would have to take. But when Greyson was before him, Cyrus couldn't do it, he faltered, pulling back at the same time Greyson did and slicing through his eye with the tip of his sword. He remembered with perfect clarity the sick sensation that pooled in his stomach as the blood dripped off his blade. He'd let him go, not chasing Greyson as he and his people retreated.

Cyrus had hoped after the war he would be able to find some way to tell Greyson how he felt and convince him to give them a chance, but it didn't work out that way. He argued with his uncle, fighting for the people of the Griseo Mountains as a way to prove he cared for Greyson and because it was the right thing to do. Then in recompense for the changes, his uncle demanded Greyson's head. Cyrus never thought Greyson would give himself up, but he did. For the next five months, he argued and fought with his uncle to spare Greyson's life, but his uncle wouldn't be swayed.

Every night he would go to the dungeons and check on Greyson after he'd fallen asleep, crying each time he saw him. One night, unbeknownst to him, his aunt followed him. She figured out how Cyrus felt about Greyson and promptly told Jade. Together, the two of them worked on the emperor. In the end, his aunt blatantly told the emperor Cyrus was in love with Greyson, and he let Greyson go, exiling him, though he placed a sizable bounty on his head to keep Greyson in the mountains.

Cyrus had escorted Greyson to the Griseo Mountains. The whole trip, he tried to rally his courage and tell him how he felt, but he couldn't get the words out. On the last night, it snowed. Together, they silently watched it. That was the closest he ever came.

"Stop."

"What?" Cyrus asked, starting.

"Stop thinking about whatever you're thinking about. It's upsetting you."

"How can you tell?"

Greyson scowled. Cyrus didn't know why, but he loved that expression. Probably because that was the only one he was used to. Greyson grabbed his hand and answered, "You're muttering under your breath, and your face did that scrunched-up thing it does when you're thinking too hard."

Chuckling, he said, "You know me more than I thought." Though as soon as the words left his mouth, jealousy stabbed him squarely in the heart. *He* should've been the one to get to know Greyson.

"Okay, I don't know this expression," Greyson said. When Cyrus didn't say anything, he continued, "Talk to me, love."

The endearment burned him, making his pulse thunder in his ears. He'd waited a long time to hear Greyson say that word. Cyrus said, breathlessly, "I like that."

"You like me calling you 'love?'"

"Yes."

"Then I will if you tell me what's going on in your head."

Cyrus could have never guessed that he'd be lying in bed with Greyson and having him demand to know his thoughts. He'd dreamed about being in bed with Greyson *many* times but not something as simple as this.

Running his fingers over Greyson's palm, he stated, "I'm jealous."

"Of who?"

"Me, I suppose."

Greyson tugged on his hand, and Cyrus looked at him. "I don't understand."

"This other me got all my firsts with you. He broke through your walls, and you fell in love with him. Me," he said, gesturing to himself, "you might not even like."

Greyson gave him a patient look. "I fell in love with you. There is only one of you."

"How do you know?"

"Because you annoy me in the exact same way."

He wanted to laugh but couldn't manage it. "What if you don't actually like me?"

"Cyrus, I have the same fear. What if I don't live up to whatever ideal you've built up in your head? Honestly, I know I'm in love with you and that's not going to change."

Pulling Greyson's hand onto his chest, Cyrus said, "I love you too, and that's not going to change."

"Good," Greyson said. "Now, we get to know each other."

He scoffed. "It's more like I get to know you while you retell me everything about yourself. Interesting for me, boring for you."

A small smile quirked at the corner of Greyson's lips.

"What?"

"You said something very similar to me not long after you lost your memory."

"Another first he's stolen," Cyrus muttered darkly.

"Not all our firsts are taken."

"Well, we've kissed already, clearly. I assume we..." Cyrus trailed off as he studied Greyson. "Have we had sex?"

"Not yet."

Heat swamped him, scorching Cyrus. "We didn't?"

"No."

He grinned. Cyrus wanted to remember being with Greyson for the first time. Almost immediately, a needle of worry punctured the happy bubble in his chest. *What if Greyson doesn't want to be with me like that?* Clearing his throat, he asked, "Did you not want to?"

Rolling his eyes, Greyson said, "Of course, I want to. Have you seen yourself?"

"Then why didn't we?"

"First, it was because I didn't want to take advantage of you. You quickly convinced me that I wasn't. Second, it was because I didn't know if you were married or not."

"You didn't know if I was married?" he asked. "Honorable."

"You're the only person that calls me that. I'm a known poisoner. Even my own people wouldn't call me honorable."

"Then why did my possible marriage stop you?"

Greyson scowled at him, cheeks pink. "I wanted you to be mine alone."

Lifting Greyson's hand to his face, Cyrus kissed the calloused palm. "I am only yours."

"I'm glad," Greyson replied. "I don't think I would share you well."

"You're not married are you?"

"No."

"Never been?" Cyrus asked. He didn't know much of Greyson's romantic past, but he'd always been curious.

"No. I never cared much for romance in the past. I've courted like three women in my life and that's about it."

"No men?"

"No," Greyson said with a shake of his head. "You're the first man I've ever been attracted to. The first man I've kissed. And the first person I've fallen in love with."

Cyrus beamed, happy for some ridiculous reason. "So what else do you think you know about me?"

"You like anything sugary."

"Yep."

"You hate tea."

"Also true. You love it, though."

"What?" Greyson asked, eyebrows raising. "How do you know that?"

It had been an easy discovery. During every meeting, the emperor provided drinks. Greyson chose tea every time. His warm expression alerted Cyrus to his love.

"You always picked it. No matter what was offered."

"I did."

Cyrus kissed his rough palm again. "Didn't you wonder why there was always tea when you secluded yourself in the library?"

His brow furrowed. "No."

Cyrus had, somewhat, obsessively stalked Greyson. Whenever he retreated to the library in a dusty, abandoned corner, Cyrus would summon tea for Greyson.

Cheeks pinking, Greyson tightened his fingers around Cyrus' hand. "Thank you, love."

Cyrus leaned back against the pillow. "What else do you know about me?"

"You like the snow."

"Yep."

"And your favorite color is a stormy grayish blue."

Staring into Greyson's unscarred eye, almost exactly how he would describe the shade, Cyrus said, "Yes."

"There's a lot I don't know. Like your age."

"You don't know how old I am? I know how old you are and that your birthday is right at the beginning of spring," Cyrus said.

"How?" Greyson asked, chuckling.

He savored the sound like it was a fine meal. "I asked other mages and people about you. I think they figured it was a 'get to know your enemy' thing, not an 'I'm tragically in love with you' thing."

"So we've established you're a bit obsessed with me," Greyson teased.

A laugh burst out of his lips. He'd always wanted this. He'd seen Greyson teasing others, but Cyrus had never been able to have that kind of relationship with him. "I'm twenty-five."

"So two years younger than me," Greyson said with a nod. "Birthday?"

"The middle of summer."

"That makes sense."

"Why?"

With a soft smile, Greyson said, "Because you remind me of summer with your golden hair, warm skin, and blue eyes."

Cyrus swallowed. He wanted to kiss Greyson, but he didn't want to hurt him.

"So you're gay?"

"Yes," Cyrus said. "I'm assuming you're not."

"I'm not entirely sure what I am at the moment. I definitely like women, but I definitely like you."

"So you're bi?"

"I guess. I've honestly never thought about it. Romance had never been important. I just didn't care."

"But you like and want sex?" Cyrus asked carefully.

"Yes, Cyrus. I do."

"That's nice." Cyrus lifted Greyson's hand again and kissed each of his long fingers. He liked this. Cyrus could never have pictured a scene like this, but now that he'd experienced it, he loved it.

"Come closer," Greyson said.

"Why?" he asked, already moving.

"I need to use you as leverage. I can't sleep on my back. I only sleep on my right side."

Not the most romantic reason, but Cyrus didn't mind assisting him. He slid closer, and Greyson held onto him, pulling. A grimace twisted Greyson's face. Cyrus helped him readjust, his shoulder and side throbbing while his head spun.

When Greyson settled on his side, Cyrus suggested, "What if I lay behind you, supporting you?"

"That could work," Greyson said, his breath coming out quickly while his face was shockingly pale.

He climbed behind Greyson, the wall at his back. Gently, he drew Greyson against him, then Cyrus pushed an arm under his neck. A sigh rushed out of Greyson after a second as his muscles relaxed.

"Better?" Cyrus asked.

"Better."

29

CYRUS

Cyrus drummed his fingers on the table, lips pursed. It was afternoon if the light streaming in from the window was any indication. The room was empty, and the fire had burned down to nothing but coals. Most importantly, Greyson was nowhere to be seen.

When he'd woken up, Greyson hadn't been there, but the ache in his head hadn't allowed Cyrus to look for him. Even the cuts on his side and thigh plus the stab wound on his shoulder didn't hurt as badly as his head did. As he sat there, he had to fight against a sudden wave of nausea. Swallowing, he searched for a bucket in case he lost the battle when he saw Greyson's staff. It leaned in the corner next to his sword.

He glowed at the sight. Greyson had to trust him, even a little, to leave his staff behind. Unable to stop it, worry poked at Cyrus. What if this was all a ruse? What if Greyson didn't love him but was using him?

Cyrus banished the thoughts. He would trust Greyson. Yet, the doubts persisted. What if this wasn't real?

Standing, he ignored the pain and the way the world tilted. He shoved his feet into a pair of boots, but his gaze lingered on Greyson's staff and his sword. He didn't mind leaving his blade behind, but what if something happened to Greyson's staff?

Shrugging, he strapped on his sword and picked up the staff. Power vibrated under his hand and traveled up his arm, inexplicably warming him.

Ready as he could be, Cyrus went outside. The sun was blindingly bright as it glared off the pure-white snow. His squinted eyes watered while his nose ran. Shivering, Cyrus bit back a swear; he'd forgotten his cloak.

A gangly teenager with a messy braid passed by, then stopped. "Prince Cyrus."

Nodding, he said, "I'm sorry I don't know your name."

"I'm Jessica, Greyson's student."

"Nice to meet you," Cyrus said, breathless. Just this small excursion was taxing. Exhaustion weighed on him, and all he wanted was to sleep, preferably with Greyson in his arms. "You don't happen to know where he is."

She pointed toward the square. "He went over there only a few minutes ago."

"Thank you."

"Of course." Jessica frowned, hands curling, before she blurted, "Thank you for saving Greyson."

Cyrus blinked. "Of course. I will always save Greyson if he needs it."

Her cheeks pinked as she asked, "Is it true he's in love with you?"

His mouth fell open for a second before he snapped it closed. "That's what he says."

"It's very surprising," Jessica said, then blushed more profusely.

"More shocking, I love him back."

The teenager's eyes widened. "You do?"

"I do."

"Widow Jones says the two of you are fated, and that because Greyson was so hardheaded, fate had to work even harder to get you two together."

He laughed, then stifled a cry. Holding his head with his free hand, Cyrus asked, "Fate made me lose my memory?"

"That's what Widow Jones says."

Controlling another laugh, he said, "I best go find my fated love, then."

The girl gave him a shy wave before heading in the opposite direction.

Cyrus ambled toward where she'd indicated, head hurting more fiercely with each breath. Thankfully, as he entered the square, Cyrus caught sight of Greyson. He spoke with a soldier, arms crossed, nodding seriously at whatever was said. With measured steps, Cyrus trudged across the open expanse.

When he got closer, Greyson scowled. "What the hell are you doing?"

He did not respond as he took in every detail of Greyson's face. The swelling had gone down in his left eye, and his nose appeared marginally better. Greyson stalked toward him, right leg dragging oddly. He stood right in front of Cyrus, frowning. Cyrus could not stop himself as he went up on his toes to kiss Greyson.

It surprised him when Greyson returned it instead of pulling away. It lasted hardly any time before Greyson swore. "Damn it. I hate my split lip. If it healed already, I could kiss you properly."

"I would like that."

"Hmm," Greyson said, not letting go of his cheeks.

Cyrus looked from side to side. People outright ogled them. "People are staring."

"That's because I'm kissing my supposed enemy. Widow Jones blabbed all over town that I'm in love with you, but no one believed her."

"Ah." Cyrus was slightly hurt, even though it wasn't Greyson's fault.

Greyson yanked his face closer, kissing him again, fiercely. Cyrus groaned and carefully placed his free hand on Greyson's hip. After a few moments, Greyson moved back again.

"Now, I'm going to yell at you for coming outside while you're injured without even a cloak," Greyson snapped.

"You were gone," he exclaimed.

"Getting us food. It's the middle of the afternoon. You slept forever," Greyson yelled back, still holding his cheeks.

Cyrus grinned. He liked this. Unable to stop himself, he said, "I love you."

With a shake of his head, Greyson said, "I love you too. Now, let's go inside."

Greyson led him back toward the house. Cyrus' teeth started to chatter, and his nose ran as he hunched his shoulders. Greyson kept peering at him with a deep frown. Even with his pronounced limp, he quickly scaled the stairs.

Taking the staff, Greyson said, "You should've waited for me or at least put on a cloak."

He couldn't respond because his teeth would not stop chattering. Greyson leaned his staff in the corner, then unbuckled the sword from around Cyrus's waist. Cyrus stared at the ceiling and silently counted, trying not to think of where Greyson's hands were. Greyson scoffed and set the sword in the corner before pushing Cyrus next to the fire.

"Next time," Greyson said, "if you want to go outside, wear these." He held up a fur-lined vest and gloves. "Also a cloak. That's why I had them made for you."

Even with his chattering teeth, he smiled as warmth that had nothing to do with the fire seeped into him. "T-those ar-re mine?"

Greyson stiffly sat in front of him, clutching his stomach. "Yes."

Cyrus grinned.

"Now, there are things we need to discuss."

"Like what?" he asked.

"First, you need to write to Emperor Caspian. Lord Darius sent a letter before you came to. I also sent a letter. Well, I gave it to Widow Jones to send to my friend Frederick who will give it to the emperor, as I doubt he would read anything from me. But you sending something would be best."

He agreed. His uncle would listen to him more than anyone else. Also, Cyrus didn't want Lord Darius' twisted words to be the only account the emperor heard because his uncle would undoubtedly dismiss almost anything Greyson said.

"Second, I need to look at your injuries," Greyson said.

Almost immediately, Cyrus opened his mouth to protest, but Greyson merely held up a hand.

"It has to be done, Cyrus. Besides, I've taken care of you before."

A blush rushed to his cheeks. He could not exactly explain why it embarrassed him to have Greyson care for his wounds, but it did.

"Third, we'll eat lunch. Then lastly, you need to take a nap."

"I just woke up."

"I am aware. But having your memory erased, then subsequently restored is taxing, and you need sleep."

"Will you nap with me?".

"Of course. I'm ridiculously sore and would not mind sleeping."

"Okay." Cyrus reached forward to grab Greyson's hand. He played with his long fingers as a wide grin stretched over his lips. It was ridiculous how happy he was. He'd wanted this for eight years, dreamed about it almost constantly, and now, he finally had it. It felt unreal, like a dream that would shatter at any moment, and Cyrus would wake up alone.

Greyson squeezed his hand before standing with a deep grimace. He set out a sheet of paper, quill, and inkwell, and Cyrus got to his feet and sat at the table. He hesitated as he thought about what to say. What would appease the emperor? Even as he contemplated it, a cloying fear cropped up in his mind. His uncle would want Cyrus to come back to the capital, but that would mean leaving Greyson behind, something he was unwilling to do.

Slowly, Cyrus scratched out the letter, the black ink flowing over the page with ease. He kept his story short and succinct. He did insist that the emperor recall Lord Darius and perhaps station him to the tower with the monks, and he also put himself up as a replacement.

The only part he did elaborate on was him and Greyson. He triumphantly told his uncle that he'd succeeded in winning the elusive mage's affections. Cyrus also added that if the emperor wanted him to come home, then the banishment order and bounty on Greyson should be lifted.

He sealed the letter, then addressed it before looking at Greyson, who sat on the other side of the table, watching him. With a blush staining his cheeks, Cyrus stated, "I'm done."

"Excellent. Now, it's time to look at your injuries."

The whole process was far less embarrassing than he thought it would be, as Greyson remained clinical. Greyson methodically cleaned the wounds, then applied a foul-smelling paste before rebinding them. When he finished, he helped Cyrus put back on his shirt and trousers.

"Can I see your side?" Cyrus asked.

Greyson shrugged and lifted his shirt with a deep grimace. Cyrus could not stop the slight gasp that escaped. Greyson's left side was colored in different shades of purple. Standing, Cyrus gently touched the bruises, only to yank back when Greyson sharply inhaled.

"Are you okay?"

"I'll be fine," Greyson answered, dropping his shirt.

"How about your leg?"

"I'm not exactly sure what they did to it, but it's not broken, and it's already feeling a bit better."

Nodding, he bit his lip. He wanted to kiss Greyson yet again, something Cyrus had begun to suspect was going to become a normal thing. When he focused on Greyson, he paused. Greyson watched him, seemingly transfixed. Greyson's gaze had locked on his lips while he went stock-still.

Slowly, Cyrus sucked his bottom lip in and watched as Greyson leaned closer like he wanted to investigate where it had disappeared. Letting his lip go, Cyrus grinned in amusement, which made Greyson scowl.

His long fingers closed about Cyrus' chin as Greyson said, "You have to stop doing that."

"Why?"

"Because I find it very distracting."

"Do you?" Cyrus moved closer.

"Yes." Shaking his head, he said, "Let me make lunch."

As Greyson started to make food, Cyrus stared at him, not even trying to stop. Greyson limped from one end of the kitchen to the other, movements precise and graceful. After a while, he placed two plates on the table with bread, cooked vegetables, and some kind of meat.

They both remained silent as they ate, lost in their thoughts. The food was delicious, and Cyrus enjoyed it immensely. He also loved to stare at Greyson, who in turn, stared back. As soon as he finished, Greyson swept the plates up and stacked them in the kitchen.

"Come on," Greyson said, coming to stand in front of him.

"Should I lay behind you like last night?"

"I would appreciate it."

He climbed into the bed first, back near the wall, and lay on his side. Greyson came next, moving slowly with a deep grimace. Gingerly, he settled on his back and repositioned with quiet cries. Cyrus pushed an arm under his neck and helped Greyson lean against his chest.

"Are you okay?" he asked.

"Yes," Greyson grunted, voice tight.

Gently, Cyrus draped an arm over Greyson's chest. "We could try a snow pack on your side to help with the pain."

"Yes, but you couldn't lay behind me. You'd freeze."

"True, but it could help."

"Just stay close, Cyrus. I'm fine."

After a pause, Cyrus pushed his face against Greyson's neck. "Please tell me this is real. That this is not a ruse or a lie."

"This is real."

# 30

CYRUS

"Mmm," Cyrus groaned as Greyson ran his long fingers through his hair.

"I'm checking your head for injuries and soft spots. You're supposed to be telling me if something hurts," Greyson said from behind him.

When he started to withdraw his fingers, Cyrus lied, "Wait, that kind of hurt."

Greyson continued to explore his head, carefully examining him before the purposeful movements transformed into a general massage. Greyson's fingers worked gentle circles over his scalp, and Cyrus couldn't help the appreciative moan that slipped from his lips as he pressed into Greyson. Well, he tried to. The back of the chair blocked him from Greyson's warm chest. Greyson chuckled as his fingers slid away.

Cyrus moaned in protest, but Greyson did not go far, his fingers sliding down and began rubbing his neck, then his un-injured shoulder. Cyrus groaned again. He liked this. The fre-quent touching and conversations they'd been having. More discussions were needed to clear the air between the two of them, but he couldn't help but enjoy these simple moments.

Greyson's fingers worked on his uninjured shoulder, then moved down his back, massaging him. Sighing in content-ment, Cyrus leaned forward to give him more access.

"You're like a cat," Greyson commented, and Cyrus didn't bother to deny it.

Only a few days had passed, and already, Cyrus' head felt so much better. The pain had completely disappeared. The cuts on his side and thigh had scabbed nicely and healed to the point Greyson no longer worried about them. He continued to fuss over the stab wound in his shoulder. Greyson nagged Cyrus, almost incessantly, about not straining the muscles and giving them adequate time to heal.

After a few minutes, Greyson pulled away.

"Where are you going?" he asked.

Greyson didn't answer and asked instead, "Are you feeling okay?"

"Yes."

Smiling, Greyson pulled a chair across from Cyrus and sat down, rather stiffly. Days had passed, but Greyson contin-ued to limp and clutch his side. The swelling around his left eye had almost completely disappeared, and his split lip had healed well. Whatever damage the soldiers had done to his side and knee had been significant, though Greyson rarely complained.

As Cyrus stared at him, anger welled in his chest. Lord Darius was at fault. He hadn't done anything since he'd been confined to his home, but Cyrus doubted they'd heard the last from Darius. The captain of the guard bore no love for the lord and seemed content to take Cyrus' orders, though he watched the soldiers closely.

In the interim, until his uncle named him or another as a representative, he'd taken over the duties. In some ways, it made his life easier. Like this home he and Greyson had been staying in, he simply had Widow Jones bill the estate for rent, and he paid her. The same for any food they needed. But he'd been busier than he liked the last couple of days and hadn't got to see Greyson as much as he wanted. On the other hand, Greyson remained practical and shrugged it off.

Cyrus looked at Greyson who sat across from him. He simply watched Cyrus with a slight smile, sipping some tea. Greyson did love his tea.

"You're limping pretty badly," Cyrus said.

"My leg, mainly my knee, is not happy. I think one of the soldiers dislocated it, so the tendons are stretched. I'm hopeful it will heal."

With a frown, he crossed his arms and leaned back in the wooden chair, making it creak. "I can't believe you won't tell me which soldiers hurt you."

"They were following orders, and I will be fine."

Cyrus glared at him.

"I know you would punish them unduly. I promise I will be alright, Cyrus."

He wanted to argue with Greyson, yet at the same time, he didn't. Their relationship rested on the edge of a knife. It was precarious at best. Cyrus and Greyson hadn't discussed anything of the past, but it hung between them like a tangible wall. Yet neither of them seemed able or wanted to cross it.

Cyrus feared the instant one of them did, their fragile relationship would fall to pieces. Because what did they have to bind them together? Nothing tangible. Cyrus had years of one-sided love, and Greyson had a new-found love with a Cyrus who didn't remember the past. It was like they both just waited for a breeze to blow their relationship apart. To salvage it, they both tiptoed around everything that would divide them.

"I better go. I promised some of the kids I would teach them a couple of spells while I'm here," Greyson remarked as he rose with a slight moan.

"I wish you'd relax."

"I'm fine," Greyson said in a clipped tone.

Greyson fussed over him non-stop, but when Cyrus tried to do the same, Greyson would push him away. "I'm allowed to be worried about you."

"I didn't say you couldn't worry. I merely said 'I'm fine' because I am." Greyson did not even glance at him as he limped to his staff that leaned in the far corner.

Scrubbing a hand through his hair, Cyrus asked, "Would you stop?"

"For what?" Greyson growled.

Cyrus jerked back. Blinking, he swallowed the sudden emotion that clawed at his throat. Greyson had barked at him before, and Cyrus had shrugged it off, but this time, it felt like he was rejecting him.

"No—ugh," Greyson said, placing the staff in the corner again before he limped to Cyrus. Greyson bumped Cyrus' chin up. Greyson's brows had formed a slash across his forehead. "I'm sorry," he whispered before gently kissing him. "I'm sorry. I don't mean to be as harsh as I sound. I shouldn't have snapped at you."

"Why won't you let me take care of you?"

Greyson closed his eyes as his face scrunched, hand falling to his side.

Cyrus took Greyson's hands. "As much as you fuss over me, I want to do the same thing to you."

"I know."

"So why?"

Greyson stared at him for several moments, swallowing. "I'm not used to it. My family died when I was fourteen. I took care of others, taught them, healed them, and later fought for them. I take care of other people; they don't take care of me."

He grasped Greyson's cheeks as he stood. "I can understand that, but I need to be able to take care of you when you're hurt."

Greyson's jaw clenched, then worked side to side as he blinked several times.

"I love you," he said. "You're going to have to get used to me fussing over you because I'm not going to stop taking care of you, Greyson. For the rest of our lives, I'm going to take care of you while you take care of me."

"Do you promise?"

"Yes," Cyrus answered, wholeheartedly.

Greyson kissed him firmly. Cyrus kept hold of Greyson's cheeks as he returned the kiss, slowly. With steady movements, he tried to ease whatever anxieties Greyson possessed about the future or their relationship. Cyrus would be here. Nothing could tear him from Greyson's side.

He put a hand on Greyson's hip and carefully pulled him until they were flush against each other. Greyson groaned, tongue pushing into his mouth. Cyrus opened his mouth wider. Greyson grasped the edge of Cyrus' shirt. Cyrus lifted his arms so he could remove it with no resistance. Greyson's fingers slid down his back, skimming over his muscles. He moaned, leaning closer. Gently, Cyrus directed him toward the bed.

When the backs of Greyson's knees hit the bed frame, Cyrus helped him lay down, then crawled on, hovering over him on all fours. He was careful not to place any weight on Greyson, as he was recovering from broken ribs. Putting most of his weight on his elbows, ignoring the twinge in his shoulder, Cyrus kissed Greyson again. Greyson explored his chest, his fingers tracing the lines of Cyrus' muscles.

Sweat gathered on his forehead as Cyrus began to tug off Greyson's shirt. Hands stopped the movement.

"No," Greyson said calmly.

"What?"

"We're not having sex."

Cyrus' breath came out in uneven bursts. "I didn't think we were. I just wanted to kiss your chest."

"Oh." His pale cheeks pinked delightfully.

"For curiosity's sake, why not?"

"First," Greyson started, which made Cyrus smile. He had always liked to list things off, even when they were teenagers. "I'm in too much pain."

That made sense.

"Second, I've never done this with another man, and I need time."

Nodding again, Cyrus said, "You can have as much time as you need. I don't want you to be uncomfortable."

"Thank you," Greyson said, smiling softly at him before continuing, "Third, I need to get to know you better. I love you, Cyrus. But we don't know each other very well yet."

"I agree," Cyrus said. "I want to know everything about you."

"As do I."

GREYSON

Cyrus rested on one elbow as he touched Greyson's cheek. Cyrus' fingers wandered over his face, coming close to his scar before skittering away. He never looked at it or touched it, which Greyson found almost amusing because when Cyrus had no memories, he often kissed or touched it.

Maybe it had been familiar? Greyson didn't know.

When Cyrus' fingers traced his face again, avoiding the right side, Greyson caught his hand and placed it directly over the scar. "You can touch it."

Cyrus swallowed as his eyes darted to the side. Greyson could easily interpret the expression as disgust, but he *knew* it wasn't that. It was shame.

"I'm not mad at you, and I don't blame you anymore."

"How could you not?"

"Because we were in the middle of a battle, trying to kill each other, and you spared my life," Greyson replied. Cyrus still wouldn't look at him. "I remember your face, and the horror I saw there. Even when I hated you, I knew you hadn't wanted to kill me. Oddly enough, I dreaded meeting you."

He shook his head, blonde hair falling in front of his eyes. "I should've stopped it."

"What? The rebellion?"

Cyrus nodded.

"While I can't condone what your uncle did, there are things I'm ashamed about. Actions I wish I could take back. But we can't. You and I alone are not plagued by nightmares, Cyrus. The war wasn't won or lost on our backs, even when it feels like that. You have to let it go."

"How?"

"One step at a time," Greyson said. "I think you and I will be hashing things out to our graves, but try to let things go. Right now, you can forgive yourself for my eye. I don't blame you. I'm not mad at you. And you can touch it."

Slowly, almost hesitantly, Cyrus' fingers moved along the scar, tracing it from tip to end. A contented sigh escaped Greyson's lips as his other eye fluttered closed. He felt a gentle pressure on his cheek as Cyrus kissed the scar, moving up the length of it. When he reached the tip, a breathy laugh rushed over Greyson's forehead.

"I love you," Cyrus said.

"I love you too."

Gently, Cyrus kissed his forehead until reaching the spot between Greyson's eyebrows. "I love the wrinkle you have here."

"I imagine when I'm old it will turn deep with all the scowling I do."

"True."

Cyrus kissed the bridge of his nose. "You always pinch your nose here when I've said something stupid or you're thinking."

"Yes."

He continued exploring, kissing Greyson and remarking on the different things he loved until Cyrus reached his mouth once again. Firmly, Cyrus kissed him before saying, "One step at a time."

Greyson nodded. "One step at a time."

Lips on his, Cyrus claimed him with firm movements and quick thrusts of his tongue, and Greyson ran his fingers over his back, enjoying the feel of his skin. He was perfect. Ignoring the persistent ache between his legs, Greyson traced every inch of Cyrus' exposed skin. Cyrus groaned in response, growling through clenched teeth, "Greyson."

With a smile, Greyson brushed light kisses along his strong jaw. He never wanted this moment to end.

Someone pounded on the door, and Cyrus leaped off, swearing as his chest heaved. "What the hell?"

"Greyson," Jessica called from the other side of the door. "What's taking so long?"

He'd completely forgotten about his promise. "The kids," he said, trying to calm his racing heart. "I promised to teach them."

"That's right." Cyrus glanced at him, then blushed profusely as his eyes landed on Greyson's lap.

Greyson frowned. He was going to need a minute. "Jessica," he yelled. "I'll be right there."

Even through the door, he heard the teenager huff. "Fine." She tramped down the stairs, stomping.

Cyrus peeked at him, and Greyson could stop the chuckle that built in his chest. It took no time at all for Cyrus to join in. He rose and wrapped his arms around Cyrus. "I'll be back later."

Hugging him carefully, he said, "Alright."

31

GREYSON

A scream tore through the air, jerking Greyson awake. His heart raced as his gaze darted around the dark room. He could not see much because the dwindling fire let off very little light. A moan came from behind him as Cyrus' arms clamped around his stomach. A vicious stabbing started in his ribs and stole his very breath. His mouth opened, and tears burned his eyes. Greyson tried to contain his cry, but it came out as a strangled whimper.

He grabbed Cyrus' arm, but he did not wake as more distressed sounds came from behind Greyson. Taking a shuddering breath, he said, "Cyrus."

Cyrus' arms tightened around him, which made Greyson grunt. "Cyrus," he tried again, patting his arm. "Wake up."

Cyrus started, gasping.

Greyson continued to pat his arm, which held him in a stranglehold. "Cyrus, love, you're hurting me."

Slowly, the pressure around his ribs loosened, and Greyson breathed a sigh of relief as tears coursed down his cheeks. Every breath felt like a knife stabbed his ribs, but it began to lessen when Cyrus released him.

Cyrus remained utterly motionless, muscles rigid against Greyson's back. Greyson held his hand. "You're alright. It was just a dream."

"Greyson?"

"Yes, love, I'm right here."

A gush of warm air rushed over the nape of his neck. Cyrus asked slowly, "We're together?"

Worry prickled along his spine, but he answered the question, "Yes."

"The war is over?"

"Yes."

Cyrus pressed his face against Greyson's neck, trembling. "It was a dream."

He stroked Cyrus' arm, trying to soothe the tension. "Just a dream."

This was the one thing he missed from when Cyrus had no memories because there had been nothing to haunt him, for the most part. Greyson wished he could banish the nightmares, but they would both be plagued with them for the rest of their lives.

"I'm sorry," Cyrus whispered.

"For what?"

"For hurting you."

"I'm fine," Greyson said, and it was the truth.

Cyrus pressed closer to Greyson.

His fingers continued to trail up and down Cyrus' arm in an attempt to soothe him, but it didn't seem to work. Greyson didn't know how to help Cyrus. They were in a relationship, but he couldn't do anything.

Greyson tried to roll over to at least see Cyrus. His ribs squeezed and stole his breath, but he ignored it. Cyrus gripped his hips and helped Greyson rearrange until he was on his back. Cyrus shoved one arm under his neck and leaned over him, brushing Greyson's cheek.

Greyson asked, "What can I do?"

"Can you take them?"

Pausing, he asked, "What?"

"My memories."

"Yes," Greyson replied, swallowing.

"Would you?"

"No."

"Why?"

Holding his dear face, Greyson said, "I couldn't just take the bad memories, Cyrus. I would have to take everything."

"We would still be together."

"Yes, but I won't do it."

"Why?" Cyrus asked again, his eyes glassy. "You loved me before with no memories. It wouldn't change anything."

"Besides the very practical reason that the emperor would kill me, I wouldn't do it anyway. I know what it's like to have dreams so real you wake up thinking you're back on the battlefield, but I wouldn't ask another mage to erase all my memories because of them. I wouldn't want to forget my family, forget my friends, or forget falling in love with you for the bad memories to be gone. I love you, Cyrus. All of you. And there are things I *know* you don't want to forget, and there are things I don't want you to forget."

Cyrus pressed his forehead against Greyson's. "Sometimes I think it would be worth it."

"As do I, but after careful consideration, I always reject the idea."

"I wouldn't want to forget you again."

"Nor would I."

Cyrus rubbed against his forehead, breathing deeply. It was the after-effects of the nightmare that made Cyrus more emotional than usual, but Greyson liked comforting him.

"Sorry," Cyrus said.

"Don't apologize."

Gently, Cyrus kissed him. Greyson wrapped his arms around Cyrus' neck and held him close. He wanted to comfort him, to let Cyrus know he was not alone.

CYRUS

Cyrus nodded at the soldiers, then walked away, stretching his shoulder. He hadn't practiced swordplay yet because Greyson told him not to strain the muscles in his shoulder, but he did meet with the captain almost every day to make sure Lord Darius didn't cause any trouble. So far, the lord had remained quiet.

The weather was cold as usual, and the sky was clear. Even though Cyrus wore multiple layers, the frigid air nipped at him. He couldn't wait to go inside and warm up. Hopefully, Greyson would be there as well.

As his thoughts turned to Greyson, Cyrus couldn't help but think about last night. Dreams of the war were common occurrences for him. But last night, he'd dreamed of Greyson, just out of reach while the battle raged on. When he finally got to him, Greyson attacked him. Cyrus kept trying to explain, but it didn't matter. He would not listen.

Then Greyson had woken him up. They were in bed together, completely safe. Cyrus couldn't believe he'd asked Greyson to take his memories. It wasn't something he would normally request, as he didn't want to forget, but at that moment, all he wanted was for the bad memories to disappear.

He'd been deeply embarrassed this morning, but Greyson had treated him no different, kissing Cyrus senseless before he left. That had buried all of the embarrassment.

Shaking his head, Cyrus banished the thoughts of last night as he crossed the square toward the home he and Greyson currently resided in. As he was about to round the corner, he stopped, seeing a familiar figure. Greyson stood in front of a group of children in the middle of the barren road. He demonstrated a motion with his staff as he spoke. Then Greyson whipped his staff at a snowball. The snowball shot off at the closest building, breaking apart.

The children hooted, clapping. Greyson organized them into a line and pointed at the snowballs not far from them. The children flung out their hands, trying to imitate the smooth, whip-like motion. None of the snowballs even twitched, except for Jessica's. Magic curled around the snowball, making it fling into the distance.

Nonetheless, Greyson clapped for them. Jessica made another snowball before standing in line with the other children. They tried again and again. It took several attempts for most of the children to be able to complete the spell. Each time, Greyson applauded them and corrected their movements until, finally, all the children mastered the great technique of magically throwing a snowball.

Cyrus had no idea what the spell could be good for besides driving other children and their parents crazy, but Greyson beamed at them like a proud father. Cyrus moved closer to the group, clapping. Greyson and the children swiveled toward him. Greyson smiled brightly, which made him pause in his step. His smile came so easily now, and each one was like a delicacy that demanded to be savored.

Jessica waved, shoving her tousled braid over her shoulder, while the other children hid behind Greyson. That small action hurt, but Cyrus could understand it.

Greyson limped in his direction, practically dragging his right leg. When he reached Cyrus, Greyson grabbed his cheeks and kissed him, not embarrassed or shy about the people around them.

After a moment, Greyson shifted back because a boy of about seven with an unruly thatch of brown hair tugged on his cloak. "What, Aaron?"

"Why are you kissing Prince Cyrus?" the child asked, his light brown eyes darting to Cyrus.

"Because he's my boyfriend."

"Oh." Aaron then looked at Cyrus, face scrunching. "Does he have magic?"

"No," Greyson answered.

"That's stupid."

Cyrus' mouth fell open as he glanced at Aaron, then Greyson. "I'm a very skilled warrior."

"Still not as cool as being a mage," Aaron argued.

"It is. Tell him, Greyson," he said, nudging him.

"I'm not getting involved in this fight," Greyson said with a shake of his head.

Cyrus crossed his arms.

Greyson kissed his cheek before saying, "Cyrus is very talented and awesome."

"If you say so," Aaron remarked dubiously.

Before Cyrus could reply, Greyson said to the children, "I will teach you more spells tomorrow. Go bother your parents."

They started to complain, but he kept shooing them with a wave of his hands.

When the children dispersed, Cyrus said, "I'm just as cool as a mage."

"Sure," Greyson said, arms going over Cyrus' shoulders. "I can set stuff on fire, uproot trees, fling large rocks, and summon lighting, but you're just as awesome."

He opened his mouth to protest, but Greyson laughed. A loud, real laugh. Cyrus' heart pounded at the sound. Greyson leaned forward and said, "I'm teasing, Cyrus. I think you're very cool."

"I knew it."

Greyson laughed again.

The next morning, Cyrus jolted awake as Greyson got up. "Where are you going?" he asked sleepily as he peered out the window. The sky had just started to lighten. "It's early."

"I promised to teach the kids some new spells."

"So?"

"Jessica cornered me yesterday evening, and I mistakenly promised to teach her how to create a mage fire."

"You did what?" Cyrus asked, sitting up. Mage fire burned hotter than a normal fire, and it was much harder to extinguish.

"Nothing to worry about," Greyson said with a wave. "I'll teach them how to control it."

"*Them?*"

"Well, I assume the other kids will want to come along."

Cyrus gaped. "Let me get this right. You are going to teach a group of children how to create mage fire in the middle of the village square?"

"Don't be ridiculous. I'm going to take them to a clearing not far from here."

"Greyson," he groaned.

"Stop worrying. I have taught many, *many* people how to do this. I know what I'm doing."

Unable to stop himself, he sighed, brow furrowing. He wanted to believe Greyson, but mage fire was exceedingly dangerous.

"Fine," Greyson snapped. "If you're so worried, you can come with me."

"Really?" Cyrus asked, perking up.

"Of course."

When they exited their apartment, a group of children were gathered by the stairs, led by Jessica.

"Well, I won't have to search for you," Greyson commented as he walked toward them, leaning heavily on his staff. Greyson's leg was not healing right, but he kept brushing it off.

Coming to Greyson's side, Cyrus lifted his right arm across his shoulders, supporting him. "Where to?"

"This way," Greyson replied, pointing with his staff.

As a group, they tramped across the snow and out of the village. Cyrus' breath came out in a cloud as the cold dug into his skin. Ignoring it, he foraged on with Greyson's arm over a shoulder and an arm hooked about his waist, careful not to squeeze his ribs. They strode under the pine boughs for about fifteen minutes until they came to a wide open space with a few boulders and surrounded by snow-laden trees.

"Perfect," Greyson said.

Pulling away from Cyrus, he lined the children up and began to explain the process of mage fire, some of which Cyrus already knew, like the fact that mage fire needed no fuel. Greyson showed them the motion required—a quick jab with the dominant hand.

Magic was a bit of a mystery to Cyrus, as no one had explained it. Cyrus knew bits and pieces. Mages were born with magic and could use magic even unbound to an artifact, but were much stronger once bound. The artifact would absorb the magic the mage didn't use and store it for later. But the danger was if the artifact broke, the mage could never use magic again.

What Cyrus was unsure about was the actual use of spells. From what he'd seen, it depended on the capability of the mage, whether they used that type of magic, and the repetition of movements.

While Greyson could fling his hand and produce a spell with no trouble, seeing these children assured Cyrus this wasn't always the case.

Greyson had the children practice the quick jab over and over again while he heavily leaned on his staff. Once satisfied, he had them try it. None of the children succeeded on the first or second or even tenth attempt. Greyson remained patient, correcting the movements and offering advice about channeling their magic.

A little girl of about four soon caught Cyrus' attention. She had the most serious face. Every time she punched forward with her pudgy fist, she would make a low growl, chin jutting out. Chuckling, Cyrus glanced at Greyson to see if he noticed. Greyson smiled at the little girl before his gaze moved to Cyrus, eyebrows raised. He couldn't help but laugh.

After a bit, Greyson told them to stop. Aaron crossed his arms and sank to the ground, the image of discouragement.

"You'll all get it. It takes time and practice. Visualize the magic traveling down your arm, growing warmer as it goes, then becoming a blazing fire on your fingertips."

When none of them, not even Jessica responded, Greyson waved him forward. Cyrus came to his side, and Greyson gave him the staff. "Watch, Cyrus can't do it either."

The kids grinned while Cyrus frowned. He wasn't a mage. He would never be able to create mage fire, even if he stood there the rest of his life. The staff vibrated under his fingertips. Cyrus, knowing he was being played the fool, jabbed the staff forward, and lo and behold, nothing happened.

All of the kids giggled, no doubt Greyson's intention, and tried again.

Greyson draped an arm around his shoulders. "Thanks, love."

He tried to give the staff back, but Greyson refused it. Cyrus smiled, staring at the ground, warmed by the show of trust. Slowly, they were making their way to each other and setting the past behind them—where it belonged.

Only Jessica and one other child were able to produce mage fire. Once they did, Greyson showed them how to put out the said fire, which took a bit. Cyrus watched the roaring flames warily as he frequently glanced at the pine trees. He'd seen firsthand how fast they caught alight. But Greyson had it under control, and his students got the fire out after a few minutes.

"Excellent," he said.

"But I couldn't do it," Aaron complained.

Greyson limped over to the boy. "Maybe fire is not your skill. What about rocks?"

"I like rocks," Aaron immediately shouted.

"Good." Greyson bent down next to Aaron and pointed to a stone, maybe the size of a child's fist. "Why don't you roll that rock?"

"How?"

He demonstrated a fancy twisting, flourish as he flipped his left hand over. Aaron watched a couple of times before he lifted his right hand which had a bracelet with blackish-purple stones and tried to move the rock. It took a few times, but eventually, the rock lifted up on its side, then flopped over. Aaron crowed in victory, jumping up and down.

"Excellent job, Aaron," Greyson said.

"Can you move that stone?" Jessica asked, pointing at a massive, snow-covered boulder.

Cyrus' eyebrows shot up as he looked between Greyson and the rock that was easily twice as tall as him and a good deal broader.

"You want me to show off," he said, staring at Jessica, who innocently twirled her perpetually messy braid around her finger. Frowning, Greyson said, "Fine."

Greyson trudged toward him, but when Cyrus held out the staff, he shook his head. "Why doesn't Cyrus help me?"

"What?" he asked at the same time Jessica did.

Smirking, Greyson came behind Cyrus and grasped the staff right below his hand. "Don't worry," Greyson whispered against his ear. Magic pulsated under Cyrus' fingers and down his arm, making his hair raise. Greyson lifted the staff in a slow arc, then prodded toward the stone. The boulder shivered, snow sliding off, before it slowly rose.

An ocean of magic poured under Cyrus' skin, making his breath turn sharp as his limbs quivered. Until that instant, he hadn't understood the breadth of Greyson's magic and just how powerful he truly was.

The boulder continued to lazily rise, did a couple of twirls in the air, then settled back in its place.

Cheers sounded as the kids exclaimed and clapped. Greyson smiled at them, but Cyrus felt him start to tremble. Shifting, Greyson wrapped an arm around Cyrus' waist and said, "Jessica, why don't you take them back? I think I'm going to stroll leisurely with my boyfriend."

The teenager rolled her eyes but complied. She gathered the gaggle of children, taking the two youngests' hands in hers, then strode off.

As soon as the group moved out of sight, Greyson dropped his arm, shaking, and bent over as his breath came out in quick gasps.

"Are you okay?" Cyrus asked, brushing the hair out of his face.

"No, I haven't used that much magic recently. I'm getting soft."

Cyrus ran his eyes up and down Greyson's tight form. "I don't see it."

"Magically speaking. It's like regular muscles, you have to keep working at it and using it or it fades."

"Well, I was impressed."

"I'm glad," he said, "but I've got to start practicing more."

32

GREYSON

Greyson glared at Cyrus who sat at the table, reading paperwork, while the fire cheerily burned behind him. He'd been in bed the last couple of days because Widow Jones happened to catch a glimpse of him dragging his leg. The old woman immediately yelled at him. It had been a long conversation, which Cyrus got involved in because the old widow got so upset about it. Long story short, Greyson had to stay off his leg and ice his knee and side.

Boredom had almost immediately set in. He was unused to inaction. At home, he hunted, foraged, made poultices and potions, taught people, helped in the village, and did a myriad of other tasks. But now, Greyson had to remain in bed and do nothing.

Glancing at Cyrus, Greyson smirked. He gripped his staff, which was on the bed next to him, and flicked it, scattering the papers Cyrus read across the table and onto the floor.

"Seriously? That's the third time, Greyson. I'm going to come over there and take your staff," Cyrus said, collecting the reports.

"I'm bored."

"I am aware. You're lucky I can work from this room, so you don't have to be in here alone."

He stared at the ceiling, his side and knee throbbing. A chair scraped on the floor followed by the sound of bare feet padding over the wood floor. Something bumped the bed and made it shift. Greyson looked to the side, and Cyrus stood next to him.

"We could do a snow pack on your side."

"Yay," he said with obvious sarcasm.

"You make a horrible patient, you know that?"

Chuckling, he said, "I know."

Cyrus shook his head, but humor danced in his eyes. "I'll be right back."

Greyson watched as Cyrus donned his boots, gloves, and cloak, then went outside. A couple of minutes later, he set the bag filled with snow on the ground.

Pulling his gloves off, Cyrus said, "Let me help you onto your side." Cyrus was gentle, but shifting of any kind hurt terribly. Breath coming out in short gasps, Greyson settled on his side. Cyrus brushed the black hair back and asked, "Are you okay?"

He nodded, unable to speak.

Cyrus draped a towel over his injured side, then slowly lowered the snow-filled bag onto him. Greyson inhaled sharply. It always burned at first, but it would help in the end. Cyrus carefully arranged the snow, in what used to be a pillowcase, until it spread over his injured ribs.

"Is that okay?"

"Yes." The snow chilled Greyson and got the bed wet, but after two days of careful treatment, his knee and ribs had started to feel better.

"After we do this to your knee, I can make you some willow bark tea," Cyrus said. Greyson's nose crinkled, and Cyrus laughed. "Fine, I can ask Widow Jones to make you some willow bark tea."

"That would be much better. I thought I would die the last time you made it."

"I don't have your cooking skills."

"Hmm, you did grow up in a palace."

"True, not much use for me to learn there," Cyrus said as he returned to the table to read the reports.

Yesterday, Cyrus read them out loud, which Greyson did not enjoy, but today, he seemed content to keep the boring expenses and mining logs to himself. After about twenty minutes, Cyrus threw another log onto the already hot fire and picked up the dripping bag on Greyson's side.

"I'm going to refill this. Don't move until I get back. I'll help you resituate, alright?"

"Fine."

Greyson did not enjoy moving this time either, but his side hurt less. He didn't know if the ice actually helped his healing process or if his staying in bed doing nothing is what actually worked. Cyrus carefully lifted Greyson's right leg and squished a pillow under his knee before putting a fresh towel on his leg and resting the bag of snow on the injured joint.

Cyrus returned to the table, and Greyson could not help but marvel at him. Cyrus had healed so much faster because of magic. His two cuts and head injury had vanished completely, without even a trace of a scar. While the stab wound in his shoulder had closed up, Greyson worried that the muscles and tendons were not fully healed, but Cyrus acted as if his shoulder didn't bother him. It grated on Greyson that he was the only one in need of care, even though Cyrus did not mind taking care of him.

He hadn't told Cyrus about Lily, the little girl that saved his life, because Greyson had promised Widow Jones not to say anything. The empire had taken Greyson's mother because of her healing ability, and she wouldn't have been able to save Cyrus. Widow Jones had a right to fear for her great-granddaughter.

Nevertheless, he would forever be grateful. Cyrus would not have lived without the child's assistance.

About twenty minutes later, Cyrus removed the bag, setting it aside. His blue eyes fell to Greyson's knee. "How does it feel?"

"Better."

"I'm glad," Cyrus said. "Did you want some willow bark tea?"

"If you don't mind."

"I don't mind at all."

CYRUS

The weather, if possible, had grown even colder the last couple of days. Thick clouds coated the sky, and the wind whistled around the buildings. Shoulders to his ears, Cyrus tugged his cloak tighter against him and slowly walked down the stairs, careful not to slip on the frozen steps.

Striding around the building to where the front door was, Cyrus came to a sudden halt. A group of people rode up the steep path. Horses, wagons, and a carriage lumbered toward the village. Cyrus moved toward the square, trying to get a better view of the newcomers. A flag bearing a familiar crest flew above the group. With a slight smile, he waited as the group leisurely made their way into Woodhurst.

A man jumped out of the elaborate carriage. "Cyrus, I thought I would find you dead."

He grinned at Jasper, husband to his cousin, Jade. "It's good to see you."

His cousin enfolded him in a hug, squeezing him and slapping his back. "Cyrus, we thought Mage Greyson had killed you. What are you doing here?"

A laugh broke out of his lips as Cyrus studied his friend. Jasper was about an inch taller than him, broad-shouldered with blonde hair a shade or two lighter than his own. His warm brown skin glowed with health while his pale green eyes remained on Cyrus.

While Jasper was not traditionally handsome with his narrow features, he was by no means unattractive. When Jasper had first been arranged to marry Jade, he'd been slightly jealous because he found Jasper attractive, but in the end, it wouldn't have mattered, as Cyrus couldn't let go of Greyson.

"It's a long story," Cyrus said.

"I'll bet. You stopped writing months ago," Jasper replied. "Why are you here? Oh, did Greyson attempt to kill you and you had to go to Lord Darius?"

"No, Greyson didn't," he said. "I will explain everything, but Lord Darius is currently confined to his home. I sent Uncle a letter with the details a little over a week ago."

"Not that I like Darius," Jasper said, crossing his arms, "but why is he confined?"

"Illegal possession of poison, which I didn't tell Uncle about, lying to me, and not assisting me when my life was threatened or when I was injured. I don't think this is a good placement for him."

Jasper ran a hand through his short hair, making it stick up in places. "Nowhere is a good placement for him." Staring at him, he asked, "You didn't tell the emperor about the poison because Greyson made it, didn't he?"

"Yes."

"You have to stop protecting him," Jasper said loudly, hands waving. "The mage is never going to like you back."

Cyrus was anticipating *that* revelation.

"I assume I can't stay with Lord Darius, so where am I and my soldiers going to sleep?"

"I'll introduce you to the captain of the guard. He'll house your soldiers, then I'll ask around and see if one of the villagers will host you," Cyrus said.

"Everyone in the Griseo Mountains hates us, especially you."

"I'm growing on people."

Jasper raised his eyebrows.

He spoke the truth; people here had started to like him. The main, and he assumed only, reason was that Greyson loved him and willingly showed that in frequent displays of affection. The people of the Griseo Mountains would always follow Greyson, which was the reason why the emperor wanted to execute him.

After he got Jasper's soldiers sorted, he led him to the room Cyrus shared with Greyson.

"Where are we going?"

"I'm renting a room."

"So I'm going to stay with you?"

"No," Cyrus said with a snort. He didn't want to live with anyone besides Greyson nor did he want to share his time with Greyson.

As Cyrus opened the door, Greyson said, "It took you long enough."

33

CYRUS

Cyrus contained a giggle when Jasper caught sight of Greyson spread out on the bed. His cousin's mouth flopped open like a fish as his eyes bulged. Jasper looked between him and Greyson several times as he pointed at them.

Greyson stayed silent for a few moments before he finally said, "Prince Consort Jasper, it's nice to see you again, though it is a surprise."

"I'm a surprise?" Jasper asked, finally finding his voice.

"Yes," Greyson replied.

It took everything he possessed not to break down in a fit of laughter. Cyrus smirked as he peeked at Greyson, who appeared utterly calm. He'd won the elusive mage's love. No one, absolutely *no one*, thought he'd be able to do it.

"Cyrus, I know you're desperate and a bit crazy in love, but you can't keep Mage Greyson captive. It's illegal and not right. I'm gonna have to let him go," Jasper said in an even tone with his hands extended as if Cyrus had finally snapped.

"He's not captive!"

"I'm really not," Greyson added.

"Oh, well, you can't use love potions either. They have horrible side effects and aren't real, okay? I talked you down from that once already."

Heat rushed to his cheeks as Cyrus waved his hands, trying to stop Jasper from speaking further.

Greyson cackled behind him. "I'm not on a love potion. Did he really try to dose me?"

"Yes. I stopped him," Jasper answered unhelpfully.

"I can't believe you were crazy enough to try and dose me with a love potion," Greyson said, sniggering.

"It was a long time ago." Cyrus' cheeks burned. He'd thought, years ago, if he could get Greyson open to the idea of the two of them, he would continue to care about him after the love potion wore off. Jasper had told him the only thing Cyrus would get was a face full of mage fire.

"So I guess your secret is out," Jasper commented.

"Yes," Cyrus said, "Greyson knows I'm in love with him."

His cousin stared at Greyson, lips pursed. "You are not being held against your will?"

"I didn't say that," Greyson said, smirking. "But the ones holding me are Widow Jones, my hurt knee, and busted ribs."

"Did you hurt him?" Jasper asked Cyrus.

"No! I would never hurt Greyson."

"Lord Darius' soldiers beat me after I saved Cyrus' life."

"You saved Cyrus?" Jasper's eyebrows rose as he pointed at Greyson.

"Yes, he saved me."

Jasper looked between them, mouth open.

"He doesn't understand, love," Greyson said.

If possible, Jasper's eyebrows climbed even higher. "I'm sorry, what?"

Cyrus took Greyson's hand, their fingers interlacing. "Greyson and I are together."

"You and he are together?" Jasper asked, motioning between them.

"Yes."

"I need to sit down," he said, flopping onto a chair next to the table. "I can honestly say, I never saw that coming."

"Well, it surprised me too, but Cyrus is persistent," Greyson remarked, smirking.

Cyrus glared at Greyson, but that smug smirk remained firmly in place. Greyson tugged on his hand, and Cyrus complied with the silent request, sitting next to him. Greyson's head leaned against him as he breathed heavily.

"Are you in pain?" he asked quietly.

Greyson nodded.

"Maybe you should tell me exactly what happened?" Jasper asked, his eyes wide.

Cyrus began with leaving the capital but came to a stop when he reached the part where he arrived at the old battlefield. Greyson seamlessly picked the story up. He concisely related the events, not even leaving out the parts where he abandoned Cyrus to die or planned to poison him, which surprised Cyrus.

What Greyson didn't go into was exactly how they fell in love. Greyson hadn't been too clear on that matter with him either. As Greyson reached the end where Cyrus awoke with no memory of his time in the Griseo Mountains, he picked it back up.

Jasper remained quiet during the whole tale, hand on his chin.

When they finished, the room fell silent with only the occasional cracks and pops of the fire to break it. Jasper studied Greyson with narrowed eyes. Cyrus held Greyson's hand tightly, chin jutting out. He silently dared Jasper to not believe Greyson, but he surprised Cyrus.

"I believe you," Jasper said eventually.

"You do?" Greyson retorted with a disbelieving laugh.

"Did you lie?"

"No, but I'm shocked you believe my story."

"Well, some of it was confirmed by Cyrus. He saw the bounty hunters before you, and schemes like theirs are not unheard of."

"Thank you."

Jasper said, "I never thought I'd hear those words out of your mouth."

"More shocking than me saying I'm in love with Cyrus?"

"No," Jasper answered with a slight chuckle, though his eyebrows rose once again and he shifted back in the chair.

Cyrus smiled softly. Greyson was getting along with his family, well, part of it anyway. A small, sputtering flame glowed in his chest. Maybe Greyson and Cyrus' entire family could come to terms with each other. He didn't want to lose anyone or have to make a choice.

"I will have to speak to Lord Darius and listen to his account of the matter, so I can report back to my father-in-law," Jasper continued. "I don't know if these grievances will be enough to arrest Darius or transfer him."

Greyson scoffed. "He's done horrible things to us and his soldiers. He should be at least taken from here."

Cyrus asked, fingers tightening around Greyson's, "What?"

"Lord Darius has abused his position here since he was assigned. He hits his soldiers and abuses his house staff. Why don't you think none of us serve him? Darius has also been stealing from us. He will request an item, clothing, jewelry, or whatever and refuse to pay for it. If we don't give it to him, we're jailed. I, for the most part, have avoided this area because he had it out for me," Greyson said.

"Why didn't you report him?" Cyrus asked.

He snorted. "Report him to who? The emperor doesn't give a shit about us. Exactly who are we supposed to tell?"

Anger coiled in his stomach like a snake. "I will make this right. I swear."

"Because you love me?"

"Yes, and because it is the right thing to do."

"I never doubted you, love." Greyson cupped Cyrus' cheek, then kissed him. Cyrus would see this matter righted.

"Please," Jasper begged as he made fake gagging noises. "I'm not ready to watch this."

Cyrus almost shifted back, but Greyson kept possession of his lips for several more moments.

"Honestly," Greyson started, "you and your wife were just as amorous."

Jasper blinked. "As I recall, I've only met you once before, not long after my marriage."

"Indeed. When Spokesperson Charlotte and I were in the capital at the time, we were, surprisingly, invited to a party. I remember you said something *you* thought was clever—it wasn't—and she smiled at you with a warm look. Then anytime someone came near her, like the servant with a tray, you'd haul her against your side. Your mutual affection was obvious."

"Well, it would have been news to me," Jasper said, shaking his head.

Chuckling, Cyrus snuggled against Greyson. Jasper and Jade had an arranged marriage. They hadn't realized they liked each other until much later in their relationship.

"I wasn't in a position to tell you," Greyson said.

"I suppose that's true."

"And it worked out, I assume."

Jasper smiled, nodding. "It did indeed work out."

Cyrus tugged Greyson's hand onto his lap, tracing his rugged palm. He hoped they worked out just as well. Jasper and Jade were in love with two children.

"Do you think you could get people to come forward and tell their stories about Lord Darius? I could have my scribe transcribe them to add to the list of our offenses. It might be enough to get Lord Darius removed," Jasper said.

"Do you think the emperor will listen?" Greyson asked, his voice hard.

"I think he might. He has no love for Darius."

"I can ask around. I will only be able to get people from Woodhurst, not any further villages unless you want to stay quite a bit longer."

"No," Jasper said with a quick shake of his head. "I want to get home as soon as possible."

"I'll talk to Widow Jones, then. She should be able to get the word out."

"I will also have to have my scribe write down your story as well. I have to be thorough."

"We understand," Cyrus said before he gently kissed the top of Greyson's head, his soft hair tickling his nose. "Why don't I go ask Widow Jones if she will house Jasper and make you some tea?"

"Okay."

Cyrus scooted off the bed, then hovered nearby, inspecting Greyson to make sure he was alright before he moved toward Jasper, whose eyebrows were high on his forehead.

They stepped outside, and the wind whipped around them as it howled. "I don't know how you've survived here," Jasper said, crossing his arms.

"I like it."

Jasper snorted, rubbing his arms vigorously. "I'm freezing and my clothes are much thicker and nicer than yours."

Cyrus evaluated Jasper's clothes. They were dark blue, thick, and all lined with fur. His own were not as thick or nice. But as he brushed his fur-lined vest, Cyrus smiled. He liked these clothes better because Greyson had them made for him.

Winding around the house, Cyrus knocked on the front door. A little girl of eight or so with long black hair and owlish gray eyes opened the door, then gaped at him.

"Prince Cyrus, why are you here?"

"Hello, I don't believe I know your name."

"Lily," she said quietly, gripping her brown dress.

"Is Widow Jones home?" Cyrus asked.

She peeked through her lashes at Jasper. "Is grandma in trouble?"

"No," Cyrus said, crouching. "She's not in trouble, I promise. I need to ask her for a favor, and Greyson wants tea. He says I make horrible tea."

She giggled. "Come on in."

Warmth enveloped them, making Cyrus groan in relief. He liked living here in the Griseo Mountains with Greyson, but winter was a bit difficult to endure.

The house was long with a kitchen to the left, a table and chairs, and to the right was a living room with a wide fireplace as well as chairs and a couch with several pillows. A blue woven rug covered the wood floor, and several paintings graced the walls. There were two doors on the back wall along with a staircase.

Lily directed them to a table, then stepped out of the room and returned with Widow Jones a moment later.

"Greyson wants tea?" She chuckled. "He is particular."

"It's willow bark tea, so I feel like it's all the same," Cyrus remarked. He didn't understand how he made it so bad that Greyson couldn't even drink it. "I also need a favor."

Widow Jones hung a kettle over the flames. "Lily, why don't you go play?"

She glanced at Jasper and Cyrus, then left the room.

"So," Widow Jones began, "what favor do you need?"

"Where are my manners?" Cyrus asked. "This is Prince Consort Jasper, my cousin. Jasper, this is Widow Jones."

"Pleasure to meet you," she said with a deep bow.

"The pleasure is all mine," Jasper replied, inclining his head.

"Besides providing tea for my picky boyfriend, I was hoping you would be willing to host Jasper while he's here. Of course, you can bill the lord's estate for any expense he incurs," Cyrus said.

Widow Jones made a noise in the back of her throat. "You won't cause any trouble?"

"I swear," Jasper said, hand over his chest.

She studied Jasper with her deep brown eyes before looking at him. Cyrus smiled. Nodding, she said, "He can stay."

"Thank you."

"Hmm." Widow Jones pulled a painted tin out of the cupboard.

He glanced at Jasper, unsure. Greyson was supposed to speak to her, but Cyrus wanted to get a move on. "We are planning on bringing our grievances against Lord Darius to the emperor. I was going to have Greyson speak with you, as he mentioned the offenses against people here."

"Many."

"I brought my scribe," Jasper offered. "If people can tell me what exactly Lord Darius has done, my scribe can transcribe them for the emperor."

"Do you think it would matter?" Widow Jones asked, staring directly at him.

"Potentially. I'm hoping to have Lord Darius removed, so he can never hurt any of you again," Cyrus said.

Widow Jones said, "I will spread the word."

The kettle whistled, and she added some of the tin's contents to it. The tea simmered for about ten minutes while they sat in amiable silence before she poured it into the teapot.

"Here. Bring this to Greyson, but let it steep for thirty minutes and strain it well."

"Thank you," Cyrus replied, standing.

"I'm gonna go with him, but I'll be back," Jasper told her as he followed Cyrus outside.

After he closed the door, Cyrus said, "You're not coming up and bothering Greyson. He needs to rest."

Jasper stopped him with a touch on his arm. "I'm happy for you."

"Thank you."

"Have you two talked about what's going to happen?"

"What do you mean?" Cyrus asked, shivering in the winter air.

"You know the emperor is going to make you come home, and Greyson can't come with you."

"I already asked Uncle to lift the banishment order and bounty."

"He won't do that. I mean once the empress and Jade find out Greyson loves you, they'll fight for you, as will I, but the emperor is not going to let Greyson leave the Griseo Mountains. He's too powerful and dangerous."

Cyrus swallowed, brow furrowing. "I won't leave Greyson."

"You won't have a choice."

34

GREYSON

Widower Smith puttered around the room, making tea. Cyrus, Jasper, and most of the village were busy telling their stories for the scribe. Widow Jones, fearing Greyson would not behave himself and stay off his knee, sent Widower Smith to watch him.

The old man had basically no hair with a few gray wisps on his pale dome. His square face was heavily wrinkled with pronounced jowls, and his back bent with age. Widower Smith had to be close to ninety, but he still got around.

Once the tea was done, Widower Smith brought him a cup with a toothless smile.

"Thank you."

"You know," he said, sitting down, "I dislocated my knee once when I was young."

"Did you?"

Widower Smith nodded. "You need to stay off it, but make sure to stretch."

"What stretches would you recommend?"

The old man frowned, hand on his chin. "I remember a few. Get up, and I'll show you."

Greyson slowly rose, knife stabbing his ribs and knee twinging. Widower Smith showed him several stretches. Greyson watched closely and copied, following the movements. The tendons pulled, stealing his breath and making him wince, but he continued. If it would help him, he would do it regardless of any discomfort.

"What are you doing?" a voice shouted as the door opened. Greyson looked over his shoulder at Cyrus. His brow furrowed as Cyrus rushed toward him with a thunderous expression.

"Widower Smith is showing me some stretches to help my knee," he stated in a calm voice.

"Ah," Cyrus said as he took a deep breath. "Why don't you sit down again, so we can ice your side and knee?"

He lowered to the bed, shaking his head. Cyrus had gotten overprotective since Jasper had arrived, and Greyson didn't exactly understand why. Any little movement on his part brought Cyrus barrelling toward him. Anytime Jasper spoke to him, Cyrus buzzed around like an angry bee.

"Thank you for spending time with me, Widower Smith," Greyson said, ignoring Cyrus' fidgeting next to him.

He patted Greyson's arm. "It's no trouble."

"I'll walk you out," Cyrus said.

Widower Smith patted Cyrus' arm as well. "You're both good boys."

"We try," Cyrus said as he led the old man out of the apartment.

Greyson imagined he would escort Widower Smith all the way home to make sure the old man did not slip. It took several minutes for Cyrus to reappear. When the door opened, Greyson smiled at him as he slowly extended his leg and moved his foot up and down.

Cyrus kissed the top of his head. "I missed you."

"I saw you this morning," Greyson said with a laugh.

"So?"

"I missed you too."

Cyrus grinned. "I knew it."

"How is it going?"

"Good," Cyrus replied, sitting next to him on the bed. "Jasper already spoke to Lord Darius, and Widow Jones has rounded up a lot of people. It will take a while."

When he fell silent, Greyson glanced at him. Cyrus had a faraway look as his hands fisted on his thighs. "Is everything alright?"

"Yes. Let me get you some snow."

"Thank you."

When Cyrus returned, he helped Greyson onto his side before placing a towel over his ribs and gently setting the snow down. After it was situated, Cyrus moved to leave, but Greyson snatched the edge of his cloak.

"Stay with me."

"I need to read some reports."

"Fine."

Cyrus stood by the bed, hovering, before sitting next to him. Greyson rested his head on Cyrus' thigh. "Thanks."

Running his fingers through Greyson's hair, Cyrus said, "It's fine. I like spending time with you."

Greyson sighed in contentment. The snow chilled his side and banished the pain, but Cyrus' gentle ministrations were what truly soothed him. As sleep was about to claim him, muttering came from above him, and Greyson cracked his eyes open. Cyrus' brow was furrowed as he shook his head, then began mumbling again.

"What's wrong?"

"Huh? What?"

"You seem distracted. Since Prince Consort Jasper came you've been upset. What's going on?"

"Nothing."

He snuggled against Cyrus' well-muscled thigh. "Well, that's a lie."

"Sorry," Cyrus whispered, running his fingers through Greyson's hair. "I'm thinking."

"About?"

He did not answer.

"Should I be worried?" he asked, tensing.

"No," Cyrus said, eyes wide. "Of course not."

"Alright."

After a pause, Cyrus asked, "Why do you call them 'widow' or 'widower' and their surname?"

"Is that what you're thinking about?" he asked with a startled laugh.

"One of the things."

"We call them that as a reminder. They lost their spouses, and it reminds everyone that they need extra support and help." Greyson had honestly never thought about it. They simply called people that when their spouses died. "You don't do that?"

"No."

"Hmm."

Eventually, Cyrus took the dripping bag of half-melted snow off his side. He disappeared for a few minutes, then helped Greyson onto his back, propping his knee up with a pillow. Once Greyson was settled, Cyrus sat next to him and cuddled close to him.

"What if I dared to tell you earlier?" Cyrus asked.

"What do you mean, love?"

"What do you think would have happened if the first summer you came, I told you I liked you? Before the animosity built between us."

Greyson had no idea what would have happened. He had not been as confident in his youth. If Cyrus had approached him, what would he have done? "I imagine," he started, "it would have gone one of two different, yet similar, ways. One, I would have been so flustered that I would've never spoken to you again. Or two, I would've stared at you, completely shocked, and walked away."

Cyrus chuckled. "You don't think we could've gotten together?"

He pursed his lips. Maybe they would've gotten together? Greyson would have been intrigued by Cyrus, and Cyrus wouldn't have given up. Images of them together, exploring the city, holding hands, and stealing kisses danced through his mind.

"It wouldn't have lasted long, as I would have returned to the Griseo Mountains for the winter."

"You don't think I would've followed you?"

Yes, Greyson could easily imagine Cyrus coming with him. He smiled at the thought of Cyrus chasing him around the mountains, the two of them together. But soon it was replaced by images of war. What would have happened when the rebellion started?

"What about the war? We would've been ripped apart, and I don't think we would have ever recovered from that."

"It might never have happened if we were together. I could've better advocated for the Griseo Mountains, and we could've banded together," Cyrus argued.

"I think all that matters is we're together now. I like us now."

"I like us now too."

Greyson limped across the room. He was steadily getting better. He imagined that in another few days, he'd feel almost normal. Cyrus had left this morning with a deep frown while he muttered unintelligible words. Something was bothering Cyrus, but he would not talk about it. As the days passed, they were discussing more and more, dismantling the wall of the past between them. Though some things, foundation bricks, as it were, stopped them dead—like the emperor and the future.

The door opened, and Cyrus came inside. "You're up."

"I am."

"And everything is alright?" he asked, staring directly at Greyson's knee.

"Yes." Greyson fought to keep his voice even. Once Cyrus started worrying, he never seemed to stop.

Cyrus captured his hand. "Can I talk to you?"

His brow furrowed. "What's going on?"

Cyrus led him to the table and then sat, facing him, but he didn't say anything. His face was a blank mask that Greyson hadn't seen since almost directly after he woke up. It reminded him of his teenage years, and not in a good way.

"You're scaring me," Greyson confessed.

Almost instantly, his expression softened as he rubbed his thumb over Greyson's knuckles. "What are we going to do if my uncle makes me come home?"

This issue was something neither of them brought up, but both of them had to be thinking about it. "Well," Greyson started, "we'll be okay."

"What does that mean?"

"It means you may have to go to the capital for a few months or so, but we will be fine." Apparently, that was the wrong answer because Cyrus frowned. "What?" Greyson asked. "You *don't* think we will make it?"

"No, I think we'll be fine," Cyrus said, starting to stand.

Greyson tugged Cyrus back down. "Talk to me, love. You've been so quiet and surly."

"I don't want to be separated."

"Okay," he said slowly. "I don't either, but that might be what has to happen."

Cyrus bit his lip. "What if the emperor lifts the banishment order and bounty? Would you come with me?"

"I don't like the capital."

"I know."

Greyson scooted to the edge of his seat. "I would come with you, but I can't live in the capital forever."

A blindingly bright grin grew on Cyrus' face. "It won't be forever."

He opened his mouth but then closed it. Greyson had some serious doubts about Emperor Caspian allowing him to come to the capital. He stared at Cyrus, who beamed. He didn't want to ruin his happiness, but at the same time, it was the reality before them, and Cyrus needed to be prepared.

"Love," Greyson said softly, "he might not let me come."

Cyrus' expression dimmed. "No."

"No, what?"

"Just no."

"Cyrus, this is a very real possibility."

He stood, shaking his head.

"We'll be fine, love."

"You would be alright being apart?"

"No," Greyson said, getting up. He grabbed Cyrus' shoulders pulling him close. "No, I don't want to be separated. But what I'm saying is we'll make it. I love you, Cyrus. I'm yours. It doesn't matter how much time passes or where you go, we will be alright. We'll write, and you'll convince your uncle to let me come to the capital or for you to return, then we'll be together again."

Eyes glassy, Cyrus said, "No."

"Cyrus," Greyson started with a sigh.

"No," he said as a tear slipped down his cheek. "Just no, okay?"

"Okay," Greyson whispered, wrapping his arms around Cyrus. "Okay, love. It'll be alright." Cyrus trembled, arms winding around his waist.

"Just stay with me."

"I will," Greyson promised. "I'm right here. It will all be alright."

35

CYRUS

Thick clouds covered the sky, the wind howled, and snow started to drift down. He held a hand out to the flurries, studying the gray expanse that covered Validus Peak. It appeared a storm was closing in on the Griseo Mountains. Cyrus didn't know exactly what a storm was like here, but he figured it would be cold. Unbearably so.

He glanced back at Lord Darius' house. The lord had tried to escape with a bag of valuables. The captain of the guard, Thad, had easily caught Darius. Cyrus couldn't believe he'd tried to flee, though it wasn't as bad as Darius hurting some-one. Cyrus had a hard time containing his laughter at the image of Lord Darius scaling down the trellis with a bag of valuables over his shoulder.

Shaking his head in amusement, Cyrus walked to Widow Jones' home across the square, snow crunching under his boots. With a rap on the door, he opened it. Widow Jones sat at the table with Jasper and his scribe, a woman in her forties with gray-blonde hair and the most serious face he'd ever seen. A woman in her twenties spoke quietly as she related her tale. He stayed silent, hovering near the blazing fireplace, until she left.

"I think a storm is brewing," Cyrus remarked.

"Really?" Jasper asked, reading the sheets of paper spread across the tabletop.

"Yep."

"We should probably halt interviews for the next day or so until it blows over," Widow Jones said, standing. "Storms can get very dangerous here."

"Sounds good," Jasper said in an absentminded tone.

A warmth suffused his chest. He and Greyson could spend a couple of days together, alone, with absolutely no interrup-tions. A smile spread across Cyrus' face as thoughts of what they could do floated across his mind's eye.

Shoving the images aside, he asked, "You'll let people know?"

Widow Jones said, "They'll know. People here don't wander in snow storms unless it's an emergency."

"Well," he said, mind going back to Greyson, the softness of his skin, the way his lips moved when he smiled, the way his cheeks pinked. Cyrus suppressed a groan. "I should go. I need to bring in wood for Greyson and me."

"I'm sure I'll talk to you later," Jasper replied as his quill flicked over a piece of paper.

Jasper would probably interrupt Cyrus' time with Greyson. Suddenly, his vision for the next couple of days changed, and not for the better.

When he entered with an armload of wood, Greyson looked up. It looked like he'd been in the middle of stretching his knee. Slowly but steadily, Greyson was recovering from his ordeal with Lord Darius. Cyrus dropped the wood near the fireplace, then wrapped his arms around Greyson, pulling him close. The smell of pine and woods touched his nose—Greyson's scent.

"Hello," Greyson said with a slight chuckle, arms going about his shoulders.

"I think a storm is coming," he commented, not letting go of Greyson.

"They are common this time of year, and I can see the clouds gathering from the window."

"Hmm."

After a moment, Greyson wiggled in his embrace, and Cyrus freed him. Cyrus watched as Greyson began to prepare a pot of tea. He wanted to laugh. Greyson and his tea—a love even he couldn't compete with.

"I should get some more wood."

"That's a good idea," Greyson said. "Let me help you."

"You're limping. I've got it."

"Thanks, love."

The wind whipped around him, unfurling his cloak and chilling him. Quickly, head down, he stalked toward the lean-to not far from the stairs. He loaded up an arm full of wood and headed inside. He dropped the wood to the floor, and he and Greyson stacked it neatly.

"I'm going to get more," Cyrus said. "It's getting really cold outside."

"Are you sure you don't want me to help?"

"Yes."

He made two more trips, so there was an ample supply in the apartment. Then he went back out again to check on Widow Jones to see if she needed him to haul wood in for her. The old woman politely declined. Her grandchildren had it covered. Finally, he headed back to the apartment, frozen.

Shivering, he stepped inside, and Greyson immediately appeared in front of him. He helped Cyrus take off his cloak, vest, and boots before making him sit in front of the warm fire.

"I'm excited about the storm," Cyrus said.

"Why?"

"A couple of days alone with you."

Greyson shook his head with a slight frown, but Cyrus discerned a blush tinging his gray cheeks. Grinning, he scooted closer and asked, "How's your knee?"

"Better."

"Really?"

"Yes, Cyrus."

"I'm glad."

Greyson sat in front of him until the kettle released an angry whistle. He made his tea, then settled back in front of Cyrus, pushing a plate of cookies toward him.

"Where did you get these?" Cyrus asked around a mouthful.

"Jessica brought them."

"They're good."

The oatmeal cookies were soft and flavorful. Greyson only ate a couple, dunking them into his tea, while Cyrus decimated the plate. He loved sugary baked goods. He didn't fancy candy, but he loved pastries.

A smile played on Greyson's lips as Cyrus ate the last cookie, relishing every bite. Wiping the crumbs from his shirt, he asked, "What?"

"Nothing," Greyson said.

GREYSON

Greyson flipped the hotcake as the wind roared outside. He glanced over his shoulder at Cyrus, who sprawled on the bed. He put the plate on the table and moved toward him. Cyrus had his eyes closed, but he was awake. There was a tension in his posture that wasn't there when he was asleep.

"Breakfast is ready."

"It smells good," Cyrus replied, cracking an eye open.

They sat at the table, and Cyrus placed a couple of hotcakes on a plate as well as a scoop of eggs, then pushed it toward Greyson before filling his own plate. Cyrus shoved a huge forkful into his mouth, then said, "I love hotcakes. They're my favorite."

"I know. That's why I made them."

"Did the other me like them?"

Greyson rolled his eyes but refrained from remarking on there only being one of him. "Yes."

He frowned slightly before taking another bite. Cyrus finished the hotcakes quickly, and Greyson slid more onto his plate. "Thank you."

"Eat up," he said before eating a spoonful of eggs.

Another howl sounded, making the windows rattle. Smoke blew in from the fire and made him cough. Greyson didn't doubt that it was cold outside, but the fire kept the house toasty warm.

"How long do the storms usually last?" Cyrus asked as the window rattled loudly.

"It depends. This low on the mountains, they're not as bad. Usually a day or two of weather like this, then it's just snowing and cold."

"What do you normally do during storms?"

"Before my family passed, my mother would tell stories or my father would play his lute. Sometimes we'd play games. After they and my sister died, I spent them alone."

Cyrus pushed his eggs around the plate. "Did your family live in the same home you live in now?"

"No. I lived in the village proper, but after, I couldn't stay in the house. A family ended up moving into it. I lived with Widow Abney, who wasn't a widow yet, and her husband for a few months. After Old Man Johnson died, I moved into his cabin."

"If you don't mind me asking, how did your family die?" Cyrus asked.

"It's okay. I don't mind."

"Did you already tell the other me?"

"There's only one you, and yes, I mentioned it but didn't go into any detail."

"Sorry. I swear I'm not competing."

"You are, and it's fine." Greyson did not understand Cyrus' jealousy about the time he couldn't remember. Greyson had been with him and no one else. "Anyway, my parents and little sister died when I was fourteen. There was a sickness sweeping through the empire. A lot of people died. My family was one of them."

Cyrus paused, mouth opening. "My parents died from that. I was nine. We were in the capital where it started. My parents got sick and passed away. You would've been eleven."

"I knew your parents had died, but I didn't know how or when."

"We lost our families to the same thing," Cyrus said with a shake of his head.

"I guess we have more in common than either of us would have thought."

Greyson lay on his back with Cyrus hovering over him. There wasn't much light in the apartment, only what the low-burning fire gave off. The wind continued to howl and shake the building while the windows juddered in their frames.

"One more question," Cyrus said.

"It's late."

"I want to know everything."

Most of the day had been spent in the same manner. Greyson did not mind per se, and it wasn't like he couldn't understand Cyrus' curiosity. "Fine," he said, "but only if I get to ask you one for each question you ask me."

"Sure."

"Ask your question, then."

"Can you really summon lightning?"

Unable to stop himself, Greyson chortled. Everyone wanted to know about that. It was a lost art that he mastered. "Yes."

"When did you learn to do it? No, how did you learn to do it?"

"Those are more questions."

Cyrus' blonde hair fell about his face, and Greyson could feel himself weakening the longer those perfect blue eyes stared at him. "Fine. I learned when I was almost nineteen. Do you remember that abandoned corner of the library you always followed me to?" When Cyrus nodded, he continued, "There's a book there that describes it, not in detail, but enough to give me a rough idea. The first time I returned home after I got my staff, I spent months trying different things to summon lightning. Finally, I could do it."

"That's crazy. You taught yourself."

"I did that for several spells, especially battle magic."

"Why don't you ever use it?"

Greyson scowled at yet another question, but he answered anyway, "It takes a lot of energy and it's not practical to use."

"That's still cool."

"I will show you sometime," Greyson offered.

"You will?"

"Sure."

Cyrus opened his mouth, but Greyson placed a hand over it. "It's my turn." Lips pursed, Greyson thought through what he wanted to ask before finally settling on something. "Why didn't you say anything to me when we first met?"

"I was over-awed by you."

"What do you mean?"

Cyrus stroked Greyson's cheek. "When I first saw you, I instantly liked you. Like crazy liked you. You were the most beautiful thing I'd ever seen. Then the ancient staff flew out of the treasury and landed at your feet. You were so calm, like you expected that to happen. You simply picked it up, and waves of power rolled off you. I was enamored and seventeen. I couldn't get a single word out even when I tried.

"My uncle yelled at me after the meeting. I was supposed to contribute, not stand there and ogle you. Especially since Jade had been sick for that first meeting. I followed you, hoping to speak, but I couldn't. Every time I was tongue-tied. The next year you came, I managed to talk to you, but by then, you already hated me, and rumors of how powerful you were started to circle."

"I summoned lightning in front of a bunch of school mages that made fun of me. You must have not been stalking me that day."

"I missed that," Cyrus said, the disappointment obvious in his voice. "Anyway, I did try. Once, I tried to hold your hand. You shook me off."

"I don't remember that."

"The third year you came, you had a bruise on your chin, and I touched your cheek, trying to look at it."

Greyson's brow furrowed. "I don't remember that either."

"I did try in my own awkward way, but I couldn't seem to get the words out, and you didn't notice. No one did until Jasper got engaged to Jade. He was the first person who realized I liked you, and he kept it a secret."

"Ah, yes, when you tried to dose me with a love potion." It would not have ended well for Cyrus if he'd attempted it. Greyson's magic would have burned through it, and he would have been pissed, though the obsessive stalking would have made sense.

A blush rose to Cyrus' cheeks. "Jasper caught me, and explained, rather calmly, that I was an idiot, and you would kill me in a painful way."

"He was right about that."

"Anyway," Cyrus said, clearing his throat, "I didn't do much more than fantasize."

Greyson smirked. "What kind of fantasies?"

"I already answered your question," he said, not looking at him.

He leaned up, ignoring his aching ribs, and asked again, "What kind of fantasies?"

"I was seventeen when I met you. You know what kind of fantasies."

Sniggering, Greyson grabbed Cyrus' face. "Did you have dirty dreams about us in the meeting room?"

Heat rushed to Cyrus' cheeks as he glared.

Unable to help it, he laughed. Cyrus refused to meet his gaze. Greyson tightened his grasp. "I'm just teasing you, love. Honestly, I'm curious."

"So you can make fun of me?"

"Partly," he confessed. "But also, I'm amazed at how much you liked me for so long."

"Most were very tame, especially at first, because I was a virgin who didn't know anything. My main one was you would suddenly kiss me in different areas of the palace, but we'd always end up in my room. It got more graphic once I had the experience to support it. My favorite one was about having sex with you on the beach at the summer palace."

"That sounds sandy."

"It's a fantasy," Cyrus said, eyes averted.

Greyson kissed his lips. Cyrus pressed into his touch, careful not to lean on him. Greyson shifted back just enough to see him. "Thank you."

"For what?"

"Loving me so long. I'm sorry I didn't notice. I think if maybe I'd slowed down and hadn't been so focused on my responsibilities and what had to be done, I might have noticed you. Or at least, that I was attracted to you."

"You're more than welcome."

36

CYRUS

Cyrus watched the snow drifting from the sky, catching one of the fat flakes. The entire village was buried in snow, piles of it. It covered the roofs, the trees, and drifts of it pressed against the homes. The storm had raged for two whole days, but this morning the wind slowed. The temperature remained chilly but manageable.

It had been a great couple of days. He and Greyson had passed them in peace, talking, and making out. Jasper didn't bother them once, which was amazing if not surprising. He didn't know why, but Cyrus was grateful.

Rounding the corner to the front of Widow Jones' house, he came to a sudden halt. Jasper stood near the door, beaming. Jasper poked him. "So, how did it go?"

His brow furrowed. "What do you mean?"

"What do I mean? You spent two days with Mage Greyson in a snowstorm. It's a romantic paradise."

He chuckled slightly. "It was very nice."

"Nice? That's all?"

"What do you want from me?"

"Details!"

"You're married," Cyrus replied, crossing his arms.

"Doesn't mean I can't hear details of your love life. If you weren't related to my wife, I would've shared."

"We didn't have sex," he confessed.

"What? Why not? Are you saying I listened to every story Widow Jones had, most about how heroic Greyson is, for nothing?" Frowning, Jasper asked, "Does he not want to?"

"Jasper," Cyrus said with some exasperation, "Greyson is recovering from broken ribs."

"Ah, yeah, that makes sense."

Cyrus opened his mouth, stalling, and Jasper raised his eyebrows in question. He ran a hand through his hair. It was longer than he usually kept it, almost reaching his chin. Should he mention Greyson's reservations? Or was this something he should keep to himself? Finally, he decided to confide in Jasper. "I'm the first man he's been in a relationship with. Greyson needs time."

"I see. You can't pressure him, Cyrus, no matter how much you want him."

"I'm not."

"Good."

"You like him," Cyrus said. "Don't you?"

"I like that you're happy and that he likes you, though he is more amusing than I would've thought," Jasper said.

He smirked. "Jade will like him, and so will my aunt."

"True," Jasper said. "But the emperor will never like Greyson, no matter how funny he is."

"Spoilsport. You couldn't just give me one."

"Nope."

He shook his head. "C'mon, let's go see who's waiting for us today."

The next few days passed in a rush. Cyrus barely saw Greyson. Jasper was desperate to get home to Jade and their children, so they took the remainder of the accounts as fast as possible. Finally, they finished, and Jasper was leaving.

"Mage Greyson, it was nice to see you again," Jasper said, standing in front of them while Widow Jones' home was behind them.

"You as well."

"Cyrus, can I have a word?"

He nodded, then said, "I'll be right back, Greyson."

They walked toward the carriage that sat in the middle of the village, waiting. Jasper turned toward him, face taking on an exceedingly kind expression. Cyrus knew exactly what Jasper planned to say.

"Don't even start," Cyrus said.

"I have to."

"No, you don't."

"Cyrus, the emperor is never going to let Greyson leave the Griseo Mountains, and you are going to have to come home."

He swallowed. Cyrus couldn't even contemplate it. Greyson said they'd be fine, but he didn't want to have to be fine. He wanted to stay with Greyson. "I'm not leaving Greyson."

"Cyrus," Jasper started.

"No," he snapped. "I said no. It's my decision, and I'm not going to leave him."

"I can't make you." Jasper shrugged.

"Thanks."

"Don't thank me. I'll plead your case to the emperor. As soon as your aunt and my wife get wind of this, they'll be on your side, but I don't think Emperor Caspian will relent."

"He will." *He has too*, Cyrus silently added.

He gathered Cyrus into a hug, slapping his back, then stepped into the carriage. Through the window, Jasper said, "Take care of yourself."

"Tell everyone I said hello."

"I will but make sure to write."

Cyrus ambled back to Greyson's side and watched the procession leave, winding down the road. Greyson took his hand, their fingers interlacing. "Will you be alright?"

"Of course."

Greyson would not meet his eyes. "Do you wish you were going with him?"

"No, I want to be with you."

"Good."

GREYSON

Greyson wandered about the apartment tent, collecting a few things. He finally felt better, and he wanted to explore the area to hunt for herbs or anything of use. Also, to be outside for more than a few minutes would be amazing. It was getting a bit tedious remaining inside.

The door swung open with a slight squeak, and Cyrus came inside. Lord Darius had tried to flee yet again, early this morning.

"How far did he get?"

"Not far," Cyrus said, rubbing his hands together. "We found him about twenty minutes from the village. Darius had bribed his maid to hire a coach for him. The girl walked over three days to the village down the mountain and brought a carriage. We found him before he left. He wasn't happy."

"I imagine. What are you going to do to the maid?"

"Nothing," Cyrus said. "She'll be confined to his house and go back to the capital with him, then be reassigned."

"He really doesn't want to live with the monks."

He shrugged off his cloak. "No, it's not that. He's afraid my uncle will execute him."

"Will he?"

"I doubt it. He doesn't like executing people."

Greyson raised his eyebrows. "I would have never guessed. He's only tried to kill me a couple of times."

"Sorry. You're the exception I guess."

He scoffed. "I'm so honored."

Laughing, Cyrus snaked his arms around Greyson's waist. "You should be."

Greyson wiggled out of his embrace, then collected a waterskin, placing it in his bag.

"Are you going somewhere?"

"Yes," he said. "I'm going to search for herbs."

"Do you want me to come?"

"No, it's alright." Greyson smiled at him, and Cyrus frowned. He paused, then draped his arms over Cyrus' shoulders. "Did you want to come?"

"I don't want to crowd you, but we haven't spent much time together."

"I'm going to tell you something. Prepare yourself."

"Okay," Cyrus said slowly.

"You can't overwhelm me. I love spending time with you," Greyson said, completely honest. He would never tire of Cyrus.

"Really?"

"Yep."

"Then I'm going to come with you."

"Good."

Greyson carefully walked under the trees, feet sinking into the snow. He rarely got to this area of the Griseo Mountains because he liked to give Lord Darius a wide berth. But now that the lord was confined to his home, he couldn't wait to explore.

Cyrus followed him. His feet smashed into the unbroken snow, often snapping twigs and such hiding underneath. Cyrus' teeth also chattered so loudly, Greyson could hear it.

Trying to ignore the ruckus behind him, silently thankful he was not attempting to hunt, his gaze scoured the area and searched for anything of use. What he hoped to find was a rare winter herb, caeruleus, that grew in the area.

He twisted around the pine trees, avoiding the fallen trees and craggy boulders, as he kept heading northeast. Greyson found berries, a white winter moss growing on a rock, but not the elusive herb he sought. He shouldn't have gotten his hopes up, but of course, he had.

Glancing over his shoulder, Greyson checked on Cyrus, who blindly scanned the trees with his shoulders hunched, teeth chattering. With a slight frown, he came to a stop. "Are you alright?"

He nodded but did not speak, probably because Cyrus could not have gotten a single word out.

"Are your feet wet or numb?"

Cyrus shook his head.

"What about your hands?"

Shaking his head again, Cyrus smiled, though it didn't appear convincing.

Greyson wanted to continue the search. If he'd been alone, he would have, but Cyrus had come with him, and Greyson didn't want him to catch a chill. Giving up, for today at least, he started toward the village.

"Wh-where are y-you going?" Cyrus chattered.

"Back to Woodhurst."

"Wh-why?"

"You're freezing to death."

"I'm fine," Cyrus said carefully.

"Clearly."

With a frown, Cyrus said, "I-I'm fine."

"Love," Greyson said, "I don't mind. I'm not upset."

Cyrus did not say anything but held out his hand. Greyson fought back a sigh. He knew Cyrus simply didn't want to disappoint him because he'd intended to spend the day in the mountains, but he truly didn't mind. Knowing he was not going to convince Cyrus otherwise, Greyson took his hand.

They set off again with Cyrus in the lead, determinedly marching on. Greyson searched for the herb, easy to spot with its black stem and bright blue leaves. As the day continued and they walked on, Greyson did not even catch a glimpse of the elusive herb, but he found a few other things to make the day worthwhile.

When the sun began to set, Greyson and Cyrus entered the village. Cyrus had fallen silent some minutes ago, apparently chilled to the bone. Greyson tried to watch him surreptitiously, but it was impossible, as Cyrus walked on his right side. When they reached the apartment, Greyson moved up the steps and ushered Cyrus inside.

He got a fire started as Cyrus shakily removed his cloak. "You shouldn't have come," Greyson said, trying to keep the bite out of his voice. "Or you should've let me take you home earlier."

Cyrus did not bother to respond as he sat next to the flames. Greyson could not stop the scowl that marred his face. Taking a deep breath, he buried the scathing remarks because he did not want to hurt Cyrus' feelings, and they truly wouldn't help the situation. Instead, he focused on getting Cyrus taken care of.

First, Greyson slipped Cyrus' boots off to inspect his feet. It would not take much for Cyrus to develop frostbite. Next, he peeled off his gloves, carefully checking each finger and pressing a kiss to each for good measure. Once assured Cyrus wouldn't lose any digits, Greyson hooked his fingers around the edge of Cyrus' vest and tugged it off.

As he looked down, Cyrus smiled at him, and his heart oddly started to pound. Greyson had done this before, many times, but for whatever reason, this time, fire rolled along his veins as desire slammed his body.

Greyson wanted Cyrus.

He didn't need time to try and sort through everything. He was not confused or scared, or anything that he thought he might feel. All Greyson felt was love. He loved Cyrus and wanted to be with him. It was as simple as that.

Greyson had no idea what he should say. He didn't know if he should be blunt and directly tell Cyrus that he wanted to have sex. Should he kiss Cyrus and let it lead to its natural conclusion? Or should he try to be romantic? Greyson hadn't wooed Cyrus, or anyone if he was being honest, but for the first time in his life, he wanted to.

"Are you alright?" Cyrus asked as his head tilted to the side.

Nodding, he shifted back. "I'm fine. Completely fine."

"Okay," he said slowly, brow furrowed.

He tried to give Cyrus a reassuring smile, but it came out more of a grimace. Cyrus blinked at him, then stretched his hands to the flames.

Pulse throbbing, Greyson pinched the bridge of his nose. How would he woo Cyrus? He didn't even know if it was necessary. He could simply let nature take its course, which sounded less embarrassing and far easier. Though he'd stopped Cyrus so many times, Greyson didn't know if Cyrus would move beyond a kiss without more obvious interest. But the thought of blatantly telling Cyrus what he wanted made him burn in embarrassment for some odd reason. Greyson couldn't do that. He would have to romance Cyrus, which would no doubt prove interesting.

37

CYRUS

Cyrus was numb. Greyson was going to break up with him. He'd been overly kind the last week or so. Cyrus kept thinking that maybe Greyson was as nervous as he was about the emperor's letter. But as the days passed, he became increasingly convinced Greyson was simply trying to find a way to extract himself from this relationship.

Greyson had made hotcakes every morning for breakfast and had been extra nice, not snapping or scowling. He'd also done all sorts of things, presenting small gifts and whatnot, but the one thing Greyson hadn't done was kiss him, not once, in the last week. Also, he hadn't let Cyrus trail along as he wandered the forest.

He didn't know what to do. Cyrus should probably let Greyson go, but he couldn't, not yet. If Greyson asked, Cyrus would honor his wishes, but otherwise, he would keep holding on in the hopes that it would change.

Cyrus didn't understand what went wrong, but he could pinpoint the exact moment Greyson changed. It occurred when they arrived back at the apartment from exploring the woods. Greyson had started to take care of him, like normal, and all seemed fine until he helped Cyrus undress. Greyson had hovered above him, looking stricken.

Maybe Greyson didn't want *this* anymore?

A knife twisted his insides. He could not even think that. Now that he'd experienced being with Greyson, Cyrus couldn't go back. Since he was seventeen years old, he'd imagined all sorts of scenarios and situations, but he couldn't have dreamed how amazing being with Greyson would actually be. He and Greyson were different, yet they matched perfectly, and he didn't want this to end.

Cyrus entered the apartment from his daily check in on Lord Darius. His gaze froze on Greyson who was straightening up the room. Cyrus wanted to draw him into his embrace, hold him close if only to assure himself that everything was fine. He didn't, though, because he didn't know if it was something he was allowed to do anymore.

"I got you something."

This had become a regular occurrence. The gifts almost came on a daily basis. Cyrus forced a smile to his lips. "What?"

Fist extended, Greyson grinned. Cyrus stepped closer, drawn in by the warmth of his expression. Slowly, he pulled Greyson's fingers straight. In the center of his palm sat a venetus gem that had been shaped into a flower. It was round with intricate petals, appearing almost like a puffy ball. Cyrus picked it up and tilted it back and forth, the light changing the iridescent gem's color with every movement.

"Thank you," Cyrus said, unsure why Greyson would give him a flower.

"I found a venetus. It probably fell off a wagon. It's not powerful enough to be made into an artifact, so it was destined to be ground up. I crafted it into this shape."

"Thank you," he said again.

"Do you like it?" Greyson asked, eyebrows lifting in obvious expectation.

"Of course. What type of flower is this?"

"A King Zinnia."

He mustered up a smile. "Thank you, Greyson. I like it."

His brow furrowed as his long fingers trailed over Cyrus' cheek. "Are you alright?"

"Of course." Cyrus closed the distance between them, wanting to feel the softness of Greyson's lips on his, but Greyson pulled back.

"I need to go."

Ice sat squarely in his chest. "Alright."

Greyson cupped his cheek, running his thumb in a soothing arc. "I'll see you later."

Not saying anything, Cyrus stared at the stone flower in his hand. It felt like a solid weight had settled in his stomach. His fingers traced the petals. Greyson had to feel something about him, right?

Cyrus dropped the stone in his pocket and went outside. The frozen wind didn't faze him as he headed around the front of the house with nowhere in particular to go. He needed out. He needed fresh air, though he'd only just come in.

"Prince Cyrus," a rough voice said and made him turn around. Widow Jones stood in the door frame of her house.

"Widow Jones," he said, unable to keep the exhaustion from his voice.

Her lips puckered. "What's eating you?"

He waved off her concern, but when he tried to leave, ice swelled around his ankles. Cyrus teetered, but the ice released its hold, and he was able to catch himself. Peering at the old woman, he asked, "Your doing?"

"Indeed," she answered. "Come in."

With no other option, Cyrus entered the house. Lily played on the rug in front of the stone fireplace with some wooden dolls as she sang in a high voice under her breath. Widow Jones waved to the table, and Cyrus sank onto a chair.

She poured him a cup of tea, setting it in front of him. Cyrus smiled but didn't touch it. Widows Jones added a dollop of milk into her own tea. "How are you doing?"

"Fine."

Widow Jones shook her head. "You are a terrible liar. Absolutely terrible. You'll probably need to work on that for your royal duties."

He chuckled, but it sounded false to his own ears.

She remarked, "Greyson has been quite busy. I've seen him running around."

"Yep."

"Uh-huh." She raised her snow-white eyebrows.

His mouth opened to confide in her, but he swallowed the words. Cyrus didn't know Widow Jones that well, but the emotions that circled in his mind were like poison. They needed out, yet he couldn't speak about them because by doing so, it might make them true.

"Problems are part of any relationship," she said, taking a sip of tea. "I've found their cure is usually communication. Clear communication. No rounding the subject or hinting. Say what's wrong and what you need."

"H-how? How did you know?"

She guffawed. "I didn't get old for nothing. Besides, I was married. I learned a few things. I'm just trying to save you from a lifetime of pointless arguments over a stupid wooden carving that your mother-in-law gave you that was uglier than the serpent's ass."

There was a story to that, but Cyrus didn't know if he wanted to know it or if he should ask. Instead, he smiled politely.

GREYSON

As Greyson stepped into the apartment, he looked around until he saw Cyrus who sat at the table, hunched over what appeared to be another report.

With a slight smile, he set the bag not far from Cyrus. A bright blue leaf escaped from the top. Greyson smirked. He'd found several caeruleus herbs in a grove, not entirely buried in the snow. It was quite the find, and he could hardly believe it. He'd harvested three of the five plants, leaving the others to pollinate future plants.

"Hello," Greyson said.

Cyrus nodded with a tense expression.

His brow furrowed. Cyrus did not look pleased to see him. Maybe he was having a bad day? When Greyson had given him the flower this morning, he seemed out of sorts, not his usual chipper self.

Letting it go, Greyson carefully removed the plants from the sack so as to not break the fragile stems or leaves. The juice would not kill a person, but it could make them sick. The herbs had to be dried before being made into a healing potion.

He set them on the table, the dirty roots spreading over the wood. Greyson leaned his staff in the corner before removing his cloak and gloves. As he turned around, he caught sight of Cyrus touching one of the bright blue leaves.

"Be careful," Greyson snapped.

Cyrus jerked back, face pinched like Greyson had struck him. Greyson had not meant to snap; it slipped out before he could stop it. He grabbed Cyrus' hand and inspected his thick fingers, not seeing any liquid.

"I'm sorry. I shouldn't have yelled."

Cyrus did not respond.

Greyson hauled him up, then wrapped his arms around Cyrus' waist. "I'm sorry," he repeated. "I didn't want you to break the leaf open and have any juice spill on you. It could make you ill."

"Are we poisoning someone?"

"No. This herb can make a powerful healing potion."

Not responding, Cyrus leaned against him, arms slowly coming about Greyson's neck. Greyson's fingers trailed up and down Cyrus' spine as he breathed deeply. The simple contact soothed him. He rested his cheek on the top of Cyrus' head, the golden strands soft against his cheek.

"I'm sorry." Greyson did not like snapping at Cyrus. He was trying to get better.

Cyrus didn't say anything as he moved out of Greyson's grasp, nodding. "I understand."

Greyson stared at Cyrus. *What is he talking about?*

Shaking his head, he let the matter go. He tied rough twine around the base of the plants, then hung them from a hook in the kitchen ceiling. It would only take a few days for the herbs to dry, especially with how hot Cyrus kept the apartment.

"What do you want to eat?" Greyson asked as he surveyed the cabinets.

Cyrus did not reply, so he turned around. Cyrus' jaw was clenched as he stared at the table with glassy eyes. Greyson moved toward him. "Love, are you alright?"

Slamming a hand down, Cyrus glared at him. "If you're going to break up with me would you just do it already?"

"Break up?" he choked out. He had no intention of ending this. Swallowing, he asked in a tight voice, "Do you want to break up with me?"

CYRUS

"No," Cyrus shouted, standing. "Of course, I don't. You're the one who wants to break up with me."

"When did I say that?" Greyson asked. "I have no desire for this to end."

"Then why are you acting so weird? For the last week, you've been tiptoeing around me. I thought you were preparing to break it to me easily. What the hell is going on?"

"I was trying to show you how nice life could be together."

"I already know that. I love being with you!"

"Well, that's good," he snapped.

Widow Jones' words floated through his mind. What did he need? The truth. Cyrus needed the truth, but more than that, he needed Greyson. Nonetheless, nerves prickled in his stomach. What if he upset Greyson or they fought? Cyrus shook his head. It didn't matter. He had to do this.

Cyrus crossed the room and stopped right in front of Greyson. Pink tinged his pale cheeks. Hand under his chin, Cyrus lifted Greyson's face so he could see it better. "If you don't want to break up with me, then what's going on?"

He did not reply, but his cheeks darkened.

"If you don't talk to me, then I can't know what you're thinking. Please, tell me."

Greyson looked at the ceiling. "This is ridiculously embarrassing."

"What?"

"I want to be with you."

"We are together."

"I mean *be* together."

"We are," he said.

Mouth falling open, Greyson gaped at him. "How are you not getting this?"

"Maybe because you aren't telling me. Just say it."

"I want to have sex with you, okay? I wanted to that night after you followed me into the woods. But I was embarrassed, so instead of telling you, I decided to woo you, which apparently didn't work." Greyson scowled, cheeks bright red.

Desire thrummed in his body as his pulse sped up. Gently, Cyrus cupped his cheeks. "You don't have to be embarrassed."

"Well, I am."

"Is it worse to be embarrassed or to have me think you're going to break up with me?"

"Maybe you should've asked me directly, instead of thinking about unnecessary things?" Greyson retorted, cheeks still bright red.

"Let's compromise," Cyrus said. "In the future, let's just directly talk. Alright?"

"I can try."

The blush hadn't lessened on Greyson's cheeks, so Cyrus smiled softly. "There is nothing to be embarrassed about. I love you."

"I love you too."

Cyrus captured Greyson's lips and kissed him slowly, fully. He wanted Greyson to feel loved and safe. His touch remained soft as he nibbled on his lips. Greyson pressed closer and kissed his mouth open, then his tongue delved inside. Cyrus groaned.

Greyson shifted back, and Cyrus released an annoyed noise. Greyson asked, voice quiet, "Are you sure you want me? This?"

"I should be asking you that," Cyrus mumbled. Before he could respond, Cyrus yanked Greyson flushed against him so he could feel exactly how much he wanted him. "I have wanted this for a very long time."

A soft smile pulled on his lips as Greyson bent down to kiss him. Cyrus ground against Greyson, which elicited a tantalizing moan from Greyson. His hand slid down and he tugged on the bottom of Greyson's shirt. He slipped it off, with a bit of assistance. Eyes wandering over his bare chest, Cyrus couldn't help but wonder about the scars and where they came from, but Greyson didn't let him get a single word out.

Cyrus directed Greyson toward the bed. When the back of Greyson's knees bumped into the bedframe, he shoved him back, then climbed on top of him, knees bracketing Greyson's hips. Greyson pulled Cyrus' shirt off before exploring his back and chest. With each touch, the kiss turned faster and more passionate.

Cyrus pulled his mouth away, breath coming out quickly, then began kissing Greyson's face before drifting down to his neck. As he nibbled and sucked, Greyson moaned. He feasted on every sound. It was music to his ears. After a bit, Cyrus moved back and examined his handiwork. A lovely little mark decorated Greyson's neck. Smiling, he continued to drop kisses on Greyson's chest.

Eventually, Greyson rolled over, pushing Cyrus onto the mattress. Greyson pressed into Cyrus. He could feel Greyson's desire for him.

"Cyrus," Greyson ground out, making him smile. Cyrus kissed him, tongue exploring Greyson's mouth. Greyson began undoing the ties on Cyrus' trousers before shoving them down. He kicked them off, leaving him in nothing but his undershorts.

"I need you," Greyson said, his voice harsh.

Slowly, Cyrus ran his fingers over Greyson's face, tracing his features. "I'm right here. I'm not going anywhere." His hands slid down Greyson's neck, over his chest, before stopping right at the edge of his trousers. "Are you sure?"

"Yes," Greyson said before kissing him.

GREYSON

Greyson snuggled against Cyrus' chest, fingers absentmind-edly wandering over his smooth skin. Cyrus had an arm slung around Greyson's waist, keeping him close. The room was mostly dark, as the fire had died, leaving nothing but coals.

Cyrus began to trail his fingers up and down Greyson's back. A sleepy grumble escaped his lips as he closed his eyes. "I should put a log on the fire," Greyson commented, not moving.

"You should stay right here." Cyrus placed a kiss on his head.

"Hmm."

He chuckled. "So what's the verdict?"

"About?"

"About what we just did."

"Obviously, I enjoyed it." If his eyes were open, he would have rolled them. It had been amazing as Cyrus well knew from Greyson's vocal and energetic responses.

"It will be even better next time."

Greyson sat up slightly so he could see Cyrus' face. "Cyrus, you enjoyed it, right?"

"Yes, very much."

Satisfied, he settled back down.

"I didn't mean anything bad," Cyrus said. "I just meant it gets better the more we know each other."

"Hmm." Greyson had enjoyed it and couldn't imagine it getting any better, but he was willing to believe him.

"You must have experienced the same with your past rela-tionships."

He shrugged. "I wasn't with anyone for very long."

"Ah."

"I hadn't been interested in relationships before now. I was always too busy."

"And now?"

"I'm with you," Greyson said as sleep began to lure him away. "I mean, you're it, so I guess I'll see if you're right."

CYRUS

A beam of light danced in his eyes, blinding him. Squinting, Cyrus looked outside. It was lighter than it should be. *I must have overslept*, he thought. Greyson was half draped across his chest, face tucked against his neck. His steady breath tickled Cyrus.

Cyrus couldn't help but grin as memories from yesterday resurfaced. Greyson's moans. The way he ground out Cyrus' name. The feel of Greyson's skin against his. His own release. Cyrus had imagined the two of them being together many times, but it didn't compare to the real thing.

While his body remained warm under the blanket with Greyson, his face was chilled. His gaze swiveled to the fireplace. He could see it from the corner of his eye. It was empty and cold. The fire must have died hours ago and let the chill of winter seep in. Despite that, Cyrus had no desire to move.

Eventually, Greyson shifted against him. "Good morning, love."

Squeezing him, Cyrus said, "Good morning." Greyson started to climb over him, and Cyrus trapped him in his arms. "Where are you going?"

"To get dressed." Greyson black hair hung around his face. "Why?"

"So I can go to the outhouse."

Cyrus tightened his arms. "Do you have to?"

He scoffed. "Yes."

With an exaggerated sigh, he released Greyson, who scrambled over his chest. Cyrus watched as he tugged on his trousers, donned his shirt, then yanked on his boots. Greyson glanced at him and rolled his eyes, probably from Cyrus' blatant ogling.

"I'll be right back."

A few minutes passed before Greyson strode in, shivering a bit. Cyrus held out his arms for Greyson, who shook his head; instead, he got the fire started.

"Don't you need to use the outhouse?"

"No," Cyrus said, stretching his arms out again. "I need you."

Smiling, Greyson climbed onto the bed. Cyrus dragged him onto his chest and kissed him, arms locked behind his back. Greyson shifted back after the barest moment. "You need to get dressed. We overslept, by a lot."

"No."

"No?" he repeated, chuckling.

"We need to stay here."

"You have responsibilities."

"They can wait."

"Cyrus."

"No," he said for the second time as he tucked Greyson's hair behind his ear. "It can wait until tomorrow." Before he could protest again, Cyrus took possession of his mouth to silence any argument.

38

CYRUS

Cyrus stared at the three letters. He knew they were coming, but looking at the familiar writing of his family, made his heart plummet. The paper crinkled under his fingertips as he fidgeted with the missives. While they remained unopened, hope existed that his uncle would relent and allow Greyson to come with him.

His gaze shot to Greyson, who sat on the ground, pounding the colorful herb with a stone pestle while muttering under his breath. The last few days he and Greyson had spent every moment together. Cyrus couldn't imagine separating now.

Greyson scowled. "Just open the damn letters. It won't get any better or worse staring at them."

"What if he says no?"

He started to grind the broken-down herbs in a counter-clockwise motion. "Just open them."

Cyrus glowered at Greyson, then peeked at the noisy bubbling coming from the stove. There was a pot full of a deep purple concoction, which unnerved him slightly, especially since Greyson hadn't put anything even close to that color into it.

Ripping his gaze away from the bubbling liquid, Cyrus looked at the missives once again. With a deep breath, he ripped open the first one, which was from his uncle.

Nephew,

Well, I'm glad you're alive. I would have bet good money on Mage Greyson killing you. The only thing that stopped me was your aunt, and that no one was taking odds. I did receive a letter from Lord Darius, who related the whole of it to me. I am inclined to believe his account.

The mage also sent one via Mage Frederick, which surprised me. The content surprised me even more. I am not sure I believe him, though your Aunt Quinn was quite taken with it and Mage Greyson's romantic notions. However, I lean toward the lord's account, as odious as Darius is.

But before I could make a decision, your letter arrived. I'm not shocked that you believe Greyson. You've always had a soft spot for him. But I am glad that you've recovered your memory that the mage probably stole in the first place. Assured of your safety, I am willing to wait to make a judgment until Jasper arrives and makes an assessment of the situation. Until that moment, your mage can live.

As far as lifting the exile order and bounty, my answer is no. I don't care if Mage Greyson is innocent of these matters, he's guilty of rebel rousing. I have sent Lady Lyra to replace Lord Darius. Even if the lord is innocent, your aunt was taken by Mage Greyson's idea to banish him to the tower. Perhaps the monks and their quiet ways will be good for him? Lady Lyra will carry my orders about your mage. Once she arrives, you are to come home. Do you understand?

I expect to see you shortly.

Uncle Caspian

Cyrus should've expected it—Greyson certainly did—but he didn't. Deep down he thought his uncle would allow Greyson to accompany him home. Of course, the emperor did not. Fighting back the waves of disappointment, he opened the next one, which was from his aunt.

Cyrus,

I'm so relieved you're alright. I knew Mage Greyson would not kill you, but when you stopped writing, I feared something terrible befell you. I, of course, did not believe a word of Lord Darius' letter. I'd hoped that man would fall into a mine and do us all a favor by dying.

I do believe Greyson's letter. He forever endeared himself to me. Your mage offered to kill Lord Darius in the manner of my choosing. My choosing. Oh, if your uncle let me, I would choose something truly horrific. I'm sure Greyson knows of some horrid spells.

He also seems to love you a great deal, son. Greyson was not even concerned about himself. He wanted Caspian to send help to protect you from Lord Darius. My husband says it's all poppycock, but I believe Greyson. You did the impossible. You won Mage Greyson's affection. I would've never guessed, but I'm happy for you.

Though Caspian did not want to share Greyson's letter with me, I snatched it from his office. I shared it with your sister. Jade sided with me. We are both firmly on your side about Greyson, and we are actively working on the emperor. He will relent eventually, my dear. He loves you too much to deny you anything. Just make him hurt by missing you.

Don't come home.

Now, I shall miss you terribly, but if you stay away, sooner or later, he will let Greyson come with you. I already spoke to Lady Lyra. She agreed to help. I promised you or Greyson would introduce her to some lovely gentlemen. Do round some up for her, dearest.

I love you dearly, son of my heart,
Mother

Cyrus beamed. The empress never called him her nephew, but always her son. He'd lived with his aunt and uncle since he was nine years old, and he loved them both dearly.

It didn't surprise him in the slightest that Greyson had offered to kill Lord Darius. He seemed to harbor a deep hatred of the lord. Of course, the empress felt the same way. Greyson's willingness to kill Darius would have been enough to sway her, even if Greyson hadn't said he loved Cyrus.

Cyrus reread the last part of his aunt's missive. He paused on the words, "Don't come home." He had much the same thought. He couldn't leave Greyson anyway.

He opened the last letter, from his cousin.

Cyrus,
I'm glad you survived. I knew Mage Greyson was too smart to kill you, but apparently, he's dumb enough to fall in love with you. I can't even imagine, but cheers. I'm glad. Now, you won't be moping around the capital. It was a pathetic sight to see.

I do hope you won't keep Jasper long. I don't like when my husband is away from my side. But at least, he will find you alive. When you stopped writing, I truly feared he'd find you dead or not at all.

Mother showed me Greyson's letter. It was horribly romantic. The man is besotted with you. You two deserve each other. You both sicken me. I cannot believe he saved your life. I can believe his ulterior motives. He spared nothing in his letter, including his plan to kill you. I'm glad he didn't go through with it. I would have missed you terribly.

I'm with Mother on her plan. Just stay away for a bit. Father already complains about how much he misses you. Simply keep yourself from his sight as Mother and I work on him.

Also, if you could bring Greyson home, maybe he could tutor Casper. My lovely son has gone through another tutor. This is number twelve, and he's only three. I have not let him be bound to an artifact because all of the tutors seem incompetent. But maybe Greyson will fare better. That's what he does, doesn't he? Teach? Anyway, it would be nice to see what he can do.

Hopefully, I will see you and Greyson soon.
Jade

Jade was one year younger than him, and they'd grown up together. Cyrus wasn't surprised she'd sided with him. Deep down, Jade was a romantic who loved her husband dearly.

He reread the bit about his nephew, Jade's second child. Casper had shocked everyone when he'd shown magical ability. But his nephew, though it was mostly Jade if he was honest, had scared away tutors quicker than Cyrus would've thought possible. He imagined Greyson could teach Casper just fine, though his nephew might not know what to do with him. He very much doubted Greyson could be intimidated by Jade either.

Biting his lip, he turned toward Greyson to share the letters, but Greyson was carefully pouring the ground herbs into the bubbling pot. The liquid transformed from a deep purple to shockingly pink. Cyrus' eyes widened as his mouth hung agape. Greyson cackled loudly as he stirred the liquid clockwise.

"I knew I remembered how to make it," Greyson said.

Never had Greyson appeared more like a mage, an evil mage at that, as he stood over the boiling concoction. Greyson kept stirring until the brew morphed into a vile green, then he began poking the bottles lined up on the counter with his staff. A couple shattered while the rest remained standing. He nodded in obvious satisfaction. Then, slowly, he began to ladle the liquid into the small bottles.

As soon as the brew hit the glass, it changed from a rather swampy green to a splendid dark blue. Greyson cackled again as he kept pouring the liquid into the vials. Once the last one was filled, he looked into the pot, then peered over his shoulder.

"Love, come here."

"Why?" he asked but walked toward him.

Greyson poured the last of the brew into a cup, maybe a mouthful or two. "Drink this."

"Why?" Cyrus dubiously stared at the liquid.

"Because it's not enough to fill a bottle, and I don't want to waste it. It's too valuable."

"Why don't you drink it?"

"Because I love you. It's a healing potion. Just drink it."

He glanced at Greyson, then back at the cup. The liquid grew progressively lighter blue by the second as it cooled. Taking a deep breath, Cyrus downed it, expecting a truly horrible taste, but he was pleasantly surprised. It tasted like coconut mixed with a tarter type of fruit that he couldn't place. When his mouth hung open in shock, Greyson laughed.

"It wasn't that bad, was it?"

"No. It tasted pretty good."

"Don't drink the others. They're worth a good deal."

"I won't, don't worry. So what do you do now?" Cyrus asked, glancing at the neat row of bottles.

"When they are completely cool, they will be a very pale, silvery blue, and I will cork, then wax seal them."

Setting the cup down, he hooked his arms around Greyson's waist. "You wrote to the emperor."

"I already told you I did." He settled his arms on Cyrus' shoulders.

"You didn't tell me it was romantic."

"Nonsense."

"No," he said. "It moved my aunt and cousin. You didn't care about yourself, just me."

Greyson frowned, but Cyrus could perceive a bit of pink on his cheeks. "I didn't want Lord Darius to hurt you. My people would've protected you. As soon as you woke up, if you hadn't regained your memories, they were going to hide you until someone else from the capital showed up."

Unable to stop it, he grinned. "Thank you."

"I would never let anyone hurt you."

"Nor I you."

With a soft smile, Greyson asked, "What did the emperor say?"

"He won't lift the orders."

"Shocking," he replied, voice heavy with sarcasm. "So you have to go home?"

"No."

"Cyrus, you can't defy him."

"I can and will."

"Love, we'll be alright."

"We will because I'm not going anywhere."

Greyson cupped Cyrus' cheeks. "We can't endanger the Griseo Mountains because we want to stay together."

"Trust me. Please. I would never put anyone in danger."

He didn't appear convinced.

"Trust me."

Nodding, Greyson said, "I trust you."

"Good. My aunt has a plan, which my cousin also supports."

"What is it?"

"Stay with you until the emperor misses me."

"Will that work?"

"I think so, but it doesn't matter because I get to stay with you."

Leaning down, Greyson whispered, "I'm glad."

39

Cyrus

Cyrus walked into the oppressively hot blacksmith's shop, biting his lip. He hoped he wasn't doing something stupid, but he had to at least try. The front of the shop was connected to the forge on the right-hand side, if the heat emanating from the wall was any evidence. While the shop itself was not large, a chipped and scratched wooden counter spanned the room, and shelves lined the wall behind it filled with various items from nails to horseshoes.

A man came out from a side room, wiping his blackened hands on a rag. He was a massive mountain of a man with dark brown hair and gray eyes a shade or two lighter than Greyson's.

"Prince Cyrus," the man said, eyebrows raised. "This is a surprise."

"Hello," he said. "I don't suppose you do small metal work?"

"Like what?"

"Like a ring." A blush stole over his cheeks.

The man grinned. "You're going to propose to Greyson."

"I am," Cyrus said, fighting the sudden rush of emotion that clogged his throat. "I'll probably bawl my eyes out, but yes."

Chuckling, the huge man said, "When I proposed to my husband, I was crying so much that I couldn't even get the words out. He just stared at me as I held out a ring, blubbering. Finally, he was like, 'Are you proposing to me?' I nodded, and he laughed. I thought he was going to break my heart, but he accepted my proposal."

"What's your name?" Cyrus asked, chuckling.

"John."

"It's a pleasure to meet you."

"You as well."

"So," Cyrus started, "do you have rings?"

"I do."

"Excellent." Cyrus didn't know if Greyson would accept his proposal, but he wanted to ask.

"In fact," John said, leaning his hulking forearms on the counter, "I have a ring that I think would be perfect." He bent down and removed a plain, wooden box. Opening it, he took out a ring.

The second he saw it, Cyrus knew it was the one. It was a black metal band, and in the center were iridescent blue stones set inside the band. "It's perfect," he said. "It's like his staff."

"The stones are the same ones we mine. The ones that are too small or weak to be made into artifacts are usually ground into dust and sold to make potions, but I buy a few for jewelry. It's a Griseo Mountain tradition to have a wedding ring with a venetus. Just because Greyson is marrying an outsider doesn't mean he should be excluded."

"You think he'll marry me?"

"I do," John replied. "It's obvious he loves you."

"How much for it?"

"This one will cost more because my husband also used magic to help craft it. He has the ability to change metal colors, like this one here."

"How much?"

"A gold."

Cyrus whistled. That was a lot of money. It was no wonder why the ring was available if John was charging that much.

"I can bill the estate if you'd like."

"I want to buy it myself. Would you take anything else for it?"

Smiling, John leaned on the counter again. "I've heard Greyson made some healing potions. I would take a bottle for that."

Chewing on his lip, he stared at the ring. Cyrus didn't want Greyson to know about the ring, but he'd rather owe Greyson than his uncle. "I'll see what I can do."

"I'll hold it for you, then."

"Thank you," Cyrus said, heading out of the warm shop.

GREYSON

Greyson sat on the floor near the fireplace with a mortar and pestle between his legs. He'd found some ignis berries—a bright orange berry that warmed the skin. Carefully mushing the berries, he added a few herbs and spices to make a poultice.

The door opened, and he glanced at it, smiling. Cyrus had left early this morning, taking himself off somewhere. "Hey, love," Greyson said, as he continued his controlled movements.

"What are you doing? Poisoning someone?"

He rolled his eyes. "I don't poison people that often. This is a poultice for Widow Jones and Widower Smith as a thank you."

"Ah." Cyrus crouched in front of him, biting his lip, gaze averted.

Greyson grabbed his chin, making Cyrus free his lip. "Don't do that unless you want this afternoon to go a very different way."

Cyrus leaned closer. "I don't think I'd mind that."

"Let me finish this first." Greyson went back to the poultice. Once it was finished, he would put it into tins.

"I need a favor."

"What?"

"Can I have one of the bottles of healing potion?" Cyrus asked, bouncing a bit.

"Why?" Greyson asked, steadily moving the pestle in a counterclockwise motion.

"I can't tell you. But as repayment, I will give two favors that I can't say no to."

A smile stretched over his lips as different possibilities played through his mind. "I would've given it to you for free, but sure. Two favors, that's worth it."

"Damn it. I should've just asked," Cyrus said, grinning.

"Don't worry. I'll think of something fun."

Cyrus straightened and walked toward the kitchen where the potions sat on the counter.

"I thought we were going to have sex once I finished this?" he protested.

"Is that a favor?"

Scoffing, he said, "No."

"Then I will be right back."

Greyson watched Cyrus leave the apartment before turning back to the poultice.

Cyrus had been acting oddly the last few days. He kept looking at him, opening his mouth before snapping it closed. Greyson had no idea what was going on, but he figured Cyrus harbored some doubts he did not want to talk about.

Greyson had some doubts as well, not about them as a couple, but about what the future would look like. He tried to talk to Cyrus about this plan Empress Quinn concocted, but the words got caught in his throat. Sharing had never been something he was good at. Also, he didn't want Cyrus to think he didn't trust him because Greyson did. He knew Cyrus wouldn't let anything happen to the people of the Griseo Mountains. If the emperor threatened them, Cyrus would leave, regardless of how much it hurt.

That wasn't what truly worried him, though.

When Lady Lyra arrived to replace Lord Darius, it would be time for Greyson to travel home. Cyrus would go with him, but he didn't know how Cyrus would do in Drakcombe and his tiny cabin. Before Cyrus had regained his memories, he liked it, but he had nothing to compare it to. Now, Greyson didn't know if Cyrus could be happy there.

This was something he hadn't even tried to convey to Cyrus. Clearly, Greyson was going to have to work on his communication skills. He frowned at the very thought.

Cyrus sank down in the chair next to him. "Are you alright?"

He opened his mouth to say the words that needed to be spoken, but they remained buried within him. Instead, he replied, "Of course."

Nodding, Cyrus bit his lip and stared at the fireplace. His bottom lip looked much plumper with his perfect teeth sunk into it. Cyrus licked his lips, then returned to chewing on the bottom one. Greyson wanted to taste them for himself, then possibly other parts of Cyrus. Greyson yanked his gaze away. This is why he loved and hated when Cyrus bit his lip. It drew him in like nothing else. Focusing on Cyrus, not his lips, he noticed the tension in his shoulders and the way his hands curled and uncurled on his thighs.

"What's going on, love?"

Releasing his lip, Cyrus asked, "What?"

"You're acting weird."

"Am not."

Greyson rolled his eyes. "You are."

Cyrus did not respond, not that Greyson could blame him.

As it was getting late and they'd already eaten dinner, Greyson collected the plates and stacked them on the counter to wash them in the morning. Then he placed a large log on the low burning flames.

"Are you going to sleep?" Cyrus asked.

He wiped his hands on his trousers. "That was the plan."

"Come sit with me," Cyrus said, holding his arms out.

Greyson stood between Cyrus' legs. Cyrus slung his arms around Greyson's waist, staring up at him. Greyson brushed Cyrus' hair, smiling as the blonde strands slid between his fingers.

Cyrus groaned, which made his smile widen. Greyson rubbed his fingers over Cyrus' head, the silky hair sliding through his grasp, then tugged on Cyrus' hair. "It's late."

Cyrus made a noise in the back of his throat.

"Come on."

"I love you," Cyrus whispered.

"I love you too."

Shaking his head, Cyrus gathered him closer, chin resting on Greyson's stomach. "I really love you."

"I know," he said. "I really love you as well"

"I want to stay with you forever."

Greyson caressed Cyrus' cheek. "That's convenient because I don't plan to let you go."

"You don't?"

"No. You're mine." Greyson could not imagine his life without him, as strange as it was. Less than a year ago, he hadn't wanted anything to do with Cyrus; now, Greyson didn't want to be separated from him.

A grin stretched over Cyrus' face. "I want to ask you something."

"Okay?"

Cyrus stared straight at him and asked, "Will you marry me?"

His mouth fell open as tingles cascaded through his body. Blinking several times, Greyson nodded, mouth still open.

"You will?"

"Yes," Greyson replied, grinning. He grabbed Cyus' face, bending down to kiss him, hard. Cyrus' lips moved frantically over Greyson's as he stood. Greyson's hands slid around Cyrus as he pressed closer, clutching his back.

Breaking away, Cyrus breathed in quick gasps, chest heaving, as he said, "I didn't think you'd say yes."

"Why wouldn't I?"

Cyrus shoved a hand into his pocket and produced something small. Greyson watched as Cyrus slowly slid a ring on his finger. He could not help but admire the black metal ring with blue glimmering stones.

"Is this why you wanted the healing potion?"

"Yes."

Greyson pressed his forehead against Cyrus. "You could've told me."

"It wouldn't have been a surprise, then."

Suddenly, he started laughing as an image shot through his mind.

"What?" Cyrus asked.

"Should we have Lord Darius perform the ceremony?"

Chuckling, Cyrus said, "Best to wait for Lady Lyra, I think."

"You're probably right."

40

CYRUS

Cyrus and Greyson stood in the center of the village as they watched a procession travel up the road. Almost six weeks had passed since he'd received the letter from his uncle. Lady Lyra had finally arrived.

A bubbling feeling grew within his stomach as he watched the carriage approach. Now, he and Greyson could get married, leave Woodhurst, and go home. Cyrus sighed. Greyson raised an eyebrow in an obvious question. Cyrus took Greyson's free hand, their fingers interlacing, in response.

Cyrus focused on the fine carriage with decorative paneling as the procession halted. The door opened and a tall woman with no curves dressed in a thick fur-lined cloak and dark blue dress stepped out.

With a smile, Cyrus said, "Lady Lyra, welcome."

Lady Lyra smiled in return. Her pale blonde hair was swept up into a bun with a few curls framing her face and her sea-green eyes glimmered. She had strong features and warm sandy-brown skin. "Prince Cyrus, it's lovely to see you."

"I'm surprised you agreed to this placement."

"Well, the emperor did not give me much of a choice. He said go, and I did."

"That makes sense." Cyrus gestured toward Greyson. "Lady Lyra, this is Mage Greyson."

She gave him a coy smile. "Well, well. Where have they been hiding you? You are fabulous."

Cyrus' jaw tightened as he started to bristle at the woman's obvious flirting. A quick glance at Greyson, who looked non-plussed, reassured him. "Greyson and I are together."

Giggling, she placed a hand on her chest and asked, "Did I suggest otherwise?"

Greyson chuckled.

"It's nice to meet you, Greyson." Turning to Cyrus, Lady Lyra said, "Your mother informed me of the plan. I have to admit, Prince Cyrus, I had no idea of your long-standing infatuation. Princess Jade said you were quite mopey and pathetic."

The empress, his cousin, and most of the court referred to the royal couple as his parents and the crown princess as his sister. The only one that didn't was the emperor, and the reason his uncle kept the distinction was so no one thought Cyrus would inherit the throne instead of Jade. An honor he didn't want in the slightest.

"I was not mopey," he retorted, though Cyrus silently agreed with the assessment.

She tittered.

Continuing with the matter at hand, Cyrus informed her, "You will have to oust Lord Darius from his home. Greyson and I are staying in an apartment we're renting."

"I figured that responsibility would fall to me. I have a small contingent of soldiers that will take him to the coast before he is sent to the tower with the monks. Your mother wasn't pleased with his reassignment."

Empress Quinn had a right to dislike Lord Darius. At every chance, he had pressed his advantage toward her. It had been widely known of his unwanted affections and attention, but because he'd done nothing more than make lewd remarks, there was nothing anyone could do. Finally, Lord Darius grabbed her arm and dragged her against him at a party. He was promptly stationed in the Griseo Mountains.

"I imagine she wasn't, but I believe the monks will be good for Lord Darius."

"Sure," she said with obvious sarcasm. "The one benefit is he will be too far away from any sort of society to do any damage."

Cyrus didn't respond, and thankfully, Greyson remained quiet. Lady Lyra would side with Greyson's idea—kill the lord in increasingly horrible ways. "We will have to go over the accounts," he said. "Lord Darius was quite the spender."

"Excellent. If there is nothing else, I would like to go inside and warm up."

"Actually," Cyrus said, tightening his hold on Greyson, "I had a favor to ask."

"What?"

"I was wondering if you would marry Greyson and I?"

"Well, I'm flattered," she said, fluttering her eyelashes, "but I have no interest in entering a throuple at this time, and I don't know either of you well enough."

He rolled his eyes, but Greyson laughed. Cyrus grumbled, "You know what I meant."

"I did, but I couldn't resist."

Greyson leaned toward her and whispered loudly, "Between you and I, I don't share."

"Oh, possessive type are you?" she asked.

"Only when it comes to Cyrus."

She laughed, and Cyrus grinned as heat seeped into his cheeks. Greyson smirked at him.

"Well," Lady Lyra said, drawing his attention from Greyson, "I would certainly be happy to perform the ceremony, but I think it would sadden your honorable parents and sister if you got married without them."

"I have no idea how long it will be before we can go to the capital. I don't want to wait," Cyrus said. He glanced toward Greyson, who nodded in agreement.

Lady Lyra's lips pursed. "I could say that you ordered me to perform the ceremony, then you could take yourselves off. I'll write to the emperor that I thought you two were secluding yourselves for a couple of weeks in the apartment you rented, but in truth, you ran away to somewhere I don't know about."

"We're just going to Greyson's village," he said.

She covered her ears. "I don't want to know that."

Cyrus lifted his hands in surrender. His uncle would know where he ran to, as he intended to keep writing to his aunt and Jade. "Fine."

"Now that's settled, I'm going inside." She walked toward the fancy house with several soldiers at her side.

Greyson shifted toward him. "Should we go with her?"

"No. She'll be alright."

"So," Greyson started, smiling, "what do you want to do today?"

With pursed lips, he stepped closer. "I'm not sure."

"Is that so?" Greyson raised his eyebrows, smirking. He moved right in front of Cyrus. "You have no plans?"

"None." Cyrus grinned, placing his hands on Greyson's hips. "None at all," he said, but was quickly forming some ideas.

"Hmm." Greyson nodded. "So you wouldn't care if I went herb hunting?"

Cyrus' mouth fell open. Greyson *wanted* to leave now?

Greyson burst out laughing. He leaned down, and his black hair brushed Cyrus' face. "You make me laugh."

"Apparently, I do," he grunted.

"I'm not making fun of you, love," Greyson said. "You just make me very happy."

He couldn't keep the smile off his face. "You make me happy as well."

Greyson rested his forehead against his. "I could never have imagined this. Not ever. I couldn't have even guessed I would be this happy or that my life would turn out this way."

"Ending up with your enemy?" Cyrus joked.

"No. Being with anyone."

Cyrus closed his eyes. "I pictured you and I together countless times, but it is so much better than anything I imagined."

"I'm glad. I promise I will keep it that way."

He shook his head against Greyson's forehead. "I promise to make you equally as happy."

"I already am."

GREYSON

The fire crackled soothingly, spreading heat throughout the darkened apartment. Cyrus held his hand, breathing evenly. Greyson knew he was awake, but they both remained silent.

Tension resided in his muscles, and it would not relent. Doubts plagued him. He wanted to marry Cyrus, was thrilled in fact, but deep down, Greyson worried it would not be enough for Cyrus. Cyrus was a prince with an entire empire at his fingertips. Greyson had very little to offer. All Greyson had to his name was the cabin in his sleepy village. Cyrus said he wanted to go home with him, but Greyson couldn't help but wonder if Cyrus would change his mind.

Closing his eyes, he sighed loudly.

The bed dipped as the sheets and blankets rustled next to him. A heavy weight settled on top of him, making Greyson open his eyes. Cyrus stared at him, hair falling around his face. "What's wrong?"

"Nothing."

Cyrus frowned. "You're lying, Grey."

That's new, he thought, though he didn't mind it. Greyson looked at the love of his life and ran a hand through Cyrus' hair, loving the feel of it sliding through his fingers. "I'm scared."

Brow furrowed, Cyrus asked, "Of what? Us getting married?"

"No."

"Then what?"

The worries for the future poured through him. Part of Greyson did not want to talk about them, did not want to open up, but he needed to. Taking a deep breath, Greyson peered into Cyrus' clear, blue eyes. He trusted him.

"I'm scared you'll change your mind."

"About you? That will never happen."

"No. I know you'll keep loving me. I'm worried that when we settle into this life in my cabin that you'll grow bored. What if the emperor never relents? What if you can never go home? What if you grow to regret staying with me and being stuck in the Griseo Mountains?"

Cyrus kissed him. It was hard and unrelenting. Lips brushing his, Cyrus said, "I don't blame you for your worries, Greyson. But I don't share them."

Unbidden, he smiled as he remembered Cyrus saying something similar before he regained his memories. "You're not worried?"

"Let me tell you some things. I'll even do it in list order, as you like. First, I'm thrilled to go home with you. Second, I don't like the hustle and bustle of the capital. Third, if my uncle never lifts the banishment order, I will be sad to never go back, but I won't blame you or regret being with you. Finally and most importantly, you are my home, Greyson. You. It doesn't matter where I live as long as you're with me."

"Do you mean that?"

"I do."

He kissed Cyrus. Greyson could not believe how much he loved him. It felt like every day his love grew stronger, rooting like a tree deep within his soul. He rolled on top of Cyrus, pinning him. Grabbing his hands, Greyson trapped them against the bed. "Marry me."

Cyrus chuckled against his lips. "I'm already marrying you."

Greyson silenced him by pressing his lips against Cyrus' mouth firmly. "Tomorrow."

"Tomorrow? Are you serious?" Cyrus asked, mouth falling open.

"Yes." Greyson had never been more serious in his life. He wanted to marry Cyrus and didn't want to wait another day.

"Yes. Let's get married. Tomorrow."

Smiling, Greyson opened his mouth to speak, but Cyrus kissed him and every thought left his mind.

CYRUS

Cyrus pulled the bottom of his fur-lined vest down as he peeked at Greyson, who was right next to him, his expression completely serene. Lady Lyra was right in front of them. Her eyes flicked between them, then at the snow-covered ground of the village square. Lord Darius'—well, her home stood directly behind her while Validus Peak loomed above them. Villagers circled them, all silently watching.

Clearing her throat, Lady Lyra asked, "You want to get married right here? Dressed like that?"

Laughter erupted from the villagers. Cyrus and Greyson replied at the same time, "Yes."

"Well," she said, "it's your wedding."

Greyson tugged on his hand, replying, "Yes, it is."

He stared at Greyson, buzzing in his ears and his pulse racing, as Lady Lyra performed the ceremony, not hearing a single word. Cyrus couldn't believe this was happening; that, finally, he was marrying the love of his life. It didn't seem possible. He still bore some jealousy for the him that he couldn't remember, yet at the same time, Cyrus was unbelievably grateful. If he hadn't lost his memory, he and Greyson would've never gotten together.

When Lady Lyra said to, he slipped the ring he'd gotten for Greyson onto his finger. Cyrus wanted to drag Greyson into his arms and kiss him, but he refrained from doing so, as the ceremony wasn't over yet.

As Lady Lyra called for Greyson to put a ring on Cyrus' finger, panic shot through him. He hadn't gotten a ring for himself. Greyson removed a band out of his pocket. It was black like his with one, small iridescent blue stone.

"It's tradition," Greyson said, sliding the ring onto his finger. "Because you're marrying me, you're now one of us."

"No one will mind?"

"No, no one will care. You're mine, Cyrus, and I'm yours. You saved my life, multiple times. You saved the Griseo Mountains. You're one of us now if you want to be."

"I do."

"You guys are kind of taking my lines here," Lady Lyra complained, arms crossed.

Cyrus and Greyson both chuckled.

The instant she declared them married, Cyrus cupped his husband's cheeks and kissed him. Greyson's hands went about his back and squashed him against his chest as tears threatened to spill. Eight years ago when he saw Greyson for the first time, Cyrus couldn't have predicted this ending. Oh, how he longed for it over the years, but he never thought it would happen. Now, he was married to the love of his life, and Cyrus would never let Greyson go.

EPILOGUE

GREYSON

Greyson peeked over his shoulder at his husband. Cyrus sat at the table, reading the book Jade had sent. Poofy orange flowers filled Greyson's favorite cup—a gift from his husband. It had been six months since they'd married, but Greyson hadn't quite gotten used to it.

The last six months had been amazing. He'd feared Cyrus would grow bored with the simple life here, but Greyson had underestimated his curiosity for everything. Cyrus had flourished, rebuilding his relationship with Widow Abney and forging new ones with the villagers. Julia and her wife Victoria had moved to Drakcombe with their two children. Charles Davies was back to hating Greyson, but the couple had become solid friends with him and Cyrus.

Annabeth had not liked living in the same village as Cyrus, so she moved to the coast. Greyson had been sad to lose her friendship, but he hoped she'd come around eventually. Elizabeth visited frequently. Even Liam had come for a short visit. They had introduced Liam to Lady Lyra, and she'd taken an interest. Greyson did not think she would leave Woodhurst anytime soon. The small village was alive with people and students for Greyson to teach, and he loved it.

Not everything had been perfect. They'd fought, of course, about several different things but usually resolved whatever was the matter after a bit. They were still working through all the issues of their past, but Greyson was almost positive they'd be dismantling what stood between them until they died, and he was alright with that.

The main contention between them was the vial of poison. Cyrus wanted to get rid of it, and Greyson asserted it was a waste to do so. Besides, they couldn't dump it in the river without killing a ton of fish, animals, and plants, not to mention polluting the area, nor could they bury it in case the glass bottle broke and poison seeped out. No, for now, they'd compromised; it sat, gathering dust, in the secret cubby in the cabinet.

Cyrus kept reading the book, completely engrossed. Smiling, Greyson put a couple of cinnamon buns, slathered with icing, on a plate. He sat next to Cyrus and prodded the plate in between them. Cyrus finally looked up from the book.

"Cinnamon buns? They look amazing, Grey."

"Thanks." He picked up one and the icing dripped onto his fingers. They took forever to make so Greyson didn't bake them often, but he hadn't made them for Cyrus yet, and he had a promise to keep, even if Cyrus didn't remember. Biting into it, the sweet icing clung to his face as the warm spice danced along his tongue.

Cyrus bit into the bun, then released a loud groan before shoving half of it into his mouth. "These are amazing," he said while chewing. "I like hotcakes better, but I can see why they're your favorite."

He paused mid-bite. Greyson didn't think he'd ever told Cyrus they were his favorite, at least not during a time he could remember. Chewing quickly, he asked, "Where'd you hear that?"

"You told me." Cyrus licked his fingers.

Brow furrowed, Greyson tried to think through the last six months.

"Why don't you make them more often?"

"They take too long."

"You should teach me, and I'll make them for you."

Greyson scoffed. Since they'd come home, Cyrus had insisted on cooking. It had not gone well. Cyrus couldn't cook a meal to save his life. Greyson figured they were better off if he did all the cooking; not to mention, the cabin was more likely to survive.

A sudden kiss on his cheek drew his attention to Cyrus. "I promised I'd help Widow Abney this afternoon," he said. "You're not checking the traps today, right?"

He fought the urge to roll his eyes or snap back. Cyrus did not like Greyson wandering too far by himself, just in case. He still did it, of course. These were his mountains, and Greyson refused to be afraid of bounty hunters who may or may not attack him.

"No," he replied. "I'm taking Lily Jones out herb hunting tomorrow. We'll check the traps then."

His mother's ring hadn't chosen Ruth Davies as he'd hoped, but instead, chose Lily Jones, which shouldn't have surprised him. Greyson's mother had been a healer and so was Lily. He was trying to teach her all he knew, but eventually, if Lily wanted to be a true healing mage she would have to go to the capital.

"I'm glad," Cyrus said. "Well, I will be back later." He flashed Greyson a smile and snagged another cinnamon bun before he left.

After the door closed, he made a pot of tea. Tea and another cinnamon bun plus Cyrus' new book seemed like an excellent way to spend the remainder of his afternoon, especially while the light remained bright enough for him to read. Once the tea finished, Greyson settled down with a cup. Opening the book, he began to read when a knock sounded.

A frown immediately pulled on his lips. No one ever knocked on his door. It was an unspoken rule. Greyson would train people and help anyone with what they needed, but it was always done in the village. He was not social by nature and liked his space. Marrying Cyrus had not changed that. Now, Cyrus was included in that space. The only time people came to his door was for emergencies. He'd already gone to the village this morning, training a new crop of students like he usually did during the summer months.

The air left his lungs as the floor dropped out beneath him. What if something had happened to Cyrus?

Leaping up, Greyson raced to the door and flung it open. The man outside his door jerked back. Greyson's mouth fell open.

"Are you going to let me in, Mage Greyson?" Emperor Caspian asked.

"Sorry, I'm shocked to see you in front of my house," Greyson quipped.

He had not expected to see Cyrus' uncle in the Griseo Mountains. The only time Emperor Caspian had been in the Griseo Mountains, to Greyson's knowledge, was when he and Cyrus stood in the center of Woodhurst and declared the rebellion over after they had already surrendered. Since his and Cyrus' marriage, Cyrus had continued to write to his aunt and cousin, and they wrote back, but there had been complete silence from the emperor.

Moving from the doorway, Greyson said, "Come in."

Greyson slowly stepped back, hands curling into fists. He had not mentally prepared to see the emperor, and the old anger for the man boiled under his skin. He took a deep breath to control the sensation. As much as he hated the emperor, he was Cyrus' uncle, and if Greyson killed him, it would hurt Cyrus. Though, he could not stop the violent thoughts circling his mind.

Baby steps, he told himself.

"Where is your staff?"

"Why? Planning on breaking it?"

The emperor frowned, furrowing his wrinkled face. Greyson loathed to think it, but Cyrus resembled his uncle. Same golden-blonde hair, blue eyes, and a long nose, but the emperor had thinner lips and an oval face. There was also an air of authority that hung about the emperor like a cloak.

"I want to make sure you aren't going to kill me."

"It's right there by the door," Greyson said, gesturing.

The emperor came inside flanked by two mages, one of whom was familiar to him.

"Frederick," Greyson called out to the tall man with pitch-black hair and pale, gray-tinged skin that marked him for who he was—a Griseo Mountain native. "Pleasant to see you. I don't know your friend."

"I'm Mage Opal," she said with a slight bow, white-blonde hair falling over her slim shoulder. "It's an honor to meet you."

His eyebrows raised; not many capital mages thought meeting him was an honor. Some would not even call him 'mage' because he had no formal training.

"Mage Frederick has told many stories about you. Can you truly summon lightning?" she asked, awe lining her voice.

The urge to roll his eyes was so strong, it took everything he had to suppress it. People were so impressed by that skill—a forgotten knowledge. He'd never found a use for summoning lightning unless he wanted to start a forest fire, which he did the first time he'd managed it, because it was too energy-consuming and too hard to control to use in battle. It was a pointless skill.

"I can."

Before she could respond, the emperor cleared his throat, and she fell silent, blushing. "I brought Mage Frederick and Mage Opal to test Cyrus to make sure he is not under a love potion."

"That's the stupidest thing I've ever heard."

"Excuse me?" The emperor's eyebrows raised.

"Cyrus and I have been married for six months and together for much longer than that. You can't keep someone on a love potion that long. It would kill them." Greyson crossed his arms, shaking his head as he leaned back against the table.

"He's right, your majesty," Frederick replied.

"Nonetheless," he ground out, "we will test him."

"Test away. Cyrus is not here, as you can see," he said, gesturing to the empty cabin behind him.

"Where is he?"

"In Drakcombe, helping Widow Abney."

The emperor glanced at Frederick, who nodded. "I'll get him."

A thick tension hung in the air. Greyson forced his muscles to relax and sat in the chair he'd earlier abandoned. "Would you like some tea?"

"From you? I think not."

"It hardly matters to me, but I wouldn't poison you," Greyson said.

"Why?" Emperor Caspian asked, hovering near the open door and Mage Opal. "Are you suddenly suffering from an overabundance of love for me?"

"Hardly, but if I killed you, it would upset Cyrus, and I won't do that."

The emperor scoffed, and Greyson shrugged. It didn't matter if he did not believe him. "I'm going to drink my tea before it gets cold." He picked up the ceramic cup, still warm beneath his fingertips, and took a drink. The strong flavor clung to his tongue as the liquid slid pleasantly down his throat. With a slight smile, he ripped a piece of the cinnamon bun off and ate it. The entire time the emperor simply glared at him, muscular arms crossed.

"I don't believe you."

"What? That I refuse to allow your presence to destroy my enjoyment of tea and pastries?" Greyson remarked.

"No!" the emperor growled. "I don't believe you care about Cyrus. You are using him to get to me. You're going to hurt him to hurt me."

Greyson lifted his hand. "Wait, you think I married Cyrus in a long plan to get back at you?"

"Yes."

"Great plan," he said, his voice heavy with sarcasm. He did not hate the emperor that much. "But it is not true. I love Cyrus."

"You never did before."

"I didn't know Cyrus before," Greyson growled, voice deepening. "If I'd actually gotten to know Cyrus when I was a teenager, maybe I would have realized it sooner." He truly meant it. Over the last six months, he'd had time to think about it. He'd always been attracted to Cyrus, his eyes had never strayed from him, but Greyson had never had a chance to get to know him or even acknowledge his attraction.

Shaking his head, he continued, "Anyway, the past doesn't matter. I love Cyrus, and we're married. Do you intend to void our marriage that was performed by a member of the court and witnessed by many?"

The emperor stared at him in silence for several long moments before his shoulders slumped and he scrubbed a hand through his short blonde hair. An action that reminded

Greyson strongly of Cyrus. Suddenly, the emperor seemed like an exhausted man. He sat across from Greyson before pushing his thick fingers through his hair again.

"He's liked you for a long time, you know."

"I am aware."

Both of them sat in silence. Greyson glanced at the open door, frustration building with each passing second. Frederick should have reached the village by now and found Cyrus. He had no idea what was keeping them.

"You and I," the emperor started, "are going to have to find a way to get along. For Cyrus' sake."

"Do we?"

"Yes," he said. "I miss Cyrus. I couldn't love him more if he'd been born to my wife and I. Also, he is all I have left of my little sister."

The emperor spoke the truth, but that did not make this easy. Greyson hated him. "We do," he agreed, "but that does not mean I won't stop fighting for my people."

The other man glowered. "I will allow no rebellions."

"I didn't start the war, you did. You refused to pay us a reasonable amount for our work. You may own these mountains, but we bled and died for them, and you stole everything."

"I pay more for the venetus now."

"Yes." Greyson sneered. "Because of Cyrus. But you still punish us. You inflicted Lord Darius on us when you knew he would abuse us, and you didn't care."

The emperor stared coldly at him in stony silence.

"I will *always* fight for my people." Taking a deep breath, Greyson continued, "But for Cyrus' sake, I am willing to not kill you. That's the best I can do. Besides, being with Cyrus and getting to know the future empress will help my people in the end. But that doesn't mean I won't fight for the Griseo Mountains if need be."

"I don't know if we will ever get along."

"Probably not, but we can pretend and refuse to be seated next to or near each other at any event. If luck is with us, we won't have to speak more than a few words to each other for the rest of our lives."

"I can live with that," the emperor replied.

Greyson could live with that as well. It would not be pleasant, but he could and would endure much worse to stay beside Cyrus. "You will have to lift the banishment order and revoke the bounty if you want Cyrus to travel to the capital."

"You would trap him here?" the emperor asked, a fist banging the table and making the teacup rattle on its saucer.

"No. I told Cyrus to go back. He refused to listen. He's the one that won't leave without me."

The emperor crossed his arms. "Stupid, lovesick fool."

Nodding, Greyson agreed with the sentiment.

"That means he's going to want you to come on family vacations and activities and everything, doesn't it?"

"I would assume so. I am his husband."

"That means we will be trapped on a boat with each other."

"At least it won't be cold," Greyson offered before taking a sip of the lukewarm tea.

"What?"

"I took Cyrus to the northern coast when he'd lost his memory. He went sailing with some fishers there. He froze half to death and terrified me, but he loved it."

Chuckling, the emperor waved his hand. "That's nothing compared to how much he scared me when he was nine. This was right after my sister died, and Cyrus came to live with us. I took him sailing. He'd never been before because his mother was terrified of open water, but Cyrus took to it immediately. At one point, he was watching the water over the railing, and then he just jumped overboard, giggling like a loon."

"He did what?" Greyson growled, terror freezing his muscles, even though Cyrus was fine.

"Yes. I thought we wouldn't find him or he'd be dead by the time we did. But lo and behold, we found him, half-drowned. The next few times he went sailing with me, I tied him to the mast. Thankfully, he's outgrown such idiotic acts." His gaze lingered on Greyson as he added, "Mostly."

Greyson scoffed. "He hasn't outgrown anything. When he lost his memory, he climbed up a half-built building because some teenagers goaded him into it. He fell off, and I had to catch him with magic."

"Are you sure you want to be with him?" he asked, hands folding. "I can tell hundreds of unbecoming stories if it would help."

"I'm not changing my mind about Cyrus."

Thankfully, Cyrus came in before the emperor had a chance to stay anything else. He smiled at the two of them. "Uncle."

Standing, the emperor enfolded Cyrus in a tight embrace. Greyson got to his feet as well. After a minute, Cyrus stepped out of the hug, then moved around the table toward him.

"Grey," he said. "I see you didn't kill him."

Greyson frowned. "You left us alone for longer on purpose, didn't you?"

Cyrus grinned. "How else would the two of you ever talk?"

He scowled at his husband. Cyrus smirked before placing a kiss on his lips. It was brief, as they had an unhappy audience who made his presence known with a lot of loud coughing, but it was enough that Greyson was willing to overlook being left alone with the emperor. Taking Cyrus' hand, Greyson faced Emperor Caspian, who watched them with narrowed eyes.

"So you won your heart's desire, nephew?"

"I did," Cyrus said, squeezing his hand.

"You went and got married without your family?"

"Would you have come so quickly if I hadn't?"

Cyrus' uncle did not answer the question but said, "I'm going to have you tested to see if you're under the influence of a love potion."

"That's ridiculous," Greyson snapped. "Just look at Cyrus. He has no symptoms. No weight loss, no bloodshot eyes or dilated pupils, no hair loss, no excessive drooling, and not to mention the fact he's still alive."

"I don't care," the older man ground out. "He will be tested."

"What does that entail?" Cyrus asked, looking at him.

"Just a prick on the finger. It's not a big deal."

"Mage Opal will test him." The emperor motioned for the young mage to start. She quickly began to pour the necessary ingredients into a brass bowl. When it came time to add the blood, she presented a thin, silver needle. Cyrus held out his hand, and she pricked the pointer finger of his dominant hand. Blood welled up, and Mage Opal flipped Cyrus' hand over, allowing a couple of drops of blood to fall into the bowl before letting go of him.

They all leaned closer and watched for any reaction. Nothing happened.

Cyrus nudged his shoulder. "What was supposed to happen?"

"Nothing because you're not under a love potion. If you were, a bunch of red smoke would have poured out before forming the shape of a heart."

"Could Greyson have faked the test?" the emperor asked, looking at his two mages.

"Seriously?" Greyson asked.

The emperor ignored him and kept staring at the two mages.

Frederick shook his head. "It can't be faked. If Prince Cyrus was under a love potion, his blood would have reacted." Mage Opal agreed.

Emperor Caspian said, "Fine, Cyrus. You win. I already lifted the damn banishment order and revoked the bounty before I left. I knew you wouldn't come home without your mage."

"Then what the hell was this all about?" Greyson snapped.

Cyrus ignored his outburst and hugged Emperor Caspian. "Thank you."

"Are you sure you want him?" the emperor asked. "I brought Mage Frederick because he can tell you all manner of unflattering stories of Mage Greyson."

Greyson's mouth fell open. "Is that your solution to breaking couples up?"

Cyrus nodded. "He told Jasper horrible stories about Jade for weeks before the wedding, and that was an arranged marriage."

He honestly did not know what to say. The emperor was an even more ridiculous human being than Greyson could have possibly guessed.

Cyrus shifted back to his uncle. "I'm sure. I just want Greyson."

CYRUS

The warm water lapped against them as Cyrus stretched out on the hot sand next to his husband. They were at the royal summer palace. The empress let them stay there as a honeymoon if they had another wedding with all the pomp and circumstance of a true royal wedding.

He'd managed to get Greyson to go through with it. Greyson's only term was that their original wedding date was recognized legally as the day they got married. The empress was more than happy to agree to that. The wedding was long and boring, and neither of them enjoyed it, but it meant a lot to Cyrus' family.

Thankfully, Greyson got along just fine with Empress Quinn, Jade, and his niece and nephew. Greyson had immediately taken to his nephew, teaching the rebellious child with surprising ease. He'd even found a bracelet artifact for Casper to bond with. Jasper and Greyson of course already got along, but now they'd grown closer.

"So," Greyson said, drawing Cyrus' attention, "was it everything you dreamed it would be?"

Cyrus had imagined, many times, making love to Greyson on the beach near the summer palace while the warm waves crashed over them. It had been his favorite fantasy. While it had been sandier than expected, he'd enjoyed it.

He rolled on top of Greyson, who grunted from the sudden weight. He stared at his husband, hair falling in front of his eyes. Greyson brushed a sandy hand through his hair.

"I liked it."

"I'm glad. It was interesting, to say the least."

He kissed Greyson as a wave washed over them. "Do you have any long-standing fantasies?"

"About you?"

Cyrus nodded, biting his lip.

"No romantic ones. Just mainly maiming and killing you."

He frowned. "You're ruining the moment."

Greyson laughed, hands settling on his lower back. "My dream is to grow old with you. I want to be a crotchety old man with you next to me."

"I like that."

As Cyrus was about to kiss him again, Greyson said, "Oh, I thought of one."

"About me?" he asked, swallowing.

"We should have sex in the library."

"What?" he asked, sputtering. "It's in public."

"We're outside right now."

"On a private beach."

"With servants right up the shore in the summer palace," Greyson said.

Clearing his throat, Cyrus asked, "You wanted to have sex with me in the library when we were teenagers?"

"No. I want to do it now. I have no sex-related teenage fantasies about you. But I do want to make love in the abandoned corner where all the magic theorem books that no one besides me reads are. You used to stalk me there when we were teenagers."

"How romantic," Cyrus said sarcastically.

"I could use one of the two favors you owe me."

"Seriously? In public?"

"We just had sex on the beach. I don't see the difference." Greyson leaned up and rolled until he hovered over Cyrus. "You'd enjoy it. I promise."

"It is one of your two owed favors."

"I told you I'd find something fun to do."

Cyrus simply laughed.

"You know," Greyson said, leaning closer, "we could go to all the places you used to stalk me and make out."

"I think I would enjoy that."

"Of course, you would." Greyson closed the distance between them. Cyrus groaned, rocking beneath him.

A wave crashed over them, soaking them both. When the water receded, Greyson and he both laughed. Cyrus held his face, thumbs stroking his cheekbones. "I love you."

"I love you too."

"We were supposed to go sailing, but I think we should get a snack, then retire to our room for a while," Cyrus commented as his fingers trailed over Greyson's bare skin.

"Hmm, you have more room-related fantasies," he said, nodding.

Cyrus glared, which made Greyson snicker. Greyson had been making serious inroads into all of Cyrus' past daydreams. He acted like it was a challenge to fulfill them all, which Cyrus found amusing, not to mention fun.

"If we did that," Greyson said, "I wouldn't have to tie you to the mast."

Cyrus' mouth fell open. "You've barely spoken to my uncle, and he told you that story?"

Greyson smirked.

"Seriously? I was nine. I never did it again."

"It's funny. Now."

"And when I went sailing with Charles Davies, I didn't fall in. I just got wet from the ocean spray."

"What?" Greyson asked, eyes widening.

"When I almost froze to death. I didn't fall in."

Greyson gaped at him, mouth open.

"What?"

"You remember?"

"Remember what?" Cyrus asked, still upset.

Greyson grabbed his face, his full weight almost crushing Cyrus. "You remember sailing with Charles Davies. I never told you that. Neither did Julia. I made sure she wouldn't."

He blinked, mouth opening, as he thought back. Cyrus could remember the cold ocean spray, Greyson's angry face when he came back, sitting in front of the fire, and after that things grew hazy again. Though, even as he thought about it, Cyrus remembered chasing Greyson after he'd gone outside and pinning him against the house.

"I remember. I also remember the night before. You told me you loved me for the first time."

"You're getting your memories back," Greyson said as his face scrunched and emotion filled his eyes.

"I am." Cyrus couldn't believe it.

"What else do you remember?"

"I don't know."

"Do you remember the first time you kissed me?" Greyson asked, his voice husky.

He closed his eyes, brow furrowing, as he thought back. Almost immediately, his head started to pound. "No, not yet."

"Maybe you will."

"That would be nice."

"Yes, because then you can stop being jealous of the past you that you don't remember."

Cyrus hooked his arms around Greyson's waist. "I can't believe I'm remembering."

"I can't believe you and I ended up together."

"I can," he said. "We're fated."

Greyson scoffed. "Fated? Not likely."

Cyrus pressed his lips against Greyson's to silence any argument. He didn't care if they were meant to be or not. They were together, and Cyrus had no intention of letting Greyson go.

AFTERWORD

I started writing this book as a way to relax from my First Being Novels, which are progressively growing more complicated. It was a side project that I wasn't sure would ever see the light of day, but the book practically wrote itself, and before I knew it, it was completed. When I reread my work, I knew I couldn't let it sit on my laptop forever. Cyrus and Greyson deserved to be read. So I began the dreaded editing.

There were so many things in this book that were a joy to research/write. First, the amnesia in romance (AIR) trope. It, of course, is nothing like medical amnesia, which I did heavily research. I wanted to put my own take and touch on this common trope used in books, movies, and TV shows. AIR was one of my favorite tropes growing up, and it was a dream come true to write my own novel with it.

Another interesting thing was Greyson's disability—monocular vision. Having one eye is a standard fantasy (or pirate romance) trope, but I wanted to do it justice with some reality. I did so much research on it from blogs of visually impaired individuals, videos, research studies, and even a hunting blog that catered to bowhunters with one eye. I wanted to put little things in the book that spoke to his disability without making it the focus of the story.

So many books focus on the bad of being disabled or disabled people being angry (which can be true, but it's not the whole truth), but as a person with disabilities, I like reading/writing about people who have disabilities but are not angry about it. I like stories that have disabled representation without making it the character's whole personality or the book's whole plot. So that's what I did.

I absolutely loved writing a romance with two men. I loved writing about different representations from Cyrus being gay, Greyson, Julia, and Jasper being bisexual, and Victoria being a lesbian. Growing up in the nineties (dating myself here), there was not a lot of LGBTQIA+ representation, and I promised myself if I became a writer I would do that. As part of the queer family, I want others like myself to find good representation in novels.

This book has fulfilled so many of my dreams as a child and promises I made to myself. I hope you enjoyed this book, and I hope you love it as much as I do. I am planning on writing more books in the world, and I hope you will stick with me.

I also want to take a moment to thank a few people. First, the LGBTQIA+ family. There are too many people to name individually, but you all supported me and encouraged me to be myself. You gave me a place to belong when I felt adrift at sea. Thank you so much. I would not be here without you all. Keep being you!

Next, I want to thank my older sister and editor, Sandra. You helped me read, edit, and even named this book. You always support me personally and in my writing as my biggest fan. I cannot thank you enough.

I would like to thank my illustrator, Etheric Designs. I didn't know exactly what I wanted for this cover, but you helped me weed through the important aspects of my book, and what kind of cover I needed. I really appreciate your patience, and I look forward to working with you in the future.

Finally, I want to thank my beta readers. You read the book and gave me much-needed advice on plot, pacing, and typos (so many typos). I could not do this without you. Thank you.

ABOUT THE AUTHOR

Katherine A. Darling can usually be found with a book in her hand and a cat on her lap. She was born and raised in Northern California. She got her BA in business from Simpson University only to decide business was not for her. She has possessed a wild imagination since childhood, which later led to a desire to write books. When she's not writing, you can find Katherine reading, playing LOTRO, crocheting, or hanging out with her truly impressive number of cats.

9 781961 972018